FLAGRANT THREE

FLAGRANT THREE

A NOVEL BY

CARL E. LINKE

ℱ

Philip-Forrest Publishing
Chapel Hill

ℱ Philip-Forrest Publishing LLC

Copyright © 2012 by Carl E. Linke
Published in the United States by Philip-Forrest Publishing LLC
P.O. Box 2053
Chapel Hill, NC 27515-2053
Visit our website at: www.carllinke.com

Cover Design by Philip-Forrest Publishing LLC

ISBN-13: 978-0-982-74219-8
Library of Congress Control Number: 2012948801

PRINTED IN THE UNITED STATES OF AMERICA
First Edition: (November 2012)
10 9 8 7 6 5 4 3 2 1

For Jack McGill.
Soldier, scholar, athlete.
Husband, father, and brother
in the Long Gray Line.

PROLOGUE

Darkness swallowed the frustration of the figure streamed to a monitor more than a safe distance away. The silhouette of a man with an unkempt Afro, full beard, and broad shoulders tapered to a trim waist, paced inside the confines of his new world where panic of the unknown surrendered to the vacuum of solitude.

The grainy background on the computer blurred as the subject moved from side to side between walls that were un-insolated, covered from floor to ceiling by wooden shelves filled with food and drinks packaged in bulk. Cartons of canned beans, Vienna sausages, soups, pasta sauce, and more, all with pull tab tops. Flats of Gatorade and water. Boxes of snacks—peanut butter crackers, cakes, cookies, pretzels, peanuts. One large orange cooler which held nothing but cold air. A box filled with used batteries of various sizes. And one sleeping bag made for someone less than his six and a half foot frame. The floor was a cold cement slab with dark, red stains covered with mouse droppings strewn about like confetti. The fetid odor was ever-present and inescapable. There were no windows and only one solid door covered by sheet metal with no handle or knob. For Malik Farqu'har there was no way out.

CHAPTER 1

Wednesday, March 30
8:47 a.m.

I don't get it McGill," Coach Riley said. He pulled his hair, stepped away then turned back toward the player, sweat soaked and seated on a stool in a locker room filled with a heavy cloud of wintergreen analgesic.

"I told the team to wait outside. They don't need to be a part of this. I'm sure they'll have their own private session with you later," he said, his nose inches from the player's face, his voice loud enough to echo off the abused metal lockers and out into the hall. "Those guys busted their asses to get to the Final Four and you piss it all away for a night of drinking and whoring." He stared into the kid's eyes, the left one swollen shut, crusted with dried blood. The coach jerked his head away, took two short steps, and creased another locker with his knuckles before he walked back toward his star player.

"Thirty-two years. Thirty-two goddamn, lousy years I've waited for this game and you…" He moved down the row of lockers, slamming doors and kicking stools, shoes, and sweats that littered the floor. "And then you come along. Mr. Hotshot, the best player I've ever coached. And, the cockiest, most self-centered, ungrateful, inconsiderate, son of a bitching prima donna I've ever met." He picked up a shoe and hurled it. The kid ducked as it flew past his head. He watched with a scowl as the coach stopped three feet short of the stool, bent down, and reached for him. At that point, the coach did not have a chance. Before his buns ever left the stool, Tucker McGill unleashed a roundhouse sucker punch that silenced the coach and ended it all.

Then, suddenly he was back. Same world, different time. His breathing stopped. He gripped the arms of the chair and sat straight up until a hand out of nowhere eased him down.

"Whoa, cowboy? Just about done. That Lidocaine wearing off?" Mel Cooper asked. "You always fall asleep in the dentist chair? Must have been some thriller of a dream; sorry to interrupt."

Tucker offered a pained nod, the best he could with the dentist's two hands jammed in his mouth. Between the dental lamp that hovered overhead like a UFO and the warm garlic breath coming through the dentist's mask, Tucker quickly pulled out of his fog; he remembered where he was. There was something about a dentist chair. Once he got past the smell of burnt tooth dust and whir of the pneumatic drill—with its jackhammer-like vibrations—he could usually squeeze in a nap, the dream not always present.

"You really should get to the dentist more often. I did some work to cap that number thirty molar on the lower right. Just finishing up with this little cavity next to it."

With another toe-tap, the drill popped into the dreaded high-frequency pitch as it carved out a hole the size of Mammoth Cave or so it seemed to Tucker. Between drillings, he bit his tongue and the inside of his mouth; both proved the numbness was painfully lacking.

"You're not falling asleep on me again are you? Open a little wider. Tilt back here to the right. I don't want to break your jaw. Everything still pretty numb in there?" the dentist asked.

"Hun-uh," he gagged, with a mouth full fingers, cotton rolls, and saliva.

Tucker closed his eyes. He could feel the warm breath around his face and sensed the movement close to his shoulder. He tuned out the endless chatter between the dentist and the assistant; then slipped back into his nap. When the light over the dental chair went out, he awoke.

"Well, that was easy," Mel said.

"Easy for you to say," replied Tucker, grabbing his jaw. "What the hell did you do? Dig a tunnel in there?," he said, as he slid out of the chair and stretched.

"Hey, your choice. Fix 'em, pull 'em or eat grits for the rest of your life."

"Yeah, well not this week. Cinderella is going to "The Ball." He slapped his numb cheeks. "I gotta get to Atlanta tomorrow to do some set-up work for interviews for the heavies around campus: the athletic director, the president, the head of the alumni athletic boosters. The glamorous life of an assistant AD in a small-time school headed to the big-time stage."

"I'm thinking about closing shop and going over," the dentist said, looking at the computer screen, not at Tucker.

"Minor problem. Tickets are sold out; have been for months. Scalpers will gladly sell you a single-game ticket for about two grand for semis. Probably looking for double that for the finals." His cell phone vibrated in his pocket. "Excuse me," he said, as he pulled it out. "Great. Another 'Call me ASAP' panicked love-note from my boss. Gotta go." He headed to the door, then turned and said, "How 'bout happy hour at the P.I. Bar and Grill. Say five o'colck?"

"Deal. See ya there," Mel Cooper said, with a thumb up.

Tucker rubbed his jaw as he left the office. It still had that tingly feeling, little pins in his cheek that otherwise felt like a piece of plaster. He was glad he had a chance to get the appointment in before Atlanta, but he had a mountain of things on his desk. It still amazed him (and the seven hundred and fifty other residents of Beech Island, South Carolina) that the smallest Division I basketball school in the country was about to make history. Over the course of the season they had lost a few games. The coach claimed it was lack of focus. But he had taken thirteen boys—not McDonald's All-Americans—and built a solid team around American diversity. Kids, actually young men, from urban, suburban, and rural high schools. Some black. Some white. Some were foreign. They were all part of a student body of just over twelve hundred. Through coaching magic, Coach Ernest "Ernie" Howells—aka "Wolfman"—had the team at their playing best and peaked for the NCAA tournament. They had kicked and fought and wormed their way through the brackets as underdogs the entire way, through three rounds to the Sweet Sixteen and then to the Elite Eight and now four days shy of playing in the Final Four. Riding on the shoulders of the hottest player ever to play the game—Malik Farqu'har—their Cinderella Team was a definite contender among the final field of powerhouse teams which included Michigan State, UConn, and the UNC Tar Heels.

Tucker dialed the athletic director's office as he walked to his car, a brisk March wind in his face. The dentist office was on the other side of town which was not saying much for Beech Island, South Carolina—which has no beach and is not an island. It wasn't much more than a crossroads on the way to Augusta, Georgia across the Savannah River. It was merely the home of Redcliffe College and a few service businesses, like a dentist, two doctors, and a coffee shop. Students had to drive five miles to Augusta to rejoin civilization. The campus was a classic example of secluded academia encroached upon only by sports, clubs, and tom-foolery of parties before technology gave them the Internet, cell phones, and social networking.

"Good morning. Athletic director's office. This is Miss Block," said a voice, sweeter than Southern iced tea.

"Hettie Belle, this is Tucker. The old man just texted me to call in ASAP. Is he around?"

"One moment please, Mr. McGill. I'll see if Mr. Burgess is available," she said. The phone clicked and the recorded music of the student band launched into the Redcliffe fight song that looped and played over and over again while he waited.

"He'll be right with you."

"Thanks."

Ben Burgess, the long-standing AD at Redcliffe College stood by pomp and ceremony. Nobody except the president of the college could call him directly and that included his own wife. Everybody had to go through Hettie Belle Block. She was sweet as a magnolia tree in full bloom but a bulldog of an assistant. Nothing and nobody got to Mr. Burgess without her approval.

"Burgess." His high-pitched voice belied his walrus appearance which included a bushy moustache that hid most of his upper lip.

"Boss. McGill. Sorry, I was at the dentist getting roto-rootered. Feels like I have a mouth full of marbles when I talk. What's up?"

"Your super-stud hero didn't show for shootaround this morning," the AD said.

"What do you mean? Who?" Tucker said.

"I said...your superstar...Player of the Year...Malik Farqu'har is missing. Nobody's seen or heard from the kid since practice last night," Burgess said, referring to the one player that had singlehandedly made Redcliffe the Cinderella team they were. "No signs of him. Tried calling his cell; no response."

The news jolted Tucker like he had stuck his finger in an electrical socket. He shook it off and said, "What about his roommate?"

"Yeah right. His roommate, what's his name? Oh yeah, Derbish, shacked with his girlfriend last night to get psyched for the tournament. Coach isn't too pleased with that little move. He didn't go back to the room after practice. He hasn't seen or heard from super-stud, either."

"So now—"

Burgess cut him off. "Meet me at The BIB in fifteen minutes. We need to talk this thing through without all the wandering ears around this building. Don't say a word to a soul. I don't want the press in on this."

"Hell there's no way we can keep this away from the press," Tucker said.

"Dammit, McGill! Just meet me at The BIB."

CHAPTER 2

Wednesday, March 30
9:09 a.m.

The BIB—The Beech Island Barista—was the official, unofficial student union for Redcliffe College. It was the only place within walking distance of the campus where students could hang out, sip coffee, and surf the net wirelessly to study or relax. Originally built in 1954 to manufacture T2 Green Golf Carts (a business that failed), the space was a small, converted, single-story warehouse divided into eight rooms, each with its own theme, mood music, and décor. Each attracted a steady set of regulars. And, of course one, small room seemed to lure the staff and faculty.

Tucker arrived first and ordered his usual, a double Americano with four sugars, forgetting that he could not feel his tongue and would likely dribble most of it down his shirt. Ben Burgess arrived five minutes later, chewing on his unlit cigar. He stopped by the counter and ordered an extra-large Cinnamon Dolce Latte before wandering into the room with a sign over the door that read "The Library." He saw Tucker in the corner furthest from the door, a mug steamed by his elbow.

"Ain't this a crock," Burgess said, as he approached rubbing his flattop.

Tucker remained seated and looked up at his boss. A group of four entered the room behind Burgess. Tucker recognized them as professors but was not sure which departments they represented. He flashed them a quick hand motion that his boss did not see.

"This little pecker-head takes us all the way through the season, sets records out the wazoo, then skips out," Burgess said, as he yanked on a chair and plopped down.

"You really think he skipped out? Why would he do that?" Tucker said. "Something could've happened to him."

"Right," Burgess said sarcastically. He grabbed his mug and went for a long swig, the result more than he expected. "Holy hell, that's hot," he said, as he slammed his mug on the table splashing some onto his wrist. He pursed his lips and pressed hard against them with the back of his hand. "Damn. Can they make this shit any hotter? Umm, umm, umm," he moaned rubbing the foamy cream off his moustache. "I'm going to need a goddamn throat transplant." With his hand over the front of his neck, he continued, "The kid's a publicity hound from Chicago. Gotta be another one of his stunts. We've been down this path before. I don't give a shit about the why or the who or the how. What I need is a six foot six shooting guard. I need him in Atlanta in ninety-six hours to play Michigan State," Burgess said, as he jabbed at McGill with his cigar.

Tucker stared wide-eyed but silent. He disagreed with Burgess's assessment of the young college basketball phenom.

"And I don't need that prick from the *Augusta Chronicle* crawling around here." Burgess took another long drink. "The last thing we need is for this to turn into a three-ring media circus. We've had our share of paparazzi for the year."

Tucker rocked back but didn't dare appear casual. "Word travels fast these days. My guess is…the word's out and rumors are flying."

"I told the coach to have his kids cool it. I told him we could explain the kid's absence. We need to figure out how. There'll be hundreds at the send-off from the arena in a couple hours, a thousand if the student body skips class and rolls out. Plus the staff and faculty. Plus the locals. Plus more press. ESPN is due in here sometime. Kinda hard to hide the fact that King Malik is not there with his court." Burgess jammed his cigar back in his mouth and began to gum the tip of it.

Tucker looked over toward the table of professors. One of them had his eyes on Tucker, attentive to the discussion with Burgess before he quickly turned back to the other three at his table. Tucker leaned in toward his boss.

"What do we tell the press and the team?" Tucker said, soft enough for only Burgess to hear. "Hettie Bell is going to pull her hair out with all the calls. She probably has them coming in already if any tweets got out."

Burgess pulled the cigar out of his mouth. His face was covered with red splotches; could have been rosacea or just remnants of another night of heavy drinking, just Burgess and his best friend "Jack Daniels."

"Get over to the arena and talk to Ernie Howells. I have a meeting in President Kline's office in about fifteen minutes," Burgess said, loud enough for the entire room to hear him.

"Has anybody talked to the kid's family? His mother? Only child I think. He's pretty tight with her," Tucker said.

"Ask the coach. If not, then you call her. I talked to her once, at a game. Her damn accent is so bad I could barely understand her. You talk to her," Burgess said, as he downed the last sips of his latte.

"What are we telling the team?" Tucker asked, as he pushed back from the table, again with an eye on the professors. The athletic director was already on his feet and moving.

"You and Howells figure that out. Just let me know what you come up with. I'll update Kline after the fact."

Burgess waddled toward the entrance to the room, Tucker a step behind. The eight eyeballs and four dropped chins at the next table watched Burgess and Tucker head out the door before the four professors reconvened the buzz about what they had just overheard.

On the sidewalk in front of The BIB, Burgess waved his stogy toward Tucker. "Meet me back in my office in an hour, after you finish with the coach. We need to nail this down before noon," he said, and continued on to his car parked a few spaces further down the street toward campus.

Tucker waited until the AD pulled away from the curb before he stepped out of the wind and back into vestibule of The BIB. He checked his phone, connected to the Internet, and pulled up his Twitter account. His hunch was right! Postings from two of the players he followed on Twitter already announced Malik Farqu'har was a no-show that morning.

While he read thru the other posts, one of the professors crashed through the inner door, the roasted aroma of freshly-brewed coffee escaped behind him. Tucker jerked back out of the way. The academic eyed him briefly but continued out with his cell phone to his ear. Tucker thought he heard the guy say something about "Farqu'har." Tucker hesitated then decided he should talk to the professor who by that time had picked up his pace into a jog headed toward campus. After a few strides, Tucker stopped and looked back toward The BIB. Even if he caught up with the guy, there were three others who had shared the same information still inside. Tucker looked at his watch. He had less than an hour to meet with the coach to get his take on what had happened to Farqu'har. One hour until Burgess would assuredly ream him on how to handle the press. It wasn't the press that concerned him; it was how to catch and defuse the sonic boom of tweets sure to follow.

CHAPTER 3

Wednesday, March 30
9:52 a.m.

Winter's fangs gnawed at Tucker's joints which made for a sluggish jog. The extra forty-five pounds he had packed on over the years did not help much either. Every step had an ache and every ache had a memory that haunted him, his legacy of a shortened professional career in Boston. With his car parked two blocks from The BIB he had seven minutes to piece together ideas while he drove to meet with Coach Howells.

At the arena the staff scrambled to pack up of gear before the bus arrived to carry them to Atlanta. Coach Howells was in his office with two assistants studying stats and various last-minute scouting reports on the Michigan State Spartans, a perennial basketball powerhouse and their opponent in the semi-final game just three days away.

The coach, deep in thought, did not notice Tucker walk through the door. One of the assistants cleared his throat and nudged Howells.

"Great, now what, Tuck?" Howells said, hoarse from practice. He slapped his pen down on his desk.

"Hey, Ernie. Tough morning," Tucker said, the tone in his voice reflected the chaos of the situation. "Can I talk to you for a few minutes? I know you're getting ready to go and all, but given what's happened I need to talk to you."

Howells raised both hands like a robber had him at gunpoint, then placed them back on the edge of his desk, pushed his chair back, and said, "Sure. What's one more distraction? I mean, I'm only getting ready to take the smallest team in Division I basketball to the national championship, but I—"

"Sorry, I need to talk to you…alone," Tucker said.

Howells looked to his assistants. "All right guys. We'll call this a wrap for now. Go check with Ike and make sure he has what he needs. I don't want him to get over there and come up short on anything. We don't have time to go into improv-mode once we hit Atlanta."

The two assistants nodded. "We'll check in with you once the bus arrives, coach," one said.

"Thanks."

After the door closed, Tucker was quiet for a minute to choose his words. "Bad morning Ernie?"

"I've had better," Howells said, his words filled with disgust.

"Any word from Malik?"

"Nothing. None of the guys have heard anything."

"Any ideas?"

"None."

"Do you have guys out looking for him?"

"Hell, Tuck. These guys are going to load a bus to Atlanta in a little over an hour. I can't have them out looking for Farqu'har now. I sent out Todd Mueller, one of my assistants. Nothing yet. He's checked the usual spots…dorms, chicks' dorms, the Tabby Townhouses. No luck."

"Have you called his mother or heard anything from her?" Tucker said. He slid forward in the overstuffed chair in front of Howells' desk.

"No. I haven't had a second to make any phone calls. Todd may have called her; I don't know. I'd just assumed or hoped he'd overslept and he would show up, at some point before we pull out."

"Obviously he's not sleeping in the dorm if that's the case. And, if he doesn't show?" Tucker asked.

"No clue. My focus is on the team and the game," Howells said. He looked up at Tucker. Wrinkles wormed across his forehead. He had seen Ernie Howells this disturbed only once before, when his wife died in a hit-and-run accident early in the season. Tucker knew Howells was as level-headed as anybody in the game. The distress written across his brow was for Malik, the one player that had a unique influence on the team.

"The AD expects me to come up with a plan. He's over with President Kline now getting his ears wacked for sure. He'll get a load over there, then come back and drop it all in my lap like he always does," Tucker said, with a wince. "What's the departure schedule? I have it on my desk, but don't recall. What press is involved?"

Howells leaned forward and grabbed a pencil. "I had Malik and Jamal Derbish, scheduled to meet with the press thirty minutes before we departed. Team would rollout to the bus right at noon, the starting five would be the last ones out of the arena."

"ESPN. Any word from them?" Tucker asked.

"Yeah. I heard from Marty Schultis late last night. He said he would be in and wanted time with Malik," the coach said. "I told him he was a little late to the show, but I would squeeze him in for an exclusive."

"So now what? We punt?" Tucker said.

"Got any other options? What do we tell these guys?"

"Have you seen Twitter today?" Tucker asked. "The word is already out. I saw tweets from both Brady and Jackson O'Bleness. They're going back and forth about Malik being a no-show for the shootaround this morning."

"Dammit! I told all of them to lay off the social networking for now." Howells threw the pencil toward the metal trash can just past the end of his desk. "Shit. The last thing we need is to get people firing up the rumor mill on this shit."

"Well, it's out there. We need to cover this for now. How about if we get the team and your staff together. Tell them that the AD's Office wants to keep Malik under wraps for the morning, to keep the press and the pressure off of him. Some interviews etc, etc. All choreographed by the AD's Office. We're working a plan to add a little Cinderella mystique to the departure, a psych game on Michigan State. Keep them guessing." Tucker improvised as he went on. "Then, we'd escort Malik to Atlanta separately in time for practice tomorrow. Tell the guys to cool it on the tweets again. Tell them not to mention any of this on Twitter or emails or anything. Hammer it home, hard. My guess is somebody will let it leak out that we're playing this psych game, blah, blah. Not a huge deal, but it could buy us some time."

"You're shittin' me, right Tuck?" Howells' frustration melted the wrinkles but turned his face fiery red. "I can't lie to my guys. It's an issue of trust," the coach said, then took a drink of cold coffee that brought a cringe as he simmered down.

"Blame it on me, Ernie. Tell folks you didn't know anything about this plan. It all came about early this morning and I didn't even tell you until now. I've been accused of much worse in my life," Tucker said.

Howells hesitated then reached into his desk drawer for a bottle of Rolaids. He took two and crunched down hard.

"What about ESPN?" Howells said, as he popped a third mint and rubbed hard at the stubble on his chin.

"Same story. No...tell them to take it up with me, not the AD. Me," Tucker said, without hesitation. "And I'll call the kid's mother to find out if she's heard from him. I'll ask if anything was bothering him outside of the obvious." Tucker paused. "Player of the Year voting? The NBA draft. That's serious pressure on a kid but could solve a boatload of problems for him, given his family and his old man."

Howells bent forward with his head slumped. Tucker grabbed a basketball sitting on the shelf next to the chair. The inscription painted in white letters read "Big South Championship 2000, Redcliffe 87 – Presbyterian 84." The entire team had signed the ball with a black felt marker. Wolfman Howells, the point guard and team captain, was awarded the ball as the Most Valuable Player in the tournament.

"Ernie, did anything happen this week in practice? Anything? Anything that might cause the kid to walk away from all of this?" Tucker asked.

Howells lifted his head and clasped his hands in front of his face, looking into space past Tucker. "Practice has been pretty intense. I need to keep these guys sharp and healthy. One thing, maybe an incident. Yeah." He tilted his head toward his visitor. "Working some rebounding drills, guys hustling under the boards. Malik spun and clobbered Rusty Reid in the mouth, knocked a tooth out or loose or something. Lots of blood. A brief shoving match. The trainer took Rusty over to the dentist to get patched up. Reid and Farqu'har never get along. Always going after each other. Sometimes it gets a little out of hand. Not sure what it is. That's the only thing. The guys are all pretty tight. Nerves. Regardless, I know Malik wouldn't just walk away because of that."

"So, when was the last time someone saw Malik?" Tucker held the ball and tapped it against his forehead.

"Last night after practice. Ike Moncrief, the trainer, said Malik stayed late to shoot free throws. The two of them left together, but Ike ducked back inside; he forgot something. When he came out, he said Malik had already left."

"Anybody else?"

"Ike said when they went out by the side door there was a crowd of about a dozen people, some fans and a few hecklers."

"Hecklers? Out back?"

"Yeah, Ike said they had on Augusta State caps and Clemson sweatshirts. The usual crosstown rivalry crap," Howells added. He lifted his mug of cold coffee but could not stomach any more.

"Do you think the Malik went somewhere with them?" Tucker asked.

"Doubtful."

"Did Moncrief recognize any of them?"

"Don't know. Look, Tuck, I've got to go. The kid's got to show before we head to the bus. I need to talk to Todd Mueller to hear if he found out anything," Howells said, as he reached for a binder with sheets sticking out, unclipped. "Right now I have thirteen other players and a game to think about, a game without Farqu'har. Not an easy task. Come Saturday night, we could end up the laughing stock of college basketball."

"Let me know the instant you hear from Farqu'har or as soon as anybody hears from him. Before you go, grab the team and your staff. Tell them our story, about how the AD's office is holding Malik back to add to the tournament mystique, humma-humma," Tucker said, placing the MVP basketball back on the shelf. "Tell them to stay off Twitter. At this point, keep the basketball world guessing. The players just need to lay off for now. It'll all come out soon enough. If you want I can meet the team in Atlanta tomorrow and fill them in, but you need to hold them on this story for now."

Tucker stood to leave.

"If the kid…" Tucker shoved his hands in his coat pockets, "if the kid doesn't show by the time the bus pulls out, I think I need to get the sheriff involved."

Howells continued to gather things from his desk but shook his head in frustration.

Tucker stepped out of the office and pulled the door shut behind him, then stuck his head back in.

"Ernie, where can I find the guy who saw Malik leave? Was that the trainer?" Tucker said.

"Yeah, Ike Moncrief. Forget about seeing him here," Howells said, his eyes very direct. "The next time you'll see that kid is at the Georgia Dome in Atlanta sometime tomorrow morning. I'll tell him you want to talk to him."

"Don't tell him why, okay?" Tucker said.

"Sure," Howells said, though he wondered why this had to be secret. "And Tuck. Find the kid," Howells said, his eyes fixed on his desk. "I need him. We need him." He pushed back, stood, slapped his desk hard with both hands and turned away.

Tucker looked at his watch. Time was ticking away and had unexpectedly become the most important thing in the world.

"Call me if you hear anything," he said, before he disappeared through the doorway.

CHAPTER 4

Wednesday, March 30
10:04 a.m.

W hat do you mean he's not here?"
Before Ben Burgess had a chance to finish his
sentence, Brent Kline came out of his seat,
bug-eyed. With his pipe shoved in his mouth and hands
stuffed deep in his pockets, the excitable Redcliffe
College president glared at his potbellied athletic
director. Any news that jeopardized Kline's primrose
path to a notable chair in Ivy League administration
brought out the best, or worst, of his South Boston
temper.

"What the hell, Ben? The kid's about to make history
for this school and he's missing?" Kline said, after he
took a breathy puff on his pipe.

"Not sure what to say. I have—"

"Shit! I'll have every know-it-all, big-dollar, deep-
pockets alum in this office when this word gets out. If
that kid doesn't play, we lose millions in gift money.
Grants already in the works all based on this kid
pumping up the school in the press. Do you realize
that?" Kline said. He slammed his desk drawer shut.
"What the hell are you doing to find him? I want

someone bird-dogging this thing every second of every minute until he's back under your wing."

"I have Tucker McGill, my Assistant AD doing all he can—"

"What do we know so far?" Kline said, as he returned to his chair. He grabbed a pen, prepared to take notes.

"I'm not sure what we know. We're just getting started with—"

"Dammit," Kline said, as he slapped his desk with his empty hand; papers flew everywhere. "If this kid doesn't show and we go into this weekend without him, we'll have everybody who ever had anything to do with this school on our backs. Alumni. Boosters. Odds makers. Networks. Sports writers. Who knows about this? The NCAA know?"

"No. Hell, the kid might have just overslept, we don't know, so just hang on," Burgess said, with his palms toward the President. "We're looking into it, but with press and ESPN on campus, I wanted you to be informed." He braced his hand on the President's desk. "Tucker McGill is with Coach Howells getting any details he can. We'll have a plan on how we're going to handle this before the team leaves at noon."

Kline scratched at his chinstrap beard. "So, for all we know, the kid could be shacked up somewhere. You talk to his family? Have we checked with Mike Hazlett in Campus Security? Notified the sheriff? Filed a missing person report? Anything? Come on Burgess. Give me some warm fuzzy feeling that we're doing something here before this becomes a crisis. You know how much I like crises," Kline said.

Burgess knew how Kline handled—rather did not handle—crisis well. Even a simple thing like a snow closure ionized Kline into mutant Kryptonite, unstable and toxic.

"McGill is doing those things as we speak," he said, stretching the truth. "Let me touch base with McGill then I can get back to you. I wanted you to be aware this was evolving. Oh, it's already out on Twitter, too."

Kline dropped his head like a rag doll. "What's on Twitter?" he rumbled, softly without looking up. "Who posted what about this? Get to whoever it was. Tell them to cease and desist. We can't afford rumors, especially not this kind. Who posted?" The tall, thin, contemplative Kline was two steps out of his chair, eyes on the clock.

"A couple of the players on the team. McGill and Coach Howells will get that stopped," Burgess said. "I'll get back to you soonest. Let me find McGill."

"Ben, what options do we have if the kid doesn't show?" Kline said.

"What do you mean options? The coach prepares a game plan without the kid and we play the best damn game we ever played," the AD said, his dark eyebrows furrowed.

"Not a prayer!" Kline fired back. "Suicide." Kline closed his eyes, interlocked his fingers behind his head and stretched back. "We need a plan. We can't play that game."

"That's why we have a coach. Howells is a good one. Coach will have a plan—"

"I mean a plan to find the kid and a plan if we don't find the kid," Kline said.

Burgess paused before he spoke again on his way to the door. "I'll get back to you."

"With a plan, Ben. With a plan," Kline yelled.

CHAPTER 5

Wednesday, March 30
11:27 a.m.

To hear Tucker tell the story, it was the weather that seeped into his joints—not his forty-one years or the scars around his knees—that caused him to use the handrail on the stairs to the second floor of Steiner Hall, the administrative building which had housed the fractured marriage of academics and the athletic departments since the early 1950s. Though he and Coach Howells had discussed the situation, the details of a plan to find the missing Malik Farqu'har remained nebulous at best. He knew Burgess expected more than he had.

On the second floor, Tucker passed a janitor with earphones whose head bobbed to private tunes while he buffed the white marble floor to a glassy shine. Photos of distinguished professors lined the corridor walls between the academic wing and the athletic director's office, the athletic "pit" as it was known. The eyes of the distinctive, handlebar-mustachioed Sebastian Pellkofer, tracked McGill's walk with an accusatory scowl. Tucker heard the other photos murmur as he moved further down the corridor. His heavy footsteps echoed the entire length of the hall. With his head down, he tried to concentrate, but the cordial greetings of others broke his concentration.

"Hey, Tucker," said June Lawlor, Dean of Students, as she passed him in the hall.

"Hey, June," Tucker said, the slightest murmur of a greeting.

"Y'all do good for old Redcliffe this weekend over in Atlanta. We'll be watchin'."

"Not my doin', but we'll give it our best. Get the bubbly ready," Tucker said, his head back down, in thought.

"They won't know what hit them!" said Ollie Look, Dean of the School of Pharmacy, who came out of his office to add his two cents.

Tucker picked up his pace to avoid lengthy conversations. He needed to talk to the athletic director but wasn't sure exactly what he would say. The plan wasn't really a plan beyond the discussion of how to handle the press and the team.

The door at the end of the hall read "Director of Athletics" and beneath that "Benjamin L. Burgess." The name on the door had not changed in nearly three decades; neither had the petite body at the desk just inside the suite.

"Hey, Hettie Belle," Tucker said, without much enthusiasm as he entered. He looked around for others. "Mr. Burgess available?" As the door closed behind him he heard soft classical music, obviously from a small radio or sound system hidden behind Hettie Belle's desk.

"He is available and expecting you," she replied, with a peculiar squint.

Tucker offered a faint smile, before his eyes shifted with anxiety. He had hoped Burgess would be tied up to allow time to generate the detailed plan expected.

"Have a seat, Mr. McGill. I'll ask Mr. Burgess if he is ready for you now."

Tucker unzipped his parka but elected to stand and stare at the glass display cases with awards, memorabilia, and letters touting the past successes of Redcliffe athletes. As he stepped from one item to the next, he thought about what he and Coach Howells had discussed. In the end, all the awards in the room combined could not begin to matter half as much as the next game and the mark this game could have on college basketball history. The potential for the college to get major recognition. The money that it would bring to the school. It was an absolute fairy tale and it could all pass if one Malik Farqu'har did not show.

"McGill get in here," Ben Burgess said, busting out his office door.

Tucker took a deep breath and passed through the doorway, he brushed Hettie Belle as she tiptoed around the two and returned to her desk. As the inner office door closed, Hettie Belle pushed a small yellow button under her desk and settled in to privately listen to the conversation via the muted internal intercom.

"You and Howells come up with something?" Burgess said, as he walked to his desk where he picked up a slimy stogy, shoved it in his mouth, and waved for his visitor to sit in the brown leather couch. Burgess planted himself in the overstuffed leather chair opposite him. He checked his watch. "We don't have all day, McGill," he said, in a grumble that left no doubt he was already pissed.

"I think we are covered for now. Coach is handling the team side of the story," Tucker said.

"How? What's he doing? Hell, he's leaving in about thirty minutes. He doesn't have time for this shit. What's he doing?" Burgess shifted in the chair as he began to seethe.

"Ernie is telling the team that you, well the AD's Office, is holding Farqu'har here for special interviews and then taking him to Atlanta later. Maybe adding a little drama to the Spartan's scouting group," Tucker said. "And telling them to stay off Twitter, the Internet blogs, all those sites. Not to post anything about any of this with anybody. Just drop it and say 'no comment' if they're asked."

"Then what? What's the plan to find the little Fuk'har," Burgess jabbed. He leaned forward and beckoned with his hand for Tucker to speed up with more of the plan.

"That's all we discussed. We didn't have much time. We hit the immediate concerns then Ernie had to leave." Tucker mimicked Burgess's body language with a forward lean that put him close enough to smell the coffee and cigar on Burgess's breath.

"Well, my man. Mr. McGill," Burgess said, the cigar out of his mouth. "Here's my goddamn plan. It goes like this. You get your ass out of this office and find that kid. Can I be any clearer?"

Tucker allowed the silence to cool the situation while anger thumped a steady drumbeat in his temples. He looked away.

"Your one and only mission in life—even more important than breathing—is to find Farqu'har's ass and get it to Atlanta. Got that?" Burgess inched even closer to Tucker's face.

No response from Tucker; he sat and listened while his pulse ticked steadily upward.

"If that kid is not in Atlanta by game time Saturday, it will be bye-bye Redcliffe, hello world for you, McGill," Burgess said, his puffy, round face beet red.

Tucker did not back down or pull away. When he finally spoke, he was loud and forceful. "Look, the kid loves basketball. It's what got him out of Chicago's South Side, out of the projects. What the hell makes you think he's playing games?" The young assistant knew he would need more than luck to prove his point, but he continued. "Hell, we have no idea where the kid is, and you think he skipped? The kid may have been in some accident. Ever think of that? With the weather he may be off the road, lying in a ditch, injured, seriously."

Tucker broke his stare and stood with his feet spread wide. "These athletes, these kids, are our responsibility. Have you forgotten that?"

"No, McGill. I haven't forgotten that," Burgess said, with pointed sarcasm. "Remember, this guy isn't some ordinary kid. And don't forget he pulled stunts like this before," he added.

"Hey, the kid's young. He made some mistakes, and he knows it. We all make mistakes at twenty."

Burgess stared hard at McGill.

"This kid is sitting on a pile of gold. You said that yourself. We don't take him to Atlanta, some bookie makes big bucks. If Farqu'har doesn't play in that tournament, his Player of the Year nod goes to someone else, right out the window. Why in the world would he kiss that off? Makes no sense," Tucker said.

"Sounds like a story I once read about a stud from Providence College. The 'golden boy'. The next basketball great. Another Michael Jordan or Larry Bird," Burgess said, with a smirk.

"Don't go there, Burgess. Don't try to compare this kid to me. Don't try to pull my reputation in here or smear his. It's a little late to question all of that now," Tucker said, his teeth clenched. The memories of how he got to where he was quickly filled him with rage.

"We're talking about one of our kids. One of our players. A kid that happens to have the most unique basketball talent of any player in the country today, possibly ever, and you want to play games? You want to play like it is the kid who is 'giving it to the man'? I don't think so."

"Sit your ass down McGill, if you know what's good for you. And if you don't, sit down and listen anyway," Burgess said, as he looked away, back toward his desk.

McGill breathed heavily, his heart pounding like a boxer after a volley of punches before the bell. He settled in, back on the couch.

"As I said before you interrupted, I know the damn story, the whole story. And since you're so damn smart, I don't need to give you the damn story again, do I?" Burgess got up and walked around to his desk. "And this kid sounds a lot like you. Big time success on a little stage, and it all goes to his head. A little booze, chicks, parties. Sound familiar?"

Tucker tried not to listen, a conscious effort to suppress images that had haunted him for years. He was beyond pissed.

"Against the better wishes of the Boosters who support this shootin' match around here, I brought your ass in. And, because I still hold the cards, what I say goes." Burgess waited for another challenge from Tucker. "And here's what goes." Burgess came back from behind his desk and stood toe-to-toe with Tucker where he used the stub of his cigar to poke at Tucker's chest. "You find the kid. Do whatever it takes. Call his mom. Call the cops. Call whomever you want, but I hold you responsible. Period." Burgess turned away from Tucker, with his stogy back in his mouth. "End of story," he mumbled. "You find that kid, and you get him to Atlanta. I can't imagine that leaves any room for questions, but do you have any?" Burgess said, as he walked back to face Tucker.

In another place and another time Tucker would have decked Burgess, but over the years he had worked too hard to expunge the errors of his youth, especially around guys like Burgess.

"I get the picture," he said, his disgust difficult to hide. "But if I don't find the kid, if he really is missing, I'll need the authorities to get involved," Tucker said.

"Ha! The local gendarmes from Aiken County? Those good old boys in the sheriff's office? I think a couple of those guys got their badge in a Happy Meal. They have less commonsense than they had fries. Hell, it'll take them till Saturday to figure out where to start on this one, and that's obviously too damn late."

"Geezuz," Tucker said, "then find some private eye, some detective dick to put on the heat. I don't have any experience in this stuff. I have a lot to do in Atlanta as it is. Besides, I have zero authority for—"

"You don't need any goddamn authority. You need to get your ass in gear and your nose in the dirt. Get into other people's business. Make the calls and track down the kid! Comprendez? The sheriff can handle the slow shit. If the kid doesn't show up, they'll bring guys in and ask questions. You just make sure you're tight with the law and get their answers. Stay a few steps ahead of them, find the boy," Burgess said.

Tucker took a step back to avoid another poke in the chest.

"Sure. You got it," Tucker said, as he relaxed the tension in his body. To argue any further would waste time and only allow Burgess the opportunity to dredge up Tucker's questioned past and uncertain future. He looked away with his tongue in cheek. "Yeah. I'm on it. I'll be in Atlanta if you are looking for me." Tucker turned toward the door. Hettie Belle Block had just enough time to slap twice at the button under her desk before the line disconnected, and Tucker walked out of the suite.

Tucker stormed out of the admin building, took a deep gulp of the wintry air, and stopped to button the collar of his parka before he walked back across campus to the Huebner Arena. *Why would that dumb bastard jump to the quick conclusion that the kid just left?,* he thought. *Why didn't he think something might have happened to him? Was there something else Burgess knows?*

The walk from Sneltzer Hall to Huebner Arena was a short ten-minute stroll, on a cold day maybe eight. But on this day the sidewalks and grassy quad were filled with the entire student body making their way toward the bus that would carry their Cinderella Eagles to Atlanta. Tucker weaved through the crowd. He hoped to get inside the arena to talk to Coach Howells; not a snowball's chance that was going to happen. Like Times Square on New Year's Eve, students were crammed together and made it impossible to get anywhere close to the arena. He toyed with a long route to the back entrance, but time would not allow. Over the loud speakers, petite Carrie Rice, the Captain of the Redcliffe Cheerleaders, announced the team, player by player, as each came through the arena double doors. Some waved. Some smiled. Some flashed a V-sign with their hands, earbuds in their ears. To the man, each rubbed the beak of the Eagle statute on the pedestal in the square, then boarded the bus. Tucker listened from a distance, hopeful to hear one name in particular. He waited to the end. The final name announced was Coach "Wolfman" Howells. No mention of Malik Farqu'har.

CHAPTER 6

Wednesday, March 30
12:21 p.m.

Students slapped the sides of the team bus as it inched its way through campus behind a security escort from the South Carolina Highway Patrol under a shockwave of fight songs and blasts from the cheerleaders' victory canon. After the bus passed through the front gate, the impromptu pep rally-sendoff crowd scurried to the warm confines of the academic buildings, out of the wintery winds and sleet. Tucker, caught in the surge, elbowed his way to his office above the campus fitness center where most of the members of the athletic department hung their hats. Only the athletic director shared residence, tenure, and status with the deans in Steiner Hall.

Back in his office he felt the post-dentist tingle in his mouth as he shook the ice off his parka and placed it on the hook beside the door. Meager as it was, the ten-by-ten office was his professional home away from home. The décor was "sweaty jock." Photos taken throughout his athletic career covered the walls. Receiving the NCAA basketball tournament trophy as a senior for Providence College. The NBA draft photo with the owner of the Boston Celtics, proudly holding up his beloved green and white number eleven. Team schedule posters for Redcliffe Eagles spring sports. Old oak file cabinets oozed papers from open drawers. Even his cluttered desk, buried under mounds of papers, magazines, and correspondence that needed his attention. Outside his window the late wintry mix had turned into a swirling spring snowstorm.

Despite the clutter, the first thing he noticed when he sat down was the message light on his phone. He pushed the voicemail button and rubbed his numb, frozen cheeks. As he listened, his stomach growled a reminder that he had not eaten anything yet today.

"Tucker, Marty Schultis, ESPN. *What gives man?"* the voice said, loud and angered. *"Tried to catch Wolfman Howells, but he's not answering his phone. Had an interview with Malik Farqu'har set up for this morning and couldn't get anybody to make it happen. Now I'm catching word that the kid didn't show for the bus. What's up? Call my cell."* Click.

And it begins. Tucker deleted the message, certain he would hear from Schultis again, probably soon. *Why couldn't this have happened to Pinckney or Sammons or somebody else on the team? Only Malik,* he thought. He pulled a yellow pad from his desk drawer, swept back the other papers on his desk, and brainstormed his course of action. Calls to make. People to question. People to notify. Cashing in favors with others on the athletic department staff, conscious to avoid a volatile flair up in the feud with the academic departments.

The campus bell tower chimed one in the afternoon which made it noon in Chicago. He decided to call Malik Farqu'har's mother first.

The athletic department made it a practice to maintain emergency notification data on all student athletes. Tucker logged into his computer and drummed his fingers on his desk while he waited for the system to pull

the information for Malik Farqu'har. A picture of the
missing player popped up, probably taken his freshman
year. Same broad smile and deep brown eyes, but with
short cropped head of hair. Malik had since reverted to a
retro look with a beard and mini-Afro hair similar to his
old-school basketball idol, Kareem Abdul-Jabbar.

The summarized information listed his father first:

NAME: Farqu'har, Rodney
ADDRESS: Metropolitan Correctional Center (1995)
           71 West Van Buren Street
           Chicago, Illinois 60605
PHONE: None
           NOTES: All visits are controlled
           and scheduled. All visitors must register
           and must appear on the Approved
           Visitor List prior to visit. No telephonic
           communications.

His mother was listed below:

NAME: Novikov, Alexandra
ADDRESS: 9157 South Princeton Avenue
           Chicago, Illinois 60620
 PHONE: (773) 568-0287 (Home)
           (xxx) xxx-xxxx (Work)

No work phone. *Great.* Chances of finding her at
home at noon were fifty-fifty since she had no work
phone listed.

Tucker recalled reading about Malik Farqu'har as a
high school player. They had similar backgrounds. Malik
came from the Chicago South Side projects while
Tucker grew up on the wrong side of the tracks in

Central Falls just outside of Pawtucket, Rhode Island. One difference was Tucker lost his father in a longshoreman accident when Tucker was ten. Malik's father, Rodney Farqu'har, who was serving time in federal prison, walked out on his wife and new son the day after the boy was born. Malik's mother, a single parent, worked a number of jobs, none that provided real income. His basketball scholarship to Redcliffe College—one for which Tucker had personally gone to bat—was the ticket out of the projects for the kid, but left his mother alone in a city with few friends. A mail-order bride from Russia, Alexandra Novikov had mastered enough English to communicate but was never comfortable in public. Her conversations in English were short and for business only. She had a few friends, mostly Russian immigrants who, like her, spoke Russian socially. None of them had more than a basic education, Soviet-style, and all were laborers.

Tucker pulled the handset from the cradle and dialed. The phone rang. Once. Twice. Three times before a groggy voice answered.

"Preevyet," the voice said, rich in an accent, not typical Chicagoan.

"Miss Novikov?" Tucker asked.

"Da. Kto eto?" she replied, a deep throaty Russian voice, the kind heard in Cold War spy movies.

Tucker hesitated long enough for a second response.

"Yes, this is Xandra Novikov. Who this is?" she said, as she breathed out and coughed.

"My name is Tucker McGill. I'm calling from Redcliffe College in South Carolina. Your son Malik is a student here."

"Yes."

"I am calling to ask if you've talked to your son today?"

"No. I not talk to him."

"Have you talked to him in the last week or two?"

"No. Why you ask me?" she said, her accent even more pronounced when she strung words together to form a sentence.

"Has he mentioned any problems with school?" Tucker asked.

"Excuse me. I no understand," she said. She coughed to clear her throat.

"Has Malik written to you or called to mention any problems he might be having in school? Anything at all? Problems with students or his courses or professors? Anything at all?"

"Nyet, no. He has not problem. He play basketball," she added.

"Yes, I know. Malik is a very good basketball player," Tucker said, to agree and hopefully build a little rapport with her before he mentioned the boy's absence. "The basketball team is in a very big tournament this weekend."

"Da, I mean yes; I know. I see in paper."

"Well, Malik did not travel with the team on the bus today. We're not sure where he is. I thought maybe you would know."

"No. Not on bus? Why he not go with team? He play on the Redcliffe Eagles team," she said. "So where is Malik?"

"Miss Novikov, we're trying to find him now," Tucker said, short and sweet to reassure her.

"Is he okay? Is Malik okay? Where is he? Where is my son?" she said, more engaged, now with a tremble in her voice.

"We're looking for him now. I am confident we'll find him soon, and he'll be all right."

There was a silence on the Chicago end followed by a phlegm-filled hack through the phone. Tucker held the receiver away from his ear confident a mucus-filled lung would come flying out at any minute.

"Miss Novikov, I'm the associate athletic director here at Redcliffe. We will do all we can to find your son, but I need to ask for your help."

"My son, he love basketball. He always say he want to play. Why he not go to tournament?" she said, still confused.

"I'm not sure. That's what I'd like to know. I'll have a group, a large group of people who will help me find Malik. But, I want to ask that if you hear from him, anything from him, directly from him or from anyone who is with him or knows where he is, I need you to call me immediately."

"I work two jobs. I work at grocery store in evening and train station cleaning in early morning. I only home a few hours to sleep here from six until two o'clock in the afternoon. Maybe I can use work phone," she said. She hesitated with her speech, nervous yet anxious to help.

"I'm sorry I awakened you. Over the next few days it's very important that you call me as soon as you hear anything, please," Tucker said. He read his number to her and reemphasized the need for her to call immediately.

"I do that. I call, sure," she said, with emotion in her throat. "You find my son. He is all I have, yes?" she said.

"Of course, Miss Novikov. We will find your son," Tucker said, though he questioned how or where or when. "Remember, please call me. Thank you. Goodbye."

"Do svidaniya!" she said, as she pulled the mouthpiece away from her head and hung up.

Tucker rubbed his temples with his fingers to suppress the starbursts that flashed early signals of a humdinger of a migraine working its way to the left side of his brain. *Strike one.*

Second on the call list, law enforcement. Tucker pulled out the campus directory. Under Emergency Contacts, it listed the Aiken County Sheriff's Office. The only contact he had in any of the departments was PJ Beedle. The two of them had played softball in a summer league a few years earlier, before Tucker suffered a career ending hamstring pull. Tucker scanned the directory past the Bloodhound Division and Patrols Division before he spotted PJ's name under the Criminal Investigations Division. Though it seemed a bit extreme, at least at this point, to report a missing person to this group, Tucker dialed the number for Captain Philip John "PJ" Beedle.

"You have reached the desk of Captain PJ Beedle. I'm unable to take your call right now, but please leave a message and I will return your call at my earliest convenience. If this is an emergency please dial extension 422 at the end of this message." The answering machine clicked. "PJ, this is Tucker McGill over at the college. We played together on the Tag-Em-All team in rec softball a few years back. When you get in, would you give me a call? I have a little something I need to ask you," Tucker said, sure that his Rhode Island accent would be enough for PJ to remember by. *Dammit! I need to get these guys involved.*

Tucker pulled his list back to review the next contact. His phone rang.

"This is Tucker McGill," he said, never one to offer his title or position over the phone. He always felt, if they dialed the number they knew who they were calling, and if it was a wrong number, it made no difference any way.

"Tucker. It's PJ. Sorry. Screening my calls. Hey, how you been? Your leg recover yet?" PJ asked, his drawl thick and as original as gravy on biscuits.

"Can't say it has. Better shift my name from the injured reserve status to inactive reserve—for life—I think," Tucker said. "You doing okay?"

"If life was any better, I'd have to pay somebody for feeling so good! What can I do for you?" PJ said.

"Need help finding a kid, one of our basketball players. Not sure how to go about submitting a missing person request. Not even sure it would be through you, but this one's kinda special, shall we say."

"Has anyone else from the school reported the student missing?"

"Not to my knowledge."

"When was the last time someone saw the kid or heard from him? Why do you think he's missing and not just off somewheres?" PJ asked.

"Well, a missing kid, a student, would probably be reported through the Student Affairs office. This kid is a basketball player. The team boarded the bus and left for Atlanta without him about an hour ago. Final Four weekend."

"Right," PJ said. "Going to be a great one, too. Who's missing?"

"Our shooting guard, Malik Farqu'har," Tucker said, pained to even think the words.

PJ offered no response. When the shock let loose of his tongue, he uttered the first words that came to mind, "No. No way. You gotta be kidding me, man. Geez."

"All I can tell you is he didn't show for the shootaround this morning. The coach, the assistants, the players have called his cell. No answer. Coach Howells sent one of his assistants to Farqu'har's room, and he wasn't there. Things looked normal, but the kid wasn't there. The assistant drove around and checked other spots where the players thought he might be, good places to check. No luck."

"When was the last time someone saw him?" PJ asked.

"After the practice last night at the arena," Tucker answered. "The team trainer, Ike Moncrief saw him last."

"Have you talked to this Moncrief kid?"

"I haven't. The coach may have, but Moncrief is on the bus, headed to Atlanta. Coach needs him there with the team especially with this kid out of the lineup. I'm scheduled to head to Atlanta tomorrow. Not sure if I'll stick to that plan. May go earlier or may need to stay here for now," Tucker said.

"Okay. Let us pick it up from here. My deputies are loaded on special assignments. A case like this, I'll handle initially, especially considering who we're talkin' about."

"PJ, needless to say this kid…well sure…any kid is important when missing, but this kid is critical to the team. They play Saturday. That doesn't give us much time to have this guy in Atlanta."

"Understood, Tucker, but we have procedures we need to follow. Our goal is to find the kid and find out what happened to him. Sometimes we can do that fast, sometimes not. Your need in Atlanta may not have a whole lot of bearing on how we approach this. We'll do the best we can to find this kid as fast as we can, but we need to follow the book. Investigations take time."

"Got it, PJ. Do what you can. Let's stay in touch. Use my cell number, and call me if you find anything or need anything. I'll do the same from my end," Tucker said.

He provided his number and suggested texting as much as possible.

"And PJ, can you keep this kinda quiet? I know you have procedures and all, but we don't need the press jumping on this just yet. We already had some players put some tweets out that Farqu'har was missing, but the coach followed up on that by telling the team the athletic department was keeping Malik back for interviews and to lay a little psych on Michigan State."

"Gotcha. We'll do our best, but at some point procedures might dictate differently," PJ said, while he fumbled through his desk for the Missing Persons Report form.

Tucker thanked PJ for the help then, and before he hung up added, "And PJ, I talked to the kid's mom. She's not heard from him, not in a few weeks. I asked her to call me the minute she hears anything."

"Okay. I might be calling her, too."

"Stay in touch, sheriff. Round up that crew, and find my man."

"Will do, Tucker. Good to talk to you."

Tucker worked back through his list, made a few calls then noticed the time. *Shit. Happy hour. I'm late. I gotta go.* He threw his list into his backpack along with his laptop, grabbed his Blackberry, his keys, and parka. *I'll grab a bite, make a few more calls, then figure out tomorrow.*

CHAPTER 7

Wednesday, March 30
5:19 p.m.

The P.I. Bar & Grill housed in the Partridge Inn— "The Great Hotel of the Classic South"—had been a landmark of the Summerville Historic District of Augusta since the late 1800s. The most stylish and sophisticated bar in all of Augusta, it served up the world famous Steve's Southern Fried Chicken alongside of shrimp and grits, not to mention the daily happy hour that made it the favorite watering hole for Generation X-ers—swinging singles, geo-bachelor businessmen, prowling professionals, and a particularly large gathering of "cougars." Clusters gathered around the room, snuggled up to the bar, hid in cozy corners, or enjoyed the view of the city from the verandahs (on warmer days). A "Little Vegas" of a place in the sense that "what happens at P.I. stays at P.I." For Tucker, it was a change of venue away from the college scene, an atmosphere to let his hair down without faculty and student involvement. It reminded him of The Greatest Bar in Boston where Celtics fans could rub elbows (and other body parts) with their favorite Celtics players.

From the looks of the crowd, everybody in Augusta wanted to celebrate Hump Day at P.I. Tucker entered from the lobby of the hotel. The place was mobbed. Groups everywhere. One exceptionally loud and wild group standing at the end of the bar caught his eye as he looked for Mel. Eight guys in business suits with ties pulled down, clanging glasses and mugs like Knights of the Round Table. None of them looked familiar, but when he got close enough to see over their shoulders, he saw Mel, sitting on a barstool wearing a clingy, long-sleeved cashmere shirt—buttoned only half-way—on top of a black pencil skirt with knee-high gray leather boots. She saw Tucker's face, shifted her posture, and immediately announced his arrival.

"Pardon me boys, but it's time for y'all to be gone with the wind. Rhett Butler has arrived on terra firm...finally," she said, Scarlett-style. The ring of admirers turned to see all seventy-six inches and two hundred and fifty-five pounds of Tucker—an unhappy, stressed Tucker. "How about a little privacy, pah-lease? Don't forget to drop your business cards here, fellas. Never can tell which one of y'all will win the drawing," she said, her pearly-white teeth in full bloom as she gathered the business cards—with some duplicates—piled around her drink on the bar. More than one offered a bit of a peck on her cheek or neck as they walked away.

Melissa Cooper, DDS, out of her white scrubs and workday pony tail unclipped, her dark red hair—the color of rich mahogany—that curled on top of her shoulders highlighted the fading tan on her thin face, a cute dimple at the end of her nose the only imperfection, but even that seemed to make her more attractive to men and loathed by women. When she stood briefly, she looked every bit of her five feet nine inches, and after she slid back onto the stool, the split in the front of her knit pencil skirt opened generously up her thighs to make her legs seem even longer. Tucker pulled up a stool close to hers.

"Drawing?" Tucker said, with a question mark on his face as he watched the suits disappear into the mingled masses throughout the bar.

"Oh, just a little game with the boys. You can enter, you know," she said, with a wink. "With the right incentive, I can fiddle with the odds." She stepped forward, her hand extended to caress Tucker's cheek, but instead she grabbed his shirt by the open collar and pulled him toward her. "But don't be late when you invite me to join you. Those odds will go to zero, cowboy," she chided, her lips pursed like a nun with a ruler.

She relaxed her grip and sat back with the same look the spider gave the fly. "A girl's gotta do something in this little bitty town," she said.

"Safe bet that a practice in Augusta and even in Beech Island is a far cry nicer than your place in New Jersey. Trenton's the pits," Tucker said. "May I buy you a drink, my little peace offering for being late?" Tucker raised his hand to get the bar tender's attention.

"That would be wonderful. The usual. Oh…and dinner," she added, "since you were real late." Her lower lip thrust out like pouty child amused her but annoyed Tucker.

"You drive a hard bargain," Tucker said, as he turned to the bartender to order a beer for himself and a Wild Turkey, Rare Breed, three cubes—the usual—for her.

"Not that it matters, but let me hear your flimsy excuse," Melissa said, with her nose in the air.

"I'm surprised you can't guess. The word's all over town, probably a topic all over this room right now," he said. He watched her cock her head and scrunch her face like she had no idea what he was talking about.

"Our superstar basketball player's missing. He didn't make it to the gym today, and the team left for Atlanta without him," Tucker said, as he grabbed his beer and handed Melissa her drink. Condensation from the glass dripped onto her knee. Tucker was quick to wipe it off, his hand lingered for a gentle pat which generated a quick, mischievous smile across her face. She flipped the red curls from her shoulder and listened.

"Nobody has seen the kid since last night. Burgess has all but threatened me to find the kid and get him to the game." He stopped long enough for a swig of beer. "I talked to the kid's mom, she hasn't heard from him. Talked to the sheriff's office. They're starting a search, sometime. I've got a million and one things to do for this tournament that all go on hold until I find this guy."

"Tell that ass Burgess to go pound sand," she said, as she preened herself unconsciously.

"Burgess thinks the kid walked away. Why he thinks that, I don't know."

"Somebody ought to check on that guy Burgess then. He's not playing with a full deck." She turned to the bar and stirred her drink. After a moment of silence she said, "Hell, in the end, it's only a game…" she paused, "and, as far as I'm concerned, a weak excuse for being late for a date you made. Let the coach handle it." She looked back toward Tucker with a grimace on her face, "Has the coach done anything or is he non-involved too?"

Tucker stuttered to find the right words, words that would appease her. "He's with the team. He's thinking bigger picture, like how he's going to win without this kid. I told him I would handle the search; he needed to concentrate on Saturday's game."

"Somebody needs to light a fire. I mean, the coach …" she said, before taking another healthy sip of her drink. "Hell, if it makes that much difference, put an APB out on him. That's what they do in Trenton. The pigs would already have an APB out on the kid and strip searched half of the female population to see if they can find evidence of him."

None of this settled well with Tucker. It was all impulse. "The sheriff might have done that here, too. We don't know much of anything for sure except we haven't heard from the kid."

Mel continued to bombard him with questions and pushed for a vigilante group, bypassing the sheriff.

"Let's talk about something else. I've had enough of this for one day," Tucker said, to put to rest the barrage of questions. "I heard you did some patch up work on one of the players the other day. Coach said one of the guys had a little shoving match with our missing stud, and you had to do some of your dental magic on the kid."

"No magic, just the usual dental doctoring. I had to knock him out while I worked on it. Should be okay, good enough to play any way," she said, then switched back to their original topic. "What else have you done to find your superstar? What's next?" she asked, as she drained the remainder of her drink, turned the glass upside-down on the bar, and motioned to the bartender to bring another round.

"I have a list of people to contact—"

"Have you talked to players? Staff? Coaches?" she interrupted.

"Not yet. They all just left for Atlanta," Tucker said.

"You need to talk to them. What about campus security? And, has the administration done anything? Anything from the Dean's Office? Has he issued a statement or initiated a search for this guy? Have you talked to him?" She sat up straighter like a teacher with school boys in detention.

"I have them on my list, but—"

Melissa inched forward, patted him on the shoulder and said, "You need to get to all those guys," then sat back. "What about enemies? Any of those? Rivals? Have you talked to anybody at Augusta State? I hear they're not too fond of the success by their country cousins in Beech Island," she said. As she talked she tapped the bar with her finger.

Tucker listened and drank his beer and another beer while Melissa fired volley after volley of questions at Tucker. Every time Tucker opened his mouth, she nipped back at him like a hyena after a wounded beast. For the remainder of happy hour, while her bloodstream flowed with bourbon, she brainstormed while Tucker— on her command—took notes on bar napkins and coasters she passed to him. Eventually, the beer on an empty stomach made him feel lethargic, and he tired of hearing what an uninvolved, disinterested but gorgeous bystander had to say.

"Hey, hey, hey. Hold on a sec," Tucker said, his hands formed a tee in front of Melissa's nose. "Do you want dinner or not? If you're just going to ramble, I'm going to eat. I told you, I've had enough of Malik Farqu'har for one day."

She nailed him with her, "Yes. That was the deal, cowboy. You owe me dinner." She ran her hand up his forearm. She hopped off her stool, wobbled but braced herself with a hand on the bar, then headed to the dining room with the assertive walk of a strong woman, Tucker in tow behind her.

Over dinner, she continued to monopolize the conversation, but eased off the Farqu'har questions. "So, you went to Providence College on a basketball scholarship, eh," she said. Tucker nodded. "Grew up down the road in Pawtucket. What? Too scared to leave home to go to college?" she said. Tucker watched her put her wine glass to her lips, her eyes closed.

"I had reasons to—"

"To stay home? Poor mom needed her little boy close to home? How sweet."

"I had a scholarship, a full ride," he said, short and sweet.

"Now I see. Just like this Farqu'har kid, young high school star from the wrong side of the tracks offered a scholarship and a big chance to change his past, except your guy left home for Redcliffe. Not sure if that's a step in the right direction," she said.

The evening was not going the way Tucker expected. He needed a break from the Malik Farqu'har search. He wanted to relax with a drink, or two. He thought an evening with Mel would do more to sooth his pain. Somehow with all the questions, accusations, and assumptions, she made matters worse. He bent forward, put his elbow on the table and his chin in his hand. "What's this all about?"

Melissa met him in the middle of the table, put her hands on his cheeks and fixed him in a deep and mysterious stare with amber eyes that burst sunset orange at the pupils like a burning crevasse in a snow field. "So, why'd you deck your coach after the last game?" she said, with a haughty sneer.

Tucker lifted her hands off his cheeks and sat back with his palms flat on the white linen table cloth. Frustrated, soft-spoken Tucker said, "Where did you hear that? What's with all the questions? What is it with you women?" He grew impatient with her, the first step toward anger.

Melissa cocked her head, taken aback at his attitude.

"I'll share a little bit of background if you want it," Tucker said, in a huff. "You want to hear about Sheila, the last girl I dated, the psycho paranoid one. She asked a million questions, too. She was convinced everybody was after her, spying on her." He relaxed and looked around the room before he rocked toward her, and in a whisper said, "So do you think those waiters are really waiters or are they CIA checking on people?"

Melissa pulled back in response, an Edvard Munch scream on her face, her eyes wide with mock wonderment. After a deep breath, she let out a hard sigh, and her face softened into a smug smile. "Oh, a little sensitive are we?" she said, in a voice so soft only he could hear. Before Tucker had a chance to challenge her, she simply added, "I just like to know a little something about the men I screw or I let screw me." Her statement came with no emotion in her voice or in her eyes.

Tucker sat, silent. He shifted his eyes to release some of his steam.

"Come on. We're going to my place for dessert," she said, finally, as she tapped Tucker on the tip of his nose. She stood and grabbed his hand. "Follow me. I'll show you the shortcut."

In less than ten minutes, despite the weather, they were in Melissa's townhouse. Strange as it was, he had talked to Melissa only three times, been out with her twice, and now it appeared he had won the business card drawing the schmucks at the bar had lobbied for earlier. He would make a night of it, maybe longer.

"Remember I can fiddle with more than just the odds, cowboy," she said, as she began to unbutton her shirt. He started from the bottom to help her until they were all unfastened. She slipped the shirt off her shoulders and let it drop to the floor. Tucker ran his hands across the contours of her soft skin.

"Let's unwrap that package of yours and fiddle," she said, while she released his zipper in slow motion.

In less than twenty minutes, Melissa had switched from fire hose of words to blazing action in a carnal way, much to the pleasure of Tucker. Despite the welcomed change he wrestled with two familiar but forgotten inner voices—one that spoke of his euphoric transgressions of youth, always ending with *Burgess has it right* and the other that simply whispered a name, *Malik*. It was too late to make any calls from his list; he knew he was too drunk to talk business. Besides, Tucker was too aroused to consider anything outside his immediate reach. He silenced the whisper, temporarily. From that point on it was all about Melissa; she had her way with him.

CHAPTER 8

Thursday, March 31
8:12 a.m.

Happy hour over drinks turned into twelve hours of debaucheries that would have Hollywood searching for a rating beyond a triple X. Tucker staggered into his apartment at five a.m., a defeated man, used and abused by the endless needs and desires of Doctor Melissa Cooper. He had planned to be on the road by six, but after two snooze-button reprieves, he overslept until eight then staggered into a hot shower which he capped with a blast of cold water to wake himself.

The night's sleep, what there was of it, was intermittent. Melissa never rested and neither did the voices in Tucker's head—a deep, raucous laughter from one and a desperate whisper from the other.

As he stood in front of the mirror he wondered where his old self had gone. His chiseled look had softened, not like he remembered himself back in his playing days. As he lathered his face, his eyes examined the reflection staring back at him, far beyond the mirror, back to another time when he was the college star, the campus king. The entire world of Providence College revolved around Tucker McGill in the spring of 1991. Banners and kiosk posters promoted the chances of winning a national championship behind the fade-away jumper of the gravity-defying hotshot named Tucker McGill, who in the end let it all slip away.

When his cell phone erupted with "YMCA"—his obnoxious ringtone à la Village People—he flinched. Tucker wiped the shaving cream, now mixed with the trickle of blood, from his face as he reached for the phone.

"Tucker McGill," he said. He dabbed at his neck with a towel.

"Mister McGill?" the voice asked. Tucker recognized the thick accent immediately.

"This is Xandra Novikov. This is joke, no?"

"I'm sorry. I don't understand." Tucker detected a trace of sarcasm in her voice which was more nasal than the day before.

She coughed and cleared her throat before she answered. "I receive, just now, a package. You know, FedEx man. He just bring a flat package with letter inside. Letter from Malik. I not understand what letter means."

Tucker tossed his towel in the sink. "First, this is not something I had anything to do with. Can you go back and explain a little more?"

"I arrive home late from job at train station," she said, clearing her throat. "I just get to sleep. I hear hard knock on door. I get up and see FedEx man in truck. He left flat package by door." While she talked Tucker ran his hand through his hair as he moved toward his desk. When he heard her turn the phone away from her mouth and cough, he found a pen and a pad of paper.

"I read the letter but not understand. I think maybe you send letter."

"Miss Novikov, I assure you, I didn't send any letter. Can you read the letter? Is it typed?" He cradled the phone between his ear and shoulder. "If you can read it to me, possibly I can help," Tucker said. "Read it to me slowly, please."

Xandra Novikov cleared her throat. "I still not read very good. I read slowly. It have my name at the top, *Miss Novikov*."

"*Mommy dear. Do you miss me? Does my...,*" she hesitated as she phonetically sounded through the syllables, "*does my ever-loving coach miss me too? Wish I could help, but I am so lost. Your little boy has had enough of the basketball bullshit. I need a little time off and it's so sad because so many people are counting on poor me this weekend.*" Once more she paused.

Tucker started to ask her a question, when she continued, "*I need a tiny cash advance of $2.5 million. Place it in a plastic Jewel-Osco grocery bag...,*" she stumbled through the words, unsure of their meaning, "*and leave it by the second kiosk on the platform for track fourteen out of Union Station for the train departing at 5:18 p.m. today. Leave the bag at exactly 5:15 p.m. according to the station clock, then leave. And please, mommy, remember days in Mother Russia where you always looked over your shoulder? I will be watching you. You will be safe if you do as I ask. Now it's your turn to listen to me.*" She stopped, again.

Tucker broke the silence to ask if she had finished. She said yes then struggled twice to clear her throat.

"I not understand. What this mean?" She grunted with disapproval.

Tucker pieced together the note. Even with Xandra's difficulty reading, it did not sound like Malik Farqu'har had overslept or was shacked up like Burgess had thought. He was cautious to explain without causing any panic.

"The letter. It not sound like Malik. He not talk to me like that before," she said.

"It sounds like Malik is with some others who need money. They want you to provide them with money."

"For why?" she asked. "Who he is with? Why he not on bus?"

"I'm not sure. I'm not sure who's with Malik," Tucker said, not willing to explain kidnappings and ransom and the potential dangers.

"I have money. I save some money to help Malik. I have money."

Tucker was surprised at what she said. He looked down and shook his head. "Miss Novikov, they want a lot of money."

"I have no big money," she said. "I work two jobs. My husband in prison. He give me no money. If I not pay, if I not leave the money, what does it mean 'someone might get hurt'? Malik get hurt? Who doing this, Mr. McGill? Why they do this to my Malik?" Her voice raised octave after octave as she rambled in strained English. "Maybe I get money from my husband."

Tucker recalled Rodney Farqu'har was a kingpin drug dealer before his arrest and imprisonment, not a clean source of money. His brain scrambled to restore calm. "Please don't do anything. I'll go to the authorities, the police here, about that letter. They will need to work with the police there in Chicago," he said, though he doubted PJ Beedle's ability to take any action from Beech Island.

Xandra fired back, "I get money."

"No. Please, Miss Novikov, wait," Tucker insisted.

"The letter. It looks like same letter papers Malik receive when he learned about scholarship. The top has crest, like shield, stamped into paper."

"You mean a letterhead. Is the crest round and have words around the outside?"

"Da. I mean, yes. But I know not these words."

Tucker did not expect her to know them. If it was the official seal for Redcliffe College, the words were in Latin: *Magisterium, Fiducia, Integritas, Obsequium*— Leadership, Trust, Integrity, Discipline. Over the phone Tucker could hear Xandra cough and let out a few expressions he did not understand, probably Russian. He made no attempt to calm her; she needed to release the shock, frustration, and fear. Her world was wrapped in one son, hundreds of miles away. One son whom she loved unquestionably. It had been just a little over twelve hours since McGill had called and gave Xandra the news about her son and less than twenty-four hours since Malik Farqu'har had been presumed missing.

Through the phone, Tucker heard what sounded like a fist pounding a table. Alexandra Novikov came back to the phone, her voice raspy. "The letter, Malik signed this letter."

Tucker did not respond immediately. He could hear the confusion in her voice.

"Are you sure it's his signature?" Tucker asked.

"Da," she said, without any hesitation. "Why does he sign letter like this? Why he not go with team? He always good boy?"

It was obvious she still did not understand what Tucker had explained. She did not grasp the fact that someone was holding Malik and forced him to sign a letter if in fact it was his signature. Xandra cleared her throat. Tucker sensed it was more than a cold that had choked her. He was lost for words that might explain or comfort. There was nothing he could do to sooth her. He knew if it was really a ransom note, they needed to get the Chicago police involved. He needed PJ to make that happen.

"Miss Novikov, I know all of this must be confusing for you. I understand you want to know what's happened to your son. Please, give me a little time. Give me until the end of the day. Let me see what I can find out, what I can do," he said, his voice quiet, calm, reassuring. "I'm confident we'll find Malik, and he'll be all right, I just need you to wait and do nothing. For now, disregard the letter. I'll get back to you later today."

"Yes, Mr. McGill. I do that, but I worry so much for Malik."

Tucker was unsure of her tone and the first part of her statement. "Please get some rest. Try to sleep. I'll call you this evening."

"I try. Please remember me," Xandra said, then hung up.

Tucker quickly dialed the number for PJ.

The machine picked up and Tucker heard the voice recording. At the beep he said, "PJ pick up." Tucker waited. PJ didn't pick up, so Tucker jumped in, "PJ, call me ASAP. The kid's mother received a ransom note." After Tucker hung up the phone, he dressed and packed a small suitcase. Before the incident, Tucker had a long list of things to do in Atlanta, all tournament-related, all business. He had told Coach Howells he wanted to talk to the trainer, Ike Moncrief. He believed Moncrief had something to say about what happened to Malik Farqu'har.

In Chicago's South Side, Alexandra Novikov used the steam from a hot shower to ease her congestion before she dressed, applied more than her usual makeup, and caught the Rock Island District Line 8:31 a.m. train to the LaSalle Street Station, a block from the Metropolitan Correction Center.

CHAPTER 9

Thursday, March 31
9:26 a.m.

His conversation with Xandra was a quick wake up, quicker than he'd liked and brought with it a killer headache that rumbled between his ears like bricks in a dryer. He swung by The BIB, grabbed his daily double Americano in a tall paper cup to go along with a bacon, egg, and cheese bagel sandwich before he jumped on his shortcut connector to Interstate 20 West to Atlanta. An hour later, the breakfast he managed to choke down laid heavy in his stomach though it eased his headache to a constant throb behind his eyeballs. The only relief was to close his eyes which he dared to do every so often as he made his way on the two-and-a-half-hour drive to Atlanta.

Cell phone coverage along the route was usually excellent, but low clouds with the late wintry weather played games with his signal. He attempted to call PJ at the sheriff's office again. The call went straight to voicemail. *Dammit PJ. Stop screening your calls and pick up the damn phone.* He did not bother to leave another message.

Next he tried to call Coach Howells. Voicemail again. This time he left a message and told Wolfman Howells he was en route to Atlanta and needed to see Moncrief at ten-thirty, somewhere—either the hotel or at the Georgia Dome.

He made other calls to arrange interviews, to arrange tickets, to arrange for a post-game department victory party, and to reconfirm his room reservation at the Marriott Suites Midtown, the designated official home away from home for the Redcliffe Eagles during the Final Four weekend.

One call he was reluctant to make was to his boss, because he did not want to listen to Burgess whine and scream; unfortunately Tucker knew he had to update him on what he had discovered since they last spoke. With his headache under control he hit speed dial and waited to hear the beeps of the dial tone and the ring at the distant end.

"Burgess," the voice said, with just enough static to interrupt the conversation Tucker intended to have.

"It's McGill. Got a minute?"

"Where the hell are you, McGill? You sound like you're in some goddamn cave? Yeah, I've got a minute. I'm headed into a press conference with Wolfman Howells. Why the hell aren't you here?" Burgess said, choked with his phone tucked between his shoulder and ear as he walked through the lobby at the hotel with his ever-present cigar in hand.

"I'm in my car on I-20 headed your way. Stayed in Beech Island to make calls last night trying to find Farqu'har," Tucker said, without confessing he actually never got around to the calls he intended.

"Give me a rundown. Make it quick. You find the kid? His lazy ass somewhere in Augusta tied to some bedpost or something?" Burgess charged.

"Nothing like that. Haven't found him but talked to his mother, twice," Tucker said. He paused to allow Burgess his usual rant, but nothing came. "I called her yesterday to find out if she heard from her son. She said she hadn't heard from him for a couple weeks. I explained he appeared to be missing and asked her to call me as soon as she heard from him. She called this morning."

"Did she hear from the bastard?" Burgess growled.

"No. She called to say she received a strange letter by FedEx this morning. It was a ransom note. Gave her instructions on how to drop two-and-a-half-million dollars in a bag and leave it at a train station in Chicago."

"What the hell—"

"I'm not sure if this is part of a prank or the real deal or what. I talked to Captain Beedle from the sheriff's office yesterday. He's working the case. Tried to get to him this morning, but all I get is voicemail. I need him to contact somebody in Chicago to see what they can do on that end. I'll let Beedle work it."

"Hey, McGill," Burgess said, as he grabbed the phone from his shoulder and stepped into an empty ballroom not in use. "You do whatever. You can have all the Aiken County Keystone Cops work this deal, but you need to find the kid. Shit, for those guys it's just another missing person and—"

"Not any more. If we get Chicago to take a look at the letter, this'll become more than just a missing person especially given who the person is. I doubt this is a prank. The letter's a threat. We can make a case to expedite this thing since this kid's a prime subject for something big or bad to happen."

Through the car speaker Tucker heard a pop then static followed by a familiar string of profanity.

"Dropped my damn phone," Burgess said. "Okay, I'm going into this conference. Call me back later or find me when you get here. We need to talk face to face."

Tucker cringed.

"And, call Brent Kline. I think he's still at Redcliffe," Burgess added. "Make sure he's aware of what the hell's going on. Make sure you give him a full status of things. At some point he needs to call Chris Gorting at the NCAA and inform him of this first hand."

"I'll call President Kline. I still need to talk to Beedle to see if he has any news and to pass on the info about the FedEx letter," Tucker said, checking his watch for the time. "If you're with Ernie headed to the conference, tell him I checked Twitter before I left Beech Island. No more tweets from any of the players about this so maybe we have it contained for now."

"And I didn't see anything on the TV news here this morning. Nothing in the *Atlanta Journal-Constitution*, either," Burgess said.

"Tell Ernie I left a voicemail for him this morning. I need to see Ike Moncrief as soon as I get there."

Tucker heard Burgess mumbling something to the coach walking next to him.

"He said he got your voicemail. He'll have Moncrief on standby. We're about to head into this press conference. Call Kline now. Find out how he wants us to handle this with the press, alumni, and etcetera. He needs to talk to the Gorting sooner rather than later. When this thing hits, the yahoos in Indianapolis are going to go ape-shit. When ESPN catches wind of this, who knows what'll happen. As soon as Michigan State hears this there'll be one huge sigh and nothing but laughter out of East Lansing."

Tucker did a yada-yada nod to himself. "I'm still a ways out. Let me get on the horn with President Kline and get his guidance. I'll pass on your comment about the NCAA."

"McGill, don't let that skinny shit out of the call to Gorting. I'm telling you, Kline's not comfortable outside academia. He'll fight it. Don't let him pussy out. Gotta drop."

The steady dial tone blared through the car speakers until Tucker ended his call, then suddenly realized he did not have a phone number for the Redcliffe College president.

CHAPTER 10

Thursday, March 31
10:11 a.m.

Tucker tried PJ again with the same result. This time he used the prompt and transferred his call to the front desk.

"Augusta County Sheriff's Office, Mary Beth speaking." Mary Beth Snew was the fifty-something admin assistant to the Sheriff of Aiken County. She joined the office right out of Westside High School in Augusta. Unmarried, her job was her life. She was a walking, flesh-and-bones archive of case histories for the past forty years, recognized as the right-hand man for the sheriff.

"Hey, Mary Beth this is Tucker McGill. Have you seen PJ Beedle around there?" he asked.

"Morning, Tucker. No. Haven't seen him at all this morning. Something I can do for you?" she said, as she smacked the wad of gum in her mouth.

"I hope. I'll find PJ. I left him a voicemail. But can you get the phone number to President Kline's office over at Redcliffe. He may have a special emergency number on file there," Tucker said.

There was a pause, "I'm checking. Hold on," Mary Beth said. "You must be drivin' or on a speakerphone.

Sounds like you're in a tunnel. Oh, here it is. Found it! Are you prepared to copy?"

"I'm driving, but I think I can remember it. Go ahead."

She sighed. Tucker could hear her gum pop through the phone.

"Well, the area code is the same as always. The prefix is the only prefix we have for campus. The last four are nineteen-seventy. Anything else?"

"No, thanks," Tucker said.

"10-4. Have a good day!" She hung up.

Tucker dialed the number while it was fresh in his memory. He had talked to Brent Kline at departmental social outings but never had occasion to call him directly for business related items; Burgess and Hettie Belle Block did all the talking for the department.

"Good morning. President Kline's Office. This is Clara Overholt. How may I assist you?" Obviously the phone number was an office phone and not an emergency cell number for Brent Kline.

"Miss Overholt, this is Tucker McGill from the Athletic Department. I need to speak to President Kline, please?" Tucker said. In the back of his head he was still scripting what he needed to say to Kline.

"Good morning, Mr. McGill. President Kline is busy—"

It's so difficult to interrupt a sweet Southern accent, but Tucker did. "I understand Miss Overholt, but what I have to discuss with President Kline is extremely important and time sensitive. I really need to talk to him."

Clara Overholt was a permanent fixture in the president's office. She had served six different presidents, all men. They came and went from behind that desk, some more honorably than others. She had heard every approach imaginable to get through her screen to the president. McGill's was par for the course. "I am so sorry, Mr. McGill, but President Kline cannot talk to you at this time. I can take a message and call you at a convenient time when he is able to speak to you."

"This is extremely urgent Miss Overholt. I wouldn't press you if it wasn't, but I must talk to him now, please," Tucker said, as politely as he could without blowing his cork. He looked down at his speedometer and noticed his frustration had pushed his speed up to near eighty-five miles per hour. He eased off the gas and backed off with his tone. "This is concerning the college championship basketball games this weekend."

"Oh, about the games? They are going to be so exciting. I truly wish I could help, but President Kline is just not available now."

Tucker bent forward, pounded his forehead against the steering wheel and silently mouthed a litany of his favorite four-letter words.

"Fine. Please call me when he is available. Thank you," he said, disconnected, and tossed his phone in the passenger seat.

Although around campus and specifically within the athletic department, Brent Kline was considered the quintessential academic, over the years he had developed a casual affection for golf. On occasion he would play with a select faculty foursome. Tucker knew that one of the standard group members was Mike Webb, the head football coach at Redcliffe. Tucker punched speed dial on his phone and appealed to Mike for Brent Kline's cell number. With a little coaxing and a simple explanation of the reason he needed it, Tucker was able to get the number and quickly dialed the Redcliffe president.

"Hello," Kline answered in a deep voice, expected from a stretched-body man who could pass as Ichabod Crane, beak-nose and all.

"President Kline, good morning sir, this is Tucker McGill from the athletic department," Tucker said, his voice strong. "Sorry to bother you at—"

"McGill, how did you get this number?" Kline asked with displeasure.

"President Kline, I need to talk to you about Malik Farqu'har," he said, ignoring the question.

"Ben Burgess told me he was missing. Have you found him? What do we know now?"

Tucker talked Brent Kline through the events of the night before and earlier that morning. He detailed his efforts to work with the local sheriff's office in the search. When he asked for guidance on how to handle the press, Kline was less than definitive.

"McGill, that's your job. I told Burgess to put a plan together. Whatever you do, preserve the name of this college as a safe and secure environment for our students," he said, "and to win that damn game."

"I realize that, Mr. Kline, but we're talking about a kid who stands to make millions in a matter of weeks when they hold the NBA draft."

"I know all that, McGill. Your point?"

"My point is there are people out there, related to the sports or not, who apparently want to get a cut of the action, the kid's potential salary money or to stop that in some way temporarily or permanently," Tucker said, as he ran his fingers across his forehead and through his thinning brown hair. "This kid was the pre-tournament choice for MVP. The entire country will be watching for this kid on Saturday. There is more money riding on these games than the Super Bowl," Tucker said, talking with his free hand while he drove. "Playing the brackets is a national pastime in March. ESPN has covered this kid the entire season. CBS has covered our games through the first four rounds and is scheduled to cover the semi-finals on Saturday."

"Okay, okay. Are you going somewhere with this, McGill?" Kline said, as he tapped his desk with his pipe.

"There's more to it now. I talked to the kid's mother. She received a ransom note via FedEx this morning."

"She what?"

"People know this kid has big money riding with him playing. We need you to get to the NCAA and have them postpone those games," he said. Again he eased his foot off the gas.

"McGill, that's NCAA business. We don't have a say in that," Kline argued.

"But Mr. Kline, if we don't approach the NCAA, they won't arbitrarily delay the game. Do they even know Farqu'har is missing?" Tucker asked. "Have you talked to Mr. Gorting, the NCAA President?"

"I told Burgess I wanted a plan. What's your plan? Tell me more about that note," Kline said, followed by a long drag on his pipe.

Tucker walked Kline through the note and his plan, piece by piece. Despite endless interruptions, he fielded all the questions, ignored the sarcasm, parried the unfounded attacks on his character, and retained his civility until the very end when he could not control himself any longer.

"President Kline, you have to call the NCAA," he blurted out. "It's not something I can do. It's not something Ben Burgess can do. It's something you have to do."

"Who do you think you're talking to, McGill?" Kline said, his rage rising as it always did when challenged. "I'm not one of your student interns."

Tucker felt the adrenaline revving up.

"All due respect, sir, you wanted a plan, I gave you a plan, and it involves you. I know these kids. I know what they need to win, physically as well as psychologically. Without Farqu'har they have a one in ten chance of winning." He took a deep breath to compose himself. "At this point, the NCAA will only listen to someone at your level. Burgess can't do this. I sure as hell would get nowhere. You have to present our case. Call the NCAA. Talk to Christian Gorting, and tell him he needs to postpone the game for the good of NCAA basketball."

"Listen," Kline said, calm, cool, and deliberate. "No pissant associate jock is going to tell me what to do. Do you understand me, Mr. McGill?"

"And all I can tell you, sir, is that if you don't call..." he paused, "if you don't try to get this game postponed, you and this school will be the laughing stock of college sports. Do you want to answer to the Board of Trustees for that?" Tucker locked his eyes on the taillights ahead and imagined a call to each Trustee to explain Kline's refusal. "You can be damn sure I would let every Trustee know we talked, and with this cell number I'm sure I can get the evidence needed to prove it."

Kline pulled his pipe from his mouth. He had climbed the administrative ladder through three schools in twelve years—Bennington College, Bethany College, and Berea College—to become the youngest serving president of a Division I school with his sights set on the Ivy League, the big time. He knew how the game worked. He knew McGill's threat was blackmail, but he had no other clear choice. He wasn't comfortable posing an ultimatum to the president of the NCAA, but under these circumstances McGill was probably right, on all counts.

"I'll take your recommendation under advisement," was all Kline said, after a long, nervous puff on his pipe.

Tucker remained speechless in thought. *You ignorant, pompous son of bitch. If you are too chicken-shit to stand up to the NCAA under these circumstances, the Trustees should send your ass packing.* Tucker cracked his window to take in some cool air.

"Thank you, President Kline. I'll continue my search and do appreciate your support," Tucker said, his pulse still elevated.

"Good day, Mr. McGill," Kline said.

"Good day to you, sir."

Tucker heard the phone on the other end click followed by the dial tone that hummed from his car speaker. It took fifteen miles of outside air to cool his boil.

Listening to Kline was the opposite of listening to Melissa Cooper. Kline did not believe in action on anything, and Melissa was ready to jump on everything, probably even the waiters—literally and figuratively—especially if they were CIA.

About the time Tucker realized his window was still open and he was quite cool, the Village People were screaming "YMCA" over his cell phone again. It was PJ.

"Where the hell have you been? You gotta stop screening your damn calls and pick up the receiver, man," Tucker said. "I've been calling you all morning."

"I'm on the road to Atlanta. I checked my voicemail before I left and figured I could call you from the road. Don't tell my boss I was drivin' and dialin', though. The office frowns on making calls on the move unless it is an 11-99. What'ya got?"

Tucker updated PJ on the FedEx ransom note. They kicked around their next course of action and agreed that Beedle would have the sheriff contact the Chicago

PD for assistance. They needed to secure the letter and begin the tracking process.

"Where are you now, Tucker? Sounds like you're in a car or a phone booth or somewheres."

"I'm in my car, just about to Atlanta," Tucker confirmed.

"Good. Tell you what I need. I need you to get with the coach, and have him get that trainer guy of his ready for me to talk to. I don't want any excuses; I need to see that kid as soon as I get there. I'm about an hour out. Should be there by eleven. Plan on eleven o'clock."

That meant PJ was about thirty minutes behind Tucker on I-20. Though the traffic had increased as he approached the city, as long as PJ did not use his flashers or drive well above the posted speed, Tucker had just enough time to sit down with Ike Moncrief before PJ arrived.

"Okay. I'll have the kid available. Plan to meet us at the Dome. I am not sure what the practice schedule is for the day but expect the trainer will be there at a practice or mending ailing joints of some kind. Ask around to find the locker room we'll be in," Tucker said, with a little pedal to the metal.

"I talked to Mike Hazlett, Campus Security," PJ added. "He gave me the security tapes from Huebner Arena, tapes from night before last, the night the kid was last seen."

"Did you see anything on the tapes?"

"Well, there were a lot of folks—kids, students— hanging around the back door, by the locker room. Most of them hoopin' and hollerin' as the players came out," PJ said, as he eyed a car that sped by him like he was standing still. "That kid Farqu'har, I recognized him from the papers, he came out kinda late with some other guy who then went back inside. Farqu'har was drinking a

Coke and did some high-fives with some guys but kept walking. Most of the crowd stayed by the door except three guys who moseyed along by Farqu'har, sorta hip bumping him as he walked. Stand by," PJ said. He listened to a report coming over from dispatch. He thought it was about the search for the missing player, but it was a missing dog someone had reported. "Not sure if they were trying to aggravate him or what. They had on Augusta State jackets. The tall kid, Farqu'har, was either playing along with them or something because he sorta staggered along like a wet noodle kinda."

"Is that all you got?" Tucker said.

"You see, the camera has a good angle out the back door, but once the kid and those three guys turned at the edge of the building, we couldn't see anything after that. Except, we did see that kid that went back inside, the one who came out with your player. That kid came back out and looked around, like he was looking for Farqu'har. I lost him when he went around the corner of the building like the others."

"So, did those tapes help you? Did you get anything out of them?" Tucker asked, as cars pulled up on either side of him.

"We were able to identify the three guys from Augusta State. I had one of our patrols bring those guys in. They weren't very happy, you know, the tough guy image and all. We questioned all three. Stories all line up. That's why I need to talk to this kid Moncrief, the trainer. You said he was the last person to see him? What about the guy walking out with the player?" PJ asked.

"Same guy," Tucker said. "I'll let you go. When I get to Atlanta I'll find Moncrief and have him in the locker room to meet with you."

"Thanks, amigo. Drive safe," PJ said, before he disconnected.

Tucker made one more call to Ernie Howells who had left a voicemail for Tucker to call him with a status. Again he got Howells voicemail but left the message to have Ike Moncrief in the Georgia Dome locker room at ten thirty, no questions. He bumped up his speed to something that would cost him a bundle if pulled over. He had a new sense of urgency for getting to Atlanta, to ask Moncrief some questions before the sheriff asked his.

Traffic on the Perimeter road around "Hotlanta" sucked Tucker into the urban rush like a New York City cabby. When his cell phone sang out its "YMCA" message, he was white-knuckled, weaving in and out between cars and across lanes, too preoccupied to answer. He leaned over to check the caller ID; it was Wolfman Howells. He snatched the phone off the console and as he looked up his eyes opened wide when he saw the La-Z-Boy chair fall from the pickup truck and splinter on the blacktop twenty feet in front of his car.

CHAPTER 11

Thursday, March 31
10:25 a.m.

B rent Kline had lectured on supply-side economics in front of student and professional academic audiences around the world, but outside the realm of theoretical modeling, he was a hopeless bag of nerves. Within his college and among the trustees, he was a voice heard and received. When it came to the physical, the real, the athletic side of the world, Kline was a fish out of water. And when it came to discussing matters of sports, he quickly turned to his athletic director to "handle it." Ben Burgess was not available to handle the challenge Kline now had; this call was a call only he could make as the President of Redcliffe College.

"Clara, get me Christian Gorting's office. He's the President of the NCAA," he said, through an intercom speaker installed about the time Truman was in office.

He rolled the tension from his shoulders, let his head fall back to look up, and closed his eyes. His Zen calm shattered when Clara Overholt buzzed back and told him his call was on line one. Perched on the edge of his chair, he stared at the phone, then reached for it like he was picking up a cactus, swallowed hard and said, "This is Brent Kline."

"Yes, Mr. Kline. This is Liz Oglesby, Mr. Gorting's assistant. A pleasure to talk to you today. This must be an exciting week for you there at Redcliffe with the Final Four coming up and all," she said.

"Yes, a big week indeed," Kline replied. "Speaking of which, I need to talk to Mr. Gorting, if he's available, please."

"He has some people in his office right now. Let me see if he can take your call. I'll be right back." The phone clicked and a recorded phone message began to play before Kline had a chance to switch to speakerphone. After several minutes of rah-rah background music with a female voice that touted the many programs within the NCAA, a man came on the line.

"Mr. Kline," the voice started, as the jittery president fumbled with the handset. "This is Stan Rice. I'm the liaison for men's basketball issues here."

For Kline it almost seemed like this guy Rice was a mind reader, a guardian angel of sorts, someone with whom he could plead his case without going to Chris Gorting.

"Hi Stan," Kline said, contemplating his message.

"Looking forward to the games this weekend. You have one helluva team down there, real Cinderella. And that kid Farqu'har. Man, he's as hot as a firecracker. Just exciting to watch that guy play."

For the next three minutes Rice blabbered on about basketball, the brackets, and the teams in the finals. Kline paid little attention, his thoughts more to what he had to say, what he needed to recommend. Question for him was who to approach? Gorting or Rice? The more

Rice talked, the more he knew he would get no decision out of this guy.

"Say, Stan, I need to talk to Chris Gorting. Any idea if he's available?" Kline asked.

Rice put a hand over the mouthpiece on his phone, but Kline could hear the muffled exchange between Rice and Clara Overholt. "Clara says Chris will be with you shortly. I just happened to stop by to drop off some papers and heard your name. Thought I'd say 'hi' and wish you luck this weekend."

"Great. Thanks, Stan. I'll let you go. Just put me back on hold, please," Kline said, his simple attempt to avoid frivolous socializing.

The NCAA promotional recording came through the speakerphone before Clara Overholt picked up.

"Mr. Kline, Mr. Gorting will speak to you now," she said. Kline lifted his receiver.

"This is Chris Gorting. How are you Mr. Kline?" a voice said, scraping and rough. "Sorry. Fighting a bout of strep throat. California blood takes a long time to thicken here in the Midwest."

"That's quite all right, Mr. Gorting. I understand. Had similar issues when I was in West Virginia a few years back. I need a few minutes," he said.

"Sure, I have time. Not often I have the president of one of our Final Four schools call me. I'll bet you're extremely proud of that coach of yours and what he's done with that team."

"Indeed. What—"

"He's worked miracles with those guys. Amazing. I sit here and watch the big schools like Carolina and Duke with their high school All-Americans and they stack wins on top of wins, but Redcliffe doesn't have a one and your guys have destroyed teams," Gorting said, with emphasis on how the team had performed. "This weekend will be a tough one. Not like Coach Howells hasn't seen tough ones all through the brackets. That guy's a hardwood genius. Better keep an eye on him. There are many schools, big time basketball schools, looking to regain their big time status on the court. Howells might just end up talking to some of them here soon," Gorting cautioned.

"Well, we have the greatest respect for Coach Howells and all our coaches. I'm sure our AD has considered all of that. In fact, I called to talk to you about Coach Howells, our team, and the tournament games this weekend."

"Sure, go right ahead. I just wanted to say good luck."

"Thanks. As you can imagine, basketball has meant a lot to Redcliffe College this year. We've actually built a bit of name for ourselves, something we had sought through academics for decades," Kline said, though it pained him to grasp the reality of his statement. "Now it comes to us in a five-month period through athletics, through basketball. We'd hate to lose that momentum regardless of how it developed. Likewise, we understand the significance of our appearance in the Final Four. A legitimate Cinderella, so to speak, with the eyes of millions watching on TV. David out to slay Goliath." Kline built a silence while he took a sip of water to quench his dry mouth.

"Mr. Gorting, we have an issue with our Saturday game," Kline said, nervous as a whore in church. His voice cracked mid-sentence.

"Chris. Call me Chris. What kind of 'issue'?"

"I guess it's more than just an issue with the game. It's a serious issue about a missing player."

"Missing? Like academic problems missing? Health? What do you mean 'missing'?" Gorting said.

"It's Malik Farqu'har. And it's not an academic or health issue. We believe he's been kidnapped." Kline hesitated and waited for a reaction from Gorting.

After a brief pause, Gorting cleared his throat. "Do you have any contact with him?" Gorting asked, his thoughts more toward the weekend.

"No, none at all. And what we know is very sketchy." Kline proceeded to summarize the events of the past two days, to include the FedEx letter Xandra Novikov received earlier in the morning. He briefed Gorting on the actions taken and planned but cautioned that working with the sheriff in Aiken County might extend the search period beyond the weekend—and Saturday's game.

"So, Mr. Gorting...Chris...I have a problem or rather, we have a problem. If our team goes into the game Saturday without Farqu'har, the chances of winning drop precipitously," Kline said, as he sucked Gorting into the real issue. "Bad for us and potentially bad for you. People would watch this game for ten minutes, then probably go find better things to do."

"Now don't sell your team short there, Brent. Howells still has a team to put on the floor."

"Agreed, but assuming we were scheduled to play in the finals without Farqu'har, the viewership would drop to nothing. Guaranteed." Kline was unsure of how to proceed. He fumbled for words while fingered the pipe in his hand to calm the butterflies that churned in his stomach. "I need you...to consider a delay. Postpone the game or games for a few days," he said.

Gorting chuckled. "Afraid that's not possible, Brent. This is basketball. This is sports. Throughout the season, teams suffer setbacks all the time. Injuries, illnesses, other family emergencies for the most part. Can't say I've ever heard of a missing player before." Gorting looked up and smiled when his assistant entered his office and placed a stack of correspondence on his desk. "At this point the network holds the strings in more ways than one. Our legal guys would think I am crazy. We have a contract with the network. I can't get them to drop those games this weekend. They won't buy that. They won't delay these games. They have too much riding on them," Gorting harrumphed.

"I'm not asking to cancel the game, just want a level playing field. We both know we don't stand a snowball's chance in hell of winning that game without Farqu'har. It won't even be a game. Ratings will eat you up if you and the network decide to play this weekend," Kline replied, his voice more forceful now. He always enjoyed a good debate but preferred to discuss topics other than sports, especially with the head of all college sports.

Gorting placed his phone on speaker to free up his hands. On the top of the stack of papers just delivered was a FedEx envelope. While Kline continued with his futile appeal, Gorting unzipped the large envelope with purple and orange letters.

"I have to report back to my Board of Trustees today. I need to give them a sense for what's happening, both with the search and with our appeal for a delay to the game," Kline said.

"Come on, Brent. We can't stop this thing. This is a moving train. This Final Four week and weekend—the coverage, specials, interviews, re-runs of previous classics—all of it, is locked and cocked. People all over the globe are set to watch this stuff," Gorting said, as he pulled the paper from the envelope.

"I know what you're thinking, but I'll bet when the word gets out that Farqu'har isn't playing, people will be more involved watching news and police reports to follow what's happening in the search and less involved with watching Michigan State destroy a too-small school from Beech Island, SC," Kline said, still nervously fondling his pipe.

Gorting continued his multitasking, his ears latched to the speakerphone, and eyes read through the text of a letter on Redcliffe letterhead. His ears registered select words over the phone: "destroy," "reputation," "classic," "Cinderella." His eyes scanned the paper and recorded a different set of words with different emotion and meaning: *"cover-up," "gang," "your little secret," "make your choice." "Dead."*

Kline wrapped up and waited for Gorting to reply. Nothing came. Kline broke the silence, "I need some answer today, Chris. I need to tell the Trustees something."

Gorting, re-read the letter with a vee-shaped brow, not listening to Kline at all. "I'll get back to you," Gorting said, then turned off his speaker and hung up abruptly.

CHAPTER 12

Thursday, March 31
10:39 a.m.

Reflexes die hard in former professional athletes, fortunately. Tucker saw the chair roll off the back end of the junk-filled pickup in front of him. Instinct allowed enough reaction time to miss the large chunks of the overstuffed chair and cars in the next lane, however, the splinters and assorted hardware scattered a proverbial minefield for his tires. As with most things, he over-analyzed the incident. His ex-friend Sheila would have blamed it on the CIA. As he figured it if he had been on the road earlier he would not have been behind that truck with the chair. He had planned to be on the road earlier, but Melissa Cooper had other plans for him the night before, consequently the late start for him. He knew she had made it to work on time and was getting her grins drilling someone's teeth while he banged up two knuckles during the roadside tire change that cost him thirty minutes and the lead he had on PJ.

Forty-five minutes later, Tucker hung his Final Four parking pass from the mirror and pulled into a spot a few yards from the box office doors at the Georgia

Dome in midtown Atlanta. The clouds remained a constant, but the wind had died down to a breeze. Inside the building a security guard, about half the size of Vermont, pointed him toward the locker room assigned to Redcliffe College. Tucker had no problem finding the locker room but spent several minutes trying to track down Coach Howells who walked him to the training room and introduced him to Ike Moncrief, the trainer. The coach explained the sheriff's request to sit down and talk about Malik Farqu'har's disappearance. He said Tucker would be with him during the questioning. The coach told Tucker he could use the coach's annex across the hall; Howells and his staff were scheduled to review more videos of the Michigan State Spartans regular season games against ACC opponents.

As Tucker led Moncrief to the office to begin his questions, PJ Beedle appeared from around the corner at the far end of the hall, black briefcase in one hand and a Styrofoam coffee cup in the other.

It was easy to recognize PJ; he was the epitome of a jock gone to seed. Broad shoulders with a puffy pillow-like chest, a grizzly in a starched shirt. The tan uniform of the county sheriff's office topped off with the Smokey-the-Bear hat would normally make it a dead giveaway, but with all the security of the Final Four, law enforcement officials were everywhere. Tucker stopped and waited for PJ to join them.

"PJ, this is Ike Moncrief; Ike, Captain Beedle, Aiken County Sheriff's Office," Tucker said. Moncrief tilted his head down at PJ in a long, cold stare with his hand extended. PJ placed his briefcase on the floor, returned the look, and proceeded to crush the kid's hand in a steady, slow squeeze. "Let's go in here and grab some seats," Tucker said.

From its appearance the room was less an office and more of a storage room for excess team promotions. Old banners, fliers, and posters. A bag of miniature footballs with the Atlanta Falcons winged logo. An old metal desk, a pair of desk chairs on caster wheels, and a stack of folding chairs on a carrier. It provided the privacy they needed and, though cluttered, was about as sterile as the interrogation room back in the sheriff's office.

PJ took his sweet time to arrange items on the desk. He put his Styrofoam cup on his right, opened his briefcase, and pulled out an iPad which he placed to his left, then pulled out an old, small tape recorder which he placed between him and Ike Moncrief. Finally he placed two pencils next to a notebook directly in front of him, closed the briefcase, and placed it on the floor. Ike Moncrief rubbed his palms together in his lap as he watched from a chair opposite his questioner.

Tucker pulled out a folding chair and sat off to the side, back away from the others to observe. He was surprised at how quiet and meticulous PJ was. He was always the loudmouth on the team and in other casual conversation. This was the first time he had observed PJ at work. It seemed almost out of character and a bit odd, PJ being quiet and all.

Thanks to PJ, in no time the small room reeked of Old Spice aftershave and Skoal wintergreen tobacco, the reason he carried the Styrofoam cup. PJ reached for the cup, held it below his lower lip and let a slug of tobacco juice ooze out of his mouth. With two pudgy finger tips he removed a piece of long cut tobacco from his tongue then looked up at Moncrief.

"Mr. Moncrief, I wanted to talk to you about Malik Farqu'har," PJ said. "I am going to record our session so I can go back over the tape with my notes to make sure

I copied your comments correctly." Moncrief remained still. PJ pushed the button on his recorder and placed it back on the desk. "This is Captain PJ Beedle, Aiken County Sheriff's Office. Today is Thursday, March 31, 2011. Time is seven minutes past eleven in the morning. Location is a…" he looked at Tucker, "coach's office annex at the Georgia Dome in Atlanta, Georgia." He turned back toward the recorder. "I am joined by Mr. Ike Moncrief and Mr. Tucker McGill." PJ reached for the recorder and pushed it closer to the trainer who had rolled back away from the desk.

"First, Mr. Moncrief, I want to make sure you understand you are not accused of anything and not suspected of anything. I am here to ask you a few questions concerning the disappearance of Mr. Malik Farqu'har."

Moncrief sat up a little taller, somewhat concerned about the formality PJ used to open the discussion. "Suspected of what? What's up with Farqu'har?" Moncrief said. "Coach said the AD had him back at school."

"We'll get to that," PJ said, his palm raised to have Moncrief ease off a bit. "Do you recall the last time you saw Mr. Farqu'har?"

"Tuesday night at practice."

"Do you recall when Mr. Farqu'har left practice?"

"Yeah. We walked out of Huebner Arena together, probably around nine or so. Farqu'har always stayed after to shoot free throws."

"Did you leave the area together?"

"No. We started out, then I remembered Coach Howells asked me to set something out for him, and I forgot to do it. So, I asked Farqu'har to wait up while I ran back inside to put those things together. When I came out, he was gone."

"How long were you back inside the building?"

"Maybe two, three minutes max," Ike said. He leaned back in his chair and twiddled his thumbs in a slow roll, his eyes momentarily mesmerized by the badge on the sheriff's shirt.

"Was anyone else with you?" PJ asked, his nose in his notebook as he recorded Moncrief's responses.

"Nobody from the team. Everybody else left probably twenty or thirty minutes before us. There were some students looking for autographs or something and a few dudes from Augusta State with their usual bullshit hanging around."

PJ looked up, his forehead wrinkled with question. "What do you mean 'usual'?" he said.

"Guys from State are always giving us shit. Back when I was playing freshman year, they'd come over and challenge us to pickup games. It got to be more a brawl. A couple of those guys were just thugs."

"Wait...so you played on the team?" PJ said, with a nod toward Tucker.

"Yeah, as a freshman. Blew out my Achilles tendon and never really recovered. My vertical is about four inches now. Since I was in a sports medicine major, Coach wanted to keep me around; he said I could work in as team trainer. Worked out okay."

"Wish you were playing this weekend?" PJ asked, with the first hint of a smile.

"Yeah, but I put all that behind me. I try not to think about that too much."

"So, when you went back inside, what was Mr. Farqu'har doing?"

"He was drinking a Coke I gave him and doing high-fives and autographs for the crowd."

"Did you ever see Mr. Farqu'har have any kind of exchange, verbal or physical, with anyone in the crowd?"

"No."

"Not any of the guys wearing State jackets? Nobody?"

"No."

"And when you came back out Mr. Farqu'har was gone? And the crowd?"

"They were gone, too. Right. Nobody was outside when I came back out."

"Captain Beedle, excuse me, but Ike, you said nobody was outside when you came back out. After just three minutes?" Tucker said.

"Yeah. It was cold, windy, nasty that night, remember? There was a bigger crowd right after practice when I went out to my truck, but by the time Farqu'har and I came out there was only about ten people."

PJ continued to ask questions about time and students in the crowd and anything Moncrief might have noticed that was unusual or different. While the trainer talked, PJ continued to write but noticed Moncrief's ability to recall details began to stutter. PJ pulled out his iPad. With a few finger taps he brought up a video player.

"Mr. Moncrief I am going to play a little clip for you." He tapped the tablet and a video began to play. "This is a copy of the recording from the security camera outside the locker room of Huebner Arena. The video was taken the night of March 29, I believe. Can you tell me if the individuals in this video are the guys you mentioned when you answered my questions…the guys and the crowd?" PJ slid the tablet toward Moncrief; Tucker scooted his chair closer to watch.

"Yeah, same guys," Moncrief said, after a few seconds, cocksure of his answer. "Lots of guys from State wear those jackets, but those look like the guys." He began to fidget in his seat. His foot began to tap the floor while he rubbed the palms of his hands on his thighs.

PJ pulled the tablet back, nodded toward Tucker and offered him the tablet.

"So when you came back out and saw everybody was gone, including Mr. Farqu'har, what did you do?" PJ said.

"I looked around. Didn't think much about it. Kinda pissed me off that Farqu'har didn't wait up, but hey…it was cold. I got in my truck and left," Moncrief replied. When he caught himself rubbing his hands, he slouched a little deeper and crossed his arms.

"So you never saw Mr. Farqu'har alone with the three individuals you identified on the video, correct?" the sheriff asked.

"No, I did not. Everybody was gone."

"Where did you go after you got in your truck?"

Ike Moncrief took a deep breath, the shaky kind a kid takes when he barely escapes being caught with his hand in the cookie jar but did not say anything. He just sat there. After the pause, he leaned forward, put his hands on the edge of the desk and said, "I told you. I left. Look, I need to get guys ready for practice. Are we almost finished?"

PJ picked up the Styrofoam cup and made another slimy deposit.

"Mr. Moncrief, I realize and appreciate your position with the team at this point, but be advised I am conducting an investigation for a missing person who just happens to be a key element of that team."

"Right. I know that. And I have eleven others on that team that have to play the game because that son of a bitch isn't here," Moncrief snapped back.

PJ sat up straighter. He took a hard look at Moncrief; a scowl formed on his face. No teeth or turned up lip, more of a frown.

"Tell me, how did you and Mr. Farqu'har get along? How was your relationship with Mr. Farqu'har?" PJ asked and again nudged the recorder closer to Moncrief.

Tucker crossed his arms and sat back, not sure where PJ was headed with his question. The session had lasted much longer than expected, and now it seemed the sheriff had shifted from simple questions to interrogation.

"What?" the trainer said, confused.

PJ repeated the question, holding the kid's eyes with his. "I said...did you and Mr. Farqu'har get along?"

"Yeah."

"I'll ask you again. Where did you go after you got in your truck and left the parking lot?" PJ put his pencil down and fixed his eyes on his tall subject on the other side of the desk.

"To my dorm. I drove to my dorm, did some packing, read a little, and went to bed," Moncrief said, his answers curt and direct while his eyes burned a hole through PJ's forehead.

"Did you go directly from the parking lot by Huebner to your dorm? Any stops along the way?" PJ asked, for clarification.

"I went to my dorm...directly. No stops," he replied. His eyes veered away, his face contorted while he chewed on the inside of his cheek.

"Did anybody see you from the time you left the gym until you got to your dorm?

"No."

"Your roommate?" PJ asked.

"Damn!" Moncrief reached up to massage the bridge of his nose then used his hands to make a point. "I thought you said I was not a suspect? Why all the questions? I got in my truck, drove to my dorm. I didn't see anybody and nobody saw me, at least nobody I know of. My roommate was on the advance party down to Atlanta. He left Tuesday morning." Moncrief was sweating more than when he'd come in, enough to soak through the warm-up T-shirt.

"Where is your truck now?" PJ asked.

"In my dorm parking lot. Davenport Hall," he replied.

PJ wrote down the last comment and leaned forward in his chair, toward the tape recorder. "For the record, Mr. Tucker McGill, the Associate Athletic Director for Redcliffe College is in the room and has been here for all the questions. Mr. McGill, is there anything you would like to ask Mr. Moncrief?"

Tucker looked to the floor and shook his head no. PJ had asked many more questions than Tucker felt necessary. Sure the kid was the last known person to see Farqu'har before he disappeared, but there was no reason for the third degree. Tucker wanted to ask Moncrief other questions but felt the kid had been through enough already.

"Mr. Moncrief, I appreciate your time and willingness to answer my questions," PJ said, folding his hands in front of him on the desk. "As I continue my investigation, if further evidence suggests a need for clarification or additional questioning, I will make arrangements to speak to you again. Do you have any questions for me?"

"No," Moncrief said, sliding forward and out of his chair.

"If Mr. McGill doesn't have anything for you, you may go." Ike Moncrief did not wait for Tucker to respond. He stood and walked out of the room without a word.

Tucker went to the door, looked up and down the hall; Moncrief was already out of sight. He went back in and sat down at the desk while PJ scribbled something on his pad. "That was a little harsh, don't you think PJ?"

PJ looked up and growled, "Hey, you want answers? You want to find the kid? I'll do my job; you do yours."

"Down, boy. Down," Tucker said. "Let's not get too feisty."

PJ finished his note and reached for his Styrofoam cup. "The kid's lying," PJ said, with conviction, before he oozed out another glob of tobacco-filled spit.

"Why do you say that?"

"Kid got a little testy. His answers got choppy, cutoff, flustered. And his words didn't match his body language. He moved around a lot. He kept rubbing his hands. Very nervous. Then he got real stiff. Did you see how he soaked through his shirt?" PJ made sure the recorder was off and started gathering things. "Did you notice how quiet he got when I asked him about what he did when he got in his truck? Always a good sign the subject is about to lie. Not normal for a guy that is on the up and up."

Tucker looked around at nothing in particular, just taking time to allow things to settle in a bit. He was no psych major, and his only experience from police questioning came when he was on the other side of the table, in Moncrief's seat. "The guy once played on this team, and now is the trainer for his buddies. What about the three punk kids from a rival school down the road? What about them?" Tucker asked.

"I'm telling you there is something about this kid." PJ He looked at his notes. "I wasn't satisfied with the kid's response when I asked him if he and Farqu'har got along."

"I guess...he did hesitate. Maybe he just didn't hear the question. As you said, the guy was tight as a knot, probably exhausted. Kid has a lot on his mind aside from all of this," Tucker said, in an attempt to explain Moncrief's answer.

PJ's cell phone rang. He looked at it, flashed the palm of his hand toward Tucker, and walked away. He huddled, nonchalantly, in the corner peering back toward the table. Tucker caught pieces of the muffled conversation. "Just finished." (Pause.) "Not now." (Pause.) "Not yet." PJ shoved his phone back in its holster and walked toward Tucker. PJ did not explain the call. "Can you check with the coach, and get his assessment of that relationship, the one between Moncrief and Farqu'har?"

Tucker wanted to ask if the call had any news on the case but with the recent outburst, let it slide. "Sure," Tucker said, looking at his watch. "Hey, I gotta run. I have a meeting with the press. Not really looking forward to this one. Could be brutal."

As PJ packed the last of his things, Tucker walked to the door and added. "I'll let you know what the coach says about those two."

PJ spit out his pinch of Skoal and dumped his cup in a trash can outside the room. He took a swig of water from a nearby water fountain, swooshed it around his mouth, and spit it into the trash as well.

"Talk to you later there sheriff," Tucker said. "What are you doing next?" he asked, walking away backwards.

PJ took a drink of cold water and said, "I'm headed back to Beech Island. I need to look at that kid's truck. I still don't believe this kid. I think we might just have something there."

CHAPTER 13

Thursday, March 31
9:40 a.m. (Central Daylight Savings Time)

Xandra Novikov stared through her reflection out the window of the northbound train into the city. Chicago invariably dismissed the notion of "In like a lion, out like a lamb." Sideways snow and slush heaped well above the curb, was proof enough of that. After three days the novelty of it all had worn off for all but the school kids on another unscheduled snow day. Umbrellas turned inside out looked like storks in crinoline petticoats stuck in mountains of snow along the centerline along Wacker Drive, as plows dumped bucket-loads of snow for nightly removal. Salt-stained cars with blocks of black-speckled ice around wheel wells crept through silver and ebony ice melt on the streets between ice glazed sidewalks that challenged those who dared.

At every station Xandra watched bundled, bone-chilled commuters board; they reminded her of the station in her hometown of Chismena, outside Moscow. The bitter-cold winters. The stark countryside. Barren platforms. Soldiers with rifles in their heavy olive-gray overcoats. Ugly memories but home. She dreamed of children, herself, her youth. Poor, the daughter of a

Communist factory worker. And her dream of dreams, to leave for America. Despite conditions and lack of education, she grew up as a wholesome girl, not too tall, not too thin. Her face was plain—pleasant, not beautiful—but good enough for Dmitry Kuzmenko to conscript her to his black-market service as a mail-order bride, selling Russian girls worldwide.

The conductor announced the next and final stop as LaSalle Street station. Xandra adjusted her scarf, re-buttoned her parka, grabbed her purse, and stepped out. With her shoulder into the wind, she pulled her scarf higher across her nose for the two-block walk to the urban skyscraper jailhouse, the Metropolitan Correction Center. By the time she made it to Van Buren Street, the exposed worm-like scar that ran from her cheekbone to her chin was frozen. She rubbed it with her gloved hand. As she did, the pain reminded her of the night, the knife, the rage, and the man she was about to meet who gave it to her.

Rodney Farqu'har was scum. The jury that sentenced him to thirty-five years behind bars in MCC-Chicago in 1990 said so. Members of Posse Diablo would disagree. After twenty plus years in confinement, Pharaoh—as he was known—still had a loyal, fearful following which he controlled without interference by the suspicious but standoffish authorities. With time on his hands and institutional prison diet, he transformed his frame from wiry to muscle-bound despite his years. His classic dreadlocks had disappeared for the more favored inmate shaved head look. Not a violent man, personally, the guards had marked his behavior as good after an incident his first year, a plus for his next parole hearing still two years away.

Xandra could feel the scan of the security cameras as she approached the guards just inside the lobby door.

The entrance area was quiet, ghostly quiet. The clock above the desk read 10:12 a.m. Visiting hours did not open until noon. With short notice, she had hoped to be in the first set of visitors for meetings. Her hand shook when she presented her paperwork to the desk officer. He scanned the papers and took a hard look at her ID, a Russian passport, outdated. When he looked up, his gaze lingered on the scar. Xandra bit her lip and, with a worried grin, covered the scar with her hand. The officer dropped his eyes back to the passport, his chin followed. He saw no scar on her photo but verified her paperwork and handed her a visitor's badge.

"Be back here no later than thirty minutes prior to your scheduled visit. In the mean time I suggest you go around the corner to Starbucks, grab a cup of coffee and relax," the desk officer said, with a warm smile.

Xandra nodded, somewhat confused. Disregarding the guard's suggestion, she stored her coat, scarf, and purse in a locker inside an adjacent coatroom then took a seat on the far side of the lobby, hidden by a large ponytail palm in a golden planter. She sat alone with her hands in her lap, her eyes focused on the floor where she watched a small cockroach shuttle from beneath the planter to the baseboard and back, with no escape. Over the echoes of footsteps, telephones, and semi–private conversations around the room, her thoughts vacillated between love and fear—love for the little boy she raised alone in the South Side projects and fear for that same boy. Love for her son, grown to a respectable man outside the life of crime that brought her to this place and fear of the animal husband she waited to see. She had to do what she had to do and say what she had to say to Rodney Farqu'har, a husband of twenty-one years and a man whom she had not visited in the last twenty.

Precisely at noon the desk officer called the names of sixteen people including Alexandra Novikov.

Four guards escorted the group onto an elevator to the eighth floor visiting room where they walked, one at a time, through a metal detector. When two men were pulled out of line, Xandra felt chills all over her body; her stomach lurched. She began to shake as she watched the guards use hand-held wands to scan the two men before they escorted the group into the visiting room. Xandra chose a table close to the wall toward the back where she waited, one hand on the table to support her shaky knees, the other covered her scar.

The Visiting Officer walked next to Rodney Farqu'har, past all the tables to the rear wall, and stopped where Xandra stood. She did not recognize the bulky black man in front of her, until she heard his voice.

"Well, I'll be go to hell, if it ain't my lovely commie wife," he said, as he fell into the chair without a hug or a kiss or any sign of affection. His time in prison had not mellowed Rodney. He'd raped and been raped during his time in MCC and to him Xandra was just another object. Not bling or blow or blast or brick. Just a thing, a used thing at that. "Finally come to see how I was doing. Ain't that sweet. Turn around, and show me that booty of yours, baby," he said, followed by a laugh which sounded more like a seal barking.

Xandra took a calming breath, closed her eyes and made one slow-motion rotation like a figurine on a music box, chin up and a slight quiver in her cheeks. When she had finished she took her seat in silence.

"Oo-ee. I needs a little piece of that. We gots everything here but that. We get three hots and a cot, a little recess time to play tag on the roof, maybe shoot some hoops twice a week. Not like that boy of mine."

Her eyes snapped up. "Malik is my son," she said, her back stiffened the same instant, a hard chill came over her.

"Well, well, bitch. You got some fire in you now. That shit is good, baby. That shit is good," he said, his head cocked to the side, his face puckered in wonderment. He spread his arms wide and grabbed the sides of the table pulling himself closer. "Now you just shut the fuck up," he said, his nose inches from hers. He leaned back in his chair, crossed his legs and drummed his fingers on the table. "You come down here to see me 'cause you miss me, baby? With a face like that bet ain't nobody touch you in twenty years." She did not respond, but he was right. "I told you when I left I be back, baby. Two more years in this can and you and me we be back together getting' nasty and shit."

As he talked, her conviction began to wane. His voice—its high-pitch and maniacal tone—brought back the memories she could never remember to forget. He was an abusive pig who abandoned her and her newborn son. He made her sick. The violent, disgusting, vomit-in-your-face kind of sick, but she needed him. She needed something from him.

"Yeah that boy of mine," he said, his smirk dared her to speak out again, "he be doin' good down there in basketball. He be doin' damn good. The brothers 'round here checkin' him out in the newspaper and shit. They tell me all 'bout him. Oo-oo, he damn good. That boy be makin' big time money. Yeah, baby. That's what I be talkin' 'bout. Big money. Soon, I gets out this place, I be his manager. We makin' real money then. Yes, sir. Real money." He popped a cocky grin and placed his hands behind his head. "You be a good girl, and stay 'round you might get some of that money yourself, baby. Ha, ha, ha…maybe we can get that scar of yours fixed, mama." His smile lingered.

"Mr. Rodney, I need money," she said, in a low but bold voice. Her accent made her plea sound more like a demand.

"Ain't it a bitch," he said, deliberately, enunciating each word. "The bitch needs money, and she comes to me. Shit baby, you ain't come to see me in twenty years and you come ask for money?" He pouted and puckered his face. "You ain't never sent me a birthday card, not sent me a Christmas present. You ain't even called to say 'how the fuck are you' and you come ask me for money?" He leaned closer to her and reached to twirl her hair. "Now where the fuck do you think I am going to get money, baby? In case you ain't noticed, this ain't exactly a country club. You ain't seen this is a goddamn prison? I ain't got no money, baby. Now when my boy hits the pros, then I have me some money."

Xandra turned away. She knew Malik was her son and only her son. Rodney Farqu'har had no right to associate with her son, but he was the only person she knew that could get her the money she needed. She turned back and bowed her head toward the table. She bent forward, wrapped her arms around her stomach and gagged back an involuntary response.

She lifted her head. "Malik is in trouble," she said, her eyes, set with pain and sorrow she was reluctant to show.

"What you mean?" he replied, as he closed the distance between their faces.

"I need two-and-a-half-million dollars or something bad will happen to him. I receive a letter. They want money."

"Who 'they' want money?" He clenched his jaw with a bulldog overbite. "I don't need nobody telling me what they want from my boy." All humor drained from Rodney's face.

Xandra sensed the sudden interest in the boy he left at birth, the son she had no intentions of sharing with him. Locked in Rodney's penetrating stare, she explained the events of the past two days in her best broken English. At times she stopped to reach inward for strength and to choose the right words. Her Slavic accent confused him; he made her repeat over and over until he pieced together her story. He pushed for names. She told him she brought the letter with her, but visitors were restricted from carrying anything into the meeting room.

"I need money," she said, at the end. "Big money. If I not show them money, they do something to Malik." She hid her face in her hands to wipe away tears that welled up before he could see them.

Rodney looked around the visiting room. At a table on the other side of the room, a visitor massaged the neck of one prisoner who sat hunched over, his head on the table. Others engaged in deep conversation. Some held hands with wives and children. Many talked to men in suits. They all had someone. They all had plans. He, too, had a plan for the basketball phenom that shared his last name.

"Punks. These punks can't get away with that shit," he said to her. "I'll tell you what we do. We invest in the boy's future, that what we do. Then we take out the shitheads," he said. He placed his elbows on the table and leaned toward Xandra. She pulled back. Rodney covered his mouth with his cupped hands, lowered his voice and said, "You leave here, and go straight home. You hear me, bitch?" Xandra nodded. "You wait at home till someone calls you. Listen to what they say, and do exactly what they tells you. No questions, just do exactly what they tells you. And you tells nobody, nothing about the call. Got that?"

Xandra nodded in silence, quiet as a nun in prayer, her eyes on the table.

Rodney motioned with his hand for Xandra to come closer to him. Scared and reluctant, she obeyed. When he reached forward with his large black finger and twisted a lock of her hair, she closed her eyes. She dared not do anything that might have Rodney change his mind. The contact lasted only an instant.

Rodney pushed his chair back fast, sat upright, and raised his hand. The Visiting Officer came to the table and escorted him out of the area. Xandra remained seated at the table. They had not exchanged any parting words. She took slow, labored breaths but did not bother to watch him walk away. She dropped her head to the table and cried. Not for him. After twenty years the presence of this one man still threatened her. Alone, again, and uncertain if the visit meant anything for her or Malik.

In the lobby she wrapped her scarf around her neck and head like she had a toothache and prepared to retrace her steps to the LaSalle Street Station. The weather had worsened. The snow on the sidewalk in front of the MCC was several inches deep, despite the constant efforts and complaints of the security guards. Beyond the building front, the packed snow on the sidewalk was even deeper along the trampled pedestrian path down the center. On the train home, she thought of Malik and, in the privacy of a nearly empty train car, she cried.

The tensions of the morning had left her little more than a shell. She stumbled with each step along the quarter-mile walk from the train station to her apartment. Thick rubber boots like anvils on her feet trudged through the new, wet snow. She used three keys—for three locks—to open her apartment, pushed the door closed with her back, and slid down to the floor where she sat, burdened under the weight of two thoughts. First, how long would she have to wait for the call Rodney promised. Second, she had to talk to Tucker McGill. She dialed the number he had given her, his cell number. He did not answer, but at the tone she left her message, "Mr. McGill, I fly to Atlanta to find my son."

CHAPTER 14

Thursday, March 31
11:17 a.m.

This is Brent Kline," the Redcliffe president said, when his assistant announced the call; it had been two hours since their first call ended abruptly.

"Brent, Chris Gorting, NCAA," the voice said, over the speakerphone. "I apologize for the short call earlier. Had a bit of an immediate issue."

"Have you given more thought to my request?" Kline said, caught off guard, unprepared to talk. His debate team experience at Princeton told him to challenge, to pursue his earlier request, so he lunged in on the offensive with a stern voice.

"Well, yes, a bit, but—"

"Chris, it would be intellectual suicide for us to think that if we play without Farqu'har that either of us could win. People would laugh Redcliffe off the face of the Earth."

"Brent, listen to me." Gorting interrupted.

Kline ignored him and pressed harder, louder. "The NCAA would take a big hit. Ratings for the network will be in the toilet; sales for the sponsors, same thing. This news will create a chain reaction—"

"Would you just listen to me," Gorting shouted. "I think we could have a bigger issue." Gorting settled a bit but continued in a voice deeper than the casual tone he had when he called. "While we were talking earlier I received a FedEx package. Get them all the time. Liz does a good job of screening these things, but she brought this one in while we were talking. It was a letter from a crazy, similar to the one you told me about, the one the kid's mother received."

"What do you mean?"

"I mean I just received a letter on Redcliffe College letterhead, signed by John Wayne just like the kid's mother. Came by FedEx."

"What did it say? Did they demand money out of you, too?"

"No. Just a threat not to delay the game," Gorting said.

His statement stunned Kline. This "John Wayne" character was fighting him from both ends. "What kind of threat? Chris...we can't play that game I'm telling you; it's suicide. What've you done? Called the police?" Kline said, anxious to privately escalate the investigation and search.

"I've called one of our directors who deals with these types of threats. He came up, and discussed actions. I believe the police are sending someone over to look at this," Gorting said, a lie on top of a lie.

"This damn thing is beginning to snowball, just like I suspected. The press involved?" Kline said.

"Not yet."

"Chris, send me a copy of that letter. I want my security guy to take a look and pass it along to the sheriff here. They're running the search. Your letter might help."

Gorting hesitated. He was the only one who had read the letter and knew the contents of the letter would raise questions. It was not worded like the one to Alexandra Novikov. He needed some time to piece together an explanation or down play this letter as some sort of hoax, an attempt to upset the Final Four week.

"I'll mention that to whomever the police send over and see if they want to handle this thing that way," Gorting said. "I'll let my guys work that out with them."

"Chris, with letters in two states, I think I need to have the South Carolina Law Enforcement Division in on this, maybe the FBI," Kline said, again posturing his argument for a delay.

Gorting closed his eyes and shook his head but responded almost before Kline had finished his statement, "No…I wouldn't do that just yet. The letter I received my not have any connection whatsoever with that other letter. We get lots of letters like this," Gorting said, one more lie in a growing pool.

"But didn't you say it was on our stationary?" Kline asked.

Gorting winced and nodded into the speakerphone.

"We don't have a lot of time," Kline said. "I need to find this kid or we don't play the game. If we get the Feds involved the investigation will get a lot more attention, fast. The alternative is to go to CBS and delay the game, for all of us," Kline added, "and I still need to find my student."

"Look, if this goes to the FBI the media will catch wind of it and blow the top right off this thing," Gorting said, unsure of how to calm Kline. "My guys can handle this and move it along. Send me the contact info so they can talk to your sheriff's office."

"You have more confidence in your guys than I have. And, if it was any other week, I would defer to your judgment, but this is Final Four week; they're going to need help, either directly or indirectly." Despite the fact that Kline was out of his arena and into sports, he felt he had Gorting in check. "Who are you going to call, Chris? One or the other, CBS or FBI? Pick one," Kline said. "We need to get this resolved."

Gorting picked up the receiver to bypass his speakerphone. "Brent, there's no way in hell CBS is going to accept any appeal—from me, from you, from John Wayne, from anybody. It's that simple."

"Then I'm calling the governor and the FBI and I'll get this damn search escalated as a kidnapping. I can see the headlines now NCAA FINAL FOUR – KIDNAPPED IN CAROLINA *Cinderella basketball star, missing*. Yeah, that'll make great news for you, won't it," Kline said, in a huff.

"I'm warning you…don't get the FBI involved today. Wait until tomorrow after—"

"I'm calling the FBI. I'll talk to you tomorrow," Kline said. He hung up and buzzed his assistant, "Clara, get Captain PJ Beedle from the sheriff's office on the phone."

CHAPTER 15

Thursday, March 31
Noon

Tucker hustled to the press conference, a buffet luncheon in the media conference room set up in a work-and-hospitality lounge high above the temporary seats on the Dome's main floor. Usually meetings with the press were casual affairs with two or three beat reporters from the local media; this one would be different. He pulled his participant pass from his pocket, draped the lanyard around his neck and wedged his way into the room packed with reporters.

Most people were clustered around the buffet lines or standing near the courtesy bar. There were no TV cameras; the event was merely the first daily update conference, too early for the networks to stream video directly to the public. Official Final Four–Atlanta banners draped the walls and hung above the raised speaker's platform up front, opposite the buffet tables. One long table with four chairs stood on a platform in front of a large blue screen with a collage of logos representing the four teams in the finals, CBS Sports, and the 2011 NCAA Final Four tournament logo—a peach falling through the netting on a basketball hoop.

Tucker noticed three men chatting behind the table. Though he did not recognize any of them, he assumed they were the representatives of the other schools. When he introduced himself, one of the men welcomed "Cinderella" to the ball which drew a good laugh from the others; fortunately none of them recognized him as a former Celtic or a hot shot hothead from Providence. After exchanging pleasantries, Tucker took a seat behind the folded place card marked "Redcliffe College." He busied himself to avoid the crowd and the other speakers. He rummaged through his backpack. He bent over a pad on the table and scribbled random, pointless notes. He knew he would be in the hot seat, soon.

A petite woman with curly black hair stood behind a lectern with a microphone at the far end of the table away from Tucker. She spoke a few inaudible words into the mike and looked around the room. When her efforts failed to catch the attention of the crowd, she launched into a Gene Autry yodel which had everybody's attention in no time.

"Sorry, old college pastime from back in the dark ages," she said. "Welcome everyone. We'd like to get started. Please grab a plate of food and find a seat. We have our four representatives here, ready to field your questions. These four gentlemen are extremely busy, as you can imagine. We don't have a lot of time, so please feel free to keep eating while we conduct this first session. I do ask that you try to keep the extraneous noise to a minimum so others can hear our guests. I know how you guys like to talk sports, but midcourt here today are these four guys up front." She paused to look down the line to ensure the four speakers were in their seats and ready. "Quick intros. Starting on your far left, my right we have Tucker McGill from Redcliffe College, Steve Kiner from Michigan State, Gary Steele from UConn, and Pete Becktel from North Carolina. If you are ready with your questions, please raise your hand. When I acknowledge you, please stand, and speak loud enough for all to hear you. Without further ado, let the madness begin! Your questions, please?"

Several hands shot up. Fortunately, the first question from the floor went to the rep from the University of North Carolina. Tucker heard the question but paid no attention; something about how many times the Tar Heels had been to the Final Four, and would they rather have a chance to play against Duke instead of the other teams. The reprieve was brief; the second question went to Tucker.

It came from the far corner of the room near the buffet line. A few turned in their chairs to see the questioner, a big woman, well over six feet tall, with a blonde ponytail and high cheekbones. She started to talk with her mouth full, choked, swallowed, and started again, "Mr. McGill, Deana Morgan, *Charleston Post and Courier*, can you tell us more about when Malik Farqu'har will be available for interviews?"

Tucker pulled the table mike closer to him. "I am afraid I can't. Like the rest of our team, Malik is preparing for tomorrow's game," Tucker said, concerned the discussion would turn to the missing player.

"I can appreciate that," the young reporter said. Tucker wondered if she was even old enough to be out of school herself. Her skin was childlike pink and dotted with freckles. "But rumor has it and some Twitter reports say he was not on the bus to Atlanta. Is that true?" she said, as she looked at her phone in the palm of her hand.

The mention of the rumor turned heads in the room, all towards the woman in back, busy with her phone.

The chatter swelled to an uncomfortable buzz before the sharp-witted girl at the lectern yodeled and said, "Let's keep the noise down to allow for a response, please. Mr. McGill, can you comment?"

Tucker used the interruption to reach for the pitcher of ice water on the table and pour a glass, a temporary stall. He could respond with the same story they told the team, the same lie, that the AD had kept Malik back to up the psych warfare against Michigan State. Of course, that answer would not fly here, not in front of the Michigan State rep or the media.

He was surprised she had mentioned the tweets; those were between two team members and not guys widely followed on Twitter. *Why would she be following them?* He had been so busy he had not seen any of the news, and only knew what the AD had told him on the call. At that point, the word of Malik's disappearance had not hit the papers. If he downplayed the question, sticking to the story to leave him back to address interviews separately, how did that play into the game preparations with the team, and how would that answer the question of when Farqu'har would be available? He knew he did not want to raise the suspicion that Malik was missing and definitely not that he had been kidnapped. Even with the letter to Xandra Novikov and after his discussion with Ike Moncrief, Tucker was uncertain. If he came out and detailed the events of the previous twenty-four hours, to explain why the player was not available, it would ignite an uncontrollable firestorm that would jeopardize any chance at all for Kline to get a delay. The NCAA would assume Redcliffe was the rogue outlier on a parochial publicity blitz.

He leaned forward to pull the microphone toward him to address the question. Further down the table the UConn spokesman turned to the Michigan State rep next to him. When he did, he accidentally elbowed his glass of ice water and knocked it into the lap of the Tar Heel rep on the end. The ice water in the crotch got quite a response out of Pete Becktel. He was on his feet brushing ice cubes everywhere. The place erupted in laughter and the usual male banter from the back to "take it off." Tucker remained quiet in anticipation of the response to the question he was about to give.

When the noise quieted to a little more than a murmur, Tucker looked down the table then nudged forward to speak. Before he could begin, the tall blonde reporter in the back yelled, "Mr. McGill before you answer my question…maybe you could explain the latest tweet from Malik Farqu'har."

Her request stirred the buzz once again. Tucker blinked his eyes several times then cleared his throat. *Malik tweeted?* "I'm not sure I understand. Not sure I've seen any tweets from Malik today," he said.

"I follow most of the Eagles basketball players," the big blond said. "Kinda my thing. I played some college ball but really just interested. The tweet says *I'm tired of the basketball bullshit. I need to take a little time off. Don't count on me this weekend.'"

Over a hundred miles away, the air inside a different room was stagnant, cold, and wet, the smell of mildew, urine and feces. Without sunlight, heat or hot water, the only warmth came from Malik Farqu'har's body and a D-cell flashlight. It wasn't the cold or the smell that bothered him most; it was the isolation from the outside world. He had no phone, no Facebook, no Twitter, no Internet. He glanced at his watch. Tomorrow would be Friday, April 1st, April Fools' Day. After two days locked in frigid, god-awful loneliness, he knew this was more than a prank or a stunt before the finals weekend. He was exhausted from attempts to carve his way out using smashed cans formed into crude knives. His fingers were raw from the cold. He was alive but did not like his chances of playing in another college game.

CHAPTER 16

Thursday, March 31
2:23 p.m. (Central Daylight Savings Time)

After she left a message for Tucker, Xandra Novikov sat hunched over her kitchen table, cuddled a cup of hot tea, and nibbled on an egg salad sandwich she bought from the vending machine at the station. The tea cut the chill that lingered in her bones, but after her encounter of the morning, her stomach fought hard not to accept food; it rippled with each bite while the comments, accusations, insults, and demands Rodney had laid on her rambled through her head. When nothing she did could settle her, she walked to the wall and pushed the flashing red voicemail button on her phone.

"If you want money for the kid, bitch, stay home and keep your mouth shut."

The message could not have been more direct. It was not Rodney's voice; it was a voice she did not recognize. What she heard did not shock her; it encouraged her to know there was a call, and maybe they would call again…and she would be ready.

Back at the table she thought about Malik, the tall, confident teen who had walked through the kitchen hundreds of times twirling a basketball on his fingertip.

His cocky grin. His manly size. His respect and love which he was never too busy to show toward her. She dared a smile as she reached for her tea, closed her eyes and took comfort in the thought of having him there, with her, now.

The ring from the phone startled her in mid-sip. Tea splattered on the table. She stared at the phone on the wall and waited. On the third ring she inched her way out of the chair and stood inches from the phone. Anxious. Trembling. She took a deep breath, let it ring one final time before snatched the receiver. "Hello."

"I'll say this one time, bitch. Listen because I'm not saying it again." The messenger spoke with an accent Xandra could not identify, but not Chicago. It was the same voice from the voicemail left on her phone earlier. "Go to the Castle Royale Motel on 103rd Street. Be there in less than an hour. Use their phone and call this number." He gave her seven digits, spoken slowly then closed. "Go alone. No tricks." That was all.

Xandra wrote down the number, unsure if she recalled the sequence of the last two digits. She checked the clock above her sink, twenty-seven past two in the afternoon.

The Castle Royale Motel was ten cold blocks from her Chicago Housing Authority apartment at Lowden Homes. It took her fifteen minutes to gather her things in a suitcase. She was going to Atlanta, but not before she followed the instructions from the voice on the phone. She decided to leave her suitcase on her bed rather than drag it through the snow for over a mile and risk someone seeing her with it. She snatched her coat and scarf off the hook, locked the door—all three locks—and headed south down Wentworth Avenue; the winds off the lake and the snow worked against her.

Under the threatening skies, Castle Royale looked as medieval as Warwick Castle without a moat. Wrought iron bars draped narrow windows across the front of the building built with a random mix of gray, red and white bricks. Saw-toothed merlons ran across the roof's edge and a drawbridge of the drive-thru was the only entrance to the guest parking lot. The rest of the street offered a mix of small, boarded-up houses and vacant lots filled with trashed appliances surrounded by fences more down than up. Heaps of black snow lined the curbs for as far as Xandra could see.

Despite the appearance, she was thankful to be out of the weather. The lobby could have doubled as a dungeon in any castle. Dark, no windows, decorated with one ripped vinyl-covered wing chair, an end table with lamp, and a display rack half-filled with tourist brochures and restaurant menus on a rainbow of papers. She shook the snow off her coat and stood in front of a glass window covered with heavy steel bars. She noticed the large digital clock by the rack of time cards adjacent to registration desk; the time was three twelve. When she pressed the buzzer beneath the window, a chubby, dark-skinned man with thick black hair plastered between his ears appeared out of nowhere with a cigarette pressed between his lips from the corner of his mouth.

"Yes, would you like a room," he said, with a Latin accent.

"Please, may I use your phone," Xandra said, her enunciation slow and deliberate to ensure he would understand.

"Lady, we no have a pay phone," he said.

Xandra turned her head and coughed before she spoke. "Please, may I borrow phone. I must make call, quickly," she said, her stare framed by the frustration smoldering behind her frozen cheeks.

"For you, on such cold day, I do favor. I let you make a call, a local call, no?"

"Yes, local call."

"See phone, there on the wall," he said, his chin extended to the wall on the far side of the lobby. "Go there, and dial zero-zero, one. I connect you to outside line."

Xandra did as the clerk had instructed. After she heard the dial tone for the outside line, she dialed the number she had written down at her apartment. She hesitated before she dialed the last two digits, concerned she might have copied them out of order.

"Yeah," was all she heard when someone answered the phone after one ring. The voice was deep and ominous, definitely Chicagoland and different from the voice that gave her the number.

"This is Xandra Novikov. I..." was all she said before the voice on the other end of the connection started.

"Go to the desk, and ask for the package for Demetrius." She heard a click and then a dial tone. She did not move, her face frozen in disbelief. She cradled the receiver under her chin, then carefully placed it back on the wall-mounted phone and returned to the window. The chubby man, now seated at the desk, turned toward her.

"Yes?" he said, as a question.

"May I have package for Demetrius?"

The man ran his hand over his greasy hair, rose and walked to the window. "Demetrius?" he said, with a skeptical, frightened face.

"Yes, Demetrius." Xandra doubted her ears. Had she heard the message correctly? Was it really Demetrius?

Smoke from his cigarette drifted through the hole in the glass window as the man on the other side eyeballed her scar. He puffed on his cigarette until he seemed satisfied then disappeared around a cloth partition. She turned and faced the door, while her eyes wandered lazily toward the small security camera bolted to the ceiling in the far corner of the room. When she heard the man return to the window, she turned as he slid a large brown envelope under the metal bars. The only marking on the package was the word "Demetrius" printed in large black letters.

Conscious of his stare, Xandra locked her eyes with his and placed the envelope under her arm. She stepped back from the barred window and covered the scar with her hand before she thanked the man at the desk. She walked out of the lobby into the cold. At the same time the man picked up the phone and began to dial. Xandra quickly dipped her head back inside to check the clock by the desk. The man said something into the phone then held the receiver close to his chest while he watched Xandra examine the clock which gave her less than two hours to meet what would be a drop-dead time at Union Station.

PJ called Tucker from his patrol car parked outside Davenport Hall on the Redcliffe campus. The front that rolled in under pewter skies three days earlier had started with a good rain before the temperature dipped to single digits and brought snow in sheets like water over Niagara. With the heater on full-high and hot, he waited for Tucker to pick up. Instead, the call went directly to voicemail. *Damn!* This time he had to leave a message.

"Tucker, it's PJ. Think we might need to talk to your guy Moncrief again. Just finished the check on his truck. Thing is covered with a thick coat of red clay mud.

Seems the boy did some off-road driving, at the very least hit some unimproved dirt roads in the woods somewhere after that practice the other night. Hadn't had rain for weeks till Tuesday. This mud's got to be fresh."

PJ reached over, turned the heater down, and turned the defroster on high to clear the condensation from the windows so he could watch the young coeds in the parking lot.

"Truck was locked, no keys. I looked inside. If this kid Farqu'har wasn't so big, I'd bet he's buried under all the shit in that truck. Based on what the kid said and the way he acted this morning, I'm off to plead my case to get a search warrant. If I find anything at all, your trainer may have some explaining to do, the serious tap dance type."

CHAPTER 17

Thursday, March 31
3:59 p.m. (Central Daylight Savings Time)

A lava-like flow of adrenaline warmed Xandra. She fell back against her apartment door and shook the snow off her coat before it melted into a pool. When she stopped she had an eerie feeling. She noticed something strange in her apartment. She took slow, shallow breaths and listened. With what she had been through for the past eight hours, she feared someone had entered her apartment, waiting for her. She moved slowly to hang up her coat, then froze, the brown envelope marked "Demetrius" clutched like a layer of skin under her arm. Whomever or whatever it was left an unusual, pungent odor. Her eyes moved left and right. No noise. She left no tension behind as she crept into the kitchen where her body fell limp when she remembered she had cleaned the sink and counter before she went to the Castle Royale. So much of her day had been a surreal blur. It was a minute before four. She took a few quick breaths to grab hold of herself. She was short on time before her next train into the city. She pulled the suitcase off of her bed and dragged it back to the kitchen, back to the phone on the wall.

"Mr. McGill, this is Xandra Novikov."

"Good afternoon," he said, surprised, excited to hear her voice. "Have you heard from Malik?"

"No," she said, her voice sounded stiff. "I pay the big money today."

Her accent made it difficult for Tucker to understand what she said. He was shocked to think he heard she planned to pay the ransom.

"How? Where did you get the money?" Tucker asked. He left his chair in the conference room inside the Georgia Dome and moved toward a window to find better reception and a little privacy.

"I cannot tell. Someone may listen to call," she said, still not convinced she was alone. "I need you to find my Malik. You must be sure he is safe."

Tucker pulled the phone away from his ear and looked at it in front of his face. He could not believe what he heard. Over the past forty hours he had checked the kid's admissions file and understood the family financial situation; no surprise it did not suggest any ability for a withdrawal even remotely close to what she needed. He heard a beep from an incoming call on his cell phone which he immediately diverted to voicemail.

"Miss Novikov, I realize it's none of my business how you came up with the money, but this is very serious. If you pay that ransom I need to let the authorities know, the ones who are investigating, searching for your son," Tucker said.

"I cannot tell where I get money," the player's mother said. "I must save for my son. I must go."

"Wait, Miss Novikov, please do not do this, please."

"No, no. I must…" she said, her loose hand reached to grab her forehead as the pressure pinched the back of her eyes, "I must go, Mr. McGill. I must go."

"The letter, do you have the letter?" Tucker pressed. "Please read me the letter again."

Xandra pulled the letter from her purse and stumbled quickly through it.

Tucker raised his voice. "The FedEx envelope. Do you have that?"

"Yes."

"On the front, please read the numbers to me."

She rushed through the numbers and said, "I must go now." Her voice was strong and defiant.

"Miss Novikov, I caution you. Please do not do this." He waited and let the silence deepen though he feared nothing he said would change the woman's mind. "Be careful." He paused for a reply that never came before he heard the click of the phone.

Tucker walked with his nose on his phone to pull up the Internet and search for the FedEx site. He punched in the tracking number and found the letter package Xandra Novikov received originated in Augusta. He called the Augusta FedEx office but was unable to get more information on the package or the sender other than the fact that it was picked up from a dropbox on the east side of town. He hung up and redialed the phone, this time to PJ.

"PJ, it's Tucker," he said, his voice rushed to pass information.

"Hey Tucker. Did you get my voicemail? Left it about ten minutes ago?"

Tucker looked at his phone. The icon for voicemail was lit. "I saw it come in but been on the phone with Farqu'har's mother. She's paying the ransom."

"What? How in hell's she doing that? Who gave her the money?"

"She wouldn't tell me. All she would say is she was paying, and we needed to find her son, safe," Tucker said. He pulled a bottle of aspirin from his backpack, popped two and washed them down with a half-cup of cold coffee. "We need to get that to Chicago."

"I'll call my contact there. What do we know about how she plans to do this? Is she meeting somebody?" PJ asked while he struggled to pull his notepad out of its holster on his belt.

Tucker talked PJ though the details based on what the original FedEx letter said. His fingers picked at the label on the aspirin bottle as he gave PJ a description of Alexandra Novikov, something the police could use. He suggested they check out a *Chicago Tribune* article about Malik from earlier in the year, one that had a photo of him standing with his mother after their blowout game against Northwestern.

The news registered with Tucker as he walked back toward the windows in the arena, his stomach frothing to a point it made him weak in the knees. A heavy cloud cover obscured the fading sun; it was nearly dark. He knew that in less than forty-eight hours, the teams would be on the court for pre-game warm-ups unless Kline had negotiated a delay. With no word from Burgess, he figured the game was still a go.

"Hey, the judge approved the search warrant request for that kid Moncrief's truck. Need to bring that guy back in. The cab had so much shit in it, it took a while to sort through it all, but I found a receipt for gas from JR's Thrifty Mart in Edgefield off Highway 23 past North Augusta. Time was 12:33 a.m., Wednesday the twenty-ninth, the day the bus left and the morning after this kid Moncrief said he went straight back to the dorm to study."

"Yeah, but he could have gone out later for whatever reason to get gas," Tucker said.

"In that shitty weather? I doubt he went out in the middle of the night. The guy was headed to Atlanta in twelve hours. The truck was going to sit at the dorm for days. He said he read, packed, and went to bed. Also… remember the security cam footage showed Farqu'har drinking a Coke. Moncrief said he gave Farqu'har a Coke, too, so I had the lab take a quick look at the cans I pulled from the truck. One can tested positive for Rohypnol…you know…the date rape drug. Don't laugh. You put enough of that stuff in your gut, with or without alcohol, and it can kill ya, even a moose like Farqu'har."

"Kind of a stretch, isn't it? I mean, how do you tie the can and the receipt to Moncrief and Farqu'har on that night?" Tucker asked, concerned PJ was trying to draw a quick conclusion.

"The lab can give an estimated time on the drug. They also checked for prints on the can. They were not small fingers. They found some prints which turned out to be Moncrief. We have his prints on file," PJ said.

"Why or how did you get Moncrief's prints?" Tucker asked.

"The kid has a record. I pulled a file we had on him. He was picked up a few months back. Involved in a bust on a gambling thing, big poker game in North Augusta. No charges filed, but we had his prints."

"Some of this might jibe with something I got from Farqu'har's mother. The FedEx package…I tracked it. It originated in Augusta, a dropbox. Couldn't get much more out of FedEx."

"Maybe I can," PJ said. "Do we have the FedEx envelope?"

"No, the kid's mother has it."

"We need it, and we need to get Moncrief back to talk to him."

"That's going to be tough. Without charges, the coach isn't going to let that kid go anywhere. He's still here in

Atlanta. The game's the day after tomorrow," Tucker said. "When can you get back this way?"

"Not sure. I need to hop off the phone and relay all of this to Chicago. Also need to get back to the FBI. This changes a lot for those guys," PJ said. "Plus the lab's checking a few other items from the truck. I should have something back from the lab first thing in the morning."

"I'll let you go. I'll go find Ernie Howells and fill him in. He's called a half dozen times to find out if we found his guy. I'll make sure he knows to have Moncrief available tomorrow, even if he has to miss practice," Tucker said.

"Okay. I'll get the Chicago police over to Novikov's place before she does anything stupid. They can also get that FedEx envelope for us. If I hear more from the lab, I'll let you know. After I talk to the FBI, I'll get back to you. Later," PJ said, then hung up.

While Tucker and PJ exchanged information over the phone, Alexandra Novikov walked to the 95th Street Station outside Chicago. With her suitcase in one hand and a white plastic grocery bag in the other, wind at her back and time against her, she caught the 4:35 p.m. train back to the same LaSalle Street Station she had left hours earlier. The train arrived a minute ahead of schedule which gave her twelve minutes to cross the Chicago River to Union Station.

The large watch in the Bulova display at the newsstand swept past 5:12 p.m. as she rounded the corner for the escalator down to the tracks. When she lunged off the last step, her suitcase wheeled to its side. She dragged it behind her trying to flip it back on its wheels as she raced to find Track 14. Through the gate she looked up at the station clock at the end of the platform. *One minute.* Using her arms and shoulders, she pushed people out of her way as she worked through the mob of arriving passengers headed into the station from their trains. She pressed so hard she almost missed the first kiosk. Frantic, she prowled trackside for the second kiosk in a race against the clock, her empty stomach flip-flopped. As the crowds cleared the deck, the kiosk appeared no more than twenty feet in front of her. She looked around, moved directly to the stand where she placed the plastic grocery bag and, without any hesitation, walked back into the station. It wasn't until three minutes later as she sat in a cab bound for O'Hare International Airport that she noticed how her heart raced; the nervous energy that had driven her for hours left her with a knot in her stomach.

The Chicago police observed the drop and the pick-up. At precisely 5:18 p.m., as latecomers with briefcases, newspapers, and brown-bagged beer cans ran to hop the train before it pulled away from the platform, a black man in a heavy, wool overcoat with red scarf reached down, grabbed the bag, and casually walked back toward the station. The CPD followed the man at a distance, not wanting to create a scene. The police noted that behind the man carrying the plastic bag with the ransom money was a much larger man wearing a blue, black and gray Georgetown Hoyas parka and a black knit skullcap. Both men strolled with no noticeable attempt to flee or avoid detection. Inside the station, the police observed the bigger man pull one hand out of his pocket and spin the pick-up man by his shoulder. The two argued. After less than a minute, the forty-something pick-up guy with the red scarf used his chin to gesture toward the mezzanine food court. The police detectives watched the man in the Hoyas parka look toward the upper floor. He saw something that caused him to stop his verbal assault; the other man walked away with the white plastic grocery bag, lost in the chaos of the crowd. The man in the parka yelled something, but like his friend who followed the woman out of the station, he was nowhere around when the police closed in, recovered the money, and took the man in the wool overcoat for a warm ride to the Chicago Police Department Headquarters.

After he talked to PJ, Tucker reorganized his notes for calls. He was unsure about PJ's assessment of Ike Moncrief, still concerned about his apparent rush to judgment. What motive would Moncrief have to kidnap his former teammate and to destroy their chance at a national championship? It made no sense. His other issue was the ransom money. Where did the money come from? More importantly, he had to stop the ransom payoff. He placed another call to Xandra Novikov; she did not answer. He left a message and asked her to call him as soon as she heard the message.

On the drive back to his hotel, Tucker's phone rang. It was Xandra Novikov.

"Miss Novikov, thanks for calling back. I wanted to talk to you more about the ransom. We have additional information about Malik and—"

"You have found my son?" she said, with a gasp.

"No, we've not found him, but we have additional information about the last time people saw him," Tucker said, leading up to the true purpose for his call. "I assume because you called, you listened to the voicemail I left?" he asked.

"No, I did not hear your voicemail. I call to tell you I am in Atlanta."

The words were like a giant icicle jammed in his ear. He was numb. On top of everything else that was going on, she shows up. *What is she going to do? How is she going to do anything?* "Where are you?" Tucker asked, his voice polite and cordial.

"I am in airport. I know not where to go or how to find Malik," she said, her voice had changed. The accent remained, but gone were the trembles, the sighs, and the sobs of previous calls; the tone of her voice bold and determined.

"Please, look around or ask. Go to the food court area where they serve food. Get something to eat if you'd like, but wait there until I arrive. Listen for your name over the loudspeaker. I'll find you. You can stay in my room tonight."

It was already past ten when Tucker got in his car. Driving from the center of town to the airport was normally an easy shot, but under blizzard conditions, the drive was slow and treacherous which gave Tucker time to think how to handle her. Possibly she could be of some help when PJ arrived in the morning. Under the circumstances, he was confident the college would cover her expenses once he could talk to someone in the admin office.

Before he reached the terminal parking, PJ called. Tucker told him he was at the airport to pick up his unannounced visitor. They agreed PJ should talk to her when he got to Atlanta.

"Bad news though, Bubba," PJ said. "The Chicago PD was all over the ransom drop. They nabbed the guy outside Union Station and turned him over to the FBI for questioning."

"And that's bad?" Tucker said.

"There was only two hundred fifty grand in the bag," PJ said.

"But the letter said two and a half million," Tucker added, as he sucked in a deep breath in disgusted.

"Yep. And on top of that, the Feds say the pick-up guy's a stooge."

CHAPTER 18

Friday, April 1
7:53 a.m.

Tucker spent a restless night on the pullout sofa bed in his suite. The night before, when he found Xandra Novikov at Hartsfield-Jackson Airport, he saw first-hand the effects of the nightmare she had lived for the past forty-eight hours. The lack of sleep and no food had painted dark circles under her puffy eyes. Her scar, which he had forgotten, now appeared thicker, rougher, and darker on her face, her skin paler than moonlight. At the terminal, she found it difficult to communicate, disoriented, unable to accept the simplest suggestions such as follow me or use the restroom, but under it all she was determined to find her son. Tucker offered his king-sized bed with hopes she could sleep in while he jumped back into his search early.

"Good morning boss," Tucker said, with no emotion in his voice, quick to overlook the friction from their previous conversation. With a cup of coffee in hand and a newspaper under his arm, Tucker met Ben Burgess in the hotel lobby. They were scheduled to attend an alumni breakfast rally in one of the ballrooms, but plans had changed.

"You look a bit rough around the edges this morning, McGill," Burgess said. "Come with me. We need to talk…" he added, his voice pregnant with another ass-chewing about to begin, "before we head over to the breakfast." Burgess headed into an open room.

"Can't." Tucker stood his ground. He left little doubt he had no interest in what Burgess might have to tell him.

Burgess stepped back to Tucker with his stubby cigar hanging from his lower lip.

"Farqu'har's mother flew in unannounced last night. She's a mess. I put her in my room; I slept on the couch. I need to get back up there before she panics and runs off doing I don't know what. I have calls to make, and PJ Beedle is due in."

Burgess lifted the stogy and opened his mouth to speak; Tucker cut him off.

"The kid's mom paid the ransom yesterday afternoon. The Chicago police observed the drop, nailed the guy who picked up the cash, and turned him over to the FBI who thinks the guy is a flunky." Tucker had his attention. Rare.

"Your friend Beedle have anything more?" Burgess asked, with his hand over his mouth, steam almost visible from his red ears.

"He should be here in an hour or so. I need to ask him when he gets in," Tucker said.

As they continued to weave their way to the ballroom, Tucker gave Burgess a recap of the session with Ike Moncrief, including the preliminary lab results.

"Does the goddamn sheriff realize we are thirty-two hours from tipoff? I knew those bozos would drag this thing out. What've you found?" Burgess said, as he stopped with a jerk.

Tucker looked at Burgess with a question mark all over his face. He had just given him the status of the search, down to the gnat's ass detail, and Burgess asked the question like he had not listened to a word of it. Tucker took a second to look up the hall where dozens of people milled around, probably waiting for their chance to shake hands with Wolfman Howells and congratulate him on the incredible season. He turned to Burgess.

"What've you heard from President Kline," Tucker asked, with not so much as a blink of his eyes. "Did he get anything out of the NCAA?"

"He's scheduled for this breakfast. I'll get to him as soon as he shows," Burgess said, with the cigar back between his lips. "As of now, I don't have anything; the game's still on. You need to find that kid, McGill," Burgess added. His round face glowed a bright red like he had been holding his breath for three minutes, which he had. Outside the earshot of the assembled alumni, Burgess poked his finger in McGill's chest and enunciated in a low voice, "I told you two days ago, you had one task and only one task. You haven't done squat. Get it done. Don't waste any time with the kid's mother. Lock her in the room," he said, turning to look toward the entrance of the ballroom. "And don't count on Kline to buy your ass any time."

Anger drove a blunt wedge into Tucker's logic. The veins in his neck grew thicker. He balked at telling Burgess to go to hell and toyed with the urge to go postal on the guy. Instead, he took a sip of coffee without taking his eyes off Burgess. He lowered the cup but not his gaze. In a low tone that left no doubt, he said, "Don't ever...lay...a finger...on me...again." Burgess pursed his lips.

"Hey Ben, I want you to meet Atlanta's biggest Redcliffe fan," cried the deep South Carolina accent of a tall, blond man in a black blazer and gray slacks who came up from behind Tucker then shouldered his way in front of Burgess. Close behind him was a man large enough to have objects in orbit around his waist, literally the biggest fan for sure. Tucker broke off his stare after Burgess and the other two men walked away.

Despite the early hour, the lobby of the hotel was filled with people wearing their team colors (greens and blues) and noisier than a tailgate Saturday at the stadium thanks to the Michigan State spirit band that marched through, full thunder, headed for a breakfast rally on the other side of the hotel. Tucker pulled his phone from his pocket to find out when PJ wanted to meet with Ike Moncrief. Before he could punch in PJ's number, Tucker's phone rang. He checked the caller ID and exhaled audibly. It was Melissa Cooper.

"Tucker McGill," he answered.

"So formal now are we. When I call my name doesn't pop up on your phone? You need to get that fixed, Tucker McGill," she said.

"Sorry. Habit," he said. With the crowd noise he strained to hear. "Just finished a little tête-à-tête with my boss."

"Just fix your phone, and look at the damn thing before you answer it," she replied, peeved at his lack of attention. "So where have you been? You walk out of my bedroom, and never call? That doesn't work, Tucker. What's going on?" she asked, her voice almost the same tone as Burgess's.

"What's going on? Well…let me see. In addition to getting my school ready for eighty million people to watch us play basketball, oh not much except a lost super-stud player, his mom who is sleeping in my room right now and—"

"Sleeping in your room?" she screamed.

"Yeah, she showed up unannounced at the airport late last night. She looks like death warmed over. I was too tired to try to deal with it last night. This city's a zoo. Hard to find an available hotel room anywhere, so I just told her to crash in my place. I'll sort it out today, one more thing I need to do."

"Any more on your kid, the player? What's the latest on the search?" Mel asked.

"Short answer, we've not found him. Long answer, the FBI is involved. Nabbed a guy in Chicago who picked up the ransom. Oh, yeah, the mom came up with money to pay the ransom."

"So there's a Chicago connection? Gang? Mob? What?" she asked, her tone more than just curious.

"Who knows. Seems the few clues we have are local. One local suspect. The ransom letter originated in Augusta," Tucker added. "Plus still trying to get the game delayed. I have my hands full with all that not to mention Burgess. The guy's an ass," he said.

"Speaking of ass, I'll be in Atlanta tonight. Booked a room at the Four Seasons. Can you do dinner? Gotta eat sometime, Sherlock," she said, her faux Southern accent sounded more like Daisy Mae.

Tucker threw back his head and rubbed his temples while he considered his response. His headache had come back, pounding like a gong with bolts of lightning strafing his vision. Last night he snatched maybe three hours of fidgety sleep. He had a mountain of paperwork and a list of things to do which was longer than the book of Job. He had phone calls to make, phone calls to return, and PJ would have even more. He quickly weighed Burgess's threat against the night before he left for Atlanta. Testosterone won. "Sure. What time do you get in?" Tucker asked.

"Let's do Park 75, my treat. It's on Fourteenth Street, in my hotel. Be there at seven," she said, with no questions asked, though she planned to be in the city long before that for other reasons.

"Okay, deal, but I need to take care of some things after dinner, so we may need to make it quick," he said.

"So now I'm a quickie? You naughty, presumptive, stupid boy. You know, I really hate it when someone tells me what I am going to do, especially when I am the one paying. I'll set the pace, cowboy" she said, her irritation inched a notch or two higher.

"All right, touché already. Hey, I gotta go."

"Okay, sweetie. You can fill me in on all the details tonight. Bring a tour guide with you. See ya." She hung up which was fine by Tucker.

Tour guide? He had to take Xandra to breakfast, then call PJ, and find Ike Moncrief. He didn't have time to go through a detailed status of the search. *What does she care? She barely knows what a basketball looks like,* he thought. But her comment about gangs. That spun some wheels.

CHAPTER 19

Friday, April 1
8:18 a.m.

Neither Tucker nor Xandra noticed the man who
followed them into the breakfast buffet and
kept a constant eye in their direction from a
table on the far side of the room. They had not seen him
on the fourteenth floor of the hotel, as well, loitering
down the hall from Tucker's room. Xandra had never
noticed him follow her out of Union Station the day
before either. He had changed out of his Georgetown
parka and now wore a UConn "Go Huskies" sweatshirt,
the same one the mannequin in the gift shop promoted,
the one worn by hordes of people on the streets in
Atlanta.

The pair of accidental roommates sipped coffee
between the questions and answers. With every lull, their
eyelids drooped. Xandra wandered in and out of the
conversation, worried about the ransom, her son, and
his release. Tucker lost sleep for many of the same
reasons. While he peeled back the paper from the
bottom of his muffin and picked at the nuts on the top,
he thought more about the connections between the
character the FBI questioned, the FedEx envelope, and
Ike Moncrief, in addition to how uncomfortable the

sleeper sofa had been. With the ransom paid—short a few million dollars—it might be best to keep Xandra close in the event something else went wrong. The ransom letter made no reference to how or when Malik would return or what might happen if the pick-up man was caught.

When they had finished eating, they each grabbed a paper cup of coffee and dodged the morning crazies (or late, late night revelers) as they walked the length of the main corridor to a small conference room reserved for the Redcliffe staff. The coach and assistants were in the alumni breakfast which allowed Tucker the chance to use the room and the phones. They closed the door behind them while the man in the UConn sweatshirt who had followed them from breakfast continued past.

"PJ, it's Tucker. Good morning," he said, making use of the speaker phone.

"Good morning to you, too, señor," he replied. "I was just fixin' to call you. I'm not going to make it to Atlanta this morning, maybe not today at all. The FBI guys are on this case like a duck on a June bug. They want to camp out here and go over the details on our end."

"Well look, I have Miss Novikov here with me in the conference room, just the two of us. Why don't you bring us up-to-date on things."

PJ nearly choked on his donut when Tucker told him the kid's mother was with him. He recalled she had arrived unannounced but thought Tucker would stand clear of her for any number of reasons. PJ brought Tucker up to speed. He went into the detailed findings from the lab, additional FedEx information he was able to uncover from the FedEx local manager, and on the happenings through the night, to include what he knew about the FBI investigation.

"The Feds say the guy in Chicago, the one who picked up the cash, says he doesn't remember picking it up or why he would have picked it up. Right! Says he has no knowledge of sending any ransom note. Right! Says he's read about the player, Farqu'har. Knows he's from the Chicago area, but that's it. Makes no sense. The Chicago PD picked him up within ten minutes of the job as soon as he walked out of the train station. Had a tail on him the entire time. The guy hired a lawyer, but the FBI plans to roll him through another session today then run a lie detector on him."

Tucker watched the expression on Xandra's face transition from sleep-deficient, to wide-eyed alert, to furrowed-brow inquisitive as PJ relayed the story.

"I'm going to need to have Moncrief back in for more questions tomorrow when I get there," PJ said.

"PJ, the game's tomorrow. There's no way Coach Howell's is going to make him available for you," Tucker replied. He looked over at Xandra across the table. He watched her cheeks sag as she closed her eyes and massaged her temples.

"Hey, he can have a choice. Let the kid meet me at a specified time and place or I'll show up at courtside with a warrant for his arrest as a suspect in a kidnapping," the officer said, no question he was serious. "There was enough evidence in that truck of his to hang the kid. The lab report came back with a positive on fingerprints on the can. They matched Farqu'har's prints on his locker and items in his locker at the arena. The concentration of Rohypnol residue in the Coke was enough to knock out a bull elephant. Whoever this kid drugged took a heavy shot, much more than he would need to get his rocks off with some chick he picked up at a bar." PJ remembered Tucker had a female guest with him. "Oh, pardon me, Miss Novikov." She did not respond.

Tucker hesitated. Redcliffe had the early game, set for five fifteen. He could possibly convince the coach to have Moncrief available early in the morning.

"PJ, from what the FBI knows any chance they can get the game delayed? Talk to the NCAA and CBS," Tucker asked.

"You crazy? Not sure they're prepared to do that. They have info, but they don't get wrapped into the schedule of events. They can put out warnings, but not their call to cancel these things. That's up to the network and the game officials."

"But we have a player that someone's holding on to," Tucker replied.

"One kid, one player, and no known threat to him, actually," PJ said.

"They might hurt him," Xandra blurted out, her face tight with tension.

"Ma'am, I appreciate your concern, but the threat was not to loss of life," PJ replied, still pissed she paid the ransom. "We're working with the FBI to find your boy as quickly as we can." PJ wanted nothing to do with the woman at this point; he had an office full of FBI agents waiting for him.

"Tucker, have him ready at ten o'clock," PJ said. "We'll check for some connection between Moncrief and this guy Charles Stocker, the guy who picked up the money. If we find one, your team's trainer will end up watching the game from the holding cell in Beech Island. Got work to do. I'll get back to ya," PJ said, before he dropped the connection.

"They found the man who picked up my money?" Xandra asked with a worried look just short of panic.

Tucker knew he had no way out of telling her the truth. She heard what PJ said, but before he had a chance to answer, Xandra continued, "So why he not release Malik? Why he not tell us where Malik is?" she asked.

"Yes, a man picked up the bag with the money, and the police have him in custody, but they don't believe he had anything to do with the letter or the kidnapping. They're not sure why or how he got involved," Tucker said.

"The one who sent the letter, if they not have the money they say they hurt Malik," she protested. She folded her hands and thumped them against her forehead until panic landed a solid body blow. She grabbed Tucker's wrists and squeezed, pulling him toward her with a grip too tight to escape. Her face, no longer cool and soft ivory white but a steamed red with a wrinkled bridge above her nose and eyebrows that slanted inward. The whites of her eyes covered with a filigree of red, moistened by a single tear in the corner of each.

Tucker fumbled for words, but the passion in the mother's grip and in her gaze choked them back. He tried to pull away, but she clenched harder with a grip that was as much a scream for help as it was a demand for action.

"We must find my son before they hurt him," she said, including herself in the search.

"We will," Tucker replied as she released him. "We'll find him."

When Malik Farqu'har placed the battery-end of the flashlight in the mouth of a gallon water jug, it splashed a dim, soft light against the twelve-foot ceiling and temporarily washed out the image the hidden camera transmitted. From the moment he staggered into the room, every move he made dangled somewhere in cyberspace, but only one computer knew how to access the portal to view him in his misery. Only one person watched him work to free himself. Only one person knew how he dumped the cans from one of the metal shelves to use the angle iron in his unsuccessful effort to pry open the door. Or how he smashed cans to use them to carve out the mortar and widen cracks in the cement block walls, to no avail. And, the camera watched him pound endlessly against the door with desperate cries for help before he collapsed on a cooler, a sleeping bag wrapped around his shoulders. The more he tried, the more he shivered, sobbed and prayed.

CHAPTER 20

Friday, April 1
Noon

It was noon on Friday, the eve of the semi-final game, before Tucker could pull Ike Moncrief away from the team. Coach Howells held the mandated, practice open to the public at the Georgia Dome which required the usual taping beforehand and the necessary whirlpools after. Tucker watched patiently in the locker room while the young trainer went about his routine with each of the players. He could not tell if Moncrief was mothering his team going into the biggest weekend of its history or whether he was intentionally stalling because the coach told him that there were more questions about Malik Farqu'har.

As the team grabbed their bags to return to the hotel, Tucker walked with Ike Moncrief to the Club level of the Dome where there was less foot traffic of spectators who had come to watch the open practice sessions.

"You want any lunch or something to drink?" Tucker asked. Moncrief pulled a bottle of water from his bag and shook his head. They settled on a tall, round table with stools in a corner, a less intimidating environment. Moncrief looked around, noncommittal, with a brief glance at Tucker before he plopped down hard on the seat and propped his feet on the rung of the stool. With his long legs hunched up nearly to his chest, he looked like an oversized jockey in a saddle.

"Ike, I'm not sure Coach Howells mentioned this to you, but Captain Beedle needs to talk to you some more concerning the whereabouts of Malik." Moncrief's eyes closed. His head shook slightly. "He may not be able to talk to you today, but I wanted to ask a few questions, some things I didn't want to bring up yesterday plus a few other things." Tucker paused and leaned forward, his hands folded on the tabletop. Behind him deliverymen carted boxes of cups, foods, and kegs of beer and soda to various concessions stands. "I need…we all need…to find Malik. Since it appears you were the last to see him, can we go back to last Tuesday, after practice on campus?"

With a movement barely noticeable, Ike Moncrief nodded in agreement.

"After our last session together, Captain Beedle took a look at your truck. He said it had a good bit of mud on it. Before it got cold, before the snow started we hadn't had any rain for weeks. Where did the mud come from?"

"I don't know," Ike said, curt and flippant. "Maybe somebody borrowed my truck. It isn't locked."

"Captain Beedle said it was locked. Obviously the mud wasn't from on campus. Where did you go after you left the gym?"

"I told you guys, I went to my dorm," Moncrief said, with a mulish expression.

"Ike, Captain Beedle found a receipt for gas from a gas station in Edgefield in your truck. The time on the receipt was around midnight on the night Malik disappeared. Obviously you left the dorm at some point."

"I don't know where that came from. I told you the truck was unlocked. Could have been anybody," he said, reinforced with a bold, disgusted stare toward Tucker.

"The clerk at the Thrifty Mart identified you by your photo, Ike," Tucker said, tapping his lower lip with his pen.

"It wasn't me." He cocked his chin to the side and looked away.

"Ike, come on. Lying isn't going to help you here. When Captain Beedle takes you through this you're going to tell the truth or put yourself in even more trouble."

Ike dropped his feet to the floor and turned to face Tucker. "Look, Mr. McGill. I have no idea what this is all about. I recall being with Farqu'har when we left the gym. Like I told you before, I went back in, and when I came out he was gone. I remember being in the truck and going to my dorm. All that other crap, I don't remember any of that—no gas, no mud, no anything like that," he said, as his final confession.

"Do you know what Rohypnol is, Ike?"

"Sure. Isn't that the date rape drug?"

"Yeah. Ever use that stuff on a girl?"

"No, sir."

"Ever use it on a guy?"

"Shit no! What do you think I am? Why would I use that on a guy?" he chuckled as he rocked back, his face puckered in disgust.

"Okay, why did the lab find Rohypnol residue in a Coke can in your truck? Captain Beedle got a search warrant, went through the cab of your truck and found a Coke can with residue in it."

"I have no idea," Moncrief said in a matter-of-fact way.

"Ike, come on. I need you to be up front with me on this stuff. I'm trying to help before the law gets to you, and all of this becomes evidence laid out against you."

"Man, I told you. I didn't do anything. I told you the truck is usually unlocked. Anybody could have thrown a can in there." Ike looked at Tucker, his forehead wrinkled, completely bemused.

"A can with Malik Farqu'har's finger prints on it?" Tucker said, frustrated with the responses and the kid's attitude. "The lab compared prints inside his locker to the prints on the can. They matched. It could have been the Coke can Malik had in his hand when you left the gym. The Coke you said you gave to him."

"Yeah, I gave him a Coke, but all this other stuff I didn't have anything to do with it." Ike's voice grew louder.

Tucker looked around the open area, his eyes unfocused, bewildered. Everything he learned from PJ, all the lab work, the security video, it was all beginning to point to Ike Moncrief. "So why did you lie about going straight to your dorm?"

"I didn't lie," he protested. "I didn't go to any convenience store or do any driving anywhere but to the dorm."

"Come on Ike, how could you forget something like that? The weather was nasty. You just finished your last practice. Had you taken anything, like drugs, like Rohypnol?"

"Me? Take that drug? You gotta be out of your f'ing mind," he said, his eyes wide open at the suggestion.

"Well then what? Medicine? Anything? How could you forget that, all of that?" Tucker asked.

"Well let's just say I don't know," Ike sassed back, tired of all the questions.

Tucker took a different tack. "Ike, tell me about your arrest for gambling, poker," Tucker said.

"I wasn't arrested," Ike said, with a scowl and a question mark on his face.

"Captain Beedle says you were brought in as part of a bust earlier in the year. Big poker game, several high rollers from out of town, not your average college penny ante game."

"What? I mean…what's that got to do with anything about Farqu'har?" Moncrief asked.

"Seems others involved with that game have been involved with other events in other parts of the country, some illegal things," Tucker bluffed. "Just wonder what the tie-in might be."

"Hey, I know nothing about those guys. Never saw them before that night. I went to play. Dudes showed up. We played. Things got too rich for my blood, and I got out," he said.

Tucker knew there was more to the story. "So you're not lying to me again are you, Ike?"

"I told you. I didn't lie before, and I'm not lying now," Ike growled. He pushed his stool back. "Geezus, why can't you guys believe me? What do I have to do, man? Come on. Give me a break." He leaned forward and buried his head in his hands.

"I'm trying to give you a break, Ike, but when Captain Beedle calls you in, there won't be any breaks, and there won't be any easy questions." Tucker looked at the kid, worn and slumped forward on his stool. "Ike, why are you the trainer for this team?"

"What?" he asked, his eyes still on the floor.

"I said…why are you the trainer for this team?"

"Because I've always liked basketball and being around basketball," he said.

"According to old scouting records, Malik wasn't the top recruit for this team; you were," Tucker said, looking straight at Moncrief who did not acknowledge the comment. "Ike, are you jealous of Malik? I mean, he's been getting all the attention for leading the team you were supposed to lead. He's the star, and you are…the trainer."

Ike Moncrief lifted his head, dropped his jaw, opened his mouth then swallowed his words. A silence grew between them. All around them vendors, media teams, delivery carts—an assortment of people—continued with their sales and preparations for the games.

Finally Ike raised his chin and cocked his head toward Tucker. "Mr. McGill, all I can tell you is after practice on Tuesday, Malik and I went out the door together, and that was the last time I saw him."

The kid's glassy-eyed stare signaled Tucker he wasn't going to get anything more out of Ike. He rubbed his palms together and knew the kid was not ready for Beedle. He wanted to believe him, but too many things did not add up. The kid denied just about everything though witnesses had confirmed it all. He had to be lying.

Tucker pushed back from the table and stood; Moncrief did the same while he pulled his phone from his pocket.

"Ike, I don't know what to tell you. I'm sure Captain Beedle will want to see you soon, probably before the game tomorrow, and neither you nor the coach can keep that from happening," Tucker said.

Ike glanced up from his phone and made brief eye contact with the hint of a smile or a smirk, then looked back to his phone. He had no interest in what Tucker had to say. He just looked at his phone with wide eyes and a smile that broadened.

"No shit! This can't be!" Ike said, as his thumb scrolled through message after message. "Tweets. Viral. Postpone the game?"

CHAPTER 21

Friday, April 1
1:51 p.m.

Tucker had turned off his phone prior to his meeting with Ike Moncrief; he didn't need any distractions, phone calls or otherwise. Turning off his phone, his lifeline, left him temporarily in the dark until Ike's outburst.

"They want them to postpone our game, postpone the semis," Ike said, as he scanned tweets that continued to stack up.

"Who is 'they?'" Tucker asked, as he moved alongside Ike.

"I don't know. Everybody. Fans. People. They're telling everybody to protest. To 'march for the madness.' To go to the CBS Headquarters in New York and NCAA Headquarters in Indy and here, at the Dome. Shit, this is awesome. This is crazy," he said. "People just keep retweeting the message *"Support the Cinderella Underdog – CU – in NYC, Indy, and Atlanta at 3 p.m. today."* That's like an hour from now." The smile on Moncrief's face slowly disintegrated. He grew reserved, more distant, and intense but continued to scroll through the messages.

Ike scrolled through messages while Tucker walked him to the cabstand in front of the stadium. He gave him cab fare and sent the kid on his way, then rushed back inside, straight to the locker room to find Wolfman Howells or Ben Burgess or somebody from the staff. Nobody. He turned on his phone and watched as the flood of tweets stacked up. He had never seen anything like it. He worked his way back to the media room; it was empty. He grabbed one of the desk phones and tried to call PJ. As the number started to ring on the other end, Tucker's cell phone rang. It was President Kline. He hung up his call to the sheriff's office and answered his cell, "Tucker McGill."

Chris Gorting's plane touched down at the Atlanta Hartsfield-Jackson Airport about thirty minutes behind schedule and thirty minutes earlier than usual for his least favorite carrier but the only flight available thanks to a clerical error. Upon landing he turned on his phone and a voicemail box filled with messages. Despite Friday afternoon bumper-to-bumper traffic into the city, he asked the driver to swing by the Georgia Dome; he wanted to see for himself what impact the tweets might have on the tournament preparations.

The tweets were more effective than he could have imagined. Thousands of people, mostly college-age students, swarmed the facility, blocking doors and access in or out. Placards and banners simplified their purpose:

CORPORATE AMERICA HOSED CINDERELLA
BOYCOTT THE SPONSORS
MARCH MADNESS IS FIGHTING MAD

Gorting realized he did not have a snowballs chance in hell of getting inside. He feared if someone recognized him there was a good chance he could become a hostage to the mob. He told the driver to turn around and head directly to the hotel.

The hotel was free of any disturbances aside from the continuous flow of over-the-top obnoxious fans, two sheets to the wind even before happy hour started, obvious crusaders from a generous hospitality suite. In the crowd, were two Latino males—sized like a "Laurel and Hardy" pairing, chubby with thin—both wearing Spartan green Final Four hoodies accessorized with bling. From behind a stand of ficus trees which separated the front desk from the sitting area they sat in conversation, subdued and private, while they kept their eyes on the front door and all that took place at the front desk. They appeared especially interested when Chris Gorting checked in, and the attendant first handed him his key then pulled a FedEx envelope from a file cabinet behind the desk. Immediately the "Hardy" observer pulled a cell phone from his pocket and made a call. His partner followed Gorting onto the elevator to the tenth floor and down the hall, three rooms passed the one Gorting entered.

Inside his room Chris Gorting fixed a drink and immediately fired off a voicemail to his comptroller to tell him how foolish it was to rein in the budget by flying Coach Class versus his usual First Class. Other voicemails and emails were less threatening. With the most pressing matters taken care of, he finished his scotch and opened the FedEx envelope the desk clerk had given him. The contents carved horror on his face—two photographs, a USB flash drive, and the words "*PAY ME NOW OR YOU PAY LATER*" in large, bold print on Redcliffe letterhead again signed by John Wayne.

Four floors above, Xandra Novikov lay face down on Tucker McGill's bed. Beside her was an opened FedEx pouch, a letter, and a digital photo printed on regular paper, the colors very dark. It was a picture taken in very low light, with a bit of a glow around a beam projected from the floor to the ceiling. On the far side of the beam was a tall figure, a one-dimensional shadow with enough definition to see the face of her son Malik. The sender was John Wayne.

Chris Gorting's mouth went dry. He did not recognize the location, and there was no indication when the photos were taken. The pictures exposed several people; he recognized only one face, his son, Robbie. In the background several men sat around a poker table cluttered with stacks of chips, cigars in ashtrays, and liquor bottles. In the second photo, the lens focus was on Robbie who held a tooter with one end up his nostril as he leaned over a mirrored plate with a lines of a white powdery substance.

He made it to the bathroom where he lost his airport supper—a burger and super-sized fries—about the same time his cell phone rang in the other room. Weak, he quickly rinsed the sour, acidic remnants of his nausea from his mouth, then answered the ring. "Chris Gorting."

"Chris, Frank Kehren, CBS Sports. What in the hell is going on?" he said, in a voice far from chummy or casual.

CHAPTER 22

Friday, April 1
3:37 p.m.

Tucker ricocheted pinball-like through the maze of meeting places in the Dome trying to find any of the Redcliffe execs. The tournament schedule listed several conferences with the press, another Eagle Boosters appearance, general public appearances and more, but none of them were in progress. With the crowd of protesters in front of the building, he ran out a back entrance concealed by big television vans and worked his way through the cables and flatbed trailers with generators the size of small houses. He flagged down a cab to get back to the hotel and went directly to a small, private conference room with a brass signboard adjacent to the door that read "President's Lounge – Redcliffe College." He knocked three times, hard. While he waited for a response, he turned to watch the stream of people behind him as they meandered about the displays of sports memorabilia along the walls. Still in his overcoat, unbuttoned and out of the weather, he knocked a second time with no response. He checked his watch. He had not touched base with PJ since early in the morning before he talked to Ike Moncrief. He knocked a third time, a persistent series of knocks before the door opened abruptly, a pissed off Brent Kline on the other side.

"President Kline, my name is Tucker McGill. We talked earlier this week about Malik Farqu'har, our missing student athlete," Tucker said, before Kline had a chance to question the disturbance. McGill looked back over his shoulder then back to Kline. "Sir, I need to talk to you."

"McGill, I'm in conference and extremely busy. Later perhaps," Kline said, and began to close the door.

"Sir, this is extremely important. I think we have a major problem," Tucker said, and with that he stepped into the room, uninvited.

The tall, thin president turned in disbelief. It was not his style to grant audience to an associate from any department unless scheduled with reason. Astounded by the man's boldness, Kline closed the door.

"What the hell—"

"President Kline, I don't know if you've seen the news this afternoon," Tucker said.

"I haven't. I've been in conference with our board members and awaiting another call," Kline said, with a long, perturbed face. He closed the door and took a seat at a desk on the back wall, still with a puzzled face.

"There is a protest over at the Georgia Dome right now. Thousands of people demanding the semis be postponed until we find Farqu'har," Tucker said, as he followed Kline to the desk. "Apparently, on Twitter, someone started a retweet campaign to protest the game just because of the schedule. And it's not just here. The tweet called for a protest here, as well as at the CBS Headquarters in New York City and the NCAA Headquarters in Indianapolis. All of the doors at the Dome are blocked by protesters. Security is trying to maintain the building. The Atlanta Police has patrolmen on the ground to maintain order."

"So, why hasn't anybody told me before this, McGill? Where's Ben Burgess? What am I supposed to do? That's police work."

"Call the NCAA, and make another plea. You have the support of thousands of fans it's not just you asking, it is you speaking on behalf of all those people."

"Look, McGill. I'm not going to tie myself to a mob, some chaotic, spur of the moment protest," Kline said, but in his head he was ten steps ahead of McGill in his thinking. It was more than representing the school or the people. It would mean his influence in the decision which, to the alumni, represented power, conviction, and strength which, to Kline, represented larger donations and financial gifts to Redcliffe, which meant even greater potential to parlay his curriculum vitae around the northeastern schools.

"It's absurd. This whole thing is absurd. What's the latest on the search for our student?" Kline said, to move the discussion back to the crux of the problem.

Tucker provided a detailed summary which highlighted the two suspects in the case, one of which was another student, Ike Moncrief. At the end, he returned to the protesters.

"At this point, sir, I think a call from you to Mr. Gorting at the NCAA could do it, could get the game delayed," Tucker said, with the slightest upturn at the ends of his mouth but not convinced of his own suggestion.

"McGill, you raise a good point, a very good point indeed. I'll consider it, but right now I'm late for another call. If you'll excuse me…"

Tucker did not move, totally numbed by the laissez-faire attitude Kline seemed to take toward the biggest event in the history of the college. He had argued with Kline on this before, and in the end, Kline told him to get lost. He made the decision to bypass Kline.

"Thank you for your time, sir. This means a lot," Tucker said, his hand outstretched. Kline shook it and closed the door hard in Tucker's face.

From the lobby Tucker tried to call Ben Burgess. No answer on his cell phone or in his room, so he called back to the college. It was late Friday afternoon. He realized his chances of getting anybody in the department were slim, but Lady Luck finally showed some compassion. Hettie Bell Block answered the phone. She did not know where Ben Burgess was, but she was able to provide a phone number to the NCAA, the number she had used earlier to call the headquarters. With another call, Tucker's luck began to slide.

Liz Oglesby, Chris Gorting's assistant, would not share Gorting's cell number, but she did let slip that he was staying in the Marriott Suites Midtown, somewhere in the nineteen stories above him. Tucker had to flirt with the cute hotel receptionist, who looked like she was all of fifteen, before she broke down and wrote something on a small piece of paper, placed the note on the counter then walked away toward another guest. The note had the four-digit number Tucker needed.

On the tenth floor, Chris Gorting opened his room door after Tucker's knock. Gorting looked a bit addled when he came to the door and even more shocked when Tucker stepped inside without invitation. Gorting, a much smaller man, put a hand on Tucker's chest and pushed him toward the wall. He made no protest to the intrusion, though his face fetched a scowl of disapproval.

"Mr. Gorting, my name is Tucker McGill. I'm an Assistant Athletic Director at Redcliffe College. I'm here on behalf of Ben Burgess the AD and President Brent Kline," Tucker blurted out.

"McGill I don't care who you are or where you're from, you don't just come waltzing into my room—"

"I need five minutes," Tucker said.

"I should call security, McGill. That's what I should do, but I'll give you five minutes."

Tucker wasted no time. He pitched an impassioned plea to delay the game scheduled to begin in just a little over twenty-four hours. For every point Gorting made against the appeal, Tucker countered with a rational, logical argument for a win-win scenario. Gorting was well aware of the protests and seemed more swayed by them than Kline had been, possibly because his headquarters was one of the locations under siege. Though Gorting made no commitment to support Tucker's recommendation, it appeared he took the appeal to heart.

"I saw the protesters at the Georgia Dome on my way in," Gorting said. "Given the late hour, any action on my part would be more than controversial, and most likely, I would be unable to get full approval from the Executive Committee, the joint Division I Board of Directors, or my legal counsel." Gorting walked toward the wet bar.

When Gorting left the sitting area, Tucker glanced over to the small writing desk in the room where he noticed a FedEx envelope partially covered by a letter with Redcliffe College stationary sitting next to a laptop computer. He started to stand for a closer look when Gorting turned.

"Water?"

"No thanks."

"Mr. McGill, if there is any chance at all I can help with this I need to be on the phone now. Unless you have anything more to add, please excuse me."

As Gorting headed toward the door, Tucker snatched a quick look at the letter. All he saw before Gorting looked back over his shoulder was that the letter was address to Christian Gorting and signed by John Wayne.

Their meeting had lasted just over five minutes, and Gorting never mentioned he had already talked to Frank Kehren, President of CBS Sports.

As he waited for the elevator, Tucker's phone rang.

"Sweetie, I'm here. You should be here too!" Melissa Cooper said, as if Tucker had missed another appointment with her.

"Hey Melissa. Well, I am not, though wish I could be. I'm headed up to change to go to a Booster Club Happy Hour. A 'command performance' event. Coach and staff. AD and department. Probably President Kline. Gotta go schmooze the alums. Besides, I need a drink. Care to join me? Great fun. Free booze. Lotsa of guys. Your kinda place," Tucker said, recalling her assembly of followers at their last happy hour.

"Sounds marvelous," Melissa said, in her best Mae West voice. "Did you say the coach was going to be there? Doesn't he have better things to do right now? I mean he's missing his stud, and the game is tomorrow, isn't it? It's still on, right?"

"Yeah, game's still on though I've spent the day trying to change that."

"Uh, well, the coach doesn't need my perfume under his nose at this point, so I'll pass. Wish him luck for me, though," she said. "I'll definitely be watching him. And don't forget we have a dinner date tonight. Seven sharp."

"Got it. I'll pass your sentiments to the coach."

"Oh, and cowboy, don't be late…again," she added, then hung up.

Tucker turned left down the hall toward his room, past a group of five people ready to board the elevator on the fourteenth floor. In the crowd, one wiry guy still in the same green hoodie he had worn in the lobby, hesitated long enough to watch Tucker enter his room before he hopped on the elevator just as the door closed.

Xandra jumped when the door opened. She sat upright on the bed and looked at Tucker. "I receive another FedEx letter today," she said. Tucker dropped his backpack and coat on the chair.

"Here? How did they—"

"This one had picture of Malik," she added, and handed it to Tucker as he approached the bed. Though the image was dark, Tucker knew it was the missing player.

"It arrive about thirty minutes ago. I had letter, too." She handed him a sheet of paper, Redcliffe College letterhead. The letter was addressed to her as "*Comrade Novikov*" and used Tucker's room number as the address. Like the letter he saw in Gorting's room, this letter was also signed by John Wayne. The message was brief:

Dear Comrade Novikov,

You failed to listen or did you disregard what I said? I am told the money in the bag was far less than I require. And you obviously told the police.

You have until game time tomorrow to provide all of the money. Place it in a black UNC duffel bag, and call Malik's cell phone for instructions on where to take it. No tricks this time. And don't call until you have the money.

If you do not do as I say, the next picture of Malik will be all black, as in lights out, as in gone for good.

s/John Wayne

Tucker could not take his eyes off the letter, definitely unprepared to look into Xandra's eyes. The sender knew that the money in the bag was far less than the demand. News of the kidnapping had traveled fast. With the FBI involvement, every news agency in the country had a nose into the crime and an ear to the ground for any word that would become an exclusive in their media. The *Chicago Tribune* had printed a small story about the arrest at Union Station in the morning edition, though Tucker had not seen the article, and he had not talked to PJ all day so he did not know what other stories were reported.

Finally Tucker dropped the hand with the letter in it and looked at Xandra on the edge of the bed where she sat, her eyes fixed on the floor, her shoulders drooped, and her hands in her lap. He searched for words that never came. He wanted to assure her that things would be all right, but he had not even convinced himself.

"Xandra, where did you get this FedEx?"

"The short man from lobby, he call. I thought it be you. That man brought it," she said, as she reached for the opened envelope.

"I want you to stay in this room again tonight. I'll order room service to deliver supper for you. Open the door only for the person who brings the food, nobody else," Tucker said. "Nobody."

Xandra looked up at him and blinked her eyes, the edges of her mouth in a frown. She remained there while Tucker placed a call for her dinner and asked for it to be delivered at six o'clock which allowed Xandra time to compose herself.

It was too late for him to shower. He changed into a starched white shirt, blue-patterned tie and black wing-tipped dress shoes.

Xandra had moved to the couch in the sitting room. She stood when Tucker came out of the bedroom. He looked at her as he walked up. He had almost stopped in front of her when she took a step and wrapped her arms around his waist with her head snug against his chest. She hugged him, tight, as she cried. He allowed his hands to drift behind her and eased into a gentle embrace while an unfamiliar surge of emotions bubbled inside him. He felt awkward with this woman, this stranger in his room, but as they lingered, close, he felt her panic, the threat of losing her son—her world—so near, so real. When he sensed the tears had stopped, Tucker stepped back and placed his hands on her shoulders, offering a slight smile, a trace of hope in his eyes. She closed her eyes and wrapped her arms over her stomach; once again her head and eyes drifted to the floor.

"Please...stay here, and don't open the door except for your dinner. If anything happens, anything at all, please call my cell phone," he said. He paused as he walked out the door. "Xandra, things will be all right. We'll find Malik. Things will be all right."

On the elevator ride to the main floor, he was less confident in his own words. He stopped in the lobby to call PJ for an update; the call went straight to voicemail. As he dialed, he looked for a short man wearing Marriott staff attire. He did not see one but aware the guy who delivered the FedEx envelope could have been on an earlier shift or out for dinner or delivering another package to another guest. In an earlier life, his friend Shelia would have him convinced the little man Xandra mentioned was not a staff member at all; Tucker discarded that notion with a grin.

The happy hour was in full swing by the time Tucker entered the room. Scheduled to start at five, hundreds of people were already there, and it was only five past the hour. He made the rounds. Checked in with his boss and updated him on the events of the day—the big discussion, the Twitter inspired protests in various cities. It was all over the evening news with live coverage from the Georgia Dome. Burgess likened them to the Arab Spring riots going on in the Middle East with a non-political impact.

"Just another excuse to get together to hoot and holler, carry on and make life miserable for us working people," Burgess said, slurring through most of the words, the obvious participant in the pre-party, party with some of his good ol' boy alumni friends.

Tucker made a point to be seen by President Kline where he waited for a sign that the politically-minded president had secured a delay. Kline eyed Tucker then turned to enter another conversation.

After he had hobnobbed for forty-five minutes Tucker rescued Coach Howells from a few overly inebriated coach wannabes who continued to lay out game strategies—how to win with Malik and how to survive without. Tucker wrapped his arm around Wolfman Howells shoulder, excused them from the crowd, and escorted the coach to a less crowded part of the room.

"So they have it all figured out?" Tucker asked, his chin pointed toward the previous group, now embroiled in their own chest pointing and tipsy toasts.

"This was not in my contract," Howells said. "All I want is for the next twenty-four hours to pass and get the game started. What's the news on Malik?"

"Nothing concrete, many ideas. His mom received another letter with another demand, well, threat. I need to get it to the sheriff. Aside from that...a few leads...nothing that you can put on the floor by tomorrow," Tucker said. He looked around the room and admired the money the boosters represented. Then he thought of the pressure they added. "Want my advice?"

"Don't tell me you have a strategy like everybody else in this room has. Geez, I've heard them all," Howells said, sipping on his ice water.

"Nah. Just relax, man. Think of something other than the game and give your head a break. In a couple days the both of us can get falling-down drunk, pass out, and nurse hangovers with all of this behind us."

Howells hesitated. He turned away from the festivities and looked out the window. "Every time I take my mind off the team and the games, it drifts back to Amanda." Howells just stared at the headlights as they crisscrossed on the street, his head and eyes fixed, unblinking. "She should be here. She wanted this as much as I did. Since the accident... She was my life. I'd give up all of this to have her back, even for an hour, to tell her how much I miss her. How much I loved her." He paused then looked back toward Tucker. "She would have enjoyed this, Tuck. She would have enjoyed this." Howells forced a smile.

"Sorry, Ernie."

"How about dinner after this?" Howells said, with a quick change of subject. "You can distract me from all of this, fill my ears with more of your crazy stories about life as a Celtic."

"Already booked. Hot date. My dentist friend, Melissa. She's in town for the game and offered to buy. If I back out of this, she'll cut off my balls and feed them to me. Seriously!"

"One of those, huh? A wild woman," Howells said, with a laugh which Tucker was glad to hear.

"She called as I was headed down here just to remind me we had a date. Damn Army screwed her up bad. You were in the Army weren't you? Didn't screw you up?"

Howells shook his head and laughed again. "Must be one of those 'Men are from Mars, Women are from Venus' phenomena," the coach said, as he downed the last of his water. "Well, I had it easy. I spent all of my time as a prison guard, the infamous Abu Ghraib prison, 'Place of the Ravens' they called it."

"Whoa. That's some tour of duty," Tucker said, his eyes wide as saucers impressed that Howells had been there.

"I got there about the time all the abuse hit *60 Minutes*. Things were pretty tight. So, maybe the Army screwed me up, too. Just hasn't materialized the same way."

"Big difference. She was an Army dentist. By her admission Uncle Sam left her with some battle scars. She's now a neat freak and a stickler for punctuality. Oh, and, apparently, the obligatory tattoo of a blackbird with a saber in its mouth. Never realized there were dentists in the Army but guess they go through boot camp, too."

Ernie Howells looked at Tucker with a question mark all over his face. "What's Melissa look like?"

"She's five nine, hundred and thirty pounds or so. Fine long legs. Amber eyes. Long reddish-brown hair that goes below her shoulders, broad shoulders. I think she was a swimmer or some sort of jock."

"I don't think I've ever seen her," Howells said, unsure of his answer. "That tattoo. I hooked up with a girl in Iraq with that kind of tattoo. Hers was under her navel. She was a big chick. Most of the chicks stuck together. The tattoo was probably one of their things. They were all kinda hard on the eyes, but loneliness can blind a guy."

Howells did not say anything more. He just stopped talking and stood there, privately, alone in thought. Tucker realized the conversation had turned to women again. Considering the coach's earlier reflection on Amanda, Tucker thought it best to change the subject.

"Anything I can do for you, Ernie? Sneak you out of here?" Tucker asked, with his hand on the coach's shoulder.

"Yeah. Find me an All-American shooting guard with initials MF," he said, as he reached to shake hands. "Thanks for the chat. I should slip back into the crowd and take a little more abuse from our booster boys on how to win a national championship. Let's just hope tomorrow gets here soon."

"Get some rest, Ernie."

As soon as Coach Howells stepped away, he was engulfed by overeager boosters anxious to tap into his celebrity status. Tucker shook his head and smiled, then headed for the exit, greeting latecomers along his way. He did not bother with an overcoat; his meeting with Melissa was in the Four Seasons Hotel, a short jog across the parking lot between the two buildings.

The room service knock on the door startled Xandra. Cooped in a strange place, left to brood over her missing son, she was sensitive to sight and sound. Armed only with instructions from Tucker to "Open the door only for the person who brings the food, nobody else," she peeked through the peephole in the door and saw the white coat of the waiter holding a tray and looking off to his right. She slipped the chain lock off the door and opened it. The short, Latino waiter smiled and took a step into the room followed by a dark skinned woman in a light blue smock with a dark blue lapel.

The waiter prepared her tray on the small desk and left quickly. The female housekeeper, wearing a white hijab around her head and cheeks, turned down the bed, fluffed pillows and placed foil wrapped chocolates on top, all the while in a full conversation mode with Xandra who enjoyed the company. When she had finished she asked Xandra if she needed anything. Xandra broke down. The housekeeper had a worried look about her, but after she had heard more from Xandra, agreed to bring some things Xandra requested as soon as she could, "Tonight or tomorrow," the housemaid whispered, as she left the room.

The next knock, less than two hours later, caused Xandra less stress; she was anxious to see the face of the housemaid that she met earlier, someone who shared a mother's sympathy for her hopeless situation. When she looked through the small peephole and pressed on the door handle, she saw only the shoulder of the burly man who busted through the chain lock and into the room. He quickly slapped his hand across Xandra's mouth and pushed her against the wall while a second man entered the room, took a quick look up and down the hall and closed the door.

"We only want to talk to you, sí?" said the big man. "You just answer a few questions and everything will be all right."

Xandra nodded her head against the pressure of his grip which he loosened enough to allow her a brief scream cut short when the big man clamped down harder, punched Xandra in the stomach, then backhanded her across the face which sent her to the floor. Before she could recover he grabbed her again and threw her onto the couch in the sitting room. He straddled her with his legs and put his hand on her mouth again. Xandra struggled for a breath, while a steady stream of blood dripped from her nose.

"If you scream again, I cut you. If you be quiet, we help bring Malik to you," the thinner character said.

Xandra froze with the mention of her son's name. For fifteen minutes, her only movement was to blot the blood which continued to drip from her nose. While the big man sat next to her, his hand snug around her wrist, the thin guy paced and asked questions about Malik, the search, and all those involved.

Before the two visitors left the room, the thin one bent down until his lips softly touched Xandra's ear and whispered slowly, "If we hear you mentioned our little visit to anyone…we make sure you never hear from Malik again."

After he closed the door Xandra could not bear to even spy on them through the peephole. She stayed on the couch, fighting back tears. She waited, hopelessly, for her housekeeper friend to return.

CHAPTER 23

Friday, April 1
7:07 p.m.

Tucker entered the Four Seasons Hotel through massive brass and glass doors that opened to a lobby rich with marble floors and columns that supported a central staircase to a spacious mezzanine piano lounge where a thirty-foot arched-glass window looked out over the grounds and the city lights of downtown Atlanta. He had spent many nights in fine hotels during his NBA playing days, but after a few years in Beech Island, SC, this place was another world altogether. The guests were not the rowdy drunks in sweatshirts wearing Trojan helmets, Carolina-blue face paint, foam husky heads or eagle feathers in a backward-facing baseball cap. Guests quietly joined friends in robust laughter and greetings from across the lobby in a fashion befitting Buckingham Palace. A teetotaler crowd immersed in March Madness. How odd.

Though he was late, he dialed PJ's cell phone; again, the call went straight to voicemail. This time he left a message. He needed to fill PJ in on his afternoon discussions with Moncrief and the latest FedEx delivery to the Farqu'har's mother. Plus he wanted to hear what PJ had heard from the FBI. His next call was to Melissa, from the lobby house phone. She agreed to join him immediately, but despite her penchant for punctuality, Melissa strolled across the lobby ten minutes later. Her heels echoed with each long-legged stride. She wore a sparkly-gold cocktail dress with spaghetti straps and a high-waist belt that cinched just below her breasts—a Liz Taylor-Cleopatra-look. Cut low in the front and lower in the back, she looked like she was covered in flowing sheets of gold leaf with frayed edge tiers of pleated silk ruffled across the knee-length skirt. Tucker experienced an uneasiness in his stomach and a sudden twitch below it. Joined by several other men in the lobby, his eyes dried before he dared to even blink. More than one flash caught her walk across the floor.

"I mean, you could've changed into something a little more presentable than your work-clothes," were the first words out of her mouth. "Were you expecting maybe a pig in a blanket and a romp in the sheets?"

Tucker laughed as did others around him, to include the women in evening dress, less presentable than Mel.

"Well, the second part sounds okay, but doubt there are any piggies around this place. Obviously you're not on the college expense account."

She flashed a sarcastic grin.

"Well then cowboy, let me show you a good time." Melissa escorted Tucker to the Park 75 Lounge where they haggled over who would order the drinks; Melissa won and ordered – a Smirnoff pomegranate martini, stirred, for her and a Wild Turkey Rare Breed Manhattan straight up for Tucker. Over the course of the first thirty minutes, Melissa dominated the conversation with questions about Tucker's search for the missing player. The details flowed as did repeat orders of drinks until he laid out everything he had done, planned to do, and what he knew of PJ's efforts which vaguely reminded him he still needed to talk to PJ. Eventually Melissa stopped, stood and pointed with her chin toward the dining room.

"Are you coming or are you just going to sit there with an empty glass in your hand all night?" she questioned.

Tucker was in no position to argue or debate. He walked up beside her. She pinched him on the butt, then wrapped her arm through his while they made their way, with a bit of a stagger, across the lounge to the dining room. As they walked, the ridiculous "YMCA" ringtone shattered the ambiance. When he looked down to pull his phone from its carrier, he caught the feral look in Melissa's eyes and politely turned off his phone.

Over dinner, Melissa rattled on and on with points and counterpoints, knowns and unknowns in the case of the missing Malik Farqu'har; for Tucker it was like listening to the monotone of Sergeant Joe Friday on an episode of *Dragnet*. Though he enjoyed the opportunity for a good meal and the company of a gorgeous date it was not much of a break from the events of the day. His headache was back with a tornado of thoughts that twisted his head into a completely different state of mind.

Need to talk to PJ. I need more on what the Feds are doing. How did the pick-up guy at Union Station fit in? And Ike Moncrief. A history of gambling? Gambling was one thing if it was poker, but if he was betting on sports, on college basketball? The evidence was against him, but his story, like the guy in Chicago, just doesn't add up. Then there's the photo in Xandra's FedEx envelope and the letter on Gorting's desk. Both arrived on the same day, same hotel. Gorting hadn't mentioned his delivery even though he knew I was running point with the investigation for Redcliffe. And, who was this John Wayne character? The previous FedEx envelopes originated in Augusta. Did these? FedEx would know. Xandra's tracking number would help to work back

through the system, maybe pick up Gorting's delivery, too. And
the appeal from Kline to Gorting and CBS. And the sit-ins.

"Earth to Tucker. Are you listening to me cowboy? I'm trying to help you here," Melissa said, with her face puckered from eyebrow to chin.

"Sure, of course, whatever."

"How about some dessert?"

"Right." Tucker nodded toward the waiter.

"No. I'm serving something special in my room," she winked. Tucker threw his napkin on the table, and without any hesitation they were gone.

As promised, Melissa charged the meal to her room, with a generous tip and led Tucker to the elevator with a delicious sway.

She tossed her handbag on the table just inside the door to her room, then placed her hands on Tucker's chest until she steered him up against the bed. She loosened his tie then pushed his jacket up and off his shoulders onto the floor. She leaned forward and kissed his neck just beneath his chin. Bewitched by the smell of her hair in his face, Tucker felt the heat of her body and the tug of her fingers on his belt. He tipped his head toward her and obsessed over the delicate pores of her milky, satin skin. He ran his fingertips through her hair, down the nape of her neck to her shoulders where he brushed aside the thin straps of her dress. With a caress, sweeter than a breath of mountain air, coral painted fingernails teased through his hair to the back of his skull as she pulled and locked lips. Her tongue probed. She moaned before she pulled back. Her amber eyes, hypnotic, reflected the gold in her dress. Tucker's hands teased their way to her backside and pulled her snug against him. The heat flared. She heard his racing heart and felt his arousal, hard.

She took a step back and ever so gently began to unbutton his shirt, one button at a time, tugged it from his arms and cast it aside. In the same motion, though slower, she reached behind her back to unzip her dress that cascaded like a slow waterfall over the curves of her body into a pool on the floor. Tucker stepped closer and lifted his hands. She dipped her head to the side and arrested him with her hand on his chest, then unhooked the clasp on her strapless bra that fell to the ground. She reached up to pull Tucker's mouth to her breast then dropped her hands to his waist, to his belt and zipper.

Breathless, weakened by the tease of his tongue, she stooped and guided his pants with a gentle nose rub across the bulge between his legs. She repeated the motion with his silk briefs, nose rub more deliberate, then shoved him with both hands toward the bed. Shackled by the trousers gathered around his ankles, Tucker tilted but did not fall. His hands moved in a slow caress until he slipped his thumbs under the waistband of her thong. She slid her hands down his forearms to his wrists, raised them above her shoulders and pushed him again, her naked breasts against his chest with a sorcerous glee. Tucker chuckled and fell onto the bed, naked. She ran her tongue across her upper lip and her thumbs past her tattoos, back and forth inside the lacy band of her panties, slowly sliding the thong past her hips, exposing herself completely.

Melissa oozed her way up his body, slippery skin on slippery skin until she straddled him. She buried her knees into the bed and rocked back, forcing him painfully deeper, but a pleasant pain worth every inch of enjoyment that squirmed inside. She rubbed her breasts and rolled her nipples with her fingers to harden them. Tucker reached up to replace her hands. Again, she pushed his hands aside and pinned them to the bed with her hands as she leaned over and traced his lips with her tongue. When she relaxed, her body lowered to meet his and they explored each other's bodies, in all ways imaginable without a word.

With a grip Melissa could not—would not—reject, Tucker rolled her onto the bed and crawled up on her, careful not to crush her with his weight, interrupted by kisses—on her breasts, her collarbone, her neck—and a gentle nibble on her ear. She arched upward until he took her breast into his mouth. She raked her fingers across his back up to his head, pulling his mouth closer to hers. She arched her back and aligned his hips. When she reached down and placed him inside her again, she gasped as he eased himself deeper. She shuddered, uncontrollably paralyzed by a passion that rolled in like a crashing tide, over and over again until Tucker collapsed on her, their steamy flesh melted into one body with four arms and four legs, in mismatched pairs; the perfume of sex filled the room.

"Wow, did you miss me," she said, her heart still aflutter. He moaned in approval while he shifted and moved behind her, spooning, his face nuzzled in her hair.

Before Tucker ever had a chance to doze off, Melissa crawled out of the bed, walked to the dresser, filled two glass tumblers—hers with gin, his with bourbon—and returned.

"To the Eagles," she toasted, as she handed him the drink.

"Here, here," Tucker replied halfheartedly. He leaned against a pile of pillows and wrestled with the sheets while she sat cross-legged at the foot of the bed, every inch of her body exposed. Her expression was hard to read, satisfaction mingled with fear or regret or consternation. He let his eyes explore her nakedness.

"Hiding under the covers now?" she teased, as she flipped the sheets off of him.

"You are one hard woman." With his flaccid maleness exposed, he took a sip and winced as the bourbon began its slow burn down his throat. "Did the Army make you this way or have you always been an animal?"

Melissa swirled the ice in her glass, then placed her finger in her mouth as an erotic display. "I was raised to be a bitch," she said, with a straight face. "Hard, no nonsense, out-of-my way, no bullshit. Biggest, baddest, tomboy around. Could outrun, outshoot, out fish, out drink, and out fuck any boy in Aiken County." She drained the gin from her glass and crunched on the ice.

"Guess the Army was a natural choice for you then?"

"Had to pay for college," she said. "My daddy, the preacher man, ran off with another woman when I was nine. She was the organist in his church. She played long and hard, just like she played his organ. Momma tried to make life good for us, but we had no money. I had to work to help pay bills. College was not an option, momma said, despite the cost. Of course, I had to pay for it. Plus all the dental school costs. I'm still in hock."

Tucker looked around. "If you ask me, by the looks of your choice in hotels, seems your lifestyle is doing just fine," he said.

Melissa stared at him, threw a pillow in his face then walked to the dresser to refill her glass. She came back and sat on top of the sheets close to him, her back against the pillows. Tucker slowly scanned her entire body from her toes to her eyes before he took an extended peek at the tattoos just beneath her navel and remembered what Ernie Howells had said.

"What's with the tattoos? What are they?" he asked.

"Two in the bush," she said, with a smug look of satisfaction. "Visual proverb."

Tucker hesitated then said, "You told me you never met Coach Howells, right?"

"Nope. I've been here six months or so. Got here right at the start of the basketball season. It appears he's been rather busy," Melissa replied. "Why?"

"Ernie was in the Army. Went to Iraq. Said he'd seen women with tattoos like yours in Iraq. Just wondered if it was some sort of 'G.I. Jane' thing. Ernie and I got to talking about it and—"

"What? You bastards stand around and talk about tattooed women? And you bring up my tattoos?" She politely reached over and scraped her fingernails down his back like a claw, just short of drawing blood. "I told you, I am not one to follow the rules, laws or groupthink kinds of stuff. I wanted a tattoo. Thought a raven with a sword would be a good one. So I went to a tattoo guy, an American doing his thing for soldiers in the Green Zone. Got myself inked and laid all in one session. A tits for tats deal."

Tucker rolled his eyes and chuckled at her honesty.

"I threw in a tooth job for a bad tooth he had, so it was a legitimate swap."

"Tooth job?" Tucker questioned.

Without looking, she placed her hand on Tucker's hip and groped around until she found what she was most interested in. Tucker flinched when she wrapped her cold, wet fingers around him. He looked her way with a shiver.

"Bird in the hand," she said, then pulled back. "All your jock buddies have tattoos. Pro basketball players are like walking billboards with all that graffiti inked all over them. Mine were my tribute to patriotism," she said matter-of-factly. "Where are your tats, big guy?" she asked.

"I was the token hold out, no billboard," he said, then continued. "What were you doing in Iraq? I know you were doing dental stuff, but—"

"If I told you, I'd have to kill you," she replied, to quote an old Army cliché. Then, she turned her head to the side and looked at him. "You know, top secret dental shit to win the hearts and minds of the enemy." She turned her head back and laughed a maniacal laugh. "It was the Army, Tucker. Dentistry in the Army. Get serious. What do you think I did? Drill baby drill! That was my mantra for sixteen months. It all went to pay back the government for dental school. You played basketball to knock out teeth, and I put them back in. How tough is that? We make a great business together," she said, as she smacked his inner thigh.

Tucker flinched with the sting of her slap, grimaced, and finished his drink.

"How about another ride, cowboy? Ready to saddle up?" she said, with a tease from a strategically placed hand. "Not another one of those arcade horse things with the gentle loping along. I mean a ride, the wild mustang, bucking bronco kind. Knees up, spurs out," she added, as she started to stroke him.

"Got work to do, cowgirl," Tucker said, thinking of the problems he had pushed to the back of his mind.

"You're damn straight you have work to do, and it's right here," she said, as she rolled her leg on top. "Giddyup!"

CHAPTER 24

Saturday, April 2
3:44 a.m.

Tucker, locked in a morning-after gaze fixed on the ceiling, was unsure of whether he awoke or came to, not even sure where he was. The clothes draped across furniture and artfully piled on the floor helped his recall. The blue-light face of the alarm clock on the night stand read 3:44 a.m. He rolled to his side and noticed Melissa was not in the bed but saw a puddle of light that fanned out from beneath the bathroom door. Then he heard her voice. It sounded like she was talking to someone, but he could not hear another voice. Possibly she was on her cell phone. *At a quarter of four in the morning?*

He remembered Melissa's evil eye which prompted him to turn off his phone at dinner the previous night. He rolled to the edge of the bed to pull his cell phone from the carrier on his belt, wadded with his trousers next to the bed. While he waited for the phone to find a signal he rubbed the sleep from his eyes with a thumb and forefinger. When the backlight finally appeared on the screen, the phone vibrated and went into the familiar "YMCA" ringtone. Startled and still half asleep Tucker dropped the phone. The Village People sang twice more before he found the phone next to his trousers.

Melissa flicked off the bathroom light and stuck her head out the door just as Tucker answered.

"Hello."

"Tucker, it's PJ. Sorry to bother you this early."

Melissa gave him a puzzled look for a second before she tapped several times on her wrist, absent a watch, then raised her hands and squinted as if to say *"What is going on?"* Tucker waved her off. She retreated back into the bathroom but left the light off. Tucker heard her talking again, something about "running" before he started mumbling into his phone.

"PJ it's a good thing you're not here, brother, because I would definitely kick your ass. Why the call?" Tucker said, as he continued to rub sleep from his eyes.

"Just got to Atlanta. Yesterday was one of those days. I saw you called a bunch of times, but no messages. Wanted to check in with you to get you up to speed before the sun came up."

"Hell, the sun won't be up for hours, man. You could've waited a little bit any way."

"The kids out at the college finished their searches yesterday. We had them fanned out over the entire area, on and off campus," PJ said, with a mouth full of donut. "They checked everything—buildings, open areas, woods, under rocks. I had them on the phones all day calling around. Checked airports. Everywhere." PJ started to choke. "Hold on."

He came back on the line a few seconds later and continued, "The FBI guys got their full readout back from their crime center, their national database. They were checking on Moncrief and more on the three from Augusta State. One guy from State had a couple piddling things, student stuff. Moncrief, same stuff we already had on the gambling, but our lab had more to add. Hold on a sec." PJ took a swig of warm coffee that he picked up in the hotel lobby. "Our guys found more than just the Rohypnol in that Coke can. In the brown paper bag they found a bunch of trash and fries, but in the bottom found a zip-lock bag with seven grams of 'Georgia Home Boy' another drug, controlled type. Sometimes used as a date rape drug, but there was enough there to kill somebody if it was used all at once."

"Wait. You think Moncrief had a backup or had planned another attack or something?" Tucker said, quietly, still with an ear on the bathroom voice.

"Sure appears he planned for something. Little doubt in my mind. At the very least, possession of a controlled narcotic. I need to haul Moncrief in," PJ said, ending with an audible yawn.

"PJ the game's today, tonight. You can't pull the kid before the game; that's not fair to the team."

"Right...and neither is kidnapping the team's best player, but looks like this kid's already done that."

"Can't you call him in, read him the riot act, charge him if need be, and then release him under somebody's recognizance? Coach? Me? Somebody?"

"Afraid not. Actually, not my call. The magistrate would need to decide, and that would not happen that fast. I need to take him back to Aiken County. I'd have the Atlanta PD pick him up and transfer him to my custody. Also—"

"More? Come on PJ."

"Not on Moncrief. Another kid. Schroeder. Andrew Schroeder. Kid's from Illinois, around Chicago. Need to ask him some questions about the money pick up at the train station. Special Agent Naujelis from the FBI needs to talk to him."

"You're killing me, man," Tucker said. "There's a game today, remember? Schroeder's not a suspect of any kind, is he? Can't that questioning wait until tomorrow or at least tonight after the game?"

"You want to find this kid Farqu'har or not, Tucker?" PJ shouted, then shook his head, and reached for his coffee again.

"Yes, but—"

"Well, then we need to ask questions fast, like yesterday," he interrupted. "If we find any link, maybe we can find the source of the ransom request, smoke out the bad guys, get the bastards to give us something—a confession, something, anything—on where they've got this kid so we can find him."

Unnoticed, Melissa walked out of the bathroom wrapped in a white terry cloth robe and sat on the edge of the bed. She struggled to piece together the conversation through Tucker's comments.

"All right, all right. Let me slap some cold water on my face and get organized. When do you want these guys?"

"Naujelis and I need to catch some sleep. We've been in a dead run since sunup yesterday, the search plus back and forth with the crime center team. It's just about four; how about eight o'clock, later this morning. Meet you in that conference room on the main floor, the one we used before?"

"Okay. I'll touch base with Coach Howells first thing and pull it together," Tucker said. "He's going to be pissed."

"Hey, I don't make the laws and I don't break the laws. I just enforce the laws. Tell him to talk to his boys, not me," PJ said, spoken like a true non-empathetic professional.

"Oh, one last thing. FBI received a call from that guy Gorting. Said he received another FedEx envelope with a letter, same letterhead. Naujelis and I will try to catch up with him sometime today, hopefully. The guy is slammed and said he doesn't want to drag his staff into this so he is not passing it through them."

Tucker wondered if it was the letter he had seen on the desk when he barged in on Gorting earlier the day before.

"Okay. Hey, thanks for the updates, PJ. Get some sleep. Catch you later."

"Roger that," PJ said, then hung up.

Tucker fell back against the headboard of the bed and closed his eyes, hoping to fall asleep and wake up to learn it had all been a dream, a bad one. Melissa had other plans.

"Didn't sound like a wrong number or a prank caller," Melissa said, without a smile.

"Nope."

"So who in the hell has the balls to call at a quarter to four in the morning?" she asked. "Or, should I say, how stupid can somebody be? Let me guess…it was your butt-faced boss, Burgess? No, better yet, it was 'Barney Fife' from the Aiken County Sheriff's Office?"

"The latter."

"I guess no news isn't good news or the news isn't what you wanted to hear?"

Tucker put his hands on his head and let them slide down across his face. "More evidence against the kid Moncrief, and possibly a link to the guy in Chicago. They need to haul in two of our guys as soon as they can."

Melissa turned a bit more toward Tucker and slapped her hands on the bed. "You should tell Dudley Do-Right to go fuck himself and the horse he road in on.

Your guys have a big game to play." She pulled back, tightened the belt on her robe and crossed her arms. "All this other shit can wait a day. Tell the bastards the kids are busy right now. Come back tomorrow."

Though Tucker wanted to agree, he knew that was not the appropriate response, certainly not one the Redcliffe administration would approve.

"They think there's an outside chance the FBI can get something out of these two. Something that will bring Farqu'har back in time for the game."

"Right. And if you feed pigs enough chicken shit, they may sprout wings and fly," she replied.

"Who in the world were you talking to in the bathroom?" Tucker asked. "You talk about me and phone calls in the middle of the night. Were you on the phone or talking to yourself...in private?"

Melissa dipped her head to one side and looked at Tucker like he was something off of Picasso's sketch pad. "Clients. Problems. Pain. Remedy. Customer service. Responsiveness. The Hippocratic Oath bit. Unlike some people...we have recently discussed...I have feelings for people. I'm all about helping. Making things right," she said, easing her posture a bit.

"I doubt that includes calls in the middle of the night. I didn't even hear your phone ring," Tucker said, as he rolled out of bed, naked.

"I keep it on vibrate." Melissa winked, her eyes admiring Tucker's full frontal. "Besides, you were so out of it, a freight train probably wouldn't have wakened you."

Tucker turned his briefs right-side-out and began to dress.

"Wait! Where the hell are you going? Don't tell me you are leaving?" Melissa said. "It's the middle of the goddamn night, and besides, I'm not sure you're finished paying for your supper, cowboy."

"Okay, then make out an IOU. I'll sign it. I need to get back to my hotel and put some things together for your Dudley Do-Right fellow. Like you, he expects responsiveness, and I aim to please, especially the law," Tucker said, as he tucked his shirt in and zipped up his fly.

Melissa stood and allowed her robe to drop open for Tucker to reconsider.

"No can do. Man on a mission for now. 'Tomorrow and tomorrow and tomorrow,'" he said, with a grin that stretched from earlobe to earlobe.

Melissa snuggled and purred against Tucker's chest. She grabbed his hands and placed them under the robe on her bare bottom, then looked up with temptation eyes. "Wanna reconsider?" she asked.

"Sorry, Mel." He gave her an affectionate slap to her tush, pulled away, grabbed his suit coat and headed for the door.

"Guess I'll see you at the game," she said, with her hands in the pockets of the robe which remained open wide.

"Maybe. My seat is right behind the bench. A couple rows up. Athletic department comp tickets," he said, as he approached the door. "I'll try to call you toward the end of the game, and we can work out arrangements for that IOU." He smiled and closed the door behind him.

The cold air sucked all the leftover heat out of Tucker the second he walked out of the hotel. He hesitated and looked around, the warm air from the lobby at his back. At this hour he expected the sidewalks to be rolled up and the streets quiet. Not the case. Cars whizzed up and down Fourteenth Street like it was four o'clock in the afternoon, not in the morning. Foot traffic from late pep rallies or early tailgaters cluttered the sidewalks. Sirens from emergency vehicles grew louder as they echoed off tall buildings. Tucker checked the time on his phone and noticed one voicemail. He listened. It was from Coach Howells left at 9 p.m. the night before. *Of course*, he thought, *after Melissa nixed the phone.*

"Tucker, Ernie Howells. Say, after you left I thought a little more about your Dr. Cooper comment. Give me a call after you finish dinner." That was the end of the recording. Tucker took note and saved the message.

As he placed the phone in his holster, it rang. "Hello," he said, expecting Melissa, though he had not listed her in his contacts for caller ID.

"Tucker, PJ. We've got a problem. I think our boy Moncrief just went through a window on the sixteenth floor of the hotel and landed with his kisser on the sidewalk. It ain't pretty."

CHAPTER 25

Saturday, April 2
4:33 a.m.

With the phone still to his ear, Tucker saw three squad cars and an ambulance speed by, sirens on, with several more sirens in the distance, growing louder. Outside the hotel, he made an immediate left and coaxed his aching body into a jog. On the far side of the parking lot which separated his Marriott Suites from the Four Seasons Hotel, he saw a cluster of blue flashing lights. A crowd formed a nosy perimeter behind the cars. Tucker ran across the lot and elbowed his way to the front. PJ was already on the scene and vouched for Tucker's access inside the familiar yellow tape labeled CRIME SCENE DO NOT CROSS which cordoned off the area. Tucker showed his driver's license as ID and signed the site access roster. A team dressed in bulky blue jump suits with "APD" stenciled across the back struggled to erect a pop-up frame for a square canopy that measured ten feet down each side. The wind made it virtually impossible to anchor the drop-down sides to hide a white blanket or plastic tarp draped, 3-D, over an object on the concrete sidewalk.

"What the hell happened, PJ?" Tucker said.

"Not sure. Looks like the kid came out the window at the end of the hall on the sixteenth floor and face planted there on the sidewalk. Some guy came to the front desk. Said he was in the parking lot and saw this guy fall. He ran to look at the guy. He wasn't moving and didn't touch him. The guy at the desk called the Atlanta PD."

"When?"

"Best they can determine about an hour ago, sometime after three-thirty. Atlanta PD, my contact, called me about fifteen minutes ago, right after we talked on the phone."

"Any witnesses or anything?"

"Nope. Just the guy who reported it. He's pretty shook up and still needs to sober up a bit before anybody will be able to get anything out of him, if they ever do," PJ replied. "Guy was beyond shitfaced apparently."

"Think he had anything to do with it?" Tucker said.

"Nah. Guy says he was outside. Even if he was inside, he's a little fat-shit guy who could never have handled Moncrief unless that kid was drunk, too. Lab will tell us that," PJ replied.

"No other witnesses?" Tucker's eyes drifted back toward the white cover.

"Nope. When the ambulance guys got here they checked for a pulse. Nada. They held on for the boys and girls from homicide to get here. They checked the guy. Had a student ID from Redcliffe College. Name, Isaac Moncrief. Driver's license confirmed. Ran it back through the NCIC and all agree."

Tucker's stomach lurched; warm bile rushed up his throat like a geyser, his knees began to melt. He turned and swallowed with a disgusting cringe. He thought about the boy he sat with less than twenty-four hours earlier—the college kid—and the look on his face as he answered questions, or avoided questions. He let his eyes drift back to the white cover.

"The homicide squad found a note in the kid's pocket. A suicide note."

"Suicide?" Tucker blurted. He shook his head and looked at the cover on the ground, then up toward the shattered sixteenth floor window. "It's not like you accidentally fall out of a window from up there. And to bust through the thing to commit suicide. Geez. Think somebody shoved him? Accidentally...or intentionally?"

PJ shook his head. "No, I don't think so. He must have come down like a rocket and face planted. Nobody pushed him or threw him out. He landed belly-flopped, splat."

"Did the drunk from the parking lot say anything about seeing anyone else up by the window?" Tucker asked.

"No, he didn't see anybody else. Could have been somebody, though. These guys are checking." He nodded toward one of the Atlanta police officers. "They've secured the window area for now."

Tucker still questioned the suicide. Why? The kid was just about to enter the grand stage of the Final Four or, at least, just off stage.

One of the homicide team members pushed PJ back to give them more room while they continued to wrestle with the canopy sides. Despite the early hour, the crowd continued to grow and grew louder.

"They have the kid's room sealed off and the hallway blocked off, controlled access. The rest of the Redcliffe team is in lockdown. APD has talked to Moncrief's roommate briefly."

"The coach? The coach is aware, right?" Tucker asked.

"Yeah, yeah he knows. I saw him down here earlier, but he had to go back up with the team."

"What did Moncrief's roommate say? Anything?"

"Said the guy, Moncrief, told him he had a headache, and he was going out to get something for it. He said he vaguely remembered Moncrief coming back in the room."

"What time was that? Not three in the morning?"

"Nah, that was earlier, but I didn't catch the time."

"Huh? The trainer didn't have anything for a headache?" Tucker asked as he scratched his head. He thought of the body under the tarp and quickly pulled his hand away.

"Well, that's what this other kid said, his roommate I mean," PJ replied. "Sounded weak."

"What'd the note say? The suicide note," Tucker asked.

PJ reached into a pocket and pulled out a small, monogrammed, leather-bound notepad. Unlike the shiny Corfam belt, holster, cuff holder, and baton clip, this notepad was brown cowhide like a piece cut from a Rough Rider's saddlebag.

"The guy from the homicide squad read it to me. It's weird. Really weird. I think I sorta got it. Not for publication. Here's what I copied: 'Desolate yet all undaunted, tomorrow will leave me from out that shadow that lies floating on the floor. To you dogs who hound me, I leave you this grim, ungainly, ghastly, ominous and unmerciful token disaster... RIP Malik.' That's it. Weird. The Atlanta PD and Feds are analyzing it now. I can't get much out of it," PJ added, "but it sounded like it was signed by this kid Malik. They also said it was on Redcliffe letterhead."

When he finished reading, PJ flipped through other pages on his pad.

"Here's another thing the Atlanta PD mentioned. When they talked to the roommate...Stifter, Joseph

Stifter…he said earlier tonight, after Moncrief left to get the aspirin, two guys showed up at the room looking for him, for Moncrief. Stifter didn't recognize them. Said they didn't leave their names or anything. They had Michigan State hoodies on. He thought it was probably some prank or something. Maybe not. Said they looked pretty hard, maybe twenty-something. Wouldn't say what they wanted. Just wanted to talk to Moncrief."

"What did they look like? Did he say?" Tucker asked, in hopes he might recognize them. "Tall? Short?"

"We have a description. Weight, height and he said they were wearing Michigan State hoodies, that's why he thought it was some kind of a joke," PJ added, with an eye on an APD guy who lifted the corner of the body cover. He nudged Tucker away to divert his attention elsewhere. The other members of the homicide team had tied down the sides to the canopy and begun a chalk trace of the body on the sidewalk.

"Where do we go from here? Without Moncrief, any other leads on Farqu'har? Where he might be? Anything?" Tucker asked, as they walked back out from inside the canopy.

"Gotta check back with Tom Naujelis. He has the lead for the FBI. Still need to see that kid Andrew Schroeder, the kid from the Chicago area. That's the only other lead. Also, need to see where we are with the local searches around Beech Island since the students have made their check," PJ said, as they stooped to move under and outside the yellow tape.

"Are you still going to try to get some sleep? We need to put our heads together. We need to find that kid," Tucker said. He turned toward the canopy with a look of nausea on his face.

"Let me touch base with these guys. The coroner's tech and body team just arrived. How about we meet at eight like we planned. Let's meet at the buffet first. That gives me a couple hours and time for the morning guys to get into the office back home." The walkie-talkie on PJ's belt squawked.

"Okay. I'll see you then," Tucker said, with one last look toward the canopy.

"That report…" PJ said, lifting his walkie-talkie, "they think they found the kid's cell phone. Farqu'har's phone."

"Where?"

"Planter in the hotel lobby. Someone found it, gave it to the front desk. One of the clerks checked through it and noticed stuff for Farqu'har. I'll check it out."

Tucker slapped PJ on the back and headed the hotel lobby entrance. Just beyond the last ring of spectators, Ben Burgess appeared, hands deep in the pockets of his London Fog trench coat.

"Where the hell you been, McGill?"

Tucker drew back; his blue eyes widened. He could not believe what he heard. No mention of Ike Moncrief's name. No comment about what a tragedy or question like *"What happened?"* No concern for the family, the team, the school. It was always Tucker who seemed to be wrong.

"I knocked on your door, I called your room. Not sure that goddamn cell phone of yours works or it was turned off. Out womanizing again? Boozing it up?"

"Excuse me?" Tucker said, through a narrow, pained squint.

"I knew goddamn well when I agreed to take you on that when things got tight, I had to watch you even closer. Just like college, eh McGill?"

"Listen, Burgess. If you have a problem with me then fire my ass," Tucker said, his face flushed red in an instant, the hairs on the back of his neck on end. "If you don't like what I do or how I do it, get rid of me, but don't stand there and preach to me like some pompous Bible-thumping evangelist. You told me to find the kid; that's what I'm doing."

"And you can bet if you don't, McGill, I will fire your ass," Burgess replied his finger stopping short of Tucker's chest.

"Like I give a rat's," Tucker said, his frustration exploding loud enough for onlookers to steal a glance toward him. He took a step toward Burgess. "There's a missing kid out there, somewhere, who desperately needs someone on his side right now." He used his chin to motion upward. "There's a mother upstairs that is probably one step away from taking the same leap Moncrief took if I don't find her son." He jerked his head over his shoulder toward the Marriott building. "There's a team in there that is holding out all the hope in the world that their teammate will show for the game, and I have every intention of making sure that happens. Not because of you. Not because of what you told me to do but because they deserve the help. All your shitty comments about me and my past, they're just that, my past. Don't bring them up again." Tucker shoved his hands deeper into his pockets with hopes one would not escape with another unforgettable roundhouse punch.

"Don't let your ass overload your mouth, McGill," Burgess fired back. "Find the kid. I'm not standing out here—"

"You're not standing out here trying to figure out why one of your best basketball recruits turned manager and committed suicide? Nah, you don't care about him. You don't care about Farqu'har, either. All you care about is yourself, Burgess." Tucker swallowed and continued. "Look, I've got a missing player and now a suicide to work. Two families who need answers. Go rub elbows with your good ole boys, and stay out of my way," Tucker gazed past the crowd of gawkers to the white canopy in the parking lot then back at Burgess, who stood flustered as Tucker walked off.

"Just like the Celtics, McGill," Burgess hollered. "A leopard can't change his spots." The crowd turned and watched Tucker step through the glass entry.

When Xandra heard the click of the door latch drop she sat up frozen in bed, her wide eyes flickered. Tucker did not notice the door chain lock that dangled from the door. The hallway light cast his long shadow on the wall. Xandra reached for the switch on the bedside table lamp, but instead clutched the sheets to her chest leaving her bare shoulders and neck exposed.

"Sorry. I tried to be as quiet as I could," Tucker said. He walked to the small desk and carried the chair toward the side of the bed. The city lights, filtered through the sheer curtain liners, allowed him to see only her silhouette. Xandra pulled the covers over her shoulders for warmth but could do nothing to slow her pulse. With slow and simple English he hoped she would understand, Tucker explained what had happened to Ike Moncrief. He explained Ike's fall. With each detail, Tucker watched Xandra drift further and further away. When he mentioned that Ike's death meant there were no other leads for finding Malik, she shrank, bent over and pressed the sides of her head with the palms of her hands.

Xandra recalled the warning in the FedEx she received. She gnawed on her bottom lip, unsure of whether or not to speak. In her mind she saw the painful face of her son and feared her son might end up like Ike Moncrief.

"Mr. McGill, I must tell something," she said, as she

wiped a tear with her fingertip. Tucker relaxed his shoulders and looked at her with a slight nod.

"Today, tonight two men knock on door. I did not let in, but they say they know where Malik is. They tell me they need to talk," she said, wiping her cheeks. She lowered her head, and as she did, her voice grew softer. Tucker inched closer to hear her better.

"They rammed door and broke the chain lock. The big one, he grab me, but I scream and he slap me, I fall and he grab me and throw me on couch there and the other man put his nose on my cheek, by my ear and told me not to scream again or he cut me. He said if I be quiet, I be all right and Malik would be all right, too. Then they pull me up and make me sit there. They tell me they know where Malik is. They ask what I know about search. About you. About who you talk to." Xandra lifted her head toward Tucker.

Though he could not see her face, he sensed this much of the story came with tears which she continued to rub away.

"So I tell them."

"What did you tell them, Xandra?"

"I tell them you were from school, and you were trying to find my son. I tell them about search, and others who look. That's all."

"Did they say anything? Tell you anything? Do you know who they were?"

"No, I not know them. Only they say they try to protect their investment. I not understand, but when I tell them about the message I receive, the one about the money..." She paused. "The letter where they say something could happen to Malik, they wanted to know more about that letter. They ask who sent it. I say maybe the Ike boy, I not know. I tell them about that boy, that Ike boy who you say you think did something to my

Malik."

Tucker dropped his chin and shook his head before he looked up and asked, "There were two of them, correct?"

She quickly looked down and nodded, silently.

"You said one was big? And the other one?"

"One man was big like bear. The other was tall, thinner, like skinny."

"What were they wearing?"

"They wear sweatshirts with hoods on shirt. Green, dark green. On front it had words, I not read and a basketball."

Tucker muttered under his breath as he stood, wiped his hands through his hair and walked back into the sitting room.

"Mr. McGill," Xandra begged, "I only want my son. I not know what to do. They tell me they know Malik. I want my son back." She bent forward and buried her head in the sheets stretched between her knees. Tucker looked out the window where the sun's first light appeared.

He walked back to the bed and placed his hand on Xandra's bare shoulder. She sighed, reached for his hand and nestled her cheek against it. She lingered awhile, then she kissed his hand and pulled back.

Tucker reached for the lamp switch on the bedside table. Once his eyes adjusted, he saw the bruise on the side of Xandra's face, her black eye, her nose swollen twice the normal size crusted with dried blood just inside the bottom of her nostrils. Parts of her face were deep purple, almost black. He bent down for a closer look, but she turned away.

"Did they do that to you?" Tucker said.

She managed a barely perceptible nod.

"Xandra, could you identify the two men who did

this?" Tucker asked stepping back away from the bed.

Xandra hesitated, afraid to answer, afraid of what might happen if she did.

"I might, but I not want them to see me," she said. "I worry about Malik."

"I'll be with you. Don't worry," Tucker said, with a strong, confident look. "We can dress and go down for breakfast. If you see them, in the lobby or at breakfast, will you tell me?"

Again, she nodded then pulled the covers tighter around her.

On their way to the breakfast room, Xandra pointed out a vendor display with the shirt her two assailants wore the previous night. Green hoodies with a basketball logo and "Go Spartans" across the front, the same shirt they saw on dozens of fans in the lobby and halls.

It was obvious this was not a normal breakfast crowd. People were awake and alive, yelling across the room to wave at friends to join them. It seemed the incident with Ike Moncrief had either not registered or had little impact, possibly because some people had not heard, some did not seem to care, and some were merely sober morning victims of the drunken night before.

"Mr. McGill, if I see men, what will you do?" Xandra asked as the waitress brought more coffee.

"I would contact the authorities, the sheriff who is investigating or the FBI agent on this case," he said, pushing scrambled eggs into his grits.

She looked down then took a small bite. "Mr. McGill, they say if I say anything to you or anyone they hurt Malik. I want my son. I only want my son. Please Mr. McGill, I not want him hurt. If they find I tell you they will hurt Malik." Her sad eyes spoke louder than her words. "Or they take him somewhere, and I not see him again."

Tucker looked at her then looked out over the room. "Do you see them? Either of them?" Tucker asked, certain something had prompted her question at that moment.

She responded with a nod but kept her head bowed hiding it from his eyes and those of the men she spotted.

"They not wear sweatshirts like last night. They are together. Two men. By window, near tree in corner," she said, with a queasiness in her stomach that caused her to push her plate away.

Tucker looked around the room. With dozens of people at the tables and more March Madness on the way in and out, he needed more in order to identify them.

"What are they wearing now?"

She did not respond.

Tucker peered over his right shoulder toward the window. There were several tables along the row. One had a small family. Another, a single woman. Nearest the tree, a busboy cleared the table of dishes and coffee mugs. Tucker quickly looked toward the hostess stand, the only access to the room. A line of people waited to enter, waiting for seats, but he saw nobody leaving.

"Xandra, there's nobody there. Look up. Can you see those men anywhere?" Tucker said, as he pushed his chair back away from the table.

Xandra slowly lifted her eyes and looked toward the window, eventually toward the table by the tree. There was nobody there. She looked around hoping to see the men but hoping they would not see her, afraid of what might happen if they did.

Tucker stood and looked around for two guys, one big and one tall but thin. Other than that, he had no detailed description. They could be wearing green or another color, maybe one of the four dominant colors in the hotel. As he turned he saw PJ headed toward him.

"PJ, this is Xandra Novikov, Malik Farqu'har's mother. Join us. Have a seat. I'll be right back," Tucker said, as he walked toward the hostess stand. In the line, Tucker saw Coach Howells and two of his assistants. The coach excused himself and walked toward Tucker when he saw him.

"Ernie," Tucker said, "I don't know what to say."

"Thanks, that makes two of us" he said, shaking his head. "I'm trying to wrap my head around it. This is not an easy one to just push aside and think about the game. I have no idea how the guys are going to focus. Do the police know anything more about what happened? I heard there was a suicide note."

"Well, they have a note, strange one that the police are going over. Other than that, nothing. They may need to talk to some more of your guys, though. The suicide thing is hard to understand."

"I agree."

Tucker nodded several times. "Yeah. Oh, and by the way, I got your voicemail this morning. The one you sent last night after the happy hour. Sorry I didn't get to it earlier. You sent it before all of this came up. Something about Melissa."

"Right, right. Forgot about that," Howells said, as he silenced a call on his cell phone. "Yeah, after you left I gave some more thought to what you said about her, about Iraq, all that stuff. Christina Morrison. That was the name of the chick I mentioned, the one I hooked up with the night before leaving. Big girl but horny. When she got back to the States she contacted me. I passed, but she kept at it. She actually stalked me via email and phone, never saw her. Finally I told her I was married and she backed off."

"Strange. When did all of that happen? Right after you got out of the Army?"

"Yeah. I told my wife. She said to tell the Army then forget it," Howells said, as he motioned to his assistants following a waiter toward a table.

"Did you? Report her to the Army I mean?" Tucker said, as Howells began to follow the others in his group.

"I mentioned it in passing to the old company commander, Damien Parker. I get emails from the guy once in a while. He's a full bull in the Pentagon now. Good guy. I think he lives in northern Virginia somewhere. Hey, gotta go. Keep me posted on all of this and on Malik." Howells walked off with a stern look on his face, locked in thought. Tucker walked back to join Xandra and PJ, his mind playing hopscotch with thoughts, still unsure of what to make from what the coach had just told him.

CHAPTER 26

Saturday, April 2
8:27 a.m.

I think we have our next lead," PJ said, as Tucker pulled up his chair. "Miss Novikov told me about last night and gave me her description of the two who came to the room. Her description is very close and confirms what that kid Stifter said. Time line fits, too. The fact that she saw them this morning also confirms they are still in the area." PJ tapped his pen against his notebook as he talked. "I need to get this over to the Atlanta PD and Naujelis. They can get people on the ground here and in the Dome looking for these guys." PJ pulled his phone and started to text a message.

"Good," Tucker said.

He turned toward Xandra and saw a concerned look on her face, her eyes unfocused in a distant look.

"If anybody wants to talk to Xandra about what she said, about the break-in last night, any of that, either you or I need to be with her. I don't think it's a good idea to have another stranger knock on the door to that room. I'll try to get a room change if they have any available, which I doubt," Tucker said.

"I'll check with management to see if they have any video of that floor for last night. Elevators and stairwells, something with a possible picture of the characters here," PJ said.

"I want to go with you," Xandra said.

Tucker looked at her with a reservation on his face.

"With me?" he said. "No, that wouldn't be a good idea. It's best for you to stay back. PJ, can you get the Atlanta PD to post a guard on that room to protect her?"

"I can try. Sounds like a reasonable request since she's one of two people who may be able to identify the guys we're looking for," he said. His phone beeped; he had the reply from the FBI. "I need to go meet Naujelis. He's at the suicide site. They've moved the body to the morgue. Moncrief's parents are due in this afternoon. They had planned to attend the game, but my guess is they'll skip that."

"Get that guard for Xandra, will ya? We can touch base later. I have a few things to check and a few others to prepare before game time," Tucker said, as he helped Xandra with her chair.

The three parted—PJ toward the door, Tucker and Xandra to the elevator. Back in the room Tucker called the front desk to request a room change. They apologized but had no available rooms to make a switch. They were quick to comply with Tucker's second request. A man from the hotel maintenance staff immediately came to the room to reattach the chain lock. As soon as the repairs were complete Tucker made sure Xandra understood nobody was to come into the room unless either he or Captain Beedle was present. She agreed. As he left the room, Tucker noticed an attractive, slender woman dressed in a blue pinstriped business suit standing close to the door.

"May I help you," he asked, wary of loiterers near the room though with her nicely coifed, curly brown hair and sleepy, brown eyes she did not appear to pose a threat.

"Sir, Lieutenant Calderone. Karen Calderone, Atlanta PD. I'm assigned to restrict access in and out of this room," she said, as she discretely flashed a badge clipped to the waist of her A-line skirt, hidden by her jacket.

"Thanks, lieutenant." He was surprised to see someone this soon but glad to know she was there.

Tucker leaned against the back wall of the crammed elevator as it stopped to load and offload people on its way to the ground floor. His head ached with all the things he had to think about today, dwarfed by the emotions from the overnight incident and other events that continued to plague the team; at this point it seemed the least of their concerns was the Michigan State team. When the elevator doors opened on the ground floor, the noise numbed him like he was sitting under to a stadium speaker. Everybody piled out of the elevator and into the mob that flitted around like schools of fishes in a shark tank. *Fans!* Tucker nudged his way upstream toward the reception desk in the lobby.

"How may I assist you, sir," said the perky desk clerk whose name tag showed the world her name was Jessie.

"Yes, can you tell me if the FedEx deliveries have been made this morning? They do deliver on Saturday, right?" Tucker said.

"Yes, sir. They deliver today. Let me check on that for you please. I'll only be a minute," she said, then disappeared behind the partition into a small office.

Tucker turned away from the desk and gazed out over the sea of people in hopes of spotting the FedEx courier who, with some luck, would be the same guy that delivered the day before.

"Sir," Jessie said, to gain Tucker's attention.

He turned back toward the desk.

"Yes, sir. We received our FedEx packages just a short while ago."

"Dammit," Tucker mumbled.

"Sir?" the attendant replied.

Tucker looked up, embarrassed at his outburst.

"There is another drop box in the hotel back by the conference rooms. Oftentimes the FedEx man will check that box after he stops by the desk, before he leaves."

"Thanks," Tucker said. As he turned around he spotted his guy. On the far side of the lobby, almost hidden by all the tall basketball enthusiasts, the scraggy deliveryman headed toward the door, his arms filled with the familiar purple and orange FedEx express envelopes.

"Hey," Tucker said, loud enough to be heard over the crowd.

The FedEx man did not slow or stop; he kept a constant stride toward the door.

Tucker upped his pace and hollered, "Hey. FedEx. Hold up."

The deliveryman was a pencil-thin man—blacker than fresh tar on Peachtree Street—with a shaved head that shined. He looked around and saw Tucker headed toward him. He adjusted his load and with his long, black fingers, he pulled the earphones out of his ears. He looked like he was in his mid-twenties and on a crusade for technology with gadgets hooked to his belt, stuffed in the pockets, around his neck, in his ears, and wore a holster to quick draw the industrial-strength scanner he carried.

"Hey, got a minute," Tucker said, as he approached the man, his hand outstretched.

The young guy shook Tucker's hand then quickly

adjusted the load of envelopes under his arm.

"Did you deliver here yesterday?" Tucker asked, with a bit of a wrinkle between his brows.

The driver hesitated and looked around before he answered with a deep, Southern voice, "Yeah."

"Do you remember accepting a couple of envelopes from someone who wanted them delivered, directly, here in this hotel?"

"I don't know what you mean, man. I deliver what they load on the truck and pick up from here, if that's what you mean."

"Scan this for me, please." Tucker handed the courier the envelope Xandra received in the hotel the day before.

The FedEx courier took the envelope and scanned it.

"So what does the scan say? Where has this envelope been?" Tucker asked, with little patience.

The young driver shifted on his feet but offered no reply.

"I need to know if someone approached you and asked you to deliver packages or envelopes to people registered here without running them through the FedEx system?" Tucker said. He put his hands in his pockets and gave the FedEx guy a "don't bullshit me" look.

"I told you, I deliver what they give me."

Tucker pulled a money clip from his pocket and peeled off a twenty, then a second twenty and held them up for the driver to see. "I'm not a cop, and I don't work for FedEx, but I want to know what you delivered yesterday. Things that were not loaded on your truck. Things someone might have given you to deliver here." Tucker pulled the money back to his pocket.

"Man, I ain't getting in no trouble 'cause of you."

"I'm not trying to make trouble, and if you come clean

with me, I'll keep it between us girls, how's that?" he said, pulling the money back up where the FedEx guy could see.

The driver remained silent while he watched the streams of people in the lobby pass by. He ran his tongue over his teeth under his upper lip and fidgeted with his envelopes, his scanner, then got ready to put his earphones back in his ears. Tucker pulled another twenty from his clip and pushed three bills toward the driver who grabbed them quickly.

"Look man, I can't be losing this job, you understand what I'm saying?" the FedEx guy said.

Tucker nodded.

"Yeah, some chick came up to me yesterday just as I jumped back on my truck. She asked me if I could take two envelopes to the desk for delivery. I said they needed to go into the system, like through a drop box or something. She hands me a Benjamin and asks again with a smile. I took two envelopes in, dropped them at the desk and walked out. All I can tell ya."

"Do you remember who they were for?"

"Man. Never even looked. I was in and out and on my way. Thirty seconds max."

"This lady who gave you the envelopes, what did she look like?" Tucker asked.

"Really can't say."

Tucker cocked his head like he had been gypped.

"Nah. I mean she was wearing a heavy coat, man. Had some wool hat with her hair all tucked up under it and all. And a scarf wrapped around her neck. She had shades on."

Tucker nodded his okay and reached into his backpack. He pulled out a FedEx envelope, the first one, the one Xandra received in Chicago. "Can you tell me where this package came from?" he asked.

"I don't know, man. That one came through the system," he said, startled that Tucker had more on him.

"Can you track the bar code back through the system and tell me where it originated?"

"Look man, I've got to go," the driver said, stepping toward the door.

Tucker dropped his arm to block him.

"I need the answer. Scan this thing, and tell me where it's been," Tucker said, his bulk no match for the skinny guy who was in no position to make a scene in the hotel lobby.

The driver took the FedEx envelope out of Tucker's hand and scanned it quickly. He punched a series of numbers, then a few more and a final set of five.

"Says Augusta, Georgia. Picked up at a drop box by Saint Joseph Hospital at 5:32 p.m. for First Overnight Service means it had to be delivered by 8:30 a.m. the next business day."

"Can you check one more package? Dropped same box, picked up same time, same service."

"Give it to me. I'll scan it, but that's it, man. I'm behind now," he said, with a stern look.

"I don't have the envelope," Tucker said. "It went to Indianapolis."

"Zip code?"

Tucker pulled out his phone, pulled up the Internet and did a search on the NCAA Headquarters.

"The zip is 46206."

The FedEx driver turned away and fiddled with his scanner. Tucker eyed the fans around them, typical gawkers. They turned their heads as they walked on with no particular interest other than to see what the two men were doing there on the side of the lobby. The driver waited, pressed the keys on his scanner and waited. Tucker waited. And the crowd continued to swirl around them. The game was still over eight hours away, but people were packed and ready for their assault on the stadium for the usual gift shopping and souvenir hunting not to mention the games and memorabilia displays. The Final Four was much more than a game; it was an experience, a spectacle, an annual extravaganza. For what they paid for their tickets, they expected a Mardi Gras event with everything short of the beads.

Finally the driver looked at Tucker. "Yeah, same box, same date, same time." The driver started to walk off again, when Tucker stopped him.

"Hey, if you see that woman or anybody else asks you to drop envelopes at the desk, call me," Tucker said, as he handed the driver his card.

The driver looked at the card. "For real? Man, you from Redcliffe. Shee-ut man, you guys ain't got a chance without that brother Farqu'har." He laughed as he walked out the door and pulled away in his truck.

Right, not a chance. Not a snowball's chance.

CHAPTER 27

Saturday, April 2
10:13 a.m.

Tucker turned back toward the elevators, headed to his room to check on Xandra. As he walked he thought about the FedEx guy. Like many service workers at the low end of the wage totem pole, he was not unscrupulous but often willing to provide a personal service for a price. No harm, no foul. Trying to put bread on the table in an economy where businesses wanted more from their people because there were fewer of them. While he waited for the elevator, Tucker recalled his brief conversation with Ernie Howells at breakfast and decided on a quick change. Frustrated with the wait, he stepped into a small conference room away from the crowds. When he entered, three members of the alumni office were packing promo spirit-bags with towels, banners, signs, T-shirts, and sweatbands to hand out to the Eagle Boosters. By the time Tucker fixed a cup of coffee, they had loaded the bags and headed to the Georgia Dome to get setup for the game.

Tucker laid his backpack on a table at the far end of the room, pulled out a few files, the two FedEx envelopes, and his notebook. He leaned back in his chair and gave himself a quick massage of the forehead before he took a tentative slurp of the hotel coffee. The instant the cold brew hit his taste buds, he spewed it across his lap, the table, and the chair next to him. Fortunately, nobody else was in the room. *Why is it so damn impossible to make a decent pot of coffee?* He puffed his cheeks and exhaled like a balloon with a slow leak with his head rocked back. He recovered quickly, walked over to the convenience bar to drop his Styrofoam cup in the black plastic trash bag and opted for a carton of OJ from a large stainless bowl filled with water from melted ice. Back to his table his first order of business was to find Damien Parker.

The Internet made the initial phase of the search rather easy. He saw three listings for Damien Parker in northern Virginia. The first Damien Parker he talked to sounded like a rather old gentleman with difficulty hearing. Tucker was patient in his attempts to have the man on the other end of the phone hear the questions. After several totally bogus replies to his questions, Tucker figured the listener was probably too old for active service in the Army or in desperate need of a medical retirement, posthaste.

The second call was much the opposite. The guy sounded like Bob Marley on the phone. Tucker did not need to ask him any questions at all. Damien Parker, number two, could never have made full colonel in the Army; he could barely speak intelligible English.

His third call held great hopes for Tucker, if in fact this guy Parker still lived in northern Virginia. Outside of the fact that Howells said this Parker guy worked in the Pentagon, Tucker was not overly confident that the coach had any contact with his old Army commander in the recent past. Immediately after he pushed the "send" button to connect his call, he heard the busy signal. He pulled the cell phone away from his ear and hung up.

Ten minutes later he tried again. Same result. Five minutes later, Tucker tried again. Busy. He listened to the tone for a second before a recorded message came on with an option to try the call again for a charge of only one dollar and fifty cents. Tucker took the offer, hung up, and waited for his phone to ring back.

The conference room door opened.

"Excuse me sir. Just need to freshen the comfort bar for you," said one of the caterers behind a cart full of noontime goodies—cookies, brownies, sodas, and a bowl of fruit. To be sociable, Tucker walked over to the pot-bellied man with the full, round face wearing striped, baggy chef's pants and a starched, white chef's jacket. He shook the server's hand and started to load a plate with an assortment of carbs and fats, when the cell phone on his table at the other end of the room began to sing. Tucker stumbled over a chair as he hurried back to his table to grab his phone.

He answered the call, but the connection was still ringing. One ring later a voice answered.

"Parker."

"Hello, is this Colonel Damien Parker?" Tucker asked.

"Yes. Who's calling?"

"Colonel Parker my name is Tucker McGill. A former member of a company you commanded in Iraq, Ernie Howells, gave me your name."

"Sure. Wolfman. Today's a big day for the guy. I've got a courtside seat right here by the flat screen for tonight. What do you need? McGill, did you say?"

"Yes, colonel. I need to ask a few questions about a woman who was in Iraq with you back in '04. Name is Christina Morrison," Tucker said, hopeful that the name would spark something.

"Cooking up something for Wolfman, eh? That guy's a hustler. Done great things in the basketball world since he got out. Let's see…Morrison…Morrison. What was her rank or what'd she do?" Parker asked.

"I can guess she was a dentist doing whatever. Not sure of her rank."

"Probably a captain or major. Would depend on her education and time in service to that point. If she was a dentist, she would not have been in my company. I had the security guys. The medics and dental personnel were assigned to the med detachment."

Tucker gave a disgusted shake of his head and muttered an f-bomb expletive to himself. "Any idea who managed them?"

"Could have been a number of guys. We rotated a lot of people through there. Around that time, we were cleaning up the mess. The one that was plastered all over the news for months. I had to rebuild a good bit of that. The med detachment not so much, but still people in and out with different assignments and projects."

Tucker shifted in his seat with his head in one hand and the phone in the other slapped against his ear. He rolled his eyes while this guy walked down memory lane in search of a name. He began to think the Bob Marley guy could have given him a straighter answer, quicker.

"Okay, why don't you try Adam Hoffman. He works in the Pentagon. He's an oh-six like me, full bird. Standby. Let me get a number for you."

Tucker could hear Parker rummaging around on the other end of the phone, so he walked back toward the snacks to pick up the plate he had filled earlier. On his way back to his table, Parker came back on the line.

"Why were you asking about this gal? What's your need?" Parker said.

Tucker talked him through a brief explanation, all concocted around some bullshit, off-the-cuff story he made up, never relating his need to Howells or

Farqu'har or Redcliffe College in any way. Parker seemed satisfied, at least satisfied enough that he gave Tucker a phone number for Colonel Adam Hoffman.

"Tell Hoff I gave you his number. Tell him this is payback. He constantly whips my ass in racquetball."

Tucker hung up and called Colonel Adam Hoffman who picked up on the first ring. After his standard but brief introduction Tucker explained the purpose of his call. He used the same bullshit story he fed Colonel Parker in the event they should ever compare notes on his calls.

"She was a handful," Hoffman said. "Seems she was always into something or someone. One of those beloved bold, audacious risk takers with a mind of her own. Spoke it most of the time, too. Rank meant nothing to her. Of course, we were both captains so she thought she didn't need to listen to me, even though I was the commander. She fraternized with the enlisted troops a lot, too much actually. She was one of three or four female soldiers assigned to Abu Ghraib. She was a big girl, liked to party. Wild one, but I guess she did a good job. I really don't know much about her job."

"What do you mean by that?" Tucker asked, afraid he would listen to a different saga of war stories.

Hoffman cleared his throat. "Well, you don't know much about the Army I guess, McGill. See, this gal was attached to my unit for admin and logistics, but she really did her own thing. She was assigned to Abu Ghraib on some special assignment. Like I said, I'm not sure what the hell she was doing other than making life miserable for me."

"So who would know what she was doing, colonel?" Tucker said, respectful of the guy's rank and service.

"Probably General Grunert, Major General George Grunert, at the time a lieutenant colonel in charge of some Special Ops projects in Iraq. Now he heads up the Army's Special Operations projects worldwide," Hoffman said, then coughed to clear his throat.

"Do you have a number for General Grunert?"

"No."

"Know where I can get it?"

"I can look around. The Special Ops guys can be hard to find sometimes. Comes with the territory."

Tucker offered his cell phone number and asked Colonel Hoffman to call if he came up with a number. In the interim, Tucker said he planned to launch a similar search into cyberspace, though he knew he did not have time to spend chasing down this Christina Morrison chick, though it seemed to mean something to Ernie Howells.

At the end of the call, Tucker finished his high-carb snack and made two more calls. The first went to PJ who gave him a status on the suicide investigation and a minor update on the missing person investigation. PJ said the hotel did not have any good video of that floor from the previous night. He explained they had seen a few potential suspects that matched the description Xandra gave them at breakfast, but they had not questioned anyone. PJ added he still needed to talk to Andrew Schroeder who might have a possible connection to the Chicago pick-up man since Schroeder was from Glen Ellyn, Illinois, a western suburb of Chicago.

Tucker made a second call; this one went to Coach Howells. He knew Howells was probably tighter than a fat lady's bikini about now, five hours before game time. He caught the coach headed out for the pre-game meal with the team. Tucker explained the situation, and how he needed to talk to Schroeder, even though it was unlikely going to bring Malik Farqu'har in for the game only hours away.

Shortly after two o'clock, a tall, muscular Andy Schroeder dipped his head below the door frame and met Tucker in the hotel conference room headquarters. Howells was willing to let Schroeder meet with Tucker as long as it would take no more than thirty minutes. Tucker agreed.

"Andy, thanks for coming. Ready for the game?" Tucker asked.

Schroeder nodded while he sipped on a bottle of blue something or other.

"You're from Glen Ellyn, Illinois. That's near West Chicago isn't it?" Tucker said.

"Yeah, about ten miles east of there, closer to the city," he replied.

"Ever hear of the Posse Diablo?" Tucker asked, looking down at his notebook and the FedEx envelopes in front of him.

"Yeah, they're pretty big in the city. It's a gang. In Chicago. They have groups out in the suburbs, mainly small ones. We had some in our high school. There were a bunch of gangs around, though. Always going at each other. Had some hits, uh, shootings. Had some guys picked up for pushing drugs at school," Schroeder said.

"Do you know of any activity out in West Chicago?"

"No. I didn't pay much attention. There are more gangs out there. More rural. Farmer guys. Low-income guys. They live out there and commute to the city. They were always hitting on each other," the young player explained.

"High school kids?" Tucker asked, confused.

"Yeah and younger, middle school kids, too."

"But no adults? No heavy gang stuff, big time pushers or drive-by stuff?"

"No."

Tucker spent fifteen minutes more trying to tie something, anything, to the gang. PJ had told him that the Chicago PD had suspicions that the two guys Xandra identified were from the Posse Diablo, based on the tattoos on the hands of the Latino guy who assaulted her in the room plus the fact that her husband was the shot caller of the gang. Tucker struck out. He could not make the connection between Posse Diablo and Stocker, the pick-up man.

"Okay, Andy. Thanks. Sorry to pull you away. Good luck tonight," he said, as Schroeder stood up. Tucker reached up and gave him a manly slap on the back.

Shortly after Schroeder left PJ called Tucker to tell him the Redcliffe staff, accompanied by a hospital chaplain and a member of the Atlanta PD, picked up Ike Moncrief's parents at Hartsfield-Jackson Airport. Per police directive, they took the parents directly to the morgue to identify their son's body and then to police headquarters where the Atlanta PD Criminal Investigations Division and the FBI sympathetically walked them through questions about their son—his background, friends, enemies, activities, and recent problems, the full gamut of topics which might shed light on the boy's actions and fate.

Tucker summarized his session with Andy Schroeder, basically another dead end. As he filled in tidbits for PJ, Tucker had another call hit his phone. It was Colonel Hoffman. He dropped PJ's call and picked up with Hoffman.

"Colonel Hoffman, Tucker McGill," he said, as he grabbed a pen.

"Mr. McGill, I found a number for General Grunert. I took the liberty to call him in advance. I didn't want him to be ambushed or you to be cut short on your call," Hoffman said. "With the game and all, I wasn't sure when I would talk to you or when you might talk to Grunert, but he's expecting your call."

"Thank you, colonel. I'll give him a call right away," Tucker said. He looked at his watch. It was already after five o'clock, less than an hour before tipoff.

Colonel Hoffman gave Tucker the number and closed, "Oh, McGill, don't give this number to anyone else. If the police need any more from General Grunert, have them call me. Understood?" the colonel said, in a tone of voice he might use to tell a recruit to drop and give him ten pushups.

"You bet," was the best Tucker could muster in response.

Tucker shoved his notebook and the FedEx envelopes in his backpack and made a beeline for the elevator. It was almost five-thirty, too late to shower. Off the elevator, he did not see the female lieutenant outside his room. Rather than startle Xandra again, he knocked on the door, announced himself, pushed the key card into the lock, and opened the door. Xandra was behind the desk, the first time Tucker had seen her there.

"Where is the policewoman? She is not outside the door," Tucker asked.

"She said, her time was up. She went to the to meet someone to take her place," Xandra replied.

That sounded odd to Tucker. He did not understand why they did not meet and replace on site, outside the room. He would look for Lieutenant Calderone on his way out to the game. He made sure Xandra had dinner via room service and asked if she was interested in watching the game. She said no, but Tucker wrote down which channel to watch if she changed her mind.

He called the front desk and asked the concierge to have a taxi meet him out front as soon as possible. Hailing a taxi was the easy part. Driving the three miles back to the Dome was a bumper car, metal-on-metal, upstream battle for the little Pakistani cab driver who spoke broken English in a nonstop monologue the entire way. Tucker paid little attention to the driver; he used the delay to make his next call.

"Grunert here."

CHAPTER 28

Saturday, April 2
5:00 p.m.

The crowd outside the Georgia Dome was a March Madness mosh pit. The number of protesters had grown overnight but was dwarfed by the tsunami of basketball fans eager to check the block of attending the Final Four. Atlanta's "Best in Blue" directed traffic, broke up a few scuffles and maintained order in the eager and unruly crowd of hardcore team followers, social elites, and the curious set of others who shelled out megabucks for tickets.

Amid the chaos, Tucker, shuffled through the security checkpoint, encouraged by the energy of the fans. He jockeyed his way to his seat, two rows up behind the Redcliffe Eagles bench. The strain of the week and excitement of the moment caused him to wobble when he stood to hear a local high school choir sing the National Anthem. The houselights dimmed as spotlights washed a silence over more than seventy-two thousand exuberant fans, all on their feet for two minutes of respectful restraint "dedicated to the greatest nation on Earth and those who defend it."

It was a surreal calm for Tucker, one that transported him back in time, to April 1st, 1991, and the Market

Square Arena in Indianapolis to a previous Final Four. He remembered hearing the same anthem on that day when his head rang like a gong with every syllable, every note, every sound and every thought that followed his previous night of binge drinking with pro scouts and agents eager to peddle his talent in the NBA. Tucker looked at the players on the bench two rows down and listened to the anthem with an attentive ear. His body ached with memories of his final college game. The crowd roar at the end of the music sucked Tucker out of his dream and spat him into the present in a most vulgar way. When the house lights came back, he thought of Malik Farqu'har, missing. Then he remembered his phone call during the madcap taxi ride to the stadium, what General Grunert had said, and how quickly he cut off the conversation with Tucker.

When the introduction of the players began, Tucker did a Texas two-step to the aisle, past ushers and security guards, into the portal, and out to the hallway where concessionaires hawked their peanuts, popcorn, hotdogs, and beer. He needed a quiet place, somewhere he could talk to Grunert again to drive home his point. He remembered the small storage room on the opposite side of the Dome, where he and PJ interviewed Ike Moncrief. He walked quickly with long strides but kept an ear on to the crowd noise and tried to make sense of which way the game was going. When he made it to the room, it was locked.

He saw a man in blue work-clothes that looked something like a tent made into an event staff uniform. The guy waddled behind a push broom with his gut displayed like pizza dough over his belt; he probably packed three hundred pounds on his five-feet-four-inch frame. Tucker asked him if he had a key or knew who might have a key to the storage room. The worker, an easy double for Jabba the Hut, looked at Tucker, shook his head and kept pushing his broom through the crowd.

With passersby looking on, Tucker pulled a thin, plastic card from his wallet, slipped it inside the dented metal door frame and jimmied the bolt on the door lock. Within a minute, undetected, he was inside the room, where the smell caused him to gag. New boxes filled with shirts, hats, trinkets, and other Atlanta Falcons memorabilia more than tripled the contents of the room in just the two days since he had been there. He squeezed past the stacked cartons to the table he used previously. His cell signal was not ideal, probably the result of his interior location, the boxes, the metal around him, and the thousands of sweaty fans hogging the signal. At a loss for any other quiet, private spot in the building, Tucker pushed the redial button on his phone.

"Grunert here."

"General Grunert, Tucker McGill. Sorry to interrupt again, but I wanted to make sure you were clear on my earlier request," Tucker said.

"McGill, I'm clear. Let me make sure you're clear," the general said, with a bit of bluster in his voice. "I told you the project that Captain Morrison was assigned was classified SECRET. The details behind the project are not for public dissemination. That's all I can tell you."

"General, I understand that. What I need you to understand is that I think that your Captain Morrison might be in trouble, and I am trying to help her," Tucker said, to take some of the wind out of the general's sails. "I realize she's no longer in the Army and is no longer governed by your military courts system, but if she were as good as you said she was I am sure you would want to help."

"Look, McGill. I have great respect for soldiers—all soldiers, anybody who ever wore the uniform—but once an individual trades their combat uniform for a business suit, there isn't much I can do. Maybe in a life-or-death situation but even then, classified documents are classified for reasons. Morrison's work is off limits."

Tucker parsed what he heard. "So, maybe there is a chance you could get details? Let me explain."

In five minutes Tucker unraveled the events of the previous week and the curious connections he saw between them. Grunert let Tucker present his case without any interruption. At the end, the line fell silent.

"Listen, McGill," Grunert said, to fill the void. "Sounds like you have your work cut out for you, but like I said the project was classified SECRET, and that's about the end of it. Good luck, trooper. Now, if you'll excuse me, I need to go," the general added.

"General, if there is anything you can do, please call me anytime on this number," Tucker said, a plea he felt headed for deaf ears.

"Rest assured I will. Goodbye."

When Tucker heard the phone click, he slumped forward, his forearms on his knees. *What bullshit.* He needed to talk to PJ to get the latest on the Atlanta PD and Feds investigations, but he also wanted to see some of the game.

Before he left the storage room, he called PJ for an update. He could hear the TV commentary in the background at the Atlanta PD headquarters. Tucker asked about the game, and PJ cranked through an abbreviated play-by-play; he made it sound like the "Jamal Derbish Show." Malik Farqu'har's roommate, the team point guard, led all scorers with twenty-three points, but they were still down—eighty-three, seventy-eight—with three twenty to play. One advantage in

Redcliffe's favor was the fact that the Spartans lost their point guard, an All-American named Eddie Himebrook, who went down early in the first half with an ankle injury and never returned to the floor. Tucker told PJ he would call back and scrambled to see the final minutes. He jogged through the crowd around the outer corridor as more fans flooded the hall coming in for the second game between UConn and North Carolina.

With the usual end-of-game fouls and timeouts, Tucker managed to get to his seat with a little over a minute left on the clock. During the final seventy-seven seconds, Derbish stymied Michigan State with glovelike defense and absolute wizardry on offense that ended the game with a step-back three-pointer at the buzzer to give Cinderella Redcliffe a one point victory and a spot in the NCAA Finals, despite their missing superstar.

Tucker found it impossible to jostle his way through students and fans to get to the court. The spontaneous celebration pushed him farther and farther away from the players, coaches and staff. He finally stopped and allowed the students their celebration with the reality that there was only one more game in this storybook season. As he watched, reality blurred the excitement of the crowd and replaced it with images and sounds of Xandra's swollen face and the voice of his spiteful boss. He remembered Malik Farqu'har.

While Tucker wrestled with the crowd and thoughts inside the Dome, a squinty-eyed viewer watched the live feed from a hidden camera in a storage shed many miles away where Malik Farqu'har huddled under a cardboard box to keep warm. He had missed the biggest game of his life, a game that would also prove to be the last for another member of his team.

CHAPTER 29

Saturday, April 2
6:23 p.m.

All eyes in Atlanta and around the country were on the David and Goliath match-up at the Georgia Dome, all except Xandra's. Her thoughts were elsewhere, too. She tried to bring herself to watch Redcliffe, but each time she turned on the game, she buried herself deeper in misery. The game was near halftime when she heard the knock on her door. She blinked and moved with caution in response. She expected room service, but the memory of her last unexpected visitors haunted her. Conscious not to place her hand anywhere near the handle or locks, she leaned her eye against the peephole and saw two familiar faces, a Latino room service waiter with a tray standing next to a housemaid with a basket of towels and other items, the same two from the night before. She did not see the replacement guard from the Atlanta PD who must have been outside the fisheye.

She watched while the housekeeper turned down the bed. The waiter placed the dinner tray on the desk and left. As soon as he was gone, the maid reached into her basket and pulled out a light blue smock with a dark blue lapel, exactly like the one she was wearing. The look she gave Xandra left nothing for interpretation; Xandra hugged her and went into the bathroom to change into the hotel uniform. The name badge read "Teresa."

The housekeeper walked with Xandra to the elevator which took them down to the tenth floor. She knocked on the door of room 1012 before she announced "Housekeeping." When she heard no answer, she looked at Xandra then placed a master key in the lock, opened the door and entered, Xandra close behind. As the two women entered the room, the maid again announced "Housekeeping." When nobody answered, they quickly checked the suite together before the housekeeper hugged Xandra and left her alone, waiting for Chris Gorting.

Xandra was uncertain what to expect. She had naively hoped to find Gorting planted in front of the television with the game on, not realizing the role he played overall with college basketball. She had his name and knew he had received mysterious FedEx envelopes like she had. She wanted to confront him about them and urge him to provide the ransom money though time had run out. She would wait for him, as long as necessary. Patiently. Silently. Optimistically.

After thirty minutes, she reconsidered. At first, she paced which only made her more anxious so she searched. She wanted to find the FedEx envelope if it was there. She needed to know what his letters said about Malik. She checked the dresser, the closet, his suitcase, his briefcase then his computer bag. Nothing. From behind the desk she pulled out the side drawers and found a copy of the New Testament, King James Version and a phone book. In the center drawer she found stationary, envelopes, and a FedEx envelope. It was empty.

On top of the desk was a laptop and a stack of sports magazines mixed with papers and folders. She rummaged through the pile. Toward the bottom she found what she was after, a letter on the same Redcliffe letterhead she had seen in her FedEx envelope. Under the letter was a sheet with two photos. Though she did not recognize the faces of the men in the photo, she easily recognized the poker chips and the snorting in the lower picture, a frequent scene in her neighborhood in Chicago. Because the sheet with the photos was beneath the letter, she assumed they were related though there had been no mention of photos when she listened to Tucker and PJ talking. She took both papers and restacked the magazines with the folders. When she stood her leg hit the desk. The stack of magazines and folders toppled onto the computer; the monitor screen lit up. What she saw disgusted her so much she wanted to smash the screen. Instead she pulled on the small, thumb drive, thinking it was a key that would turn off the computer, but the image on the screen did not disappear. She panicked and closed the lid. With the letter, photos and small drive in her hands, she left.

She rode the elevator to the main floor. The anonymity of the staff uniform and the hijab, gave her a false sense of safety. She thought she had something her two attackers could use, something with information, something that would buy her freedom for her son. She had to find the men in hoodies.

CHAPTER 30

Saturday, April 2
10:01 p.m.

The Redcliffe players watched the second game from the stands opposite the bench they occupied an hour before; the tension was less threatening. They joked with Jamal "Whirl the Pearl" Derbish for his over-the-top performance in their earlier game. Overall, they were neutral spectators with little concern for outcome of the game. To be in the finals against either UConn or the Tar Heels—ranked number one and two most of the season—was more than a dream for the previously unknown team from South Carolina.

From the stands, between games, Tucker had called PJ, but the crowd noise made it difficult to hear him; they agreed to talk when Tucker left the Georgia Dome after the second game.

Meanwhile PJ wrapped up things at the police headquarters and drove back to the hotel. In his room he loosened his tie, grabbed a Bud Light from the wet bar, and sat down in front of the tube just as the officials tossed the ball for the start of the second game. Somewhere between the seventh minute of the first half and the bottom of his second can of beer, the lack of sleep and go-go pace of the day got the best of him. He never saw halftime or the second half.

"This is Captain Beedle, Aiken County Sheriff's Office," he said, his voice was raspy as he blinked his eyes several times to clear his vision. His neck was stiff from sitting scrunched over and motionless in a chair for two hours.

"Hey PJ, Tucker. Great games, huh?" he said.

"Eagles pulled out a squeaker. I kinda missed the end of the second game. How'd it come out?" PJ asked, hoping Tucker would not notice his yawn.

"Heels by seventeen. Not much of a game," Tucker said. "What's the news on your end? The Feds find out anything on the Moncrief case? Anything from back home?"

PJ barely had time to answer one question before an energized Tucker fired another and another in a barrage of questions that lasted minutes.

"I need to grab some sleep," PJ said. "The Atlanta PD has a security watch set up to monitor the Redcliffe team on sixteen. I told them I would take the second shift because I'm here, and they are stretched kinda thin with everything going on around the city. How about we meet at the usual time for breakfast?"

Tucker agreed.

PJ set the alarm on the clock for two a.m. which gave him a little less than four hours of sleep and an hour to hit the snooze button, shave, shower, and get ready for his shift.

At three a.m. he met with Sergeant Tom Legg of the Atlanta PD by the elevators on the sixteenth floor. They exchanged the usual chatter about the game, the spirit of the players coming back, and special instructions from headquarters before Legg headed out. After the elevator door closed PJ was left with only the silence. Oddly enough, on a floor occupied by college "boys" who had just won a national semi-final basketball game, there was no noise from any of the rooms, the universal response to Coach Howells' orders to get to bed, get some rest, and be prepared for an early morning shootaround at the Dome before breakfast.

PJ yawned, endlessly, as he sauntered down the hall with the ever-present Styrofoam spit cup in his hand. The hall reeked of the floral-scented carpet spray used in most hotels; it made him gag. At one point he choked so hard he swallowed the pinch of tobacco he had under his lip. Near the far end, the site of Moncrief's fall the day before, he stopped to gaze at his reflection in the new window. He looked down at the parking lot below as he adjusted his patent leather Sam Browne belt loaded with radios, weapons, and accoutrements.

On his stroll back up the hall PJ placed his ear against each door. Nothing. Not a sound from any of the players. A good thing. With his inspection complete, he passed the time slouched low in a Naugahyde barrel chair by the elevator closest to the stairwell, his eyelids almost closed.

At half past three, exactly, he pulled out his cell phone, dialed the front desk and asked them to connect him to room 1628. The phone rang four times before a groggy voice answered. When the voice yelled "Hello" a second time, PJ hung up without saying a word. He then started another walk-through inspection, only this time he went directly to room 1628, the room of Jamal Derbish, the hotshot star of the previous night's game. Derbish lived with Malik Farqu'har on campus and always shared a hotel room on basketball trips. With Farqu'har missing, Derbish had the room to himself, optimistic that his roommate would show up at some point. For the past thirty minutes the floor had been quieter than snowfall in the forest, but out of habit, PJ looked up and down the hall before he knocked on the door. When nobody answered, he knocked again, then grabbed the doorknob and rattled the door against its frame. And another knock. As he went to unclip something from his belt, the door opened halfway and a sleepy-eyed Jamal Derbish appeared.

"What the f—" Before he had a chance to finish his question, the deputy mashed his left hand across the player's mouth, then slammed him back three feet to the wall. The door eased shut with a click. Derbish whipped his head to the side to breathe. When he raised his arm to push his assailant's face, PJ used his right hand to shove a stun gun directly into Derbish's abdomen, inches above his crotch, just like Sergeant Stevenson had taught him years earlier in the police academy.

"The stun gun is a mighty fine tool to incapacitate an aggressor. For instant gratification, so to speak, position the electrodes somewhere in the torso, between the shoulders and the hips. As an FYI it is most effective in the groin and in the neck."

Nearly six million volts snatched the air out of the stunned player's lungs like he had sucked on a Shop-Vac hose. Muscular legs that provided a forty-four inch vertical leap hours before, softened like pasta in a pot. His body went into convulsions the instant he hit the floor. Panicked gasps sounded like dry hiccups. PJ grabbed the kid under his arms and dragged him over next to the bed then zapped him again, this time in the chest. While the lean, long body convulsed on the floor, PJ grabbed a pillow from the bed and placed it over the face of his victim, then dropped his knees on the pillow on either side of the kid's head. With his back on the floor, Derbish used his spastic arms to reach for PJ's head and felt for the hand with the device in it. PJ pushed the arms to the side, reached under the pillow and fired a full five-second blast of current into the player's neck. All the flailing stopped. PJ knelt there until he watched the palsied chest of Jamal Derbish jerk and fall one last time.

When he was sure the kid was not breathing, PJ laid the body on its side in the bed, facing away from the door with a pillow wrapped in his arms, then pulled the covers back over him. After he had the body positioned the way he wanted, he wiped his shirt sleeve across his brow, straightened his gig line, adjusted his tie, and walked out of the room with his stun gun securely fastened in its pouch on the belt. The eerie quiet welcomed him back to the hall.

At four o'clock, from the chair by the elevator on the sixteenth floor, PJ pulled the police radio from his belt and made a hurried call to the Atlanta PD to report a code one-eight-seven—a homicide—at the Marriott Suites Midtown. Within minutes, the hotel again buzzed with the response. First a squad car with two policemen, followed by the paramedics in a box van and then a team from criminal investigations, the homicide squad. A steady flow of fire, police, and medical units added to the scene, most of whom left, the void created quickly filled by media. The scene in the hall soon looked like a replay of the previous night. Police sealed off the hall and told all the players to stay in their rooms. PJ talked to Coach Howells, then called Tucker.

"He's dead? How?" Tucker said, with his cell phone cradled against his shoulder. He pushed his shirttails into his trousers and dashed out of the room. "Meet me at the stairwell door. I'll be right there."

"I was on my rounds. I was down around the corner there toward the other end of the hall," PJ said, when

Tucker showed up. As PJ talked, he rested his hands on his belt; Tucker could see his arms tremble. "When I came around the corner I saw a guy leaving the kid's room. As soon as he saw me, he bolted. He headed toward the stairwell. I started after him, dropped my hat at the door to keep it from closing all the way then yelled in the room for a response. Got nothing." PJ took a deep breath and continued. "I started after the guy but doubled back to check on the kid." PJ looked over his shoulder at the activity in the kid's room. He rubbed a finger under his nose before he turned back toward Tucker. "When I found him he was in the bed. Not breathing. Couldn't feel a pulse. Called for paramedics."

The police moved in and out of the room. Some in uniform, some in plainclothes. The homicide squad—many of the same faces Tucker recognized from the previous night—hovered around the bed and throughout the room pulling evidence that would or could become clues in their investigation. Redcliffe players watched the scene with their heads poked out of their rooms like horses in stalls while assistant coaches went between rooms to provide the few answers they could.

"PJ how did the guy get in the room?" Tucker asked.

"Got no idea," he replied.

"Did you get a good look at him?"

"It all happened damn fast. I saw him. He saw me. He ran. I ran. He was wearing a green sweatshirt or something it looked like. I didn't get a good look at his face. Kind of a big guy, but from that far away kinda hard to describe," PJ said, pointing over Tucker's shoulder.

Tucker turned to look down the hall. The corner was probably a good seventy feet or a bit more, he figured.

"Excuse me," one of the Atlanta police said as she approached. "We need to ask Captain Beedle a few more questions. If you don't mind, sir, please follow me."

When the officer led PJ into the victim's room. Tucker walked down the hall, away from the scene, to call Ben Burgess to fill him in on the incident. He was sure waking Burgess in the middle of the night would be like rousting a grizzly from hibernation and the outcome probably the same—a growl served up with a ravenous appetite to chew on something like the caller's ass. At half past four in the morning, it did not take much of Burgess at all to make Tucker's temples throb.

"Just shut up, and listen," Tucker shouted, filled with the electricity of the moment. "Jamal Derbish is dead. Police think he was murdered in his room. The scene's blocked off. Wolfman knows, and he's keeping the players in their rooms. They know what's happened. You need to call President Kline and fill him in."

"For Christ's sake, McGill, I'm going to need more than that for Kline," Burgess said, fumbling for a pad and pencil. "Details. What details do we know? Who? What? Where? When? That sort of thing."

Tucker butted his head against the wall unsure which was harder—the wall or the skull on the other end of the phone. He paced the hall for ten minutes going over what details he had and answering all the questions. It would have taken less time to do all of that in person, but Burgess told McGill not to bother coming to his room. Tucker got the impression Burgess was not in his room but had no idea where he might be.

"When you talk to Kline, push him," Tucker said, as he rounded the corner in the hall and watched the homicide squad wheel the body out of the room on a gurney. "Kline won't like it, but push him to go back to the NCAA, and the network if he needs to, but Kline needs to get a delay in Monday's game. These kids can't deal with all of this and then be expected to go out and play in the NCAA final." Burgess hesitated, so Tucker continued, "We definitely don't have a level playing field anymore."

"They'll be more ready to play tomorrow than they will Tuesday or Wednesday or next week," Burgess said, his disgust poorly hidden. "What's one day going to do?"

The thought that the athletic director would not be behind the delay floored Tucker. He had to wonder if Burgess was a quitter or had personal intentions to sabotage this team and the game. Why would he even question the suggestion or intention, naïve as it must have sounded?

"One day gives them a chance to go through some counseling, to try to get their heads straight. To find themselves or find an anchor in all of this, something that will encourage them."

"Geezus, McGill. You sound like one of those namby-pamby bow tie professors from the psych department," Burgess said, pompous and bullheaded. "These kids need—"

"I know what they need," Tucker said, loud enough for people down the hall to hear. "What they need is time. What they need is a leader on the court and in their corner. It gives me time to find Malik Farqu'har and maybe learn what in the hell is happening."

"You've had four damn days, McGill. So where's Farqu'har?" Burgess screamed, spraying his phone. "If you haven't found him by now, what makes you think you'll have him here in the next thirty-six hours?"

Tucker fired back, louder than Burgess, loud enough to cause the Atlanta police officers outside of room

1628 to turn with concern on their faces. "I can tell you there's a better chance to have Farqu'har here on Wednesday than there is to have him here tomorrow. Even Tuesday would be better. Look, it's no skin off your back and no skin off Kline's back either. Just ask for the damn extension. We have nothing to lose but a game and...everything to win."

Again, Burgess paused, but this time Tucker let the silence grow. He had said his piece. Short of meeting with Burgess to talk some sense into him—at the risk of decking the guy—Tucker was finished with his argument. Burgess committed to nothing. He told McGill to meet him in the breakfast area at eight, a little over three hours away. Without a farewell, Tucker hung up.

Tucker was not a sound sleeper. For most of his life he had relied on sleeping pills to get a decent night's rest. After a two-hour nap on the couch, he shaved, showered, ordered a room service breakfast for Xandra who did not want to leave the room before he left to catch PJ in the breakfast area around seven-thirty, prior to his scheduled meeting with Burgess.

"I don't drink this much coffee normally," PJ said.

Tucker watched PJ guzzle cup after cup before the waitress left a pot for him at the table.

"That stuff's nasty," Tucker replied, with a sour look on his face.

"Atlanta PD kept me for debrief and questions until six-thirty. I need a caffeine transfusion. I have reports to fill out, more details around last night."

Tucker saw Burgess next to the cashier's stand with his phone in hand just before eight o'clock.

"I need to go. Burgess just walked up. It's Sunday, PJ. Get some sleep. If I don't talk to you, I'll see you here tomorrow morning, same time."

"Deal. I'm going to grab some shuteye then catch up with Tom Naujelis and go over our notes again. See if he has anything more from Chicago."

Tucker slapped PJ on the back, nearly spilling the cup of coffee he had at his lips, then walked toward Burgess. Burgess saw Tucker approach and turned away. Tucker expected to hear the riot act when they met, but the ass-chewing would have to wait. Burgess had actually turned to greet President Kline.

"Brent, you've met my associate, Tucker McGill, haven't you?" Burgess said, as he turned and placed his hand on Tucker's shoulder.

"I certainly have. McGill," Kline said, extending his hand.

"President Kline. Good morning," Tucker said, with a heavy pump of the president's hand.

The three men passed by PJ as they walked toward a corner table on the far side of the room. For the next thirty minutes they exchanged questions and answers regarding the deaths of the student athletes, the impact the events had on their teammates, and how they would address the press concerning the incidents. Once they had addressed the details of the death and arrangements for families, Tucker forced the discussion back to the team and the tournament; he outlined a perfect case for Kline to present to the NCAA, one they could not dispute.

Based on an early morning phone call from his staff, Chris Gorting was scheduled to meet with Brent Kline at ten a.m. in his small field office on the main floor. Gorting never ate breakfast but used the hours before the meeting to watch the news and catch up on paperwork. The reaction to the murder filled every channel. The calamity on top of the other incidents troubled Gorting, but his immediate concern was to the threat in the FedEx envelope he received on Friday. When he sat at the desk, he could not recall closing his computer, not something he normally did, but in his troubled state of mind, he realized anything could be possible.

He reached for the stack of magazines and folders on his desk to pull out the buried letter with photos; he did not see them. He thumbed through each magazine, rummaged through each folder but could not find the two sheets of paper. He leaned back in the chair, his eyes belonged to a man about to fall from a tightrope. He opened the center drawer to the desk and pulled out the FedEx envelope; it was empty. Then he remembered the thumb drive that came in the envelope; it, too, was missing. He searched his entire room with no luck. He had agreed to share the letter with the FBI, but now he had nothing to share. In one sense, a blessing; there was no evidence. On the other hand, they had to be somewhere; somebody had the letter, the photos, and the drive. He had to get them back, but it was time for him to meet with Brent Kline.

Kline was completely out of character and out of his mind—so he thought—when he pitched his appeal for a two-day delay. His argument was grounded in the tragic loss of two players and a trainer in what appeared to be a conscious effort—a plot, criminal acts—to destroy the Redcliffe team, their morale, their efforts, and any chance they had at winning a national championship. Gorting agreed and sympathized with Kline but argued vehemently with a red face that it could not be done. The rejection gave Kline chest pains. Subconsciously, the pressure of the Board of Trustees to win this appeal felt like a noose around his neck. The fact that Jamal Derbish was from Atlanta and had a special hometown following for these games bolstered his case. The city would be in mourning; they, too, needed the time. With protesters already at the site, things could turn ugly in more ways than they wanted to consider. Gorting, reluctant at best, agreed to consider the request a bit further, a consummate lie wrapped in a collegial bluff.

Gorting was back in his room before noon when he received the call from Frank Kehren at CBS Sports. The call was shorter than the discussion he had with Brent Kline. Both men were torn by the loss of the players. Gorting offered a token solution which he knew would never fly—to play the game in secret, closed to the public at an undisclosed location. Kehren instantly dismissed that idea given costs, advertising revenues, national appeal, a gamut of reasons not to go that route. He opted for a different solution.

The headline story for the *CBS Sunday Evening News* and across all the networks was the unprecedented decision to delay the NCAA basketball championship game for two days. The game would be played on Wednesday, April 6, not Monday as previously scheduled. The lobby of every hotel in Atlanta, every airline company, and most businesses in the country were flooded with angry, anxious fans who needed to extend their stays, their time away from work, their airline plans. CBS, in concert with their advertisers for that time block, had agreed to the delay the game. The network activated their operations center in Atlanta to coordinate with local businesses, hotels, and airlines—in consideration of the horrendous chain of events surrounding the Finals—to consider waiving all change fees associated with the decision to delay the game.

Without fail all hotels and airlines agreed. But for Chris Gorting, he had failed and, in private, feared what might come of the threats in the letters he had received.

CHAPTER 31

Monday, April 4
7:26 a.m.

On Monday morning, the buzz was all about the murder at the hotel and the unprecedented decision by CBS Sports to delay the final game. Sentiments were mixed as people queued up at the reception desk, panicked to secure their rooms through Wednesday night.

Outside the scene was quite different and usual at the same time. Another busier-than-normal workweek. On Fourteenth Street, traffic sped past like links on a chain, tight and connected, in a race to offices uptown, downtown, and around town. On the sidewalk beneath sun-splashed gray clouds that looked pregnant with spring snow, steam billowed from a lone vendor's cart as Melissa Cooper shortened her stride to appreciate the smells of boiled footlongs and the flock of pigeons clustered nearby waiting for handouts. Her ankle-length wool coat and cashmere scarf were no match for Mother Nature. In the parking lot between the Four Seasons Hotel and the Marriott Suites, she saw the two-day-old yellow crime scene tape that buzzed in the wind.

Melissa stopped just inside the Marriott lobby doors, taken aback by the activity at the desk. She had not seen the morning news nor was she aware of the NCAA decision about the game. She figured the presence of the black Atlanta police officer she spotted near the dining area and another near the doorway to the elevators was a response to the Moncrief suicide. She drifted toward the newsstand gift shop with one eye on the front desk and the other on the security camera behind it, glancing frequently at her watch. Between two small palm trees on either side of the desk, three, tall—basketball tall— men chatted with the curvy, chatty female desk clerk while a long line waited their chance to bargain for a room.

When the desk clerk walked into a back office, Melissa moved quickly. From her purse she pulled three FedEx Sameday envelopes. Masked by the too-tall threesome, she placed the envelopes quietly on the desk, undetected, excused herself as she passed through the line of guests then moved deeper into the lobby. When the attendant returned to the front desk, she spotted the envelopes, gave a quick look around, and then flashed her toothy smile to the three broad-shouldered hunks in front of her.

"Whoa," Tucker said, as he came around the corner off the elevator, nose to nose with Melissa. "Fancy meeting you here."

"I thought I would come by to weasel some breakfast out of you," Melissa said, her surprised response. She was shocked to run into Tucker and worried how a two-second delay might have been very troublesome for her. "I thought maybe I could surprise you, do a little breakfast together at your place, but it appears you already have a date."

"Oh, sorry. Melissa, this is Alexandra Novikov," he said, as he extended his open palm toward Xandra.

"Xandra, this is Doctor Melissa Cooper. Melissa is from Beech Island and a huge fan of the basketball team," he added with a wink.

Melissa extended her right hand and began to unbutton her coat; her eyes could not leave the scar or the black eye on the face of the other woman. Xandra shook Melissa's hand and abruptly turned away.

"Xandra is Malik Farqu'har's mother. We've been sharing a room for the past few days," Tucker said, with a smile, a tease for Melissa who did not seem to be the least bit amused. She merely nodded. "Why don't we grab a seat over there?" Tucker extended his arm toward a table well to the rear of the room.

Quiet at first, the shock of the news about the murder did little to slow Melissa. She made a quick remark about how sad she was to hear about Malik then launched into her own story about how she grew up, her runaway dad, sports, and the Army. Xandra made no attempt to talk or enter into a conversation at all. She remained quiet with her head turned slightly away from Melissa to hide her scar. Eventually when Xandra made an effort to enter the conversation, Melissa could not break through the Russian accent, so she repeated the questions over and over, each time her mouth drooped lower and her sighs grew deeper.

Finally she turned to Tucker and peppered him with her never-ending questions about the game and ongoing investigations, pressing for details like she was cross-examining a witness. Tucker noticed Melissa never acknowledged the deaths, never showed any sorrow, never asked about their families. She never seemed to care how the rest of the team was handling it. That bothered him. His whole existence for the past week had been this team and this one player, the son of the woman sitting next to him. The first break in the questions came when PJ appeared at the table.

"Thought we had a date this morning, kemosabe," PJ said. He pointed his finger toward Tucker then curled it like he was pulling a trigger on a pistol.

"Had prettier offers today, Tonto," Tucker replied with a cock of his head and a Cheshire cat grin which he quickly dropped. "Have a seat and join us."

"Morning, Doctor Cooper. Miss Novikov," PJ said, as he took a seat across from Tucker. Others in the dining room, sensitive to the events of the past two days, stared at the uniformed officer with his shiny belts and weapon.

As soon as his cheeks touched the chair, Melissa fired her questions at PJ, along with a sassy smirk toward Tucker. For the first ten minutes PJ sat, never had a chance to eat. After a decent night's sleep he had planned for a hefty breakfast with his friend, but as it turned out, his dentist had him on the ropes with questions even he had not considered.

"Look doc, I'd like to help, but quite frankly it ain't my yob and ain't yo business, so can I just get something to eat?"

As a waitress with a beehive hairdo, wearing more color in her makeup than the Rose Bowl Parade, stepped up to fill his coffee cup, PJ begged through a big tobacco-stained grin, "Can you leave the pitcher, please, darling. I have a feeling I'm going to need it."

"Just for you, shoog," she said, with a wink.

Melissa took the hint and the opportunity to excuse herself. She leaned over to Tucker, spread her thumb and pinky out and mouthed "call me" before she gave him a peck. As she pulled away she noticed the lipstick marks she left on his forehead. Without hesitation her hand went straight into Tucker's crotch, grabbed

generously, with an extra squeeze, pulled his napkin up
to wipe off the smudge, then tossed it onto the table and
walked away.

"That's one fired up chick," PJ said, as Melissa headed
toward the door.

"Yeah," was all Tucker said, though he thought much
more. "Hey, stay here. Get something to eat. I'll be back
down, but let me walk Xandra back to the room. She
doesn't need to sit here and listen to what we have to
discuss."

PJ nodded.

Tucker helped Xandra out of her chair and walked
beside her to the elevator. As they turned toward their
room on the fourteenth floor, Tucker spotted something
under the door. Most rooms had copies of *USA Today*,
but Tucker had picked up his on the way down to
breakfast. When he opened the door he saw a FedEx
envelope. The envelope was addressed to Alexandra
Novikov, marked SameDay service. Xandra looked up at
Tucker. Her eyes were glassy, bulged with emotion. She
walked past Tucker and sat on the corner of the couch
where she closed her eyes and rubbed the pain from her
temples.

Tucker handed the envelope to Xandra. "You need to
open it." He offered her the envelope in his outstretch
hand.

"No. You open," she said. She wrapped herself in a
hug, her hands under her crossed arms. "I cannot. Not
another. Please?"

Tucker hesitated. He was sick of the FedEx messages
because each one brought an increased threat. He
wondered if this would be a thorny rebuke for failing to
comply, for not anteing up the cash demanded? A
photo? A grim finale to his week of endless worry? He
questioned all he had done to find the boy. What PJ had

done or the FBI. He second-guessed being in Atlanta and not out looking for Xandra's son. And the motive. Why? Why this team, this player? Was it gang related? His father's rivals? And the others?

Tucker pulled the tab on the back of the envelope. Inside was a single sheet of paper. Like the others, it was Redcliffe College letterhead. Undated. Centered on the sheet, three words, all caps, *MALIK IS NEXT*. Tucker was not sure what to do or say. He dropped his arms to his sides and walked to the window. The clouds that squeezed out the sunlight seemed thicker, heavier. The traffic down below continued to flow without skipping a beat, though for Tucker it seemed as if time had stopped.

"What is it?" Xandra asked, her fears chasing the words.

"It's a note," Tucker said, as he walked back and stood by her on the sofa. He hesitated, placed a hand on her shoulder and added, "It says *Malik is next*." Her reaction took only seconds. Sobs turned to a steady flow of tears. She placed her head against his leg. When Tucker placed is hand on her head, she pulled back and leaned over the side of the sofa. When she sat up she had her purse in her hand.

"Mr. McGill, I must show you," she said, as she reached into her purse and handed Tucker the papers she took from Gorting's room.

Tucker quickly read the letter then looked at the photos. "Where did you get these?" he asked while he stared at the photos.

"I took from his room last night."

"But how did you get...." He turned to face her. "What were you doing in his room?"

"I went to talk, to ask for help. To ask about his letters. He did not come. I find these and—"

"Why did you take them? The police need to have these," he said, unsure if he should scold or share her fear.

"I tried to find men who hit me who wanted to know more about the letters for Malik. I thought maybe this help them and they help me find Malik. I look for them in lobby but did not find."

Tucker just looked at her unable to understand what might be going through her mind.

"And this, maybe, too?" Xandra said, as she fished for the thumb drive in her purse and handed it to Tucker. "I take this, too."

Tucker looked at the thumb drive, then at Xandra, before he took it from her. He could not make the connection between the letter, the photos, and the drive. He hoped something on the drive would explain. He snapped it into his computer and pulled up the only folder on it which contained several files marked *Robbie Gorting* and *Christian Gorting*. He did not look at many items before he ejected the drive.

"Xandra, I'm sorry," he said, as he moved toward the door. "I'll be right back. I need to go to the lobby to talk to Captain Beedle. I'll be back soon. Please...please do not leave the room." He considered taking her with him but opened the door and ran to the elevator alone.

"Did the FedEx guy leave this envelope this morning?" Tucker inquired of the tall, thin girl who had noticed the envelopes on the reception desk earlier. He flashed the FedEx envelope he found under his door. "Did the FedEx guy deliver it to my room or did someone on the staff bring it up? Who delivered it?" His tone was less than amiable.

The young receptionist opened her mouth not sure of what to say. Tucker intended to frighten her, and he had.

She folded her hands like she was praying and raised them to her mouth.

"Is the FedEx guy still around?" he demanded, looking back over his shoulder to the foot traffic in the lobby. He turned back, and the color in his face turned a ghostly white.

"Sir," the attendant offered from behind her hands, eyes popped bug-eyed, "I have no idea if the FedEx courier is in the building. I found that envelope and two others like it on the desk about thirty-minutes ago," she said, then realized she was holding her breath. "I didn't see who placed them there, but because it was SameDay service I asked one of my colleagues to deliver them. I couldn't leave my desk, you know—"

"Do you recall where the other envelopes were going? This one was sent to Alexandra Novikov in room fourteen-ten. Where did the others go?"

"I don't recall the names, but the room numbers...I wrote them on my pad," she said, as she rummaged for her notebook.

Tucker drummed his finger tips on the counter.

"One was going to room six-o-seven and the other to room ten-twelve."

"Can you look up the names and tell me which guest is in six-o-seven?"

"Sir, I'm sorry, but I can't disclose the names of our guests. I can call the room and you can—"

"No, forget it," he said, and wandered away from the desk with hopes he would find his newest FedEx friend. Instead, he saw PJ.

"Just had a call from Naujelis. Said someone slipped a FedEx envelope under his door, probably while he was in the shower. Says he wants to meet me down here for breakfast. Should be down any time now," PJ said, looking around the area.

"Yeah, Xandra got one, too," Tucker said, with a twist of his wrist to show the envelope in his hand, "Another went to Chris Gorting."

"There's Naujelis," PJ said.

"Let's grab a cup of coffee and go to the ops center conference room down the hall," Tucker suggested.

In the conference room, Naujelis wasted no time. His FedEx was just like the others—the John Wayne signature, Redcliffe letterhead, the message—except his message was text, top to bottom, with assertions that Robbie Gorting, the son of the president of the NCAA, was the person who had organized the ransom note and pick-up. It contended that the younger Gorting was over his head in debt—gambling and drugs—and his father was siphoning off NCAA money with bogus accounts to cover for him.

When Naujelis finished, Tucker showed them the sheets Xandra had pulled from Gorting's room. "I think this is the FedEx Gorting mentioned, his second package."

"When I talked to him on the phone he never mentioned photos or the thumb drive," Naujelis said.

"If this stuff is real, that's not surprising. I looked on the thumb drive. Not good," Tucker said.

For a brief moment, they remained speechless. Tucker broke the silence when he showed the others the SameDay FedEx letter Xandra had just received. The accusation of foul play at the NCAA was disturbing news but faded quickly with the threat of another murder.

"I checked with the front desk before I ran into PJ, Tucker said. "They're not sure how the envelopes got there. They said there were just three of them."

"I'll try to get more out of them," Naujelis said, taking down a quick note. "Let's go."

The three men left the conference room headed for the front desk. Tucker stepped away from the others and told PJ he would catch up with them shortly. He had to make a pit stop.

While PJ and Agent Naujelis talked to the desk clerk, Tucker walked down the hall to call his boss. Although Burgess reacted strangely on the previous call, Tucker felt compelled to keep his boss in the loop not only regarding the letter to Xandra but also on the new development which brought Chris Gorting into things, even though they did not appear related. When Burgess did not answer, Tucker left a brief message to say he had an update on his investigation and a new development. Next, Tucker called Brent Kline. Since Tucker had pushed the college president to put pressure on the head of the NCAA, he felt Kline should know about the latest potential wrinkle to impact their championship game. Kline's phone went immediately to voicemail; Tucker did not leave a message.

The halls were much more crowded than they were when he came down for breakfast. On his way back to the lobby to catch PJ, Tucker spotted his FedEx friend headed toward the back of the hotel where the FedEx drop box was located. He sped up and trailed him by twenty feet.

"Hey." Tucker hollered to get the guy's attention. The FedEx courier turned. When he saw Tucker, he stopped.

Tucker approached him, all smiles, to counter any lingering animosities or fears from their previous meeting.

"Have you made any deliveries this morning," Tucker asked, his smile washed clean from his stern face.

"No, just got here."

"Did you drop this envelope on the front desk," Tucker said, with his hand and the SameDay envelope raised.

"No. Besides, SameDay envelopes are door-to-door. Special courier. I don't handle those things," the man said, pained that Tucker was back in his face.

"Can you scan it to see if it is in your system?"

"It's not in my system. I can tell you that. It runs in its own system."

"Can you call anybody to see if it's in the FedEx system anywhere?" Tucker asked, with his hand in his pocket. The courier looked around at the crowd. Tucker looked at the FedEx Express logo on the man in front of him and lifted a pair of twenties. The courier lifted his scanner in one hand then snatched the cash with his other. He took the envelope, pulled out his cell phone and walked a short distance away. Tucker heard him read the tracking number over the phone. Two minutes later he returned.

"Nah, man. This ain't in no system..." he said, "no FedEx system."

"Thanks," Tucker said, and headed back toward the lobby. If Xandra's envelope was not in the system, he assumed the one to Naujelis was not in the system either. And the third envelope the clerk mentioned, probably the same. One step inside the lobby he literally ran into PJ and Naujelis, or vice versa.

"Come on. It's time to pay a visit to our friend Mr. Gorting. He's on the tenth floor." Naujelis pressed the button for the elevator. While they waited, PJ explained what was going on. They had called Gorting's room on the house phone and tried a cell phone number he left at the desk. No answer at either.

Chris Gorting's room on the tenth floor was located as far away from the elevators as he could get, by his request. In the hall, the radio on PJ's belt yelped; he reached down, pulled it to his mouth, and nodded. Tucker heard a voice crackle over the handset as the trio passed by a dad with his three sons, all wearing Redcliffe College shirts. Tucker gave them a thumbs up and "Go Eagles" as he passed.

Naujelis was first to the door and knocked. Not a rattle-the-door knock, just a casual early-in-the-morning knock. The other two men joined Naujelis who knocked a second time with a little more oomph. When there was no response, he knocked a third time and announced loud enough to be heard through the door, "FBI." Still no answer.

"That call was from the Atlanta PD," PJ said. "They want Tom and me to meet them on sixteen, the kid's room, Derbish."

Naujelis nodded in agreement, "Nothing we can do here now any way. I'll follow up and make contact with Gorting to find out if he received that third envelope. In the meantime I'll have guys back at the office pull a background check on the guy's son, Robbie."

As they waited for the elevator, Tucker told them he would let them do their thing with the Atlanta PD. He had a few calls to make and wanted to try to visit with Jamal Derbish's parents, if he could find them. PJ said he would check. He knew the homicide team had sent the body to the morgue but did not want to meet with the parents there. He was not sure if the police had them down at the station for any reason. With family in town for the game, most likely the parents were still in shock and with the extended family, not up for outside visitors, especially someone from the college. When the elevator bell rang, the up light came on; the two law officers boarded. "PJ, I'll give you a call," Tucker said, as the door closed.

Tucker elected to take the stairwell back down to the main floor. He knew he needed the exercise and walking down was much easier than hiking up. The isolation also gave him time to reflect. He remembered what PJ had told him about the guy he saw come out of Jamal Derbish's room and how he headed for the stairwell, this set of stairs. It also gave him time to rewind to the calls he had the evening before. When he exited the stairwell on the main floor, he had a strange feeling, like a criminal sneaking off into the crowd, but the crowd showed no interest in him at all. He walked directly to the ops center conference room in the back of the hotel where he expected quiet surroundings to make his calls; the first of which was to General George Grunert.

CHAPTER 32

Monday, April 4
8:30 a.m.

Room 1628 looked like something out of *CSI: Miami*. Yellow tape, flood lights, special criminal investigators, uniformed police, plainclothes detectives, admin people, hotel management, hotel staff. The police controlled access to the hall with officers at the elevator and stairwells. All hotel staff—room service, housekeepers, maintenance workers—when not totally restricted, were escorted to and from, then back off the floor. Players, escorted by coaches escorted by police, left the floor as a group for the morning shootaround rescheduled at the Georgia Dome. Even FBI credentials could not go unescorted. PJ and Naujelis walked with an Atlanta police escort from the elevator to the crime scene.

A line of people remained outside the room, questioned by an investigator in plainclothes seated in one of the barrel chairs from the elevator landing as he made entries on a laptop computer. The investigator recognized PJ from his earlier visit to police headquarters. He motioned with his chin for PJ and Naujelis to go into the room. Sergeant Hank Sandusky met them just inside the door where they put on shoe covers then walked around the yellow crime scene tape on the floor toward the back of the suite near the bathroom door, away from the other investigators.

"Captain Beedle, I was the one that called you to the room," Sandusky said. "We've got a few guys tailing leads on the guy in a green hoodie. The description you gave us last night was similar to the one we had from that kid Stifter, the kid who roomed with the suicide case." He opened his notebook and continued to outline what they had discovered with the case. "The morgue sent over a preliminary report. They believe the victim died of suffocation. Time of death approximately 0330 hours or about the same time you indicated you saw a man run from the room."

PJ nodded since that was the initial response from the night before.

"From what the team has been able to piece together here, last night and this morning, it appears the assailant used a pillow to smother Derbish either in the bed or near the bed."

"How could that happen?" Tom Naujelis said. "The kid was a good size, more fit than most, which meant whoever took the kid down had to overpower him somehow. Any signs of force?"

Sandusky shook his head.

"Any blood?" Naujelis asked.

"It appears the kid let somebody in the door, somebody he knew or expected," the sergeant said, then pointed to the two strips of yellow tape on the floor that ran from the door to the bed. "What it looks like is whoever came in the door either cold-cocked the kid and knocked him out or put something on his face to put him to sleep, then dragged him over to the bed where he smothered him. The morgue is checking for bumps or signs of something like chloroform."

"Any clues to support that?" Naujelis said.

"They didn't see any redness of the skin on the kid's face. They're checking his liver for signs. Other than that we have some hair and some fibers we are checking. Beedle, here, said he wasn't very good about entering the scene last night when this went down, so we expect we'll see a good bit from him," Sandusky said, looking back at PJ who remained still with his eyes at the bed, not on the speaker or Naujelis.

"Any other tests back from the morgue or lab? Anything in the kid's system? Drugs?" Naujelis asked. "Any evidence of what was used to drop the kid so fast?"

Sandusky stepped back toward the bathroom, PJ stood facing Naujelis. The police sergeant looked hard at Naujelis then turned toward PJ. A sudden flash in the other room caused all of them to turn. A photographer had snapped a photo of the crime tape on the floor and proceeded to take more pictures from points around the room. As they turned Sandusky stared at PJ who returned a curious look.

"The guys at the morgue found a few marks on the victim's body. They think the kid was tasered, well, stunned with a stun gun. There were three places on the kid's body where the examiner found two dots, uniformly spaced in all three locations. The marks are consistent with those found when a high-powered stun gun is placed on a body. They asked me to check with Captain Beedle to see if he had a stun gun."

Both Sandusky and Naujelis looked toward PJ's gear.

"Sure, standard issue. King Cobra. 5.8 million volts. Riot control and takedown," PJ offered, as he reached for his belt.

"Mind if I let the boys at the lab take a look at that thing?" Sandusky asked.

PJ pulled the stun gun from its holster. Sandusky opened an evidence bag; PJ dropped the stun gun into it. Sandusky flipped it over, took down the serial number, then handed PJ a receipt for his property with exact nomenclature, manufacturer, and serial number on it.

"I'll get this back to you as soon as they're finished with it, captain," Sandusky said.

"No rush. I've carried that puppy around with me for years and never used it. Not even sure it would work now if I needed it," PJ said. "Can't imagine I'll need it anytime soon." He smiled, but there was nothing funny about his face.

Tucker, hunkered down in the ops center conference room on the main floor, pulled up the history on his phone, found the cell number for General Grunert and tried to connect.

"Grunert here."

"General Grunert. Tucker McGill calling again. Could I get two minutes of your time?"

"Roger. Go ahead," Grunert said.

"The questions I raised last evening and the background on the special project, I think it's more critical now. Last night, not sure if you heard about it in the news, but actually earlier this morning one of the Redcliffe basketball players was murdered. I think information about the special project might have something to do with the kid's death," Tucker said, in a rush to deliver his spiel before Grunert cut him off again.

"Look McGill, you're starting to piss me off," the general said. His voice left no doubt he was tired of McGill and his questions. "I told you the project was classified. It's closed. Been closed for years and has nothing to do with you, basketball, Redcliffe College, or anything else outside of the military."

"Is there no way you can get any information on that project? I don't need full details," Tucker insisted. "I don't need the classified stuff. All I need is some general information?" Tucker added. He thought back to what Coach Howells had told him about the military system of document declassification. "Possibly a declassified, redacted version for public use?"

Grunert pulled his notebook from the cargo pocket of the old BDUs—Battle Dress Uniform—he always wore at work and around the house, military-chic for the soldier's soldier. Tucker held his phone tighter to his ear and waited. In a whisper that sounded much like a dog's growl, General Grunert said, "The project was an OADR. That stands for Originating Agency Determination Required. Which to you means I had to track down the bastard who wrote the document. Got that?"

Tucker offered a simple yes in a whisper similar to the general's though he did not understand why.

"The document was reclassified in 2009 to Controlled Unclassified Information. I can give you a pissant summary. I don't have time to go through details with you," he said, with a curt emphasis on his last word. Tucker closed his eyes and shook his head in silence.

"The project, code name Project Lenore, was to plant transceivers into Iraqi prisoners at Abu Ghraib before releasing them back into public to allow US authorities to track and to communicate, subconsciously, with those people."

Tucker was immediately confused. "How—"

"Just shut up, and let me finish, McGill. I don't have all damn day," Grunert said, his voice raised well above his previous whisper, still a growl. "The Army special operations projects team worked with the Academy of Health Sciences at Fort Sam Houston in Texas to develop a microtransceiver small enough to implant in a tooth. The device would receive voice signals via classified telephone channels. Messages were sent while the person slept. The device would detect when a subject entered into REM sleep. At that point the special ops project team would transmit voice messages. Apparently...this shit gets too technical for me here...somehow the voice vibrations were transmitted through the jaw to the ear so the subject actually heard a voice. The subject was previously programmed to listen to the voice given a unique identifier code and then take action."

Tucker did not know what to say. The whole project sounded more than shady. Mind manipulation. Zombies.

"The project was a success. It provided the White House great intel that was never released. When the shit hit the fan at Abu Ghraib, they canned the project and destroyed all the codes, the classified telephone number list, and the transceiver equipment. The destruction notice was signed off on by the project leader, Captain Christina Morrison."

Adrenaline rose through Tucker's body. He had heard more than he had asked for, but the key was, now he knew or was close to certain, that the woman who had stalked Coach Howells, was the same woman who had now latched onto him. She may not look the same, but according to all the info Tucker had, this was the same tattooed dentist asking all the questions.

"General Grunert, thank you for that. That was far more than I expected. I do appreciate all you've done."

"McGill, if anybody asks, don't tell anybody how you got that information. I'll deny every goddamn bit of it if it ever gets back to me. Understood?"

"Yes, sir. Understood. Thanks again."

Before he could disconnect, he heard the phone on the other end click off. What he had learned from Grunert validated a suspicion, but still not something he was ready to share with PJ although there were some things he needed to discuss. He pushed his speed dial number to connect with PJ.

"This is Captain Beedle, Aiken County Sheriff's Office."

"PJ, Tucker."

"Hey, Tucker. We're still up on sixteen. Where are you?"

"Down in the lobby. Hey, good you're there. Need a favor. Can you have the Atlanta PD run those FedEx envelopes through a fingerprint screen?"

"Say what? Man those envelopes pass through any number of hands," PJ said. "You trying to prove the 'six degrees of separation' thing or something?"

"No, just a point. Okay, then how about the letters inside? Those pieces of letterhead haven't been touched by that many people. Have them check those sheets, and let's see if they have the same prints on them."

"What, did your supersleuth dentist friend make some deal with you or what? That chick has more questions than—"

"No, no deals, just a hunch on my part."

"Given the nature of all that's gone down, as a betting man I'd say there are probably prints," PJ said.

"Okay, okay, okay. Thanks PJ. Just let me know when you get something will you?" Tucker asked.

"Yes," PJ replied. Somehow he pronounced a simple three-letter word using two syllables, a true Southern "yea-us." "Should be able to have something back to you by tomorrow or sooner."

"All right. Gotta run. Just call me. No, hey, meet me for dinner down here in the dining room tonight at four-thirty," Tucker said, and hung up.

He made a few calls trying to locate Jamal Derbish's parents. The police headquarters said they were not asked to come in today or had not been in as of yet. Tucker asked the desk sergeant for the phone number for the Atlanta morgue. He called and talked to the receptionist there; the parents had not been by. Next he checked with the basketball office at Redcliffe. Lucy Ann Winn answered the phone. She went on and on about all the tragedy in Atlanta, crying toward the end. He did what he could to comfort her; eventually he got her to a point where she could check emergency files and provide him with the emergency contact information for Jamal Derbish. There were two numbers listed. The first number was a home phone for his parents on the Atlanta south side; the second number was listed as a sister, Tameeka who lived north of Atlanta in Alpharetta.

Tucker went to the convenience bar in the conference room and poured a cup of coffee. *Disgusting!* He added extra cream plus four more packets of sugar to break the burnt-bitter taste and went back to his table. Situated but not satisfied, he called the Derbish home phone. Immediately the answering machine clicked on. There was a message, recorded recently that announced the death of Jamal and asked the caller to keep him and the family in their prayers. Then the machine-automated voice informed him that the *"mailbox is full"* and *"please call again later."* He dialed the second number.

Tameeka Derbish answered the phone on the second ring. Tucker introduced himself and immediately offered his condolences. Tameeka told him her parents were not accepting guests at this time. She was a recent graduate of North Carolina Central University where she played on the Lady Eagles basketball team and had recently returned to Atlanta to be closer to family. She said the entire family was in shock. Tameeka promised to pass on Tucker's kind words and would call him as soon as her parents felt up to visitors. On behalf of Redcliffe College, Tucker offered any assistance they needed. She said she appreciated the gesture.

By late morning Tucker had made all his immediate calls. For hours he had stifled the urge to call Melissa Cooper. He knew she coveted sleep. During normal workweeks she was up before the sun, running or swimming, but on weekends and holidays, she pulled the shades and remained wrapped in bed until noon. It was a few minutes past eleven when Tucker asked the Four Seasons switchboard to connect him with room 1005.

"Hello," Melissa slurred from deep slumber.

"Good morning sunshine," Tucker said, sounding as chipper as a child on Christmas morning. "Are you up?"

"Does it sound like I was up?" she said. "Oh sure, I've been up for hours. Just thought I'd disguise my voice in case you were planning to sell me something."

"Well, you don't sound like yourself, so I'm guessing you were not," Tucker said, with a chuckle. "But now that you are, got a minute?"

"Hell, now that I'm awake, I've got all damn day."

He had heard this same pissed off tone before. "Just wanted to find out if you were staying in town since the game has been delayed? People are scrambling to change their departure dates. Just thought—"

Melissa cleared her throat. "Well, I guess I'd consider it if you can make it worth my while, cowboy," she said, with a suggestive softness, total reversal of her previous tone.

"How about if we start by me buying you lunch?" Tucker asked, though what he really wanted to do was crawl into bed, without her, to correct his state of sleep deprivation. "What are you up for?"

"Actually, right now I could use a cup of coffee, black. Food?"

"Your call. A little Japanese, some sushi maybe?"

"Oh God, no."

"Something light? Soup and salad? Maybe a sandwich? Something a little more substantial?"

"Something close that includes wine," Melissa said.

"South City Kitchen it is," Tucker said, without any hesitation. "It's around the corner."

"Sounds like a soup line for the homeless. What time is it? It'll take me an hour to wake up and get ready, if I get some coffee in me fast," she said.

"It's eleven-ish now. How about I stop by at noon," Tucker replied.

"That works. See you then," she said, her voice trailing off. "Oh, Tucker, any news on your player?"

"We can talk at lunch. Get some coffee. See you in about an hour," he said. After he hung up, he leaned back in the chair, closed his eyes, and shook his head.

Tucker went back up to his room where he asked Xandra to join him in a walk to the lobby conscious of her fears, but concerned she would grow stir-crazy in the room with everything that was going on. He bought her a sandwich at the deli which she took back to the room. Before he left, Tucker urged her to stay in the room. Xandra listened and nodded but looked toward the suitcase in the corner where she hid the housekeeper smock and hijab. She offered half a smile and agreed.

The walk to lunch for Melissa and Tucker was a four-minute gauntlet of slush piles, street splash, and few words in puffs of frozen breath. Inside the restaurant they thawed at a warm, cozy corner table draped with a white linen tablecloth adorned with silver place settings; it appeared the South City Kitchen was a soup kitchen for only the rich and famous.

They drained a pot of hot coffee while they looked at the luncheon specials menu. When Melissa ordered a glass of Shiraz, Tucker ordered a Tuborg beer. Melissa latched onto the young waiter and quizzed him on pairing a dinner wine with the selection of soups, offering a bit of a tease on the side. Tucker picked at the label on his bottle of beer, eyeing it like a masterpiece in torn paper art. The waiter bowed to point out a specific vintage of wine which offered Melissa a chance to put her hand on top of the waiter's for a cheap thrill, for both. Tucker took advantage of the distraction to collect the specials menus. He placed one in his backpack.

With drinks in hand, they shared light conversation while they waited for their food—soup and salad for her and the house specialty buttermilk fried chicken for Tucker. Revived by coffee and refills on the alcohol, the table talk turned to Farqu'har and the latest details around the investigations for Moncrief and Derbish.

"All I can say is this has been one bizarre week," Tucker said. "It hasn't allowed much time to really appreciate the fact that Redcliffe is playing in the national championship. Just amazing when you to think about it. But these deaths…" He looked across at Melissa who looked up while she stabbed at the salad on her plate. Then Tucker looked back at his plate, sawed at his chicken and nonchalantly tossed out a complete change of subject. "Did you ever get up close to death in Iraq? I mean, ever see anybody die?" Tucker asked.

"Wow, that one came out of left field," Melissa said, then just as casually replied, "I was in the Green Zone in the center of Baghdad. It was pretty secure there. Rarely left the place at all," she said. "Dentists don't do much shooting, not bullets any way. Shot my fair share of lidocaine and xylocaine though," she said, with a smirk before she took a bite of salad.

"Were there any suicide bombers or crazies who tried to drive through the gates?"

"There were lots of those. Seemed to happen all the time. You read about them in the paper I'm sure," she said.

"Did you ever see any of that?"

"I'd always go down after the dust cleared. See the body parts. Sick, idiot bastards. Must have been that seventy-two virgins idea they have over there. Most of those guys would be hard pressed to find seventy-two women, period, that they could shack up with. And who knows about that virgin part; they're all covered up."

"Ever see one of our guys die?" Tucker asked, as he reached for his beer.

Melissa took a long moment to answer. "I saw an IED take out a hummer in a Lenore convoy once. Not a pretty sight. I swore if I ever had a chance I'd kill every one of those hodgies. Those little pricks. That whole area, I'm still not sure why we're there. I'd like to tell them what they can do with their fucking oil," Melissa said, with a face contorted with scorn.

"What's a 'Lenore convoy'?" Tucker asked.

Her eyes showed surprised concern over Tucker's curiosity and her slip. She reached for her glass of wine, fidgeted, brushed the hair away from her eyes, and grabbed her napkin before she answered. "Routine Army SOP. Over there you never go out alone so we put vehicles in groups, convoys. We gave them names. Usually the guys named them after their wives or girlfriends. Everything had a goddamn code name or acronym. Guys would dream up code names for meals in the mess hall. Stuff like "Marios" for spaghetti and meatballs. "Shit on a shingle" for creamed beef. Stupid stuff." She sat back, relaxed, with a noticeable sigh of satisfaction.

Tucker latched on to her mention of Lenore. General Grunert had mentioned the code name for a project at Abu Ghraib project. "Why the hell did they send a dentist out on a convoy?" Tucker said.

"Gotta go where the soldiers are, cowboy. See, not everybody's sitting in the Green Zone and not everybody gets back there to have dental checkups," she responded. "Sometimes, if we had to, we stayed near Baghdad, some other makeshift camp."

"Wasn't that prison, the one in the news, uh Abu Ghraib, wasn't it around Baghdad?" Tucker said, leading her on. He looked down and cut another bite.

Again, a silence, longer than the last time. Before she answered she tilted her soup bowl and dug several times to get the last spoonful. "You know, I think so, but I would get so lost just inside the Green Zone, I couldn't tell you where that place was."

"I thought you said your dad took you hiking and camping all the time as a kid? I thought you'd be all over maps. You never saw it, not even on a map?" he said. "Hell, that place was big news probably about the time you were there."

"Well, aren't you the curious one all of a sudden," Melissa said, with her hands flat on the table. She leaned toward him and, with a Joker-to-Batman smirk, said, "Curiosity killed the cat, cowboy." She clinked her wine glass against his beer bottle and sat back with a frozen smug look on her face, the tone of her voice said the subject was closed.

Tucker sensed he had struck a nerve, enough of a nerve to satisfy his curiosity for now. He changed the subject back to basketball and her stay. She said she had to get back to the hotel and check on her request to extend. They had placed her on a waiting list before they left for lunch. She might be leaving today; Tucker wanted her close. He made a heavy pitch for a little rendezvous later in the evening. Melissa was anxious to do just that—another opportunity to get an up-to-date status of the goings-on around the Redcliffe College basketball team. A quick look out the window convinced them it was better to negotiate another drink than to negotiate the wintry mix Mother Nature had in store for them.

At 2 p.m. Melissa gave Tucker a nibble on his ear and left him in the lobby at the Four Seasons Hotel. She went to her room, threw her coat on the couch, logged into the cloud, and pulled up a private website that only she could access. Tucker trudged the additional two hundred feet through the parking lot, passed the windblown crime scene tape, and into the Marriott Suites. From inside the lobby he immediately placed the call that would put an end to his curiosity.

CHAPTER 33

Monday, April 4
2:12 p.m.

G eorge Grunert reached for the phone, he noticed Tucker's cell number on the caller ID; he ignored the call. Ten minutes later Tucker called again.

"McGill, goddamn it. What do you want now?" Grunert said, before the phone even reached his ear. "I thought you had all you needed. Don't go dragging me down some rabbit hole with you. You understand?"

"General, I understand and I apologize for calling you back so soon. I just need to ask—"

"There's no more to ask about, McGill. I've given you the damn summary. I'm not about to 'Dick and Jane' you through the project."

"Sir, in any of the paperwork you saw on Project Lenore, were there any photos, any pictures? Pictures of the work? The subjects? Any photos of the lead for the project, that Captain Morrison?"

Grunert laughed which relieved Tucker for an instant then he thought maybe the general was about to unload on him, once and for all.

"McGill, you're in luck, ace. I went back through all completed and suspended projects. I pulled up anything that had to do with Project Lenore. Read through them all. Boring stuff. Mostly technical, too technical. One of the items that popped up with my query was a comment from a promotion board for the project leader, Captain Christina Morrison. My guess is, because this project was classified SECRET, all personnel actions had special treatment by promotion boards and that's why her packet was in the project file. Stand-by a second." Grunert switched phones while he put on a headset and started to search his computer. "That promotion packet attached included a photo. Standard Army full-body photo in service uniform. I could send that to you, but first, tell me again why you need this."

Tucker summarized the events of the past week, from his conversation with Coach Howell to the strange happenings surrounding the Redcliffe team, though he did not mention the tattoos or the fact that he was sleeping with the person he believed was Christina Morrison.

"The photo would certainly be a great help. Very much appreciated, general," Tucker said, with noticeable excitement in his voice.

"McGill," the general paused, "I'm not doing this for you, you understand? In the Army we practice what we preach. We preach 'mission, men, me.' Those are our priorities, in that order. You understand? You have a mission, McGill. You have a responsibility to your men. None of this is for you; it's for those kids playing basketball and for Coach Howells. Make it right, McGill and don't let anything stand in your way. Understand?"

"Don't worry, general. I intend to do just that," Tucker said.

"Oh, and McGill," another pause, "don't call me again." The general hung up before Tucker had a chance to agree.

Tucker grabbed two saucer-sized chocolate chip cookies from the tray in the ops center conference room and walked back to the guest business center on the far side of the lobby. He used one of the computers to pull up the email with the attached photo General Grunert agreed to send. He also sent comments sheets from Morrison's promotion file. As the photo came off the printer Tucker studied the face of the female officer. Pudgy cheeks. Soft jaw with a few ripples into a thick neck. Well-endowed, her uniform jacket seemed stretched, the sleeves tighter than one would like. To Tucker those were symptoms of overconsumption and minimal exercise. What he also recognized was the tiny dip at the end of her nose and the burning amber eyes. No question, it was Melissa Cooper. He imagined her twenty-five pounds heavier and seven years younger. Just out of college, in a foreign land, in a strange suit— an Army uniform. Anger began its slow burn.

Tucker caught Coach Howells in his room before he left to study game films ahead of the afternoon shootaround at the Dome. Howells all but confirmed what Tucker had suspected; Melissa Cooper was Christina Morrison, the woman who had stalked Howells years earlier.

While he waited to meet PJ for dinner, Tucker tried to make sense of what he had learned. He replayed memory tapes of his visit to the dentist the prior week. He could not recall seeing the usual set of framed diplomas professionals display in their offices: the usual undergrad diploma, the special dental school diploma or the usual certifications from state agencies and national organizations. None of those appeared in Melissa's office. He thought maybe she had them on the wall in her personal office and not where the dental chair was, but he recalled sticking his head into that office where the walls were covered of pictures of her. A few had others along with her, but most of them were pictures of Melissa at some celebrity event or touristy location. Nothing of an official nature with her name in print.

"It's about time, PJ," Tucker said, as he stood to shake hands. "What'd you do? Take a nap and oversleep?"

"It's the middle of the afternoon, man; I'm working," PJ said, coughing in jest. "Been on the phone working with Naujelis all afternoon to coordinate with the college to get students out to comb the area further out of town, outside Beech Island." PJ leaned back, reached into his pocket, and pulled out a tin of tobacco. After he offered some to Tucker, he shoved a pinch in his mouth and worked it around with his tongue. He grabbed a Styrofoam cup before he sat down. "With the few students left on campus, the Dean of Students cancelled a day of classes and asked the student council to organize the effort. They're doing a great job. I worked with one kid, some geology major. He asked if he could work with the others to do some soil samples for the guys back in our lab."

"Soil samples? For what?" Tucker asked.

"Our little heaven there around Augusta has a boatload of soils. If we can match a soil sample to what we found on Moncrief's truck, we might be able to narrow our search, maybe an idea of where he went," PJ answered. "Say, have you ordered any food yet?"

Tucker shook his head. They studied the menu while the waitress went for drinks.

"Where's your dentist friend tonight, Tucker?" PJ asked.

"Not sure. She's still in town. We had lunch. I'll check in with her later," he said. "Anything back from the

Atlanta PD on the fingerprints on those envelopes I gave you?"

PJ gave him a thumbs down.

"What about Gorting's kid?"

"The FBI ran a background check on the guy. Quite a résumé. Somehow they tracked him down, found him in Atlanta. I think the Atlanta PD has taken him in for questioning," PJ said.

"How about old man Gorting? Have they found him? Confirmed he received the third envelope the desk clerk mentioned?" Tucker said.

PJ pointed at McGill's shoulder. Tucker looked up and nearly knocked a tray of drinks out of the waitress's hands as she approached the table.

"They found him, but he said he didn't receive another FedEx envelope, none today."

Tucker recoiled. "He actually said he didn't receive an envelope?"

PJ nodded.

Tucker cocked his head but said nothing; PJ let him think.

"There would be no reason for the desk clerk to lie about the three envelopes. She had the room numbers. She had someone deliver them," Tucker said, scratching his head. "Granted, there was no confirmation that someone, anyone answered the door or accepted the envelope. Most likely, because of the early hour, someone slid the envelope under the door. Anybody inside could've picked it up. If Gorting didn't get it, who else was in the room? The kid? Where did they find his kid, Robbie?" Tucker asked with a furrowed brow.

"I think they told me he was in some sleazy motel outside Atlanta, southwest side."

"Did he have a room there or just visiting?"

"Don't have the details. Any chance he's staying with his old man?" PJ asked.

"I don't think he's registered in this place, but he's probably been around. He may have been at the game on Saturday," Tucker said.

As PJ talked more about what the FBI had on Robbie Gorting, Special Agent Naujelis and Sergeant Sandusky approached the table from behind PJ.

"Evening guys," Naujelis said. "Tucker how's your day gone? Did you meet with the Derbish kid's parents?"

"The day's been up and down," Tucker said, not offering to explain his sessions with Grunert or Howells. "No. Not able to talk to the parents. I talked to one of their daughters, the kid's sister. She said her folks aren't up for visitors. Apparently they have family in from out of town for the game, so they have a good support group with them right now. Surprised they aren't pressing you guys for more," he said, with a nod toward the police sergeant.

Sandusky stepped closer to the table with a cold look on his face. "Captain Beedle, I need you to come with me down to headquarters. You've been identified as a person of interest in the Derbish investigation."

The words were a body blow to PJ. He dropped his knife and fork and leaned his head back in the direction of Sandusky. "You what?" he said, his face twisted. "I'm what?"

Naujelis stood on one side while Sandusky stood close PJ on the other. "We can't go into any of the details here."

PJ pushed his plate toward the middle of the table and leaned forward to rest on his elbows, his fingers intertwined beneath his chin. He puckered his lips and ran his tongue across his top teeth. Once he had given some thought to what he had heard, he turned toward

Sandusky, and said, politely, "You gotta be shitting me. I've been bird-dogging this case and all the damn things that have happened for the past week, living on a few hours of sleep, eating lousy hotel food and you want to take me in?" He spoke with a deep, deliberate voice, absent his usual humor.

Sandusky did not say anything. PJ had years of experience on the guy which left Sandusky a little uneasy.

Naujelis placed a tight hand on PJ's shoulder. "Look, Beedle. Obviously a formality. These guys have the lab work. They gathered the forensics on this one. They can explain all of that downtown. This homicide is all theirs," Naujelis said.

"I've been down there twice already. I've told you what happened. And now, after all of that, you mark me as a person of interest because I was the first one there, no other witnesses and—"

"There are prints," Sandusky added.

"Of course there are prints. I went into the room trying to save the kid," PJ said, as he shook his head. "Okay. I'm not going to make a scene here. I have people on the ground as we speak, looking for the missing player. Let's make this quick. I have work to do."

PJ dropped a twenty-dollar bill on the table and told Tucker he'd settle up with him later. The two uniformed officers—PJ and Sandusky—walked ahead of Tom Naujelis as they left the dining room, headed for a squad car to take them to the Atlanta PD headquarters.

Tucker watched them until they were out of the dining room. He wasn't sure what to think, though he had doubts about PJ. He had worked closely with the guy for a week. He had no reasons to believe PJ would do anything to jeopardize the Redcliffe team and certainly had no motive to murder anyone.

Tucker remained at the table, nursing a cup of the world's worst coffee, with hopes that it might become drinkable. The dining room had cleared considerably; those who had witnessed PJ leave with the others had finished their meals and were long gone. Tucker shifted his focus from PJ back to Melissa. He wanted to learn more about Christina Morrison. He made another call.

When Colonel Hoffman answered the phone, Tucker was quick to apologize for calling during dinner.

"Late? McGill, I'm still at my desk. It's difficult to practice clock management here at the Pentagon. It's not like a basketball game. Workdays are twenty-four-seven propositions. What can I do for you?" the colonel said, with a grunt, his phone lodged between his shoulder and ear to free his hands to multitask with the action papers on his desk.

"I wondered if you could elaborate a bit more on Christina Morrison. You mentioned she was tough to handle back in Iraq," Tucker said.

"Like I said, she was one of four women in the unit. It was no secret that she was sleeping around with just about every swinging Richard in the barracks."

"Barracks? Weren't you in the Green Zone? On the news, I thought that was all hotel living?"

"Not hardly. We lived at Abu Ghraib, at the far end away from the cellblocks, just like the guards. Occasionally we would get a break and go back to the city for a night of R&R," Hoffman said.

"And those four women, they were—"

"They were there with the male guards and medical staff. We set up a separate living area for the women. We had times assigned for female showers. We built separate latrines outside. Primitive, but hell, the whole place was primitive."

"What else about Morrison?" Tucker said, pushing his cold coffee out of the way so he could write in his notebook.

"Well, I could probably go through notes I have. I kept a personal journal while I was there; have ever since, too. Good practice. I recommend it. But, I'll bet in my notes I could name all the guys who hooked up with Morrison. Ten, twenty, a couple dozen," he chuckled.

Tucker rolled his eyes and shook his head.

"The accommodations were less than basic, Spartan-like, but troops find ways to get it on. There were very few electrical lights in the buildings. Areas ran on generators for the most part. Hiding was easy," he said. "I do recall two classic incidents, though. Our CQ, uh Charge of Quarters, like a barracks guard, was making the rounds and found Captain Morrison in a somewhat compromising position on an exam table in the dispensary with one of the guards. But, the best one was when one of the guards watched one of the other male guards in the dental chair with Morrison 'riding him like a bucking bronco', if I remember the quote from the report. The guy surprised them with a flashlight and snapped a picture."

Tucker showed no surprise. After what he had learned over the past three days he had no interest in jealousy.

"Colonel Hoffman, if it's not too much trouble, any chance you can get me a list of names of those guys, the ones Captain Morrison did? Any of them still in the service?" Tucker asked.

"I could look at my Iraq journal. Should be easy to put together a list. Why do you need that? No clue if any of those guys are still on active duty," Hoffman said. "Why do you need all of this, McGill?"

"The names, just references is all. I might need help from one or two to verify some things, that's all," Tucker answered.

"McGill you gotta remember, those guys were young, most of them just out of high school, away from home for the first time and horny as hell. Most of them could have cared less who was balling whom, as long as they got a piece of the action. The married guys, they actually seemed to stay clear, turned their heads, and used their hands, just my guess," Hoffman said. "I'll email that list. I don't have those journals here in my office. When do you need the names?"

"Well, yesterday, as they say. I need it as soon as you can get it. I'm trying to help our buddy Wolfman. I appreciate all you can do."

After his talk with Colonel Hoffman, Tucker made a series of calls. First he tried Melissa, no answer. Then he tried PJ, no answer. Next he called the Atlanta Police Headquarters. The system bounced his call several times from department to department, desk to desk, but eventually he talked to a sergeant who told him Captain Beedle was still under investigation; it appeared he would be there overnight and released sometime on Tuesday. Since he was unable to talk to PJ, Tucker called Tom Naujelis to hear his take on what was going on at police headquarters. Naujelis told him PJ had a solid story, nothing of what he said conflicted with what he had told the police before. When they asked him to explain the stun gun marks, PJ told them he had no idea how they found Derbish's fingerprints on it; he had not seen or spent any time with the kid until he saw him in the room, dead.

"He said he 'would swear that on a stack of Bibles and take a lie detector test' if they wanted him to. If he's lying, he's a great liar," Naujelis said.

None of it made sense to Tucker. One thing Tucker knew for certain; he was tired. The events of the previous week had caught up with him, drained him, not to mention sleeping on a pullout couch. Nonetheless, he called Melissa again with the same outcome, no answer. From what he had heard earlier, she could be romping in the sheets with somebody right now. He was headed for the sheets, too, this time by himself. What he had to do next could wait until tomorrow.

CHAPTER 34

Tuesday, April 5
7:23 a.m.

For the first time in a week, the sun rose in a cloudless sky. Its rays poked through the drapes and nudged Tucker—Mother Nature's au natural wake-up call. The nine hours of sleep, even on the stiff pullout bed, made for a good morning. Tucker shaved and, as he came out of the shower with a towel wrapped around him, he was startled to see Xandra, still in her nightie, brushing her hair at the mirror. Tucker noticed a bit of an electric twinge when he brushed her backside as he tried to pass behind her to get to the other room where he could put on some clothes. Xandra flinched at his touch then hurried to draw bathwater. By seven-fifty a.m. they were both ready for a shot of coffee and some breakfast.

Tom Naujelis played a hunch and found Tucker by the continental breakfast bar on the main floor. Though he was not surprised to see Xandra with Tucker, he felt awkward discussing any of the details of the case in front of the mother of one of the subjects.

"Good morning, Tucker. Miss Novikov," the agent said.

"Off to an early start again, eh," Tucker said. "Care for some coffee? It's not all that great but does have caffeine in it."

Tucker poured a cup and passed it across to the tall federal agent as he pulled up a chair. Tucker thought the guy needed something to jump-start his morning. He had deep bags under his eyes that never quite opened all the way; his suit coat looked like he had slept in it.

"How did it go last night?" Tucker asked.

"Beedle is still there. They kept him overnight. Not sure why. The evidence they have made it look bad for him, but his story never changed."

"Why? What are they calling evidence," Tucker asked.

"Fingerprints all over the room—door knob, wall, pillow. Fibers on the carpet and on the body. The fact that he was the first one in the room. No witnesses of that. No witnesses that saw PJ or the guy he claimed left the room. No witnesses saw the guy in the hall or on the stairwell. The security camera did not show a guy at all."

"It all sounds basic. I mean, PJ was the guard on duty. He was the guy who had any chance of seeing any action," Tucker said.

Naujelis was quick to respond, "The examiner at the morgue and one of our lab techs examined the markings on the victim's body. The burn marks, the ones they thought might be from a stun gun, they matched exactly with the electrodes on Beedle's gun. They also think they have the kid's fingerprints on that gun which Beedle can't explain."

Tucker wrapped his fingers around his coffee cup and shook his head.

"They haven't charged him with anything. He actually got to bed early in the holding cell. They might have more questions for him this morning, but I expect you'll see him back this way at some point."

Tucker nodded. Naujelis planted his elbows on the table and cradled the cup of black coffee.

"While I was at the headquarters last night, I saw the police report on those fingerprints you'd asked about." He took a long sip. "The report said the prints matched. Both envelopes had the same prints. Whose are they, do you know?"

Tucker put his cup back on the table and sat back, not surprised but concerned. "Can they run another fingerprint check on something? If I can get this checked, I might be able to answer that," Tucker said, looking over at Xandra and pulling something from his backpack.

"Yeah, don't see why not. It's worth a shot," Naujelis said.

Tucker handed the Special Agent a folder. Inside was a sheet of paper—a menu from the South City Kitchen—in a document protector.

"Have them check this for prints. I put it in the plastic sleeve. The prints would be on the paper inside." Tucker finished his cup of coffee and continued. "What did your guys get from Robbie Gorting? Anything?"

"Well, I told you, the guy has a file history that goes back a long way. Started back when he was an MP, military police, in Iraq. The guy was a guard at that Abu Ghraib prison. He got in some sort of trouble for something he did with the prisoners. He never made it to the big time, not one of the ones who went to jail or anything. Just enough to get busted twice," Naujelis said.

Tucker listened as Naujelis rattled off a series of close calls with the law over a period of ten years; somehow he always managed to avoid conviction.

"They kept him at the police headquarters overnight, too. I am sure they kept him away from Beedle, though," Naujelis said. "Can't hold him. No charges. He'll be out today, too."

Tucker stared at Xandra who returned the look. Tucker could almost see the wheels turning in Xandra's head. He rubbed his eyes and looked down for a second before he turned to Naujelis. "Tom, could you get that guy's military records? Not his personnel file. His dental records?" Tucker asked.

Naujelis shoved back from the table and crossed his legs with his hands folded around a knee. "I'm going to need to give folks some sort of reason for a request like that. It's a bit out of the ordinary, but don't see why not. The Bureau has its ways with just about everything and everybody. I'll give it a shot," Naujelis said. "Give me a little more. What's this all about?"

"I'll tell you later," Tucker said.

"I can't request or waste assets on something if I don't know what it's about. I have credibility to protect here."

Tucker looked back at Xandra, then to Naujelis. "I'll tell you later," he said, his eyes pointing back toward Xandra.

Naujelis caught the gesture and understood.

"So, the Gorting guy has never been arrested or jailed?" Tucker said.

"Nothing in his record. Seems to me something or someone influenced some decisions about some of the raps listed on the sheet, but who knows."

"Interesting. Coincidences?" Tucker said, while his eyes wandered around the room with nothing particular in focus. "Tell you what, I need to go check some things. If you can jump on those records that would be great. Call me when you hear something or get the file, if you would please," Tucker added as he began to stand. "And let me know if you hear anything about PJ."

Naujelis stood and shook hands with Tucker, then smiled at Xandra. "I'll call as soon as I have anything, but Tucker you're going to have to fill me in on what you're up to. This is an ongoing investigation and if what you're doing is significant to what we are doing..."

"Understood. I'll give you what I have and let you decide if it's anything. Right now you have plenty to keep you busy as it is," Tucker said. "Thanks. Adios."

Tucker walked Xandra by the gift shop to buy her a book or something to occupy her time. She selected a magazine with crossword puzzles; she said they helped her with vocabulary. Back in the room Tucker explained he had a few calls to make and some emails to catch up on.

He took his laptop and his backpack down to the ops center on the main floor. He read through his emails, many of which addressed the events of the past week. Others were from high school student-athletes who still had an interest in Redcliffe College sports and needed assistance in providing information to team coaches. Tucker was pleased to see the school had not lost the appeal it had for talented, sports-minded teens.

After he finished his emails, Tucker googled "Coach Ernie Howells." He found a lot about Ernie's success as a coach, how he took the Redcliffe team from the cellar to the top of the Big South Conference and now to the top of all NCAA Division I schools in basketball. He also found an article about the hit-and-run accident that killed Ernie's wife, Amanda. The *Augusta Chronicle* story had one detail Tucker was after. The name of the man driving the car that killed Amanda Howells was Sam Hutchinson. Based on the eye-witness accounts and descriptions of Hutchinson's car, he was picked up in New Jersey ten days after the incident, brought back to South Carolina, charged with second-degree murder and sentenced to fifteen years in a South Carolina prison. Tucker jotted down names and details of interest until he felt a tap on his shoulder. It was PJ.

"I thought I'd find you in here," PJ said. "Damn phone needs a recharge or I'd have called you. My brothers in the Atlanta PD had me for a sleepover last night," he said, with a hint of sarcasm in his voice.

"Yeah, I heard. I talked to Tom Naujelis this morning after breakfast. You can share all the details later. So, you back on the case or cases such as they are?" Tucker asked, anxious for a follow up question.

"Yep, I need to check in with my boss first. When he finds out about last night he'll either blow his cork or laugh his ass off," PJ said, with his own smirk. "Also need to hear back from the guys on campus back at Redcliffe to see how their search is going. See if they have anything for us on Farqu'har."

"Okay, I've got one for you. Can you go through your interdepartmental channels and get some records for me? Need you to network up some records on a guy in the McCormick Correctional Institution. The guy's name is Sam Hutchinson. In for fifteen years on second-degree murder."

"Name's vaguely familiar," PJ said. He pulled out a tin of Skoal Wintergreen, tapped the rim on the table, and stashed a pinch under his lower lip.

"He was the guy accused of the hit-and-run death of Ernie Howell's wife late last year."

"Yeah, gotcha. What do you need that for?"

"Just do me this one will you? I'll explain later," Tucker said.

PJ bugged his eyes out then relaxed. "Man...that might take me all day. I have a million other things to check, but.... You mind if I use the ops center for the calls, at least to get started. My cell will take hours to charge," PJ said, with his lip jutted out beyond his nose, his tongue pushing the tobacco into place.

"Stay here if you want. Use the phone as much as you need. They can fax files here, too or have them email them to you or me," Tucker said, sliding his used Styrofoam cup toward PJ who grabbed it like a drowning man for a lifesaver. He immediately spit into it; a string-like leaf of tobacco clung to his lip.

"I'm going to run out to the car to grab a few things. I'll be right back," he said, with another spit.

With PJ away, Tucker called Melissa. After five rings, her voicemail kicked in. He hung up and tried her office, a long-shot hunch she decided to blow town and go back to work. Janet Curio, the petite and bony, middle-aged receptionist at the dental office answered.

"Good morning, Janet. Tucker McGill. Is Doctor Cooper in?"

"Now Mr. McGill, you know she up and went to Atlanta to watch basketball. You haven't seen her?" she asked.

"Have not seen her for a few days," he lied. "Is she there?"

"No, sir," she said, with a smack of her chewing gum lodged between the two one-syllable words.

This puzzled Tucker. His frustration confused him momentarily, but then her absence allowed for another white lie. "Janet, Melissa and I were talking when I was there last week. Sounded like we had a mutual friend, Sam Hutchison. Melissa said she might have his address. Can you check for me?"

"I can't give you any personal information from our files, Mr. McGill," she said, pompous as a Southern judge.

"Can you at least check to see if he might be the same guy? Just tell me when he last saw Melissa? I can probably track him down from that if I know he is still around," Tucker said, voiced slow and easy to comfort, coax, and cajole the reluctant assistant. "Melissa would do it if she were there, I'm sure."

"All right. Hold on just a minute while I check our records."

Janet was neither the brightest bulb in the box nor the fastest computer whiz when it came to technology. She meant well and was cordial to patients, somewhat of a contrast to Melissa herself; that's why she kept her on.

"Mr. McGill, I found a Samuel Hutchison. And, yes, it looks like Doctor Cooper saw the man last October, right after she got here, but I can't give you any more information than that. Privacy Act, you know."

"Okay, understood. I can find him from my old Christmas card list, probably," Tucker lied. "Thanks, Janet. Say, if you hear from Melissa, would you ask her to call me, please?"

"You're welcome, Mr. McGill. I'll let Doctor Cooper know." She hung up without any further ado.

Tucker scratched notes on his pad. He drew a line across the top and scribbled dates against it, his weak attempt at a timeline to map out events that seemed related. The YMCA ringtone once again interrupted his thoughts.

"McGill, it's Tom Naujelis. I got the field test back on that menu you gave me this morning. They had a bit of a time with that paper. Had plenty of partial prints, only a couple full prints, but those prints matched the ones on the FedEx envelopes we checked. What's going on? Whose are they?" the agent asked.

"I believe the prints are from a woman named Christina Morrison," Tucker said, one more little white lie wouldn't hurt. Before he dragged Melissa into this case as a suspect, he wanted to verify one or two more things, irons he had in the fire. "I picked up the menu yesterday when she ate at a restaurant near the hotel here."

"You randomly go around picking up souvenir menus? Who is Christina Morrison?" Naujelis asked.

"Look, I've got a hunch on something, okay? When you finish up at the headquarters, let's plan to meet for supper. I'll explain what I have," Tucker said. He noticed PJ walk through the door.

"All right. The dining room there at the Marriott. Make it six o'clock."

Tucker agreed and hung up.

PJ stopped at the convenience bar just inside the door to pour himself a cup of coffee. He reached in his mouth to pull out the wad of tobacco then dropped it in the trash can with the used coffee stirring sticks and sugar packets. He spit out a few strings of tobacco that he had missed with his fingers then rubbed the inside of his lower lip with his tongue to make sure it was clear as he walked to rejoin Tucker at the table.

"PJ," Tucker said, "you ever go to Doctor Cooper for dental work?"

"Yeah, right after she bought the place and opened up back in November or so. Had my teeth cleaned and checked," PJ said, sipping on his coffee. "Uh, nasty stuff." He cringed as he swallowed. "Then went back in January, right before my Super Bowl party to get a filling. She also gave me a crown on one of my molars. Temp one day and the final crown a week later. It took her awhile, but I didn't mind the view when she bent over me to work on my mouth," he said, as he gagged on another sip of coffee.

"Yeah, I agree. I had the same work done. She finished my crown same day," Tucker said. "Hey, I know you were out of the net last night."

PJ rolled his eyes.

"Did you find out anything on the Moncrief case? The Atlanta PD share anything with you?"

"They weren't a very friendly bunch last night, but before I left there this morning, they said they were still tracking it as a suicide. The green-hoodie thing doesn't help them much; too many of those around."

PJ put his coffee down and pulled out the Skoal again, one pinch at a time.

"They checked hotel records. From the general registration checks they found two guys with cards from Chicago," he said, with a slight tobacco lisp. "They passed the names over to Naujelis. He worked them with his Chicago office. The Chicago PD ran them against their files. Somehow these two names popped up on their gang watch list. Posse Diablo."

Tucker rolled his eyes. "Damn, it's getting late. Check on that Sam Hutchinson stuff for me will you?" Tucker said, with a sudden need to disconnect with PJ. "I need to go check on our female friend, Xandra, to see if she wants some lunch. She's so damn conscientious about her English she won't order anything for herself."

Tucker gathered his things, put them in his backpack, and slapped PJ on the back as he headed toward the door. He remembered the Posse Diablo was the gang run by Rodney Farqu'har, Malik's father and Xandra's imprisoned husband.

CHAPTER 35

Tuesday, April 5
12:09 p.m.

When Tucker slid the key card into the door lock, it startled Xandra. She shoved the blue smock back into her suitcase and moved to the bed, hunched over like a puppy cowering from a rolled newspaper. Tucker gave a quizzical look but apologized and eased the door shut. She relaxed and straightened but not totally. Tucker sat on the corner of the desk adjacent to the couch and invited her to join him in the sitting room. He noticed the crossword puzzle book was on the ottoman footstool; very few of the clues had answers, across or down.

"Would you like lunch?" Tucker asked with a pleasant smile.

She shook her head, yes, as she took a seat on the couch.

"Downstairs or up?"

"Here," she said, then turned away.

"What's wrong," Tucker asked. No response. "Did something happen?" Tucker slid forward on the top of the desk.

She appeared more withdrawn than she had been earlier, but Tucker moved on.

"Xandra, I need to ask you a few things. Captain Beedle and Special Agent Naujelis have shared some information with me about Malik and about those men that visited you, the ones who threatened you."

Tucker rose and walked toward the woman on the couch. As he approached, she slid to the cushion at the far end and pulled her knees up to her chest. Tucker found her reaction strange, cold. From the day she arrived, she never seemed relaxed; understandable he thought, though he had hoped she trusted him when he said he would find Malik.

"Xandra, I need to ask you about those two men in the green hoodies," Tucker said. He took a seat on the ottoman in front of the couch; Xandra cowered even more. "I need to know…did you know them?"

His question did not settle well. She gave him an ugly look and turned away.

"You told me and you told the police that you didn't know them? Is that true?" Tucker pressed. "It's important that we know. It's important to help us find Malik."

Xandra clammed up. She bowed her head and looked down at her arms wrapped around her knees pulled tightly against her chest. Tucker felt sorry for her but needed answers before he could follow the path he hoped would lead him to Malik.

"Xandra, I know where you got the money for the ransom."

She looked up. Her face showed insult and fear.

"Those two men, they were in the gang, your husband's gang in Chicago, the Posse Diablo weren't they?"

Xandra turned sharply and ignored his words as if he had never spoken them.

"You got the money from them didn't you?"

"No," Xandra said, with an outburst. "I did not get money from them. I not know them."

"But the money, it came from the gang. Your husband, Rodney, set you up with money?" Tucker said, at this point pure conjecture based on a hunch and the pieces of information he had received from both Naujelis and PJ. He also believed the two guys in the hoodies had something to do with the cash, either to give it or retrieve it and, by extension, find the kid.

Xandra shook her head and clutched her legs tighter. She struggled. Her breathing grew deeper, faster. She choked on her words, "I only want my son."

Tucker reached to touch her hand, but she pulled back. He needed answers. "Where did you get the money? Did those two guys give it to you?" he asked.

"Mr. McGill, I only want my son. I go to Rodney. He always told me he had money. He had ways to get money. I talk to man. He say pick up money at motel. I not know who," she said, then paused with a deep sigh. "I see those men in lobby. I look for them but not find them again. I not want trouble. I only want Malik."

"Xandra, I think we are getting close," he lied to comfort her. "Can you identify those men now?" Tucker asked.

Xandra dropped her feet to the floor and bent forward with her hands in her lap. Her head rocked ever so slightly. Tucker waited. He had asked the question; it was up to her to reply. She broke the silence with a whispered, yes.

Tucker exhaled with a heavy sigh, swiveled off the footstool, and walked into the bedroom aglow with pale, afternoon sunlight. He pulled his cell phone from his pocket and stood by the window, fogged by his breath as he looked down on Fourteenth Street. Midday traffic flowed to the sounds of the city—horns and sirens against a continuous pounding of a jackhammer down the street.

"PJ, Tucker," he said, as he looked back toward Xandra on the couch. "Hey, can you get the guys from Atlanta PD to send a sketch artist over to the Marriott? I believe Miss Novikov can help us identify the guys in the green hoodies. We can match what she gives us against what the FBI has on those two guys from Chicago."

"I'll give my buddy Sandusky a call then call you right back," PJ said.

Five minutes later, he was back on the phone. "They have someone and they will be on the way soon. Should be at the Marriott within fifteen or twenty minutes. I'll meet them up front."

"Thanks. Bring him on up to my room when he gets here. I've ordered some lunch for Xandra and me. You want anything?"

"No thanks. I'm good. See you shortly," PJ said, then hung up.

Room service rapped lightly on the door when they brought the sandwich and salads. A different waiter than the one Xandra had seen so many times before. Shortly after room service left, PJ arrived with Sergeant Sandusky and a female police sketch artist. Over the ninety minutes that followed, the artist gradually built a rapport with Xandra as they sat side by side on the couch. The sketch app on the laptop allowed the artist to cut and paste facial features as Xandra answered questions and gave her description of the two men that came to the room, the same two she saw at breakfast. Rough but better than nothing, Sandusky had the artist pull up mug shots of the two suspected Posse Diablo members registered at the hotel. The sketches, though not perfect, matched the police records. They appeared to be the same two guys who visited Xandra.

Tucker made a quick call to Coach Howells to coordinate another meeting with the assistant trainer, Joe Stifter, to verify the sketches and photos were the same two looking for his roommate, Ike Moncrief, the night before his apparent suicide. Coach Howells was already at the Georgia Dome preparing for the afternoon shootaround but said Stifter was still in the hotel resting before the bus picked up the team for practice. Howells agreed to the police visit provided Tucker was there to supervise and support Stifter. Tucker agreed and took the group to Stifter's room. "Without a doubt" were Stifter's words. He identified the two just as Xandra had.

In the ops center on the main floor the four men— Tucker, PJ, Naujelis and Sandusky—discussed their next move. After a conference call with headquarters, Sergeant Sandusky had approval to bring the two Posse Diablo gang members in for questioning in the death of Ike Moncrief. When the other three left to locate and apprehend the two suspects, Tucker remained to cross-check his notes and review messages. His phone showed no voicemail, nothing from Melissa. No emails from her either, only routine notes. When he got up to get some water, his phone sang. It was Agent Naujelis.

"Tucker, Tom Naujelis. I got the file you requested, the one on Robbie Gorting," he said.

"Can you look through there and tell me if he ever saw Doctor Christina Morrison?" Tucker asked, as he grabbed the bottled water from the tray at the convenience bar.

"Typical medical stuff. Impossible to read, but there is a stamp here for Christina Morrison, DDS, Captain, DC. If I am reading this correctly, she did some work on a molar, number thirty. X-ray looks like lower right. What's this for?" Naujelis asked.

"I'll explain at supper," Tucker said. "Thanks. Hey, you're from around here. Do you have a good dentist?"

"Why? Psychosomatic pains all of a sudden?" Naujelis said.

"Yeah, something like that. I feel a pain coming on, killer. You have a dentist?"

"Sure. Doug Athey. He's out in Buckhead, north Atlanta, just off Peachtree Road. Don't have his number handy, just look him up. He's a good man. I'm sure he'd love to get his hands on a former Celtic like you," he said, with a laugh.

"Thanks. I'll give him a call. Don't forget supper tonight," Tucker said, before he hung up.

Back at his table, he ran a quick search on "Doug Athey, dentist, Buckhead" and got the phone number he needed. He called the office and asked if he could come by for an emergency. The receptionist asked if he had been in before; Tucker said no. He explained he was in town for the Final Four, and a friend recommended Doctor Athey. The receptionist said she would check with the doctor and try to work him in as soon as possible. With the appointment made, Tucker called PJ.

"PJ, Tucker. You still in the hotel?" he said.

"No. Sandusky and I found those two green-hoodie guys. He has them in his car, I am following them headed back to police headquarters to meet with Naujelis," PJ said. "I was going to call you when I got there. News for you. New lead on Farqu'har. Soil samples came back from the kid on the search. Samples from the Sumter Forest matched those on Moncrief's truck. Less clay, more organic matter than on campus. Mineral content very similar. Layering on the truck indicated a travel route. I have one of my guys in the office checking a few possibilities right now."

"Great. When will you know more? Any way to pinpoint a location?" Tucker said, as he fumbled with the words in his excitement.

"As I said, I was going to call you as soon as I got to the headquarters and—"

Tucker was amped up. "PJ, radio Sandusky or leave a message with dispatch. Tell him you had to take care of another matter, and meet me in north Atlanta by two p.m." Tucker said, then gave him the address.

"What's going on? What's there?" PJ asked. "Things are beginning to roll, and I've had enough distractions."

"It's a dentist office. Let's just say I need some dental work done, bad, and I need you there for support," Tucker said.

"Ten-four. Aiken County Sheriff's Office. We serve to please."

CHAPTER 36

Tuesday, April 5
2:15 p.m.

Outside the Peachtree Clinic, sitting in the Aiken County Sheriff's car, Tucker walked PJ through the search process that brought them there which included a detailed chronology of events that linked Christina Morrison to Melissa Cooper. The next step was to convince the dentist.

The haggard Doctor Athey was an older alum of the Medical College of Georgia located in Augusta and, as luck would have it, a rabid Recliffe basketball fan which was quite a contrast for a guy five feet six inches tall with black hair combed over his bald dome that had a headlamp growing from his forehead. He was intrigued by the request and excited to get to work. Almost before he knew what had happened, PJ was in a chair, numbed up with two hands in his mouth. While PJ underwent the procedure, Tucker called Tom Naujelis and asked him to join them at the clinic.

As soon as Dr. Athey completed the first part of the request, the gentle extraction, Tucker was forced to call General Grunert again; he looked forward to this less than PJ had looked forward to having the dentist pull the cap from his tooth. He had promised he would not bother the general again, but when Doctor Athey showed Tucker the cap he pulled, Tucker had little choice. He shrank when the voice answered on the other end.

"McGill, I have no idea what you are up to, but I am sick and tired of answering these calls," he said, his breathing labored. "You're lucky. I'm just coming out of the Pentagon gym, climbing my way back to my office. Whatever you have, make it quick. When I get to my office this call is over."

"I'll make it quick, sir. From what you read in the Project Lenore file, which tooth was used? Lower right?"

"Yeah, bottom jaw, lower right."

"I'm looking at what we think might be one of the devices used in that project," Tucker said.

"Can't be. Where the hell are you, McGill?"

"Still in Atlanta, Peachtree Clinic to be exact. Huge dental clinic. Do you understand the electronics in the device? Can you explain the general functions of the device? How it worked? What it did?" Tucker asked, seated in a stiff plastic chair next to PJ, now missing a tooth.

"Short and sweet. I told you all of this before. As I understood the project notes, a microtransceiver—we're talking nanotechnology here—is placed in the cap for the tooth to receive calls via a cellular phone system. The project intent was to track al-Qaeda prisoners released in Iraq. Project personnel would send voice commands to the receivers while the person was sleeping," Grunert said, as he quickened his stride down Corridor 7 headed to the C-Ring. "Similar to hypnosis I believe it said but done completely without the person's knowledge. Commands could be given to the subjects, and they'd execute the command, but all recollection of the command forgotten by the subject. Mind control so to speak. Commands were sent while the person was asleep. The implanted device could determine blood flow and pulse. The project was discontinued when the new administration won the White House. McGill, what I am telling you is not classified, but don't go spreading this around, got it? We have enough to do here."

Tucker looked away from his phone. He looked at the dentist. Athey raised one finger and responded in a whisper, "I can explain part of it, I think."

Tucker put the phone closer to his mouth. "Do you have or does the file show diagrams, technical drawings of this device? And, is there a way to intercept these commands?"

"The file has all that info, McGill. Dammit! I have a meeting in the Chief of Staff's Office in fifteen minutes. I don't have time to walk you through all of that stuff. If you need it, I'll have one of my staff officers get it to you," he said, as he walked into his office and motioned for one of his "Iron Majors" to follow him. "Those cell numbers were all classified, government toll-free. Not sure what their status is now."

"Is there any way...any way at all, to check the history of the calls made on those numbers, even those used after the project was cancelled?" Tucker asked.

"Possibly but would take a while to retrace all the numbers and tracking info. My guess is someone can trace back to the phone used to call the subject, but I doubt there are any voice records of the calls," Grunert said. He pulled up the chair behind his desk and turned on his computer.

"General, is there any way to determine what cell number is assigned to a specific device?" He noticed PJ was asleep in the chair.

"Well, the old numbers might be in the files. Those would be numbers placed in units back when the project was active, 2003 or so. Other than that, records were destroyed, and according to the file, so were all the devices. I remember reading that the numbers were preset, burned into the firmware on the device like a serial number when the device was built."

"So, if we had the list and knew the device number, we would probably be able to match the number to a specific device which would allow us to check history of calls or trace a call, maybe even tap a call and listen to it as it comes in?" Tucker said, over the loud snoring from the chair.

"Correct. Well trace history any way. Look, McGill, I've spent more time than I can afford on this. I'll give your number to one of my guys and they'll call you. You can continue with your questions, but I've gotta go," the general said.

"Thank you, general. I hope I don't have to call you back," Tucker said apologetically.

"Well, you can bet I am done answering your calls." He hung up.

"Interesting," Doctor Athey said, as he approached the chair and shook his patient on the shoulder. He turned on his headlamp and leaned over PJ. "Very interesting. Okay, you asked how this would work," he said, looking at Tucker, the light from the headlamp at point blank range. He flicked it off. "Old technology actually. Bone conduction technology has been around since 1977. You implant a screw. I've seen it done behind a person's ear, then attach a receiver, maybe half as big as your thumb; well, my thumb." He held up his thumb as a reference. "Sound goes in the receiver, sends vibrations into the bone, and directly to the inner ear, bypasses the external auditory canal and middle ear. I've never seen it in a tooth. The nanotechnology they used here is something else. Wish I had thought of that," he said. "I can't tell you how all the cell signal stuff works though."

While they waited, Tucker asked the dentist to do a little more of his dental wizardry, to include forming a new, not so technical cap for PJ. Naujelis arrived shortly after three p.m. After a brief explanation of why he was called in, Naujelis suggested they reconvene at his office a few miles east of the clinic.

Inside the conference room of the Atlanta FBI office, Tucker walked Naujelis and PJ through his sequence of calls and checks surrounding the disappearance of Malik Farqu'har, as well as the deaths of Ike Moncrief and Jamal Derbish. He downloaded an email from one of Grunert's staff officers with the attached diagrams and lists from the Project Lenore files.

Tucker's leg work was more than enough for Naujelis and his team to pull together a plan. He ramped up an expedient conference call with his Chicago office and his technical experts in Virginia to examine the device diagrams and functions in conjunction with one Army technical expert familiar with the original design. He had the Georgia Bureau of Investigation and the South Carolina Law Enforcement Division dial in as well. After he read everybody into the situation, Naujelis released his technical experts to reverse engineer the device and decipher the listed pairings by number. The others remained on the call to brainstorm for over an hour. Before the call ended, the technical experts checked in with their findings and comments. Finally, Naujelis led a recap of the meeting, line by line, what they collectively agreed to do—an operation he code named Nevermore.

CHAPTER 37

Tuesday, April 5
5:21 p.m.

The groupthink at the FBI office ran long, longer than Tucker wanted. Headed back into Atlanta, he was in the thick of rush hour, bumper-to-bumper gridlock. He fiddled with the car radio until he found the local ESPN station—680 AM "The Fan"—to listen to the latest happenings in sports, especially the latest buzz around Redcliffe and the Final Four. He was relieved when PJ called him on his cell to break the stop-and-go monotony.

"Tucker, I'm stuck in traffic," he said.

Tucker could hear some country female voice in the background.

"Not sure when I'll get back in the city. Have half a mind to flip on the blue lights and cruise past all this. Had a call from my boss. He said he was out in a helicopter from over at Fort Gordon back home. Standby. Got another call on the radio."

Tucker signaled to cut over one lane to the right where traffic seemed to move quicker. As soon as he did, the lane stopped, and his previous lane picked up.

"I'm back. Boss said he flew the search area, mainly the wooded parts and spotted several small structures through the trees which he identified on an old map of the area. Most were small, isolated buildings, storage sheds or hunting hooches on the edge of the Sumter National Forest. He saw one cluster which he identified as Plum Branch Hunting Lodge over near Edgefield. Evidently it's used primarily during deer season. He's sending someone out there."

"Hey good news. Yeah, I'm in the same traffic you're in. Hard telling when I'll be back. I might pull off and grab something to eat while all this is going on, so let's skip meeting for dinner tonight," Tucker said.

"Okay, just wanted to update you. Actually, I'm headed crosstown, back to police headquarters. Should be back for the business tonight. Can't imagine this traffic will last more than an hour, two at best. Makes me miss Aiken County for sure," PJ laughed.

"Right. Better run. I'll talk to you later," Tucker said, and dropped the call. Instead of pulling off to eat, he called Melissa. She answered on the third ring.

"Well, hello stranger," Tucker said. "Thought maybe you'd run off to the Riviera with that debonair French manager at your hotel. Where have you been?"

"Shopping," Melissa said, while she scrolled through the text on her computer screen.

"Shopping? For almost two whole days? You've been shopping the entire time?"

Melissa kissed her middle finger, held it in front of the phone and fired back, loaded for bear, "Uh, no messages from you, cowboy. Never knew you called," she said, no longer focused on her computer. "You and all the crazies around here whooping and hollering about basketball. Even shopping takes forever. After the last two days, that French Riviera idea of yours sounds like a good one to me," she laughed, an extended laugh to force the same out of him. "So, what's new with you?"

"Since you asked," Tucker said, anxious to update specifics for her. "We think we have a solid lead. We think we've found Malik Farqu'har. The sheriff and the South Carolina Law Enforcement Division are checking a hunting lodge near the Sumter National Forest."

Melissa fumbled her phone then cradled it on her shoulder while she keyed a URL into her browser. When her search engine cleared, the screen went almost black, but with a closer look, she could detect movement by a lone figure across her display. She smiled with the knowledge her secret was still safe.

"Great news, cowboy. I'm sure his mom is anxious as anything to close this ordeal and have her son back, safe and sound," Melissa said, as she toggled the remote webcam with the keys on her laptop. Her voice dropped an octave and her tone shifted from lyrical to Greta Garbo seductive. "So, for two days you call, so you say. Interested in something, cowboy?" She paused, this time for self-admiration. "Why don't you come over. Maybe we can figure out a way to celebrate your great find, the kid I mean."

Tucker smirked at her suggestion. The traffic had opened enough that he was moving again, just about to merge onto I-75 where the traffic would choke down to three lanes.

"I'll need another rain check on that one? Too much going on with the game tomorrow and all. Besides, we lost PJ Beedle, the Aiken Sheriff's Department guy."

"What happened to Dudley Do-Right?" Melissa asked, still focused on her computer but listening with both ears.

"The Atlanta PD arrested him yesterday. He's now the prime suspect in the death of Jamal Derbish, the player that was murdered. Beedle's in the Atlanta jail, awaiting a hearing," Tucker explained, though his details were as far from the truth as he could make them.

Melissa looked away from her screen, checked her watch, looked back at the bedroom then back at her watch. She had not given much thought to Beedle since the night of the murder, but the fact that he was locked up concerned her.

"That's a swift kick in the ass," she said. "The guy busts his butt to find the kid's roommate and they hold him for murder? They have a motive?"

"Not sure. All I know is he's been on the case from the start. If the sheriff doesn't find Farqu'har in that lodge, it puts us back to square one; we lost a week. We have another lead on the ransom though. Hold on."

Tucker merged into the stream of cars headed into Midtown Atlanta. The merge was easy enough, but as soon as he positioned himself in the middle lane, everything around him came to a stop.

"Dammit. This traffic is killing me. Yeah, looks like the son of the NCAA president was the wheel behind the ransom; he needed cash to cover some gambling and drug deals. The FBI is still talking to the guy; could book him tonight. Keep that one under your hat. Given the issues around the Final Four and everything, this Gorting bit is all on the hush-hush." Tucker worried about how good it felt to lie.

Melissa scrunched her face in disbelieve that they had somehow pulled Robbie Gorting into this investigation but smirked at Tucker's suggestion that Gorting was behind the ransom scheme.

"Burgess found me today. The bastard jumped down my throat, still pushing. I told him about the lead on Farqu'har. He just blew it off and told me to find the kid," Tucker said. "So, I need a rain check. I'm going to wait for the sheriff to get back to me on what they found, then I'm hitting the hay. Tons to do tomorrow before the game."

"I'd just tell him to go fuck himself..." Melissa said, "but he'd probably screw that up, too. So, if you're wrapped up with all of this, guess I might as well head back to Augusta. Some of us have real jobs you know."

"Leave tonight? Come on, the game's tomorrow! Stay for the final," he said. "This is a big deal. This is history. And if we have Farqu'har back here, our chances are really good."

"I've seen about all I need to see," she said. "Besides, if you're more comfortable sleeping on a couch with that live-in wench of yours..."

Melissa noticed a change on her screen. A line appeared close to the left side, a straight gray line that grew whiter. She saw the figure in the room move toward the line then realized it was light coming from under the door. Adrenaline began a slow march through her body. *McGill was right. They found Farqu'har,* she thought. With the kid back, they could win that game. Howells would win the championship. *How'd they...* No time to track that back and Beedle is down for the count.

"Come on now; be nice. She's been through a lot and may be too nervous to sleep at all tonight," Tucker interjected. "Just stay. Tomorrow we can celebrate. I can promise you the ride of your life, more historic and exciting than the game." Though everything about his tone and proposal seemed jovial, his heart mourned the two deaths which had become more than motivators.

"Whatever. Have it your way. Spend the night with good old Scarface what's-her-name, the grieving mom, okay. But I am smokin' hot, wearing only chaps and ready to ride that bull. Bring your A-game, cowboy. Oh the rain check of yours expires tomorrow," she said, looking back at her screen.

Tucker dropped his head back and shook it. *If it was only that easy.* "You're on," Tucker said. He knew her tease was not just talk.

"Sweet, sweet dreams," Melissa said, before she hung up. She placed her phone next to her computer on the desk and studied her screen. The line she saw earlier was brighter now. What she could not see were the two deputies with the angle grinder and bolt cutters on the other side of the door. Minutes later the screen was awash with light. The figure that had moved closer to the door on the dark screen was now fully visible, all six feet six inches of him. When the officers entered, they looked up at the exhausted face of Malik Farqu'har.

She slapped her desk and said to herself, "Headlines. Breaking news: MISSING REDCLIFFE COLLEGE SUPERSTAR FOUND. Will he play in The Finals tomorrow in Atlanta?" *I doubt,* she thought. *I doubt.*

At the Atlanta Police Headquarters, Naujelis and Sandusky stormed out of the interrogation rooms, each according to the plan.

Sandusky cracked his knuckles and told the Posse Diablo gang member he was tired of sparring with him. Francisco Hernandez-Agoya, one of the two men in hoodies from Chicago, slouched in the unpadded wooden chair, pushed back from the table in the interrogation room with his legs extended, ankles crossed, and arms folded. The chair in the opposite corner was empty, intended for Agent Tom Naujelis. Sergeant Sandusky had been behind a small table opposite Hernandez-Agoya. Every response from Agoya, even to the simplest questions, came with a sneer and run-on sentence where every third word started with "f." No body language, no movement, and no confession of any sort. The suspect sat back and looked at the ceiling. Sandusky did not say anything else; he just got up and walked out.

Naujelis had a completely different experience. Robbie Gorting was loose, calm, cocky, and told Naujelis he didn't need an attorney because he had not done anything wrong. When Naujelis asked him why he was in Atlanta, he responded that he had come to watch the Final Four. He denied any suggestion he had anything to do with the disappearance of Malik Farqu'har or the death of Jamal Derbish. While Gorting blathered on and on about how he could never kill anybody, Naujelis noticed him constantly drumming his fingers; that's when he interrupted him to suggest "there's always a first time."

Gorting grew frustrated with the agent putting words in his mouth. Each time he spoke, Naujelis moved his chair closer and lowered his voice to almost a whisper. In response Gorting shifted and rubbed his hands through his hair. When Naujelis told Gorting that the word on the street was he owed a lot of money, gambling money, Gorting stiffened, his answers and explanations slowed. The more Naujelis pressed him, the less he wanted to talk. When questioned about the FedEx envelope sent to Alexandra Novikov, Gorting denied ever hearing the name. Likewise, he rebuffed the suggestion that he had anything to do with the ransom money.

After several hours, the suspect broke down. Naujelis dropped his scowl and laughed when Robbie Gorting refused to answer any more questions and demanded a lawyer. Gorting balled his fist on the table and replied, "You can go to hell."

"Got it," Naujelis said, with a nod as he stood to walk out and join Sandusky for supper, leaving Gorting to think about it, alone, in the interrogation room.

After hours stuck in March Madness traffic, Tucker made it back to the hotel. He entered through a door on the side of the building and found the lobby pre-game revelry was in full swing. Shades of blue separated the two camps. The Carolina-blue fans spilled out of a conference room rally into the hall. The crowd of Redcliffe Eagle fans had outgrown the bar area and formed a sea of navy blue and teal. Tucker wormed his way back through crowds where he watched and waited more than five minutes for the elevator before he decided to climb the fourteen flights of stairs to his room. Fortunately, the elevator landed and discharged a cabin full of Tar Heels about the time he started into the stairwell. He quickly opted for the elevator.

When he entered his room, he found it dark, illuminated only by *Wheel of Fortune* on the television, the volume turned down low. He flipped on the lights and saw Xandra relaxed in concentration. When Tucker shared the news about the strong lead on Malik, she cried with a smile from ear to ear as she squeezed his hand with a grip of hope. Although Tucker explained this was not a certain thing, it was the first solid lead that polished her dimming hope. Tucker asked if she had eaten; she replied she had not which prompted his immediate call for room service. After waiting for over an hour the regular Latino waiter arrived. He apologized repeatedly for the delay citing a flood of requests from others unwilling to hassle with the madness on the first floor.

For the first time in a week, Xandra jabbered while they ate. Filled with questions about the efforts to find

Malik and other investigations, it was almost ten o'clock
when they finished their meals. Tucker was certain his
anxious roommate would never sleep so he suggested
she take a sleeping pill which he provided, his last,
before he waded through emails and other messages.
The absence of phone calls from Tom Naujelis at the
Atlanta Police Headquarters or a report from PJ about
the lead in Aiken County concerned him, but there was
little more he could do than sleep which he needed. He
went to the wet bar and reached for a beer but decided
against it. Without the beer or his sleeping pill, he spent
thirty minutes on his back on the pullout bed,
mesmerized by the fire sprinkler on the ceiling above his
head before he dozed off.

Half a block away, the backlight of her laptop reflected
the face of Melissa Cooper as she rolled the bowl of
another glass of pinot noir across her lips. She eased
back in the chair where she had spent the past four
hours. The warm bouquet of the first sip, teased by the
office lights of the tall building across the street,
blossomed into a Mona Lisa smile.

When a synthesized chirp sounded from the speaker,
she looked down. The computer screen flickered and a
webpage appeared. Bold caps under the toolbar read
SUBJECT: US-A-01207, beneath that more text
NAME: BEEDLE, PHILIP JOHN. Down the left side
of the screen was a menu of items, only one highlighted
in a pale green.

The remainder of the screen was split in half. Each
half displayed three graphs labeled simply EEG, EOG
and EMG—electroencephalogram, electrooculogram,
and electromyogram. The top portion of the screen had
a blue box with white letters that read: static baseline.
The bottom of the screen had a blue box that read

ACTIVE. Under the graphs, top and bottom, was a rectangle with the word hypnogram. All but one graph was displayed. The hypnogram on the bottom half of the screen, the active portion was missing. Beside it in bold red letters were the words *UNAVAILABLE-CONSCIOUS*. Melissa Cooper could tell by the density of the active graphs that PJ Beedle was awake. She selected the *LOCATION* item from the menu on the left. It gave her coordinates that she placed into another open window which identified his location at the Atlanta Police Headquarters. *In jail; McGill was right.* She used her mouse to scroll through the items along the left side of the screen. She selected one and a dropdown list appeared. She clicked on the entry. Her screen flickered, new graphs appeared as well as new text under the toolbar which now read *SUBJECT: US-A-10330, NAME: McGILL, TUCKER.*

The graphs at the bottom were active, refreshing on screen every thirty seconds. The hypnogram at the bottom of the screen was a stair-step graph that indicated the level of sleep the subject currently enjoyed. The graph for Tucker McGill started very high at about eleven o'clock the night before, then slowly slipped through stages two, three, and four then into REM for about twenty-five minutes before he slipped back into stage one to restart the sleep cycle. Shortly after three in the morning, the active EMG graph went flat and the hypnogram confirmed Tucker had entered REM sleep for the second time, a period which would last about thirty minutes during which his brain could function without the limitations of the physical world around him.

While she finished the glass of wine, Melissa pulled up an audio controller for a systems check of a microphone and a collection of sound effects which included the tinny ringing from a small bell. *Nobody makes me their bitch. Nobody!* When the system was set, she clicked a telephone icon in the top right corner of her screen. "Here we go, cowboy," she said, as the phone icon changed in color from red to amber then to green.

By 2 a.m. Tucker had enjoyed a deep, restful sleep for three hours. Then, though in a deep sleep, he heard a familiar voice and images started to appear in his sleep.

I am the key to the national championship, the voice said, in a strong but soft tone.

In his mind Tucker saw himself lift the Division I basketball championship trophy, the seven-pound five-ounce walnut trophy trimmed in gold plate.

I am the key to the national championship, the voice repeated.

I am the key who found Malik Farqu'har to save the season, said the voice, softer and slower.

I am the key who found Malik Farqu'har to save the season. People admire me. Everything I do helps save this final game. I choose to keep the coach away to let Malik play. I can do what it takes to save the season.

Tucker stirred, rolled over on his side. His movement shifted as the voice continued.

I will get dressed, go to the front desk, and ask for the FedEx box addressed to me, the one with the Post-it note that says 'hold until Wednesday morning.' I will take the box to Coach Howell's room.

The voice, with a marshmallow-softness, quickened in tempo.

I will take the room key out of the box, open his door, enter quietly, and close the door. I will shoot the coach in his bed, go down the stairs, and bury the gun in the planter on the seventh floor by the elevator. I will then go back to my room.

The instructions repeated in his head. The voice was slow and soft and familiar.

If you understand grind your teeth two times.

Tucker complied in agreement.

Now sleep tight cowboy. When you are finished, forget everything you've heard.

The next thing Tucker heard was the soft ding of a tinny bell. He awoke to the sound of the elevator bell and gave no thought to how familiar it seemed.

Melissa Cooper watched her screen change. The hypnogram on the bottom half of the screen disappeared, and a message popped up in its place in bold red text *UNAVAILABLE-CONSCIOUS*.

CHAPTER 38

Wednesday, April 6
2:08 a.m.

Xandra snored ever so softly in the other room, compliments of the sleeping pill Tucker shared earlier. He dressed quickly, the only available light coming through the sheer curtains on the window behind the desk. As he reached to grab his room key card from on top of the desk, Xandra sat bolt upright in her bed.

"You leave again?" she said, with a gentle voice, almost sorrowful.

Tucker froze. Xandra sat there and looked straight at him from the bed in the other room. She tilted her head to the side and added, "Maybe you just coming back?"

Tucker remembered he was in the room when she went to bed earlier, though he stayed up to catch up on emails and tasks while she dozed off. The silence tightened.

"Oh Malik, it's good you back," Xandra said, before she laid back in the bed. "So good."

Tucker realized she was talking in her sleep, likely a side effect of the pill. He put his room key in his pocket and made his way toward the door. Half way, he stopped to look back. He listened for her quiet snore in the back room. Confirmed, he reached for the door latch and stepped out into the hall.

He took the elevator to the main floor where he found a few merrymakers still engaged in their pre-game prep at the bar, open under extended hours for their special March guests. The crowds were gone. The noise was gone. It was rather quiet. One man slumped over in a lobby chair, another stood near the window dazzled by the lights along Fourteenth Street. One attendant behind the desk rummaged through a stack of room vouchers as Tucker approached.

"Excuse me," Tucker said. His voice startled the petite, red-haired attendant.

"Sorry, may I help you, sir," she said. Her name tag read "Riley." Tucker was not sure if that was her first name or last.

"Miss Riley, I'd like to pick up a package I was told would be here at the desk."

"Certainly, sir. May I have your name?" Riley said, with a smile; her green eyes were sure to knock the socks off any of the male guests.

"McGill. Tucker McGill."

"You're a guest with us, sir? Your room number, please, Mr. McGill?"

"Yes, I'm in room fourteen-ten," he said. Everything about him seemed normal. Awake. Calm. Coherent. He looked back over his shoulder to the man slumped over in the chair, then toward two overly intoxicated fans in Carolina blue headed toward the elevator.

The desk attendant walked from behind the wall partition and handed Tucker a FedEx box with a yellow Post-It note attached. He smiled and crossed the lobby to the elevator. The Tar Heel duo boarded the elevator and motioned for Tucker to join them.

"Come on, dude. We got places to go, people to see, things to do," one said, with a slur that elongated his slight Southern drawl.

Tucker waved them off and opted to wait for the next elevator which arrived, empty, a minute later. He pushed the button for sixteen as the door closed, then turned to face a corner, away from any surveillance camera. While the elevator made its way nonstop to the sixteenth floor, Tucker pulled the zip tab on the FedEx box. Inside he found a room key protruding from a small envelope taped to a piece of card stock. Under the card was a red, black, and white Atlanta Falcons hand towel. As he pulled back the towel, the elevator door opened. Tucker quickly stepped to the door to block it from closing. Under the towel he saw a handgun with an extended barrel which was, in fact, a silencer for the Heckler & Koch .40 caliber.

He stepped into the corridor and hesitated when he noticed a man and a woman falling all over each other trying to use a key card. First she would try then he would snatch the card from her while she giggled quietly with her arms around his waist as he tried. Tucker did not recognize either of them. Though he knew the floor was reserved for the team, he did not question their efforts. When he walked by, he smiled and heard the woman whisper to her male friend, "Oops, this is sixteen-sixteen. We're on the wrong floor." The man softly banged his head against the wall by the doorframe; the woman rolled her arms around his waist and stumbled to his other side.

Tucker continued to the end of the hall to Coach Howell's room. With his ear to the door he listened but heard nothing. Other than the virtually unconscious couple laughing further down, there was nobody else visible on the floor. He slid the key card into the lock.

The LED on the handle flashed double-green, he took a breath and depressed the door lever. The door popped open with a faint click.

Tucker slipped into the room, closed the door, and immediately noticed the chill. He was not sure if it was him or just that the room was cold. The splash of light from the hall allowed him to check the layout of the suite. It was exactly the same as his. A small entrance hall led into a sitting room with fold-out couch, an overstuffed chair, ottoman, and coffee table. By the drape-covered window was a simple desk with lamp. A set of double French doors opened into the sleeping area and bathroom. He placed the key in his pocket and pulled the H&K pistol from the box. With the silencer it looked more like a long barrel six-shooter Wyatt Earp might have carried.

The opening between the drapes in the sleeping area allowed for enough street light to find the bed. Tucker saw the outline of the body facing the window with knees tucked slightly—a loose fetal position—and the plush-feather tick pulled up around the pillow. He sensed movement and froze. Again movement. This time he noticed it was the drapes in front of a partially open window. The blue digits on the alarm clock cast a dim glow on the bedside table; it was two twenty-four. He kept his arms down next to his legs as he side-stepped around the foot of the bed toward the window where he had better light and a clear view of his target. With his back to the window, he began a robotic slow-motion movement to lift the pistol, doubled one hand over the other on the pistol grip, aimed it just below the pillows, and blasted four quick shots. The silencer muffled the noise into a series of thumps. Tucker watched the bedding twitch with each round. And, as he pulled the trigger, he silently repeated the words the voice left with him: *I am the key. I am the key.*

On the way out the door Tucker grabbed the FedEx box. He closed the door and walked with a purpose to the stairwell where he took the steps two at a time from the sixteenth floor down to the seventh. At this hour he did not expect anyone in the hall, but with the craziness of basketball in the air, he wanted to make sure he was alone. He opened the door, looked both ways up and down the hall—like a schoolboy crossing the street—and stepped into the hall, around the corner toward the elevator area. He saw a potted palm tree between two peach-colored Naugahyde wing chairs. He pushed the button to call for the elevator to take him back to the fourteenth floor. While he waited, he sat in one of the chairs, worked himself down deep into the cushion and carefully dug two holes in the potting soil of the planter. In one hole he dropped the pistol; in the other, the silencer. He covered both with dirt and wiped his hands on the Falcons souvenir towel. When the elevator door opened, he grabbed the FedEx box and took the elevator up to his floor.

Conscious of Xandra, Tucker opened his room door quietly, then heard her soft snore in the other room. He undressed next to his sofa bed and within a minute he was under the covers, asleep, his actions over the past half-hour completely expunged from his memory. The towel that once covered the pistol sat undisturbed in the Naugahyde chair on the seventh floor.

CHAPTER 39

Wednesday, April 6
2:09 a.m.

Melissa Cooper emptied the last splash of wine into her glass. She pushed back from the desk and took one last glance at her computer screen. The graphs remained unchanged; the text across the bottom read *UNAVAILABLE-CONSCIOUS*. She smiled. *Head 'em up, move 'em out, cowboy.* She had been the voice on six other occasions since she left New Jersey and dozens before, but none had seemed to satisfy her more. The voice was batting a thousand. Every call, every action, every task had been received and performed to perfection. If the current administration in Washington had not cancelled Project Lenore, she— Christina Morrison aka Melissa Cooper—could have controlled the world, almost. The water-boarding and the many other perceived tortures from Abu Ghraib, Guantanamo, and undisclosed black sites would have been considered Elizabethan compared to her ability to get inside the heads of people. The government's misfortune was her advantage, and she planned to even the score with all the bastards who took advantage of her—who had her—and never called again.

After that final screen check, she shut down her computer. Her business with Tucker McGill was done; he was of no further use to her. Besides, she doubted he would be seeing much of anybody in the near future. With the drapes open, she took her time as she sipped wine and repacked her suitcase under the blanket of lights across the way.

Long before Melissa Cooper turned on her computer on Tuesday night, while Tucker McGill was stuck in traffic headed back into Midtown, even before the interrogation sessions with Robbie Gorting and Francisco Hernandez-Agoya began, Special Agent Naujelis and Sergeant Sandusky started to weave the web that they had discussed with PJ and Tucker at the Atlanta FBI office.

By eight o'clock the FBI Field Office – Atlanta, supported by the Atlanta Police Department Criminal Investigations Division personnel, became the new base of operations for "Operation Nevermore." A team of experts monitored cellular signals assigned to a range of numbers which included those pre-set for the devices they inspected with Doctor Athey earlier in the day. Naujelis briefed his field agents on the background of the case and then provided them with detailed instructions on their roles for the evening. He positioned two Atlanta plainclothes policemen in the lobby of the Marriott Suites Midtown. He assigned his two best field agents—one male and one female—to the sixteenth floor. The couple was to monitor and film any suspicious activity which might involve Tucker McGill.

Tucker shared all he had learned from Coach Howells. The speculation was that Melissa Cooper—or Christina Morrison or whoever she was—would cause something to happen to the coach before the game or during the game sometime within the next twenty-four hours. As a security precaution the FBI moved the coach to another room at the opposite end of the hall, the room previously occupied by Jamal Derbish and still marked by yellow crime scene tape. The coach was furious for being moved the day before the NCAA final and livid when they told him he would move to the room where the murder took place. Reluctantly he moved.

At ten minutes before ten, Al Seaman, a plainclothes detective from the Atlanta PD reported that a hotel guest had approached the reception desk at the Marriott Suites with a FedEx box he found by the elevator. He relayed the verbal exchange to the Atlanta FBI operations center:

"HOTEL GUEST (speaking to the desk attendant): McGill. That's what the Post-It note on the box says. I have no idea who the guy is.

ATTENDANT (RILEY): Thank you.

HOTEL GUEST: I found the package on the floor by the elevator over there.

ATTENDANT (RILEY): The note says to hold it until tomorrow. I can do that. I'll make sure Mr. McGill knows. Thank you so much for bringing this to the desk."

Officer Seaman noted the guest was a short, white male, roughly mid-thirties, dark hair, dressed in casual gray slacks with a green sweater over a white-collared shirt. He said there may have been more to the conversation, but with the noise it was difficult to hear. He happened to be standing near the desk reading a Marriott Rewards brochure when he saw the guest approach the desk and heard McGill's name. The ops center contacted Special Agent Naujelis who had just begun his interrogation of Robbie Gorting at the Atlanta Police Headquarters. His instructions back to the head of the ops center were to inform the agents in the field, post two Atlanta police officers in the Four Seasons Hotel lobby but not to contact McGill. He was concerned McGill might take actions prematurely or retrieve the box. Besides, he needed McGill to get some sleep.

At one minute after two in the morning, the cellular number assigned to the micro device planted in Tucker's tooth rang. The ops center experts awakened Special Agent Tom Naujelis, sleeping on a cot with his sport coat over his head. The FBI sound expert who had used earphones to monitor through the night, switched to external speakers and increased the volume so Naujelis could listen. The initial contact started with two light, tinny rings, followed by a voice.

"Get a trace on the call," Naujelis ordered to the expert at the desk.

"Tried. Call doesn't appear to be from a cell phone. Can check for landline. Standby," the agent said, and went to another monitor to check a different scanning device. Less than a minute later he returned. "Not landline either. Could be some VoIP—Voice over IP—set up like Skype or something."

"Keep checking," Naujelis said. He walked to the far side of the room and called Field Agent Deana Morgan in the Marriott Suites Midtown to alert her and her male partner, Agent Roy Lovegrove, to the instructions McGill just received.

"10-4. We'll be ready," she said.

Naujelis then had Sandusky alert his officers at the Four Seasons Hotel to be especially watchful for Melissa Cooper in the event she tried to influence the situation by her presence.

At a quarter past two, Officer Seaman was slumped in a chair in the lobby of the Marriott Suites when Tucker

McGill approached the desk. After McGill secured the box and headed around the corner to the elevators, Seaman squawked Agent Morgan to alert her on McGill's movement. She and Lovegrove stood near a doorway to the right of the elevator area on the sixteenth floor. When the elevator doors opened, Morgan began a pixie-like giggle as she fumbled with the key card and the door, then whispered they were on the wrong floor. As McGill passed them and smiled, she rotated to the far side of her partner and pulled out a small video camera to film McGill's walk to the coach's room and his entry through the door using a key he pulled from a FedEx box. Hours earlier, after the FBI had relocated the coach down the hall, they prepared the room for night operations—set the drapes to allow some light onto the bed, positioned a motion-activated camera in such a way that it could use the light to monitor any activity, and arranged a ballistics mannequin under the heavy feather covers to look like a body in the bed when there really was no body at all.

As McGill closed the door to the coach's room, the FBI agents posing as the drunken couple moved to the fourteenth floor and watched from the stairwell for McGill to return. Once they saw the unsuspecting McGill return to his room, they went to the seventh floor, donned surgical gloves and removed both pistol and silencer from the potted plant. They noticed the Atlanta Falcons towel but left it in the chair and took the elevator back to the main floor.

Across the parking lot to the east of the Marriott, Melissa Cooper wrapped her hair in a bun and pulled an argyle wool knit ski cap over her head. She wrapped her scarf around her neck twice, enjoying the softness the cashmere offered before she left her room. With her computer bag over one shoulder, she pulled her suitcase behind her off the elevator toward the front desk, her spiked heels clicking on the marble floor. The reception area appeared deserted until she came around the grand staircase in the center of the lobby. She froze. Two Atlanta police officers stood, in casual conversation, near the front door. Confident she had nothing to fear, she found it strange to see them there. She wondered if they were merely a precautionary measure given the events down the block. Maybe it was routine at the Four Seasons when the activities in town potentially presented a threat to their guests. Maybe there was a dignitary staying in the hotel, one which required special security.

Not willing to run the risk of happening into a conversation or leaving a trail of any sort, concealed by the mass of carpeted marble steps leading to the upper floors, Cooper changed direction and headed toward the terrace exit on the side of the building, while she watched over her shoulder for any police pursuit.

"Morgan, I want you and Lovegrove to go back up to fourteen and wake up McGill," Naujelis said, over the phone. "Don't explain anything; just tell him I want him to meet me in the Marriott ops center on the main floor in thirty minutes. No…make that four o'clock; that gives him a little more time."

"Okay. Do you want Lovegrove and me to meet you there, too?" she replied.

"No, I want you two to go across the parking lot and apprehend the suspect. Check in with the Atlanta PD plainclothes guys in the lobby first. Ask them if they had any activity at all through the night," Naujelis advised. "Then go call on Doctor Cooper. Use SOP, read her the Miranda rights before you take her anywhere," Naujelis insisted.

"Got it," Morgan replied.

"I want you present in the room the whole time. I don't want any charges for sexual assault or any of that nonsense."

"Check."

"Call me when you have her. I'm going to leave the office and meet with McGill then I'll catch up with you and Lovegrove. Tell the night manager at the Four Seasons you need to use his office or you need a room where you can detain Cooper until I get there."

Morgan and Lovegrove trekked back to the elevator and rode to the fourteenth floor. They called Tucker on his cell phone; no answer. They knocked twice on his door before he opened it, still half asleep. He squinted from the bright hallway lights as he looked at their IDs. "Why the early wake-up?"

"Sir, Special Agent Naujelis needs you to meet him in main floor ops center at four a.m."

"Why? Can't he wait till breakfast? What time is it?" Tucker asked, rubbing the sand from his eyes.

"We were instructed not to go into details. He will explain when you meet at four," she said, with a fatigued, deadpan look.

Tucker agreed. He stood in the doorway rubbing his scalp while the two field agents walked down the hall and around the corner. He heard the ding of the elevator, then the usual hallway silence broken shortly thereafter when Xandra loosed a loud snore in the bedroom. *I should have kept that last pill for myself,* Tucker thought. He had no recall of her sleep talking or snoring earlier but envied her luxury of sleep. He did not bother to shave or shower. As he dressed he thought about the plan the group had discussed at the FBI Office the afternoon prior. He sensed something had happened and he decided not to wait for Naujelis. He had time. He grabbed his coat and headed for the Four Seasons.

Morgan and Lovegrove stopped in the lobby long enough to find their overcoats in the cloakroom adjacent to the concierge desk. They opted to stay indoors as long as possible to avoid the pre-dawn chill in the air. They took the main hall back toward the conference rooms and exited the hotel via the side door which led to the parking lot between the two hotels.

A bitter cold wind blew out of the northeast, across the open lot, and slapped their faces. They lowered their shoulders into the wind and staggered down the tree-lined walkway that led to the terrace entrance to the Four Seasons. They passed two people—a grounds keeper spreading Snomelt pellets across the icy concrete and a woman headed to the parking lot. After a frigid four-minute walk, the sliding glass doors at the Four Seasons greeted them with the warmth of a mother's hug.

Melissa Cooper found her car in the back part of the lot. "Dammit. Ice." She threw her suitcase and computer in the back seat, dropped her purse on the passenger seat, and started the car and the defroster. Her American Express card made for slow work as an ice scraper on the windshield. She would scrape for a few seconds then stop to blow warm air onto her frozen fingers and wipe the ice off her coat. She had gloves somewhere in her car but did not want to waste time rummaging through it to find them.

Inside the Four Seasons the two agents linked up with the two plainclothes detectives who reported no activity. Morgan and Lovegrove flashed their badges and asked the clerk at the front desk for Melissa Cooper's room number; she was in 1105. They requested a key for the room. Though the clerk was initially reluctant to provide a key; with the proper persuasion, he changed his mind. Escorted by the night manager, they took the elevator, hidden behind the grand marble staircase, to the eleventh floor and knocked on her door. No response. They knocked a second time, still no response. When they announced themselves as FBI, the manager unlocked the door, and the two agents entered, hands on their concealed Glock 22s. The room was empty and appeared unoccupied, except for the empty bottle and wine glass on the desk.

Tucker finished putting on his coat while he waited for the elevator down the hall from his room. On the main floor he ran down the hall past staff and early bird guests then out the side entrance where the cold and wind had no mercy. In a slow jog, his nose dripped, his eyes watered, and his fingers froze after a few steps toward the Four Seasons. Fighting the wind, he slowed to dial PJ, but his numb fingers and the light from a car headed toward the exit gate made it difficult for him to read the numbers on his phone. He was half way across the parking lot when the car passed in front of him; it was a sporty 2009 Lexus ISC with Melissa Cooper behind the wheel.

The car stopped at the barrier gate to pay the parking fee. It took Melissa a minute to dig through her purse to find the parking stub she received when she entered the lot the day before. Frustrated with the delay, she tossed her purse at the passenger door. She opened her window and reached for the card reader, but her hand was still inches from the slot. She flipped the switch for the locks and pushed her door open just enough to reach the machine to insert her parking stub.

When Tucker saw the window move he shoved his phone in his pocket. Before he had a chance to yell, he noticed the door open which gave him enough time to skirt the rear of the car and open the passenger door. Melissa gasped and sat back when Tucker pushed the purse out of the way, fell into the empty seat and closed the door behind him.

"Damn it's cold out there," he said, blowing into his hands.

"Tucker you scared me," Melissa said, wide-eyed.

"Little early for shopping isn't it?" Tucker asked, his head cocked toward her. His comment was meant to sound casual, but his tone of voice was all wrong. "Well, I guess Wal-Mart and Target are open all night. Oh, no...that's only for holiday shopping. Let me guess. Making a run for groceries?" he said, his sarcasm lost in the surprise.

She turned away from him and inserted her credit card into the slot on the automatic attendant. "No, not shopping. Going to work. You're coming with me," she said, as she pushed buttons on the keypad to accept her transaction. With her back toward him, Tucker reached across and turned off the car.

"Now, Tucker, I really need to get on the road. I need to go to work," she said, eyeing the barrier gate as it lifted.

"What? I didn't convince you to stay through the final game? With a big win, I could show you some real cowboy passion. You wouldn't want to miss that would you?" he said, with a snicker.

"Well, cowboy, I know you'll be all wrapped up in the game and the post-game falderal. It would be like *Gone with the Wind*. Me pining away for you while you smoke your cigar and hang out with the boys," she said, whining with a forlorn, dimpled smile.

"Oh I doubt," Tucker replied. "Isn't hot sex an elixir of sorts for you? Seems that would be just what the doctor ordered. But, if you insist. If you have to get back to work, how about I take you to breakfast? I'm supposed to meet Tom Naujelis here in a few minutes. What do you say about a threesome? A good way to start the day. We could all have a little breakfast together, just the three of us."

Melissa's face tightened, and she said, "No, really Tucker, I need to go. I—"

"Hell, since you're leaving maybe I can get Coach Howells—you remember Ernie—to come down so you could meet him. You won't be able to see him face to face if you're not here," Tucker said.

The groundskeeper tapped on the window and gestured for Tucker to move the car away from the gate. Tucker held up one finger and nodded. The guy continued on about his business.

Melissa knew something that Tucker could not remember, the fact that Ernie Howells was dead. Tucker couldn't get Howells to come down now or later, but Tucker did not know that.

"Too bad you don't do house calls. PJ Beedle had a real problem with a tooth you fixed for him a couple months back. I had to rush him to a local dentist here in Atlanta just yesterday—while you were shopping."

Melissa crossed her arms; her face grew long. "I thought he was under arrest?" Melissa said, her eyes opened wide.

"That dentist over in Buckhead said that crown you put on Beedle's tooth was a piece of work, real art. He had never seen anything like it before. I asked him to check my tooth, too, the one you fixed a week ago. Damn if he didn't find the same thing."

"Would you just get out or you're going to Beech Island. I have work to do," she said. Her eyes narrowed like a cat stalking its prey.

"Whoa. Are you finished with your work here, Melissa or should I say Christina?" Tucker said.

Melissa laughed then her expression shifted. Her cheeks dropped. "Really I need to get going. I have an appointment at eight o'clock back at my clinic," she insisted. She pursed her lips, her eyebrows bowed into a vee. She quickly started the car and reached for the shifter in the console. Tucker placed his hand on top of hers. He remembered her touch in bed, but somehow this touch moved him more. She pressed hard to put the car in gear, but Tucker's hold was too much for her.

"Why don't we just go inside and wait for Tom Naujelis so we can talk about some of this with him," Tucker said.

Melissa pulled her hand back then stretched to grab her purse from the floor. Tucker grabbed it first. With his other hand he grabbed the keys.

"Tucker, you're starting to piss me off. Give me my purse."

"What do you need? Maybe I can get it for you." Tucker reached into the purse. Her eyes wandered, first to the front then to the side window inches from the gate. Tucker pulled a small .38-caliber pistol out of her purse. Melissa reacted immediately. She threw her hat at him as a distraction, planted her shoulder in the door, and pushed with her legs. The door opened but stopped short. She was next to the cabinet for the parking lot gate. She turned to push the door with both hands and began to squeeze through the opening when she saw Agent Morgan with her leg against the car door.

"Melissa Cooper, you are under arrest on suspicion of two counts of murder and one attempted murder. You have the right to remain silent. Anything you say or do may be used against you in a court of law. You have the right to an attorney." Morgan slapped a handcuff around Melissa's left wrist. When she had finished reciting the Miranda warning Morgan said, "Ma'am, please step out of the car."

With Melissa standing next to Morgan, Tucker stood and turned to Lovegrove outside the passenger door. "What's going on? How did you know where to find us?"

"Cell phone. Your cell phone is still on," he said. "Captain Beedle has been listening on the other end. He relayed a message to us. We were in the Four Seasons to pick up this chick and Beedle radioed you were with her in the parking lot."

Tucker pulled his phone from his pocket and ended the call.

Tucker still knew nothing of his actions earlier in the morning. Agent Lovegrove took the keys and parked the Lexus while Tucker and the two women walked through the Marriott side door, down the hall, and into the Redcliffe ops center where they saw Tom Naujelis. They never stopped for that breakfast Tucker had offered.

At 4:17 a.m., Naujelis put Melissa Cooper in his car along with one of the plainclothes detectives from the Four Seasons and drove to the Atlanta Police Headquarters. Though Naujelis had scant sleep—on a cot in the back of the ops room—he interrogated Melissa Cooper for hours before she requested legal counsel. She selected an attorney friend from Augusta, one with whom she had spent time between the sheets. Sergeant Sandusky placed her in a separate holding cell while she waited for her lawyer. She never had a chance to watch the NCAA championship game, but, then again, she never had any real interest in knowing who won; her interest was in who lost.

CHAPTER 40

Wednesday, April 6
And beyond…

Melissa Cooper answered questions from the same stiff wooden chair that Francisco Hernandez-Agoya had warmed the night before. During three, uninterrupted hours of cat and mouse—without breakfast—Special Agent Naujelis peppered her with questions while Sergeant Sandusky observed. Like whittling a hunk of aged oak, slowly he removed layer upon layer of lies in her fantastic story, each layer with another personality—the practical doctor of dentistry, the philosophical spurned romantic, the monster of Abu Ghraib and war, the freakish, technical wizard in her Frankenstein experiment, the vindictive victim, the spiteful daughter of an unfaithful father, and a mother's abandonment. That's when she asked for a lawyer.

The FBI technical team from the laboratory in rural Virginia, pressured by a certain general in the Pentagon as well as Naujelis, offered a quick analysis of technical aspects of the crime. After he left the dentist office the day prior, Naujelis submitted an urgent request for technical assistance on the ground. A short hop later, a computer specialist was in Atlanta to crack the passwords and filters on Melissa Cooper's computer. The efforts of the Bureau's special Cyber Crimes Task Force provided the keys into the history behind the activities of Christina Morrison aka Melissa Cooper— aka Rachael Rush in Texas and Katie Traska in Chicago. She was a traveling technical road show bent on revenge.

Fortunate for the FBI, the Army Intelligence and Security Command had archives of data from Project Lenore which helped unscramble known and suspected use of the technology. They had secretly tracked the phone numbers and activity of the defunct program that provided key information which led to the prosecution of Christina Morrison, brought back on active duty for punishment under Courts Martial in addition to her civilian criminal cases for murder.

Robbie Gorting enjoyed the final game. His request for legal counsel delayed further questioning until after the apprehension of Melissa Cooper; therefore, he was no longer a suspect in any of the crimes that plagued the Final Four. He was, however, called as a witness in her trial. As a former Army MP at Abu Ghraib, Robbie Gorting was one of the first victims of Cooper's revenge when she capped his tooth in Iraq. From early 2005 until the tiny fuel cell in the device lost its ability to charge, Melissa transmitted messages to Gorting, each with instructions for him to send money to various post office box numbers under the threat of death. Gorting gambled with his life to save his life, sending hundreds of thousands of dollars to Melissa. His compulsion to gambling under the subliminal threats allowed for a reduced sentence, suspended while he underwent therapy and treatment for cocaine addiction.

His father, Chris Gorting, was not as fortunate. He was convicted of fraud and embezzlement of funds from the NCAA. The circumstances of the Melissa Cooper trial extenuated his sentence, most of which was suspended, but he lost his position as President of the NCAA. Some felt the sentence was unfair, others felt he was canned because of the way he handled the disappearance of Malik Farqu'har and the deaths at the Finals. Still others believed he totally botched everything about his dealing with CBS Sports despite the fact that he was influenced by the threatening FedEx envelopes he received.

The South Carolina legal system relooked the conviction of Sam Hutchinson for the hit-and-run death of Ernie Howells' wife. When Hutchinson's attorney provided dental records that showed Hutchinson had been a patient of Doctor Melissa Cooper, he followed through on a request for a hearing based on the evidence. Later, the court reversed his earlier conviction for second-degree murder. He was immediately released from prison and made every attempt to show his regret to Coach Howells. They became close basketball friends for years.

The Chicago Division of the FBI continued to investigate the gang connections between the Posse Diablo members, Francisco Hernandez-Agoya and Jesus Gutierrez, and the ransom money paid. In return for a reduced sentence plea bargain during their trial for assaulting Alexandra Novikov, two stuffed-shirt attorneys from South Side cobbled together evidence which indicated Rodney Farqu'har had arranged for Posse Diablo to float a loan in the amount demanded. Well aware his kid Malik, was worth far more alive and healthy and playing in the NBA, the imprisoned Farqu'har dispatched two of his long faithful Posse Diablo disciples to safeguard the investments—cash and kid.

The evening of April 6, the night of the NCAA championship game, Malik Farqu'har made it to Atlanta in time to play. Though tired and a little hungry for a warm meal, he gave a phenomenal performance that amazed everyone in the Georgia Dome and earned him the unquestioned unanimous and sentimental selection as the Final Four MVP, though he had played in only one game. The Cinderella team from little Redcliffe College in Beech Island, South Carolina—which has no beach and is no island—ran with the Tar Heels for the entire game until their Naismith Award winning shooting guard fouled out. From the bench, Malik Farqu'har watched the final minute and seventeen seconds of the game slip away with a towel draped over his head. Xandra Novikov sat in the stands, five rows up behind the bench, tears streaming down across her scar, her bruised and swollen face lit by the brightest smile. It was her birthday, and for a mother there was no finer gift to receive than to have her son back.

ACKNOWLEDGEMENTS

First let it be known, as a work of fiction, I truly hope the events of this story remain that—fiction—and never plague young athletes and their coaches or the administrations that work so hard to provide for the development of young women and men through sports. I believe each of them deserves credit for the dedication, sacrifice, and commitment they make to participate in their respective intercollegiate programs.

To special people who took the time to read early drafts of this story and coached me back when the words of the tale wagged me in the wrong direction: Jan and Phil Bardsley, Barb and Alex Dunlap, Stacie Knasiak, Janelle Proctor, and Wendy Wilson. I offer special thanks for your comments and encouragement.

Many thanks and apologies to Susanne Jackson, DDS, for the nap time in the chair and the technical advice, though I managed to twist a good bit of it.

In memory of two wonderful and incredible people in my life who founded a publishing company long before they even realized, Sister Mary Philip Thacker and Forrest Sharrock. They remain at my side and in my heart.

To my son Jay, who attacks life with a special fire.

To my daughter Carrie, who shines brighter than any star.

To my wife Penny, without whom none of my world has meaning.

ALSO BY THE AUTHOR

Haint Blue

Comments on this book?
Please send to:

pfpublishing@carllinke.com